BRUSHSTROKES

GINA DALE

Gina Dale Publishing
United Kingdom

Printed by IngramSparks Inc

Disclaimer
This novel is entirely a work of fiction. The names, characters and
incidents portrayed in it, while at times are based on historical
figures, are the work of the author's imagination.

A CIP catalogue record for this book is available
from the British Library
ISBN 978-1-9996103-0-2

Also available as an eBook
ISBN 978-1-9996103-1-9

ACKNOWLEDGEMENTS

I would like to thank the following for their help, expertise and encouragement in producing my debut indie novel 'Brushstrokes':
Editor Rachel Gregory, pedanticpolly@gmail.com
Cover designer Jenny Quinlan, USA historicaleditorial.com.
Typesetter Catherine Cousins, 2QT Limited.
Reading Group: Fay Blackburn, Jane Buckley, Rita Jones, and Sian Marshall.
Website design Joey Williams, ginadalepublishing.com

Images from Wikimedia Commons
Le baiser (The Kiss) self-portrait of French painter Carolus-Duran with his wife as newlyweds 1868 - used on book cover. *Manet and his Easel* drawing by Jean-Frederic Bazille 1868 used on back cover.

1

Marie heard the carriage coming up the drive. She ran to the first floor window and furtively looked outside. A well-dressed young man alighted from the carriage and a groom started unloading his baggage. He ran athletically up the stone steps to the front door and rang the bell. The door was answered by their footman and she heard her brother Henri go running down the stairs to meet Charles Carolus-Duran, a famous artist who was here to paint Henri's portrait for his twenty-first birthday. She was also having her portrait painted as she was approaching her seventeenth birthday. She heard Henri greet Charles and heard them walking through the hall as he took him to Papa's study.

She knew she had better get back to the library and resume her studies, just in case Papa brought him to meet her. She picked up her Greek textbook but soon realised she wasn't taking the words in. She was concentrating on the brief glimpse she had caught of Charles. Marie was herself a skilled artist, having been tutored by a Russian artist. She was born in Russia but they had returned to Paris last year. Her father had been a musician, teaching at the St. Petersburg Conservatoire, and had insisted that both Henri and Marie received expert tuition in all academic subjects as well as the creative arts. He specialised in portraits and had painted many aristocratic ladies in France, Italy and Spain. Marie knew his paintings were well executed and particularly detailed and he had a knack for bringing faces to life. Her thoughts were interrupted by her maid Jeanette entering the room and informing her that her mother was expecting her to join them at lunch. She left the library to go to her room and insisted Jeanette redid her hair.

At 1 p.m. the dinner bell rang and she went down to the salon, meeting her mother in the hallway. Papa was stood at the window showing Charles the formal garden outside, and Henri was with them. They turned as the ladies entered and she caught her breath when Charles turned round. He was extremely handsome with thick, curly, brown hair and a beard and moustache… and the most startling, deep brown eyes. He stepped forward and Papa introduced Mama first, then he introduced Marie. She curtsied low and his hand was offered to support her rising.

He said, 'Enchanté, Mademoiselle Croizette.' She rose carefully, avoiding eye contact, as she did not wish him to know what an impression he had made on her.

Charles could not believe his luck. He had not exactly been looking forward to a week's work painting portraits of what he had assumed would be two spoilt, aristocratic French children. One of the reasons he had accepted the commission was that a ball was being held in honour of Henri's 21st birthday and he had hoped to pick up some more work from the influential guests attending. He was totally taken aback by the beauty of Marie; she had the most beautiful face he had ever seen. It was perfectly symmetrical, which was so unusual as most people have asymmetric faces. Her bright blue eyes and perfect complexion combined with her thick auburn hair and her slender figure was just an artist's dream of perfection personified. He realised he would have to be extremely careful not to alert Marie herself, or her family, to his profound interest in her.

He was careful to chat amicably to her parents and Henri over lunch and did not direct any questions at Marie. He could tell she was studying him surreptitiously but she carefully averted her eyes when he looked at her. Monsieur Croizette suggested that he and Henri might show Charles around the estate and the area, to find a suitable place for Charles to paint Henri.

Marie addressed her father, 'Papa, may I join you on your ride as I could do with some fresh air as I didn't get out yesterday due to the inclement weather?'

Her father smiled and replied, 'Provided your studies are all up to date I don't see why not... and you can be ready within the hour?'

Charles knew instantly that Marie had engineered this on purpose but from her father's response it was obvious she was the favoured child, which meant he must be even more careful. Marie excused herself from the table and left to get changed.

Marie called for Jeanette and ran upstairs to her

room to select which riding habit she would wear. She knew she should wear an ordinary plain wool dress as she was just going out on a simple hack. However, she knew her black velvet habit was far more impressive, but if her mother saw her she may suspect something. Finally, the black velvet habit won the day after she sent Jeanette to find out where her mother was and she was relieved to find out that she was in her private drawing room, which overlooked the back of the house.

They assembled in the hall and she was able to make an impressive descent of the stairs in full view of Charles. He could not take his eyes off her. She reminded him of the goddess Diana, but even more beautiful. Her black velvet habit fitted like a glove, accentuating her tiny waist. She wore a black top hat and veil and the contrast of her pale skin and blue eyes against the black gown gave her an ethereal quality. He felt like he had died and gone to heaven. *Oh my God.* She was practically half his age, in fact he was old enough to be her father. He must pull himself together.

They went outside; the horses were ready. Charles was given a black cavalry horse and he was amazed to see that Marie had the most elegant bay Arab Cross mare which was being held by her groom, and was anxious to be off. Monsieur Croizette had a grey Lusitano cross and Henri, a chestnut French saddle horse that oozed quality. Thankfully, Charles knew a lot about horses as his father had been a horse dealer, so he knew his riding ability was adequate to cope with whatever transpired. The three men rode abreast down the drive followed by Marie and a groom who appeared to be there purely to assist with the horses should they dismount, but may have been designated as Marie's chaperone.

They rode out into a wood with a wide path weaving through the trees and Henri started to canter. They followed, culminating in an exhilarating ride to the other side of the woods. They came out of the woods and within a few hundred yards dropped down onto a deserted sandy beach. The three men engaged in conversation but Marie and her groom set off at a trot towards the sea and then cantered along the beach. How he yearned to follow her as he realised she was an expert rider and had the mare collected in perfect harmony and balance. He forced himself to concentrate on the job and suggested the beach would be a perfect setting for his picture of Henri.

He asked Henri, 'Where did Marie learn to ride?'

Henri laughed. 'Marie rode as soon as she could walk as she was fascinated by horses. She rides better than any man and has far more empathy. She can get any horse to do anything she wants. She went bear hunting in Russia and has never lost a race against anyone. She doesn't need to break horses; she just gets on and rides them. I have seen her jump five barred gates, solid walls and wire while out hunting. She caused quite a sensation in Russia for her riding prowess. To be truthful it should be her joining the cavalry rather than me.'

Charles was even more convinced that Marie was a reincarnation of Diana, the hunting goddess. She returned at a hand canter, her cheeks glowing red, and she looked totally serene.

He couldn't resist saying, 'You are a very accomplished rider, Mademoiselle.'

She smiled and trotted over to her father and he told her that Charles was going to use the beach as a backdrop to paint Henri.

'Papa that will be a perfect setting. May I also have my portrait painted here too?' Charles nearly fell off his horse in shock.

Her father replied, 'But Marie, surely you would prefer to be painted in your new ball gown. I'm sure that is what your mother is expecting.'

She shrugged her shoulders and replied, 'Papa, you know I'm not into ball gowns and dressing up like a lady. Surely, you would prefer a painting of me riding, which I have done since childhood, rather than looking like a painted lady.'

Her father turned to Charles. 'What do you think, Charles?

He pulled himself together and said, 'Mademoiselle Croizette would make the perfect model on horseback as she is such an accomplished rider and I am sure I would be able to convey that in her portrait.'

Her father laughed. 'Very well Marie, I do see

your point but I'm not sure your mother will.'

Marie flashed Charles a triumphant smile and she rode with her father back to the house whilst he and Henri chatted amiably, following behind.

oOo

The next day, Charles started painting his portrait of Henri. He had spent a difficult night tossing and turning and dreaming of the goddess Diana. They set up camp down on the beach. The weather was calm and bright. He was anxious to get Henri's portrait done so he could have more time to work on Marie's portrait. Henri was wearing the uniform of the French cavalry so the red and navy contrasted well with the chestnut coat of his horse. He chatted to Henri, gaining valuable insight into their lives in Russia. Both of them had studied Latin and Greek but were also multi-lingual speaking Russian, French, Italian and English. Obviously, Russia was more cosmopolitan than he had realised. They had both ridden from an early age but Henri had taken up fencing and Marie, ballet. This would explain her wonderful balance on horseback. Their father insisted they both study music and learn both the piano and violin. Henri said he did not have his father's musical talent but again, Marie shone and had a beautiful voice. She had sung in many concerts at St. Petersburg in the Conservatoire Choir. He questioned Henri about his fencing lessons in Russia as he had taken tuition in fencing to a high level.

At midday, he saw Marie and her groom riding towards them with two unusual dogs. Henri explained the hounds were Russian Borzois and they had brought a breeding pair back with them to France. They looked like Greyhounds but had long hair to keep them warm and they were used to scent bears, deer and game in Russia. Marie's groom had a pannier attached to his saddle and proceeded to set out a picnic lunch for Henri and himself so they could have a well-earned break and rest the horse. Marie tied her horse up too and perched on a flat rock next to them. Every move she made was so elegant and athletic. They chatted about the two hounds, Lily and Monty. Lily was brown and white and Monty black and white. They were very tall, sleek and elegant and built for speed. Monty picked up a scent and they ran off tracking a rabbit but soon returned without a kill. Charles thought they completed his image of Diana so well he would have loved to have painted them all together. Their small lunch was soon consumed and they prepared to recommence the painting. Marie, her hounds and her groom cantered off to complete their ride.

oOo

Henri's portrait took Charles two days on the beach and then he returned and set up in the library to complete the painting. Marie joined them on the pretext of studying and she came closer to see his work. To his surprise she asked questions about his drawing technique, such as how he had interpreted the light shining from the sun onto the horse.

Henri noticed his surprise and laughed saying, 'Oh Charles, I forgot to mention that another of Marie's many talents is drawing. Ask her to show you some of her pastel drawings of animals. She also had art lessons with one of Russia's skilled realist painters, Pavel Fedotov.'

Charles was again amazed and said, 'Marie, I would be most interested in seeing your drawings. Perhaps when I have finished with Henri today you could show me?'

Marie smiled and said, 'Charles I would be very happy to have your opinion of my work and your advice on how to improve would be most appreciated. I have my own studio on the top floor but my efforts will be insignificant compared to yours.'

Charles was quick to reply, 'I doubt that very much but I would love to see them, perhaps before dinner tonight.'

Charles met Marie in the library at 6 p.m. and she showed him up to her studio. He wasn't prepared for the emotions he felt when he saw her work. Admittedly, many were painted when she was very young but her animal portraits were very good – even those she had painted when she had been as young as 8. The majority were in pastels or charcoal but the detail in her drawings displayed a talent beyond her years. Her still life pictures of flowers and fruit were average but her study of animals portrayed her love of wildlife. She had drawn her Borzois from puppies and the heads of the animals were lifelike. She could also scale up or scale down her subjects with explicit ease, which is a skill that most artists struggle to acquire. She had drawn pastel portraits of her dogs and horses and he could not fault her anatomical skill.

She produced a folder of her work with Fedotov and her first attempts at oil painting. Fedotov lived and worked in St Petersburg and had seen a pastel horse portrait she had painted for one of his friends and he asked to meet her. He knew her father and suggested to him she came to his studio lectures weekly from the age of 14. Her skill at painting people improved rapidly and her ability to produce light and shade in her paintings increased. Her depiction of faces became more detailed and he taught her to sketch her subjects individually and then reduce them down to paint on canvas. Her ability to paint landscape improved but her portrayal of animals was stunning, almost lifelike. She was able to reveal expression in their eyes and show feeling. She admitted she found oils a difficult medium to work with and much preferred her pastels. She also showed him a set of enamel miniatures she had drawn of Lily and Monty's heads. The detail was incredible.

He put the miniatures down and said, 'Marie, you are a very talented artist and I would be honoured if you would join some of my tutorials on portrait painting at my studio in Paris. I lecture once a week and currently have a mix of twelve students from France, Italy, England and Spain. Perhaps you could persuade your father to let you attend?'

Marie sighed and said, 'I would be delighted to study with you Charles.'

That night, he found it impossible to get off to sleep. Marie's pictures flew round in his head and he was overcome by her potential as an artist, but even more so by his attraction to her as a woman. He had been attracted to several of his portrait subjects but had been well aware of the consequences of dabbling with married women and had managed to avoid temptation to date. However, he had taken many a tumble with some of the women he had engaged to sit for him.

He had been too busy building his career to consider settling down but Marie had stirred such feelings of emotion within him that were overwhelming. He wasn't stupid – he knew that her father's intention was to find her a wealthy husband – but the prospect of Marie being confined to the salon as a token wife to some pompous aristocrat filled him with dread. It would be like confining a rare bird in a cage. She needed to be free to gallop off into the countryside. Moreover, she was an educated woman who had an opinion and was not afraid to voice it. Her grasp of politics and philosophy was evident and she would die of boredom living as second fiddle to a man.

2

The next morning, they set off to the beach with the groom in attendance to see to the horses. The weather was obliging with just a touch of sun and only a slight breeze. Charles realised he would have to be careful not to overshadow Henri's portrait with Marie's. Thankfully, Henri was a handsome young man but dark-haired like his mother, but he had more of his father's facial features. Charles had concentrated on capturing Henri's youthfulness and vigour and portrayed him as a young man entering the cavalry rather than as a seasoned campaigner. Henri would experience the horror of death and destruction in war soon enough when he went into battle. He was the epitome of the optimism of youth, prepared to fight for his country but unaware of the reality of war.

It took a while to set up Marie's pose as in order to centre her in the frame he needed to have the horse facing forward and slightly bent to the right. Normally, he discouraged his subjects from looking directly at him but not Marie; he wanted to drown in those beautiful blue eyes. Although her body was facing forward she held her head to the left with the slightest tilt of her chin, with an expression of coquettishness she probably wasn't even aware of. Her black velvet habit tumbled in generous folds to the horse's left shoulder and she had added a red rose as a buttonhole. The collar of the white blouse set off the cut of her jacket and she was wearing blue leather gloves and carrying her cane in her right hand. Her top hat framed her forehead and the veil gently fluttered in the breeze with a few strands of her luscious auburn hair escaping from her chignon.

He concentrated on drawing the bay mare first as he needed to fix her position in the frame and get the outline drawn. He normally refrained from small talk with his subjects but he wanted to find out as much as possible about Marie. He asked her whether the mare had come from Russia to which she laughed and said a resounding 'no'. Favorit had been bought by her father on their return to Paris. She would not have survived the cold in Russia or the heavy terrain on her delicate legs. Apparently, horses needed to be strong and supple to cope with the treacherous Russian steppes and boggy ground. She chattered away while he swiftly outlined the horse on the canvas, realising the hours spent in childhood, painting horses had been well worth it. She described the use of sleds in winter rather than carriages and the extreme cold endured travelling in winter as no bare flesh could be exposed for fear of frostbite and wolf and bearskins had to be worn over clothing. In the depths of a Russian winter it was often too cold to go outside at all.

Realising that he had been painting for over two and a half hours, he suggested a break. He moved towards Favorit and offered to help her dismount. Marie disengaged her left leg from the stirrup and threw her right leg over the pommel of the saddle. He lifted her from the waist and she slid down the saddle and their bodies were pressed together for a brief moment as she was suspended in his arms. He stepped back quickly, releasing her before he did something he would regret. His body was telling him to kiss her and instantly, Marie knew the effect she was having on him but smiling, she turned back to Favorit and put the reins over her head. Her groom came to her side and led the mare away for a rest.

Marie busied herself with the food pannier, laying out the lunch on the nearest rocky outcrop. He returned to his palette, fussing with his brushes to try to cover up his awkwardness. *What was happening?* He felt like a bumbling teenager and vowed he would not touch her again for fear of the consequences.

She came over to the easel to survey his progress and asked a question and before he knew it he barked, 'Mademoiselle Croizette, I do not discuss my paintings with my pupils until I have finished my work.' Realising he sounded too harsh he said, 'When I have completed the portrait Marie, you can ask as many questions as you like.'

'Very well Charles, I will save all my questions on technique until later.'

They resumed the portrait and Charles was overtly embarrassed at his rebuke of Marie but he was ashamed that he had reacted in that way. How many times had he painted women, even in the nude, and rarely stepped out of line although plenty of his subjects were more than happy to go further and on occasions he had obliged. He began to think he was becoming obsessed with Marie and that he would have to finish the portrait as quickly as possible to avoid becoming more emotionally involved.

He looked again at Marie and was sure she was reading his mind and realised that any attempts to ban sexual thoughts of her were doomed. As an artist, he knew precisely the beauty of her body under that black velvet habit and his desire to drag her off the horse and remove her dress and carry her off into the sea was only held in check by the presence of her groom. He concentrated on drawing the dress and finishing the horses' legs in an effort to avoid her hypnotic eyes. He would work on her face back in the library as it was forever imprinted on his soul. They finished by 3 p.m. as Marie had a dancing lesson with Henri prior to their ball in two days' time. It would at least give him time to work on both paintings as Henri's required final touches as well.

oOo

He set to work on Henri's portrait, finishing his face and his horse's head. He pondered on the difference in facial features of the two siblings. In the background he could hear the music from the ballroom and the occasional raised voice of the dance master shouting instructions in Italian. He slipped out of the library and made his way upstairs to the door of the minstrels' gallery above the ballroom. He quietly slipped in, leaving the door minutely ajar and went as near to the front as he dared, using the cover of a convenient curtain. Marie and Henri were dancing a gavotte and the dance master stopped the pianist and referred to Henri as a 'buffoon', which seemed rather unfair, but amused Marie. After an improved repeat performance they moved on to a slower waltz. Poor Henri was instructed exactly where to place his hands on his partner and Charles was thankful it wasn't him undergoing this scrutiny as he would have had great trouble in keeping his hands under control. Thankfully, dancing was another skill Charles had mastered so he hoped he would at least get the chance to have one dance with Marie. Any more would be suspicious but seeing her dancing with other men was going to be a difficult task. He realised he must get back to the paintings as time was moving on.

He worked on his pencil sketch of Marie's face, attempting to get the eyes, nose and mouth in perfect proportion with the tilt of her head. Her top hat and veil were harder to get right, allowing for the movement by the wind and the shadow cast on her face by the hat's brim.

He realised that he was becoming engrossed and breaking for dinner would be a nuisance. He went to the salon hoping to find someone so he could excuse himself from dinner. Marie's mother Louise was having tea alone and she welcomed his arrival with delight. He declined to join her for tea and apologised profusely that he was going to request to miss dinner this evening so he could continue his work. She graciously accepted his request and promised to ensure he was sent a tray. Charles was able to assess Louise's facial features and there was no doubt that she would have been a beauty at the same age as Marie. The eyes were bright blue and shaped like Marie's, but Marie had the better nose and mouth.

He returned to the library and carried on with the sketch of Marie's face. At 7:30 p.m. a servant arrived with dinner and he paused to eat it, realising how hungry he actually was. He had decided to use pastels to colour her face as this would make it easier to select the colour in oils on the main drawing. Getting her complexion correct was going to be easy but accentuating the light and shade would be more complex.

At 8:30 p.m. he heard footsteps approaching and Pierre, Marie's father came into the library with a tray, holding a bottle of port and glasses.

'Charles, you must take a break and join me in a drink or two. All work and no play isn't good for you. Besides, I want to know what's going on in Paris society and you artists are usually in the know.'

Charles laughed and put his crayon down at the same time as turning over the sketch of Marie's face.

'Well, perhaps just one drink, Pierre.'

They chatted about various prominent figures and he was delighted to hear that Pierre had invited fellow artist and friend, Edouard Manet, to the ball, which would at least give him someone familiar to talk to. They discussed politics and the art scene in Paris. Finally, Pierre brought up the subject of Marie becoming a pupil at his atelier. *She had asked her father so must be keen.* He explained that Marie was very talented and since working with Fedotov her work had improved and he was sure he could help her with portrait work. Her father was concerned that she would not be painting any nudes and he reassured him that although drawing nudes was necessary to have an understanding of anatomy and physiology, life sessions were only open to his full-time students at his invitation. Charles was amused that he had promised she wouldn't paint any nudes but she would be the perfect model to paint nude. *Still, he had better banish that thought from his head.* He told Pierre that Madame Theodore attended his Tuesday afternoon sessions so Marie would not be the only woman. They chatted for a couple of hours, consuming a bottle of wine as well as the port and he hoped this would help him sleep better that night.

oOo

The next morning he was up bright and early for breakfast, eager to get on with Marie's portrait. He was disappointed that Marie had chosen to breakfast early so she could do some studying prior to her sitting. However, Louise chattered away about the arrangements for the ball and he listened intently. He knew two of the house guests who would be staying overnight and was surprised to hear that 100 guests had been invited. Louise told him that Marie was having a final dress fitting at 4 p.m. and she would appreciate Charles's opinion of the dress as he was more 'au fait' than she was with current Paris fashion. Marie had designed the dress herself and Louise was a little concerned that it would be at odds with current fashion. He eagerly agreed as a preview of Marie's dress would be a bonus. *Was there no end to Marie's talents; horse rider, linguist, scholar, musician, singer, artist and now dress designer!*

The morning sitting transpired with no problems as he let her groom deal with getting her on and off the horse and he kept chatter to a minimum as he needed to get as much done as possible; this would be their last session on the beach. They had a quick break for lunch and he told her that her mother had invited him to her dress fitting, to which she seemed highly amused. She wouldn't respond to any questions about her dress so he would have to wait and see. By 2:30 p.m. he had done his essential drawing and Favorit was getting bored of standing still.

Marie suggested, 'Charles, I think Favorit needs a bit of exercise. Could we have a ride along the beach to let her stretch?'

'Of course Marie, I have done all I need to do out here. Perhaps your groom could pack up my paints whilst we go for a ride?'

Marie smiled, accepting that he had skilfully dismissed her groom. Charles mounted his horse and they set off quickly. Marie couldn't resist letting Favorit gallop along the water's edge and he followed willingly. After a while Marie headed up the beach to where two fishing boats were overturned and they dismounted and sat on an upturned boat, holding the horses' reins.

He told her that her father had agreed to her becoming a weekly student and her eyes lit up. Tempted as he was to inform her that she wouldn't be painting any nudes, he thought it would be improper and too embarrassing for her as she was only 17, after all. She asked about his classes and what she would be doing and he told her that he would help her with portraiture and knew of a miniaturist in Paris who could coach her in the technique. They chatted for about half an hour and then reluctantly decided to return to the chateau.

This time he could not avoid the mounting procedure and she had to gather up her skirt to expose her left foot so he could leg her up into the saddle. He threw her up and she was as light as a feather and he helped her rearrange her skirt after she had put her right leg over the leaping head. He rested his hand momentarily on her right knee and as she leant forward to untwist the reins, her hand brushed his face. He felt as if he had been struck by lightning.

'I wager you can't beat me back down the beach!' and with that she whirled round and galloped off down the shoreline. He mounted his fractious horse who was anxious to follow and galloped after her but he knew there was no way he was going to catch her mare with his heavier cavalry mount. She was at least 50 yards ahead already. She reached the spot they had used for the sitting, slowed to a halt and turned round, waiting for him to catch up.

As he reached her she shouted, 'The winner demands a forfeit of a kiss to punish you for your tardiness, Monsieur Duran!'

He could not believe what he was hearing but he knew there was no way he was going to turn down her invitation. He looked round to check there was nobody in sight, moved his horse as close to Favorit's offside as he dared, leant over and put his arm round her shoulder, drew her close to his chest then tipped her chin back and kissed her gently on the lips. He was aware of Marie's hand caressing his neck but before either of them could go any further he let go and moved his horse to the right saying, 'Your servant begs your forgiveness, Mademoiselle.'

Marie laughed and they headed back to the chateau, both wishing the spell had not been broken.

However, Charles knew he had to control the situation and refuse to do what his body was telling him to do (and what Marie's body was tempting him to do).

oOo

Thankfully, he had an hour before the dress fitting to recover his composure and treated himself to a drink in the library to steady his nerves. He reflected on their kiss and congratulated himself on his considerable restraint. He knew that Marie had been unwise to tempt him but she had probably realised that this was her only chance to let him know she was interested in him. Perhaps she had not realised the danger she could have been in but she had seen how infatuated he was with her and wanted him to know she felt the same way.

Her maid came to summon him to the dress fitting and he took a deep breath at the top of the stairs. She opened the door and Marie was standing looking in the mirror with her back to the door, her mother and dressmaker adjusting the gown. Their eyes met briefly in the mirror and she slowly turned round to face him. The dress was in sapphire blue silk with an empire line bodice trimmed with pearls, and fitted like a glove to her body. The neckline was low and round and the sleeves came to her elbow and were finished with silk gloves. She had a necklace of sapphires and earrings of a square sapphire with a droplet of pearls. Her hair was in a semi chignon with the back left loose to her shoulders. *God, he had never seen a woman as beautiful as her and he was speechless.*

Her mother came over and asked him what he thought of the dress – would it be too 'avant garde' for Parisian society?

Charles replied with sadness. 'No Madame, she will have men falling at her feet with offers of marriage when they see her in that gown. If you will excuse me now I must continue with my work.' He saw the look of shock on Marie's face and she raised her hand to try to stop him leaving but he needed to get away and back to his room. He was devastated at the prospect of losing her to another man or worse still, to some aristocratic youth. He knew that she would be the talk of Paris after the ball and she would have marriage proposals from all over Europe within a month. He returned to his room to change for dinner, too dejected to go near her painting.

When he came down to the salon before dinner, Henri and Pierre were already there, chatting about Henri's impending move to his barracks in two weeks. Charles felt so bad he thought of joining up with him. What a dreadful prospect the thought of never seeing her again was. He felt like he had been stabbed in the heart. When the ladies joined them they moved into the dining room and he was thankful Henri had plenty of chat to cover his silence. He hardly dared look at her and was relieved to find a candelabra shielded his face from her. He could feel her eyes on him but he had no intention of looking directly at her. He excused himself straight after the meal, feigning tiredness as he was in no mood to make small talk. He went straight to bed and tossed and turned all night with the vision of Marie in the gown imprinted on his memory.

3

At breakfast the next morning, Charles was relieved to find just Marie and her mother at the table. He took a newspaper in and hoped he could avoid direct conversation. He saw Marie give him a forlorn look and he realised she had done nothing wrong and it wasn't her he should be angry with.

He asked her, 'Marie will you be able to join me in the library around 2 p.m. so I can put any finishing touches to the painting? You don't need to wear your habit, just your hat and veil.'

Marie replied, 'Certainly Monsieur Duran, I will be at your service.'

He grimaced at the emphasised title and assumed 'service' referred to his mention of being her servant yesterday.

He turned to Louise and said, 'Madame I hope I will be ready to reveal the portraits to you all before dinner this evening. Perhaps you would ask the family to come to the library around 7 p.m.' He then headed to the library to continue finishing his work.

Before he could start on her portrait he had to sketch her in the ball gown whilst her image was burnt into his memory. If he charcoal sketched it now he would be able to draw it later in his studio but until he did, he could not concentrate on the other portrait. It took him about an hour and he did it from her mirror image as he had first seen it when he entered the room. This way he could play around with the light to pick out reflections in the sapphire necklace and earrings, and the sparkle of her eyes. The window had been directly to her left so he knew instinctively how the light would fall across her body.

Pleased with the result, he hid the sketchbook out of sight and settled back to her portrait. He started to paint her face and he was determined to transcribe it absolutely perfectly. The almond shape of her deep blue eyes and her tiny button nose with her bountiful lips looked out at him from the portrait and reminded him that he had kissed those lips less than twenty-four hours ago.

A servant brought him lunch at around 12:30 p.m. and he stopped for a few minutes but he was now anxious to continue and didn't want to break off. He then moved both easels at a 90-degree angle to the library's French doors. He was rewarded when the sun came out from behind a cloud and a shaft of light shone through and instantly illuminated both Marie and Henri's faces. Marie's face was just lifelike; the black velvet habit and the black top hat reflected back the light. Henri's face was reflected back from the brass work on his blue jacket and the sword at his side. He just needed to fill in the tails of both horses to indicate the gentle breeze on the shoreline.

Marie arrived promptly at 2 p.m. and he had made sure her easel was turned away from the light and the door and had selected a suitable chair for her to sit in for him to put the final brushstrokes to her painting. She gasped when she saw Henri's portrait.

'Oh Charles, it is wonderful. You have captured the horse perfectly down to the last muscle in his neck. Where did you learn to draw horses so accurately?'

He laughed and replied, 'From many hours spent in muddy fields sketching horses as a boy. Now sit down sideways on that chair and tilt your head at the same angle you did outside so I can finish your hat and veil. As I promised, I will discuss technique with you when I have finished your portrait.'

She didn't get the angle quite right so he could not resist going over to her and cupping his hands on her cheeks to correct her position. He resisted the temptation to kiss those luscious lips again but stroked her lightly on her right cheek with his fingers before he withdrew his hand. He was rewarded with the most beautiful smile from her and a long, lingering, quizzical look from those deep blue eyes.

He worked away in silence to speed up the final touches and then stood back and assessed his work. He was pleased with his sky and sea and the few shells that had been close to Favorit's back legs. He could have painted the horse horizontally on the canvas to produce the best angle for it, but he had been right to centre everything on Marie.

He moved the easel back to its position next to Henri's portrait and there was still enough light to cast a beam across her face. Marie jumped up and took off her top hat and ran over to the painting.

'Oh Charles, it is stunning. I will treasure it forever.'

He answered truthfully, 'Marie, I hope I have done justice to you. You are the most beautiful woman I have ever seen and to paint you has been an absolute pleasure.' He turned to face her and realised that she was crying. 'Marie, what is the matter, don't you like it?'

'Of course Charles, I am just so overwhelmed by its beauty!'

'Marie, come here.' He put his arms round her and hugged her, then wiped a stray tear from her eye. 'Now you can ask me any technical questions you like about either portrait.'

She astonished him with her questions and eagerness to learn. He showed her the sketch he had done first and explained how he had scaled this down to fit into the portrait. She cheekily asked what he was going to do with it now and he truthfully admitted he would be keeping it to remind him of her. They chatted about the portraits and as she stood at the easel directly in front of him he could not resist replacing a stray tendril of hair that had escaped from a plait. He realised he had done it without thinking, just as he would have done with any of his models.

They parted company to go and change for dinner and he made sure he was back in good time to rearrange the portraits in the library now the light had faded. He placed them in the centre of the room underneath a crystal chandelier. It didn't have the same effect as sunshine but it would have to do. Henri and Pierre arrived together and as they walked in he was delighted to see their astonishment at the two portraits. Henri was first to speak.

'Charles, I feel like the horses are stood in the room.'

'Good, that's what I want you to feel, Henri.' replied Charles.

Pierre was studying Marie's portrait carefully. 'You were right to paint her on horseback; she looks so alive.'

The ladies arrived and her mother approached the canvases first, her eyes fixed on Henri and she reached out to almost touch his face. She moved over to Marie's portrait and then turned to Charles.

'They are exquisite. Charles, you have captured their life and soul in these paintings.' Again, tears were rolling down her cheeks.

'Madame I can only paint what I see, I have done nothing to enhance either of them. It is you and your husband that should be congratulated for having such beautiful children.' He could feel Marie's eyes boring into the back of his head and he turned to give her a reassuring smile. She looked so vulnerable he wanted to hold her tight and never let her go.

They adjourned to the dining room and enjoyed a delightful meal. The conversation ranged around the preparations for tomorrow's ball and he learnt that Marie was responsible for the flowers in the ballroom so he knew where she would be but was disappointed that she would not be alone.

oOo

The next day, Charles made his way to his bedroom to start getting ready. He removed his dress uniform from the wardrobe and gave it a brisk brush over. He hoped his outfit would elicit as much surprise from Marie as her dress had from him. He set to polishing his leather boots to perfection.

He had been asked to assemble in the hall at 7 p.m. as the house guests would be arriving earlier than the party guests. He had been fiddling with his clothes for the last half hour and had been particularly fraught fighting with his red over sash. He took a peek from the first floor landing to ensure that all the family were downstairs before he set off. As he reached the final flight of stairs, he paused and took a deep breath. He started his descent and Henri was the first to look up when his sword caught on the bannister rails. Marie was looking directly up at him and she gasped as he continued his descent. He was wearing the full dress uniform of the French hussars and his red sash had his newly awarded Légion d'Honneur knight insignia pinned to his chest.

Henri started applauding as he reached the bottom of the stairs and exclaimed, 'Charles, when were you ennobled, you rogue? You never told me!' He came over and patted him on the back along with Pierre, who shook his hand.

He replied, 'I was awarded it last year for services to art when I returned from Rome. I was even more impressed when I was told I could wear full dress uniform.'

Louise offered him her hand and he kissed it and she said, 'Charles I am so delighted for you. To be recognised as the great artist you are by your country must indeed be a great privilege.'

Marie approached him and swept into a full curtsy and said, 'Chevalier Duran, may I offer my heartfelt congratulations.'

He offered her his hand and leant forward to kiss her hand and noticed she had tears in her bright blue eyes.

'Thank you, Mademoiselle Croizette, for your good wishes.'

Suddenly, the first guests were arriving and Charles moved into the salon as he was not part of the family greeting party in the hall. He was pleased with the effect of his knighthood on the family and hoped it would make Pierre warm towards him. He had the room to himself at the moment and a servant brought him a glass of wine whilst he daydreamed about what life might be like with Marie at his side.

He let the house fill up with guests and moved

towards the ballroom to join the party. Marie was at the far end with her mother, surrounded by her family, welcoming everyone. She was strategically placed underneath a chandelier and her sapphires sparkled in the light.

Suddenly, a hand patted him on the back and a familiar voice said, 'Charles, I didn't recognise you in your uniform, it's the first time I have seen you in it, may I offer my congratulations.'

Charles turned to shake the hand of Edouard Manet, another French painter he had become acquainted with since his return to Paris.

'Edouard, I am so glad to see you here. Now I have someone decent to talk to.' He steered Edouard towards the bar in the salon and they chatted about their lives as they hadn't seen each other for a while. Charles explained what he was doing there and pointed out the Croizette family.

Edouard said excitedly, 'You mean you have had the pleasure of painting Mademoiselle Croizette. Her face is the most beautiful I have ever seen and her bone structure is astonishing. Where has she been hiding? I have never seen her in the salons of Paris.'

'In Russia – the family has only just returned to Paris. Her father lectured in music at the St. Petersburg Conservatoire. Would you believe that Marie is an excellent painter and was taught by Pavel Fedotov for four years? I hope we can slip away later as I would like to show you my paintings and her portfolio.'

The orchestra was playing a polka. He ushered Edouard into the ballroom and found a suitable secluded alcove from where he could observe the dancing. There was an excited hub of young men at the far end of the ballroom, all discussing the delights of Mademoiselle Croizette. He was shocked at how desperate it made him feel. He realised Edouard had been watching him closely and gave him a sardonic smile. Marie was dancing with a captain in the hussars who was in his early twenties. But this was not the girl he knew; her head was down, her eyes never made contact with her partner, she did not smile and her body was stiff. When the dance ended she curtsied and turned quickly away, refusing to be engaged in conversation. For one moment he actually felt sorry for the young captain – the expression on his face resembled a puppy rejected by its mistress.

Marie's next partner was lining up to escort her onto the dance floor. He was older and obviously all too aware of the beauty before him and when he bowed to her before the dance, he slightly overbalanced. To his horror, Charles realised he must be drunk. The music started and he pulled Marie into his arms far too close for comfort and had his face within inches of her mouth. She tensed her shoulders to push him away and when she couldn't move from him she stamped heavily on his toe with her heel, which released his vice like grip. Marie escaped his clutches and left the dance floor. Anger flooded through him and he was about to stride across the ballroom when

Edouard pushed him back against the wall saying, 'No, Charles – leave it and take your hand off that sword – she dealt with the situation well.' He hadn't realised he had even picked up his sword; thankfully he hadn't removed it from his scabbard.

Edouard said, 'Come on now Charles, it's time you introduced me to Mademoiselle Croizette so I can claim her on the dance floor. I promise not to ravish her but maybe I should be wearing boots rather than shoes.'

Charles had to laugh and was grateful for the release of tension. They left the ballroom and entered the salon to find Marie. She was with two ladies he had seen her chatting to earlier. She saw him approaching and a look of relief was evident on her face.

He announced, 'Mademoiselle Croizette, may I introduce my friend and fellow artist Edouard Manet, who would be grateful if you would grant him the honour of a dance.'

Marie extended her hand to Edouard who bowed and bestowed a delicate kiss and replied, 'Monsieur Manet, I have seen your work and would be delighted to dance with you provided Charles will agree to dance with me afterwards.'

Edouard laughed and said, 'Mademoiselle, I doubt wild horses would be able to keep him away.' He took her arm and led her back out to the ballroom.

Charles followed at a distance, surprised at the extent of his feelings. Edouard was five years younger than him and although happily married to Suzanne, he knew he had a keen eye for the ladies. He watched them closely and could not fault Edouard's propriety. Marie relaxed and engaged him in conversation while they performed an accomplished dance. They walked over, chatting amiably and Edouard was amazed to hear that Marie was to become a pupil of Charles's.

He led Marie back to the dance floor and was relieved to find the next dance was a slow waltz. He would have to be careful as he knew he was being observed by several people including Marie's mother, who was dancing with someone he didn't recognise. He kept his eyes away from Marie as he knew it would give him away, but he was content to relish in the closeness of her body, his hand on her back. As the waltz was nearing the end he manoeuvred them towards the far end of the ballroom and twirled her behind a marble pillar. He bent over and gently kissed her right ear, pushing her gently back against the pillar so he was in direct contact with her body, and heard her gasp. Then quick as a flash, he released her and led her back down the ballroom.

She was accosted by her next partner and as he moved away, he turned to see the look of total desolation on her face, but he knew he had to leave her or people would begin gossiping. He returned to Edouard, who suggested they slip away as he was desperate to see the portraits. He went to the bar and talked his way into getting a bottle of wine and furtively, they made their way to the library. He told

Edouard to wait while he went in and checked there was nobody there as he was concerned her father may be around. He moved the easels back under the chandeliers in the middle of the room and then opened the door for Edouard.

Edouard walked in and then stopped dead around twelve feet away from the portraits. His eyes were looking at Marie's and then he slowly moved on until he was about six feet away and stopped again. He then moved to the left and then again to the right. Finally, he stopped about three feet away from the easel. Charles held his breath as he had never sought Edouard's opinion of his work before. He had been to his studio a few times and had commented on some of his paintings but he was anxious now as he had put his heart and soul into this one and if Manet hated it, he would be devastated. Edouard finally turned to face him.

'Charles, it is exquisite. The execution of her face and the interpretation of the light is breath-taking. I expected to see her in a typical, formal dress portrait but this is outstanding. You have brought her to life and you can feel the passion directed at you in those beautiful eyes. God Charles, men would die to have a woman look at them like that. They would fight battles purely on the strength of that gaze. I have studied the Great Masters' work, especially Da Vinci, and I can't recall a painting with a woman as beautiful as her.'

Charles sighed with relief as praise like that from a

fellow artist was praise indeed. Edouard moved over to Henri's portrait and scrutinised it intently from every angle.

'Your drawing of the horse is superb and although stationary, still conveys the power and speed within. Where did you learn to paint horses so well? I could do with some tips.'

'I started sketching them as a boy as my father was a horse dealer and that's when my riding skills evolved. Some of the horses my father bought were damaged and unrideable, having been brutally treated because they didn't conform. Once you get through to the mind of a horse you can rehabilitate them but it's all a matter of trust. Some will eventually trust men again but sometimes they would only trust you and so you couldn't resell them. I continued in Spain where the horses with that touch of Arabian blood were a dream to paint. I knew it was likely I would be commissioned to paint them as models so I reckoned if I got the horse right then I would have more time to concentrate on the subject.' answered Charles.

Edouard said, 'Henri looks the picture of innocence and youth, unsullied by the ravages of war. Let's hope it stays that way.'

Charles fetched Marie's folder and gave it to Edouard for inspection. After he had sifted through the pictures he turned to Charles, with Marie's pastels of her Borzois.

'She's good Charles, especially with animals; like

you, she can bring them to life on paper. Her horses don't have the muscular frame of yours but she conveys their temperament and spirit well.'

Charles was delighted that Edouard had confirmed his opinion of Marie's work. He refilled their glasses and they sat down in front of the portraits.

Edouard said, 'When are you going to ask her to marry you?'

Charles gasped, 'I'm old enough to be her father and I hardly think her parents would consider me a suitable match for their daughter. I can't offer her a chateau, land and a decent lifestyle. I'm just an artist like you and we all know that our work is never valued until we are dead.'

Edouard laughed. 'Very true, Charles, but it's not all about money. With Marie by your side you could conquer the world. She understands your work; she is madly in love with you and would follow you to hell and back. This would be a marriage of minds as well as bodies and never have I seen a body so stunning. Imagine the beautiful children you will have. You see her father tomorrow and beg, on your knees if necessary, for his daughter's hand in marriage. You said she could twist her father round her little finger; she got him to agree to her studying with you.'

Charles interrupted, 'And what if he refuses?'

'Then you will have to elope with her. Go back to Rome or Madrid; you are well respected there. Marry her and spend a month examining every intricate detail of that superb body and don't stop until she's safely pregnant. You won't have time to paint for at least two months but it will be the most wonderful experience of your life. You have awakened her sexuality, Charles, and if you don't fulfil her expectations you will have turned down a gift from God. Can you imagine standing back and letting another man lay a finger on her? You were ready to slay that drunkard tonight. If you let her go, Charles, you will become a bitter and twisted man and you will lose your desire and ability to paint and your career will be ruined.'

Charles sighed as he realised that Edouard was probably right; he hadn't thought of how it would affect him to see her marry someone else. But he wasn't so sure that Marie would want him badly enough to give up her family and lifestyle for him.

The door opened and Marie appeared. Before she could speak, Edouard leapt to his feet and said, 'Mademoiselle Croizette, I was just inspecting your portrait to check that Charles had done you justice. I am pleased to report that he has, but then painting perfection is such a pleasure, not a toil. He has shown me some of your pastels and I agree you have a talent worth pursuing.'

Marie seemed shocked but replied, 'Monsieur Manet, you are too kind but thank you for your compliment.'

Edouard said, 'Now if you will excuse me, I will leave you as I think Charles has a proposal to discuss with you.' He flashed Charles a quizzical smile and left the room.

Charles didn't know what to do. The fear of rejection was uppermost in his mind but he knew that time was of the essence so he was now forced into asking her.

He walked over to a startled Marie, took her hand and said, 'Marie I know we have only just met and I have nothing to offer you financially, but I would be honoured if you would consider becoming my wife.'

Marie's hand shook slightly and he hardly dared breathe or look at her fearing the rejection that must surely follow. After a pause she squeezed his hand and said emotionally, 'With all my heart Charles, I want to spend my life with you.'

He sighed and hugged her close, burying his head in her hair. When he finally released her, the tears were flowing.

'But Marie… Will your father allow it? I'm not the catch he would have wanted for you.'

She replied, 'I don't know but my happiness is important to him and I am sure we can make a success of your career so he would be proud of our achievements.' Charles took her in his arms and gave her a slow, lingering kiss. He could feel her heart beating and he just wanted to hold her in his arms forever.

Marie left to go back to the ballroom as she would be expected to be present as guests departed. They had agreed to tackle her parents tomorrow after the house guests had left.

He sought Edouard in the bar and his friend patted him on his back saying, 'Well Charles, you don't look very happy; don't tell me she declined your proposal.'

'No, of course not but how am I going to convince her father I am worthy of her?'

'Charles, stop this now! You are no longer a starving artist, you are honoured by your peers and your country and you have a great future. Leave the finances to Marie; she will be more than capable of overseeing them and you get on with what you do best.'

While the party wound down they found a secluded table and chatted about his favourite master, Velazquez. When Manet was ready to take his leave, Charles accompanied him to the door. He was hoping to slip quietly to his room to plan his campaign for tomorrow and made his way by a servant's staircase, avoiding the main hall.

oOo

He woke early the next morning and pondered the problem in great depth, convinced her father would refuse. By 7 a.m. he couldn't see a solution to the situation and he decided to go outside for a walk. He made his way down the back stairs and outside from a door in the deserted salon. He wanted to be alone to gather his courage and consider his options. He knew if he eloped with Marie, her father would be outraged and could he really expect Marie to sever all ties from her family for the life of a wandering artist?

He followed the route down to the beach, to the scene of his paintings. The sea was rougher today due to a sea breeze. The sun was just peeking through the clouds and a shaft of light enveloped him. Manet was right. Marie was a gift from God and if he didn't fight for her hand he wouldn't be able to tolerate seeing her marry someone else. He walked slowly back to the chateau and joined the guests for breakfast. Henri was the only family member there and he offered a pleasant distraction by regaling him with the names of the ladies who had taken his fancy. *Oh the joy of youth,* he was now so besotted with Marie that he doubted he would ever desire another woman.

Pierre arrived surrounded by some of his friends, so Charles stayed at the table, hoping he might be able to catch him leaving the dining room. He had decided he would ask him for a private meeting later in the day. Pierre would think it was to finalise his commission fees so it should not alert him to any other reason. He seized his opportunity when Pierre left the table alone and he followed him into the hallway.

'Monsieur Croizette, perhaps I could have a moment of your time later today.'

Pierre replied, 'Of course Charles, when everyone has gone, perhaps later this afternoon. We weren't expecting you to leave today anyway.' He then greeted a guest coming towards him.

Charles went to the library, hoping for some

solace. He settled down to study his portraits but he found his eyes were magnetised to Marie's face. He hoped he would get some time alone with Marie before his meeting with her father.

His opportunity came at around 12 p.m. when Marie found him and suggested they walk her dogs down to the beach. They discussed all the plus points he must give her father, including a long engagement if her father objected to her young age. The prospect of waiting months to marry was unbearable, but if it would allow him to marry her he would just have to be patient. They stayed out an hour and made no contact apart from holding hands – he was too agitated to risk another kiss.

On their return, he retired alone to the library, conscious that Pierre would expect to find him there. He sat there morosely thinking over his options, convinced he was doomed.

He heard footsteps and Pierre came into the library. He chattered away about the party, giving Charles no opportunity to raise the subject. Charles thought he would be better leaving him to chat as it would keep him relaxed and he would have to wait for an opportunity. Finally, Pierre became distracted by Marie's portrait and he seized his opportunity.

'Monsieur Croizette, I would like to ask for your daughter's hand in marriage.' Pierre looked shocked so he carried on, 'I know that you would not consider me an ideal match for your daughter as I am only an artist of limited means, but I assure you that I would work as hard as I can to provide a suitable home and life for her and I would cherish her until the day I die.'

Pierre said, 'I assume you have consulted Marie on this proposal?'

'Yes, of course Sir.'

Pierre moved over to the house bell and rang it and for a moment he thought he was going to be thrown out of the house. A servant arrived promptly and Pierre said, 'Would you ask my wife and daughter to join us in the library?' Pierre turned his back on Charles and moved towards the window.

Charles didn't know what to do. Should he get down on his knees and beg like Manet had suggested? Before he had time to do anything, Marie and her mother arrived. He felt as though he was about to be hanged and gave Marie a look of pure desolation. Pierre turned to Louise.

'Charles has asked for Marie's hand in marriage. What do you think?'

Louise gasped and turned to Marie. 'Is this what you want, Marie?'

Marie replied, 'Yes Mama, with Charles I would be able to help him achieve even greater heights as an artist.'

Louise interrupted, 'But it will be a hard life for a woman, with no respite. Artists work as long as it takes to do the job. You will hardly have time to see him. What if he has to go away?'

Charles interrupted, 'Madame if Marie can't join

me then I won't go.'

Pierre spoke, 'Marie, don't you think you need more time to consider this? You hardly know Charles yet.'

'No Papa, I know that I love him and couldn't bear to be without him.'

Louise sighed, 'Then provided you have thought long and hard about the lifestyle you are going to leave behind, then I have no objection.'

Charles couldn't believe what he was hearing.

Pierre turned to Louise. 'Then how can I stand in their way?'

Charles responded quickly. 'Sir, I promise you will never have cause to regret your decision. I shall devote my life to your daughter's happiness.'

Pierre shook his hand. 'Congratulations Charles, you have my permission and it might as well be sooner rather than later.'

Marie threw herself into her father's arms, sobbing with relief.

Louise offered him her hand for a kiss saying, 'I am sure you will make a wonderful husband Charles, but you do realise she is quite a headstrong young lady.'

Charles felt like he had been trampled by a horse. He could not believe that her parents had agreed so he hadn't even considered what action he would take if they said yes. He would have to buy a ring and he couldn't possibly expect her to live in his tiny cramped flat.

Louise suggested they leave them to discuss their plans and meet again tomorrow.

After they had gone he looked at Marie and said, 'I never expected for one moment they would agree. I am speechless.'

Marie laughed and said, 'I hope you are not changing your mind, Charles?'

'No, never in a million years Marie, I just have to work out how I am going to provide a marital home suitable for you.'

'Charles, I would live in a stable with you.'

They chatted until it was time to change for dinner and came to the conclusion that they would announce their engagement immediately but set a date for the wedding in the autumn.

4

When Charles finally got to his room that night, his head was spinning. He had been so convinced that her parents would turn him down that he had not even thought of the logistics of marrying Marie. He would need to rent a house across the Seine within walking distance of his studio and large enough to raise a family, undoubtedly requiring some servants. How much this was going to cost he had no idea, but it would certainly not be cheap.

He would also need to buy his fiancée a ring and that would require a fair investment. He favoured a large sapphire set in diamonds to match those beautiful deep blue eyes. However, it would have to be big enough to match the sapphire necklace and earrings she wore at the ball so again it would cost him dearly. He did, however, know a diamond dealer well who would be able to make him the initial contacts and advise on a price.

It was March 16th 1868 and although it would seem a good idea to marry before the holiday migration from Paris in August that would be too soon to organise and guests may have already left to go on holiday in July. A July wedding would have suited him better from a teaching point of view as he closed his studio in August for a month anyway, but if they waited until mid-September then most of his overseas pupils would be returning and he would see if he could enrol them at the Academie Julian for the period of his honeymoon. Hopefully, his French students could get work for a month at the Louvre, copying whilst he was away. If not, he would have to find an alternative solution. As a last resort he might be able to send them to other artists but there was a huge financial risk in doing so as they might not return to him.

He appreciated that he was going to have to work non-stop and extremely hard to raise enough money for all this lifestyle upheaval and the chances of having any time to court Marie in the meantime would be negligible. She would probably continue to come to him for tuition once a week but he could not afford to spend the weekends with her as he needed to make as much money as possible so he doubted he would be able to see her more than once every six to eight weeks. He realised that he could easily tolerate this as he honestly thought the chances of him being allowed to marry had been negligible.

oOo

The next day after breakfast, he and Marie had a meeting with Pierre in his study. They had a general discussion about a suitable date for the wedding in the autumn and he confirmed that he would be looking for a ring as soon as he got back to Paris. He had been happy to discuss his finances in front of Marie but her father did not think it appropriate.

Pierre said, 'Marie I wish to discuss finances with Charles alone, please leave the room.'

He could feel her anger rising when she said, 'If there are any financial details which affect my future, I would expect to be consulted.'

Pierre retorted, 'Marie do not be so insolent, and do as you are told.'

He hardly dare breathe as although he appreciated her point, now was not the best time to make it. He stood up and offered her his hand in the hope that she would go quietly. He could tell she was very angry at her father's words but he could see her considering her options and thankfully she rose to her feet and swept out of the room and made her feelings known by slamming the door.

They discussed his plans for finding a suitable house for them but admitted he had no idea of how much the cost would be. He accepted that he would need to provide a minimum of staff to run the house. He also assured him that he would be working hard to raise as much income as possible to provide for them but he admitted that he had few savings to fall back on as his artistic career was in its infancy. He agreed to do some investigating on the property front and said he would appreciate Pierre's advice when he had found a house that both he and Marie considered suitable.

Pierre advised that Marie would have a dowry of 20 000 francs and if they chose to put that towards renting a house then that would hopefully support them for some time. He warned him not to rent something too big to start with as once his family expanded he may be in a better position financially to buy or rent a house in a better area of Paris and perhaps move his studio as well.

He also confirmed that the cost of the wedding would be met by him and if he wanted them to be married in Paris, rather than locally, then he would agree to cover the cost. Charles assured him that both he and Marie agreed that marrying locally would be their preferred choice.

Charles promised to look into all these matters and update him when he had purchased the ring so they could officially announce the engagement. He left the office and went in search of Marie. He found her in the salon, reading, and he could tell by her face she was still seething at being dismissed by her father.

She asked him, 'Well am I to be privy to my future, courtesy of you and my father?'

Charles replied, 'Marie, your father only has your best interests at heart. He just did not want to discuss finances in front of you, which is understandable.'

'But it is my life you were discussing without any consultation whatsoever.'

'I assure you that I will include you in selecting our future home and in approving your engagement ring and the wedding planning but until I do some research and calculations I have no idea of the costs involved. Your father has informed me of the amount of your very generous dowry but I cannot reveal this to you, so if you wish to know you will have to consult him yourself.'

'Oh, you make me feel like one of my father's broodmares rather than his precious daughter!'

'No my cherie, you are a cherished work of art with an inestimable value. Please do not be so hard on me Marie; I just need time to seriously consider our future and it will be undertaken with your complete knowledge and consent. I have to get back to Paris now but if you are coming for your class next Tuesday I may have more information on the ring.'

oOo

The next day, Charles set off to visit a Dutch jewel dealer, Van Dries, who had an office in Paris. He was hoping he would be able to source him a Ceylon sapphire and diamond engagement ring to match the set of sapphire jewellery Marie had worn at Henri's party. He had asked her father for permission to borrow them so that he could take them with him and Pierre had brought them round to his studio last week.

He was ushered into Van Dries' office on arrival and he was made very welcome. He showed him the sapphire set and Van Dries examined them under a bright light and with a magnifying glass.

'Monsieur Duran, these are excellent sapphires and I confirm they are from Ceylon. They have such colour and depth and have been set with the diamonds so beautifully. I am certain that these were set in Russia and can only have been made by Carl Fabergé. They are exquisite and would have a value now of at least 10 000 francs, possibly more. Finding a ring to match these will not be an easy task… and expensive, too.'

Charles said, 'Even Pierre never said they were made by Fabergé. I suppose he may not have known. He did say he purchased them in St. Petersburg but did not reveal the cost.'

'Monsieur Duran, you will be looking at a cost of anything up to 2000 francs and that's assuming I can find one or make it myself.'

'Well, Van Dries you had better start looking and I shall need two wedding rings as well. As Marie's will be worn next to her engagement ring, they had better be the same so I shall leave you to decide on the metal.'

'How soon do you require the engagement ring? I need time to send messages out to all my contacts, particularly in Russia and it could take me some time.'

'Well, take as long as you need; my fiancée will have to wait patiently. Just let me know when you have something for us to look at.'

That night he settled down with a brandy and reflected on how his life was going to change. Charles contemplated how he was going to handle the wedding night. He remembered his first initiation into the art of lovemaking at the age of 18. He had been an art student in Toledo, Spain and attended life classes at the academy. One of the sitters was a 40-year-old Spanish woman called Isabella. He knew she was the mistress of his tutor and he had painted her as a model several times, but up until then, fully clothed. She was very pretty in a typical Spanish way with dark brown eyes, jet black hair and a dark, sultry complexion. He was pleased to see that her body exceeded his expectations. He had been at the back of the class when the session had commenced as he preferred to draw the background and setting first before coming in closer to sketch the sitter. She lay on a chaise longue, which was on a raised dais. He had noticed she was looking directly at him with a challenging, flirtatious expression. He looked behind him in case there was someone else she was looking at but there was nobody there. He thought she might even be looking at his friend Pablo to his right, but it wasn't aimed at him. He thought no more of it and concentrated on his work.

During the break, he had gone to get some wine and she was over by the sink drinking a cup of coffee, her body now concealed by a sheer robe. They exchanged greetings and as he turned to go back she placed a piece of paper in his hand and then returned to the dais. He went back to his easel and surreptitiously opened the note. His Spanish was still in its infancy and her writing was difficult to decipher but it basically said 'meet me at 25 Calle La Traviata at 8 p.m. tonight'. The shock of this caused him to sweep his brushes off his easel in his haste to hide the note. This did not go unnoticed by Isabella. What a dilemma he was in. He vaguely remembered the other students saying she was married to a Spanish soldier but while he was away she had become his teacher's mistress. He was aware of what she probably wanted with him and it wasn't to teach him to dance the flamenco. But the prospect of his tutor's wrath if he was found out and the possibility of being sent back to France in disgrace was uppermost in his mind. However, his natural optimism and his awakening desire got the better of him and he decided to accept the invitation.

oOo

He found out where the house was and did a quick survey to check the escape routes should it prove necessary to make a quick exit. He had half a bottle of brandy to steady his nerves and found himself knocking on her door at the appointed time.

Isabella answered the door and ushered him in to the salon. As far as he could tell there was nobody else around. She offered him a drink and was chattering away in Spanish, far too quickly for his level of understanding. He also found himself responding to her questions in half Spanish and half French which was no use at all, as she could only speak Spanish. However, it was obvious Isabella hadn't invited him there to discuss politics or the weather.

She proceeded to stroke his chin and wrap her fingers in his hair and within seconds he was kissing her. Bearing in mind he had kissed no other female apart from his mother up to this point he thought he hadn't done too bad a job. It obviously didn't pass muster with his Spanish beauty as she proceeded to demonstrate at great length how she wanted kissing and he began to warm to his subject. She moved on from kissing his lips to his ears and neck and at the same time was deftly removing his jacket and undoing his shirt. By the time she got to his nipples and then ran her tongue down the front of his chest it was he who was undoing his trousers.

What followed was the most amazing experience of his life so far. Isabella proceeded to use her tongue, mouth and fingers to explore every inch of his body right down to his toes. He climaxed at least three times but despite his best entreaties he was not allowed to explore her body below her breasts, which were to die for. Whenever his hand strayed further down, all he got was a resounding, 'Not yet, Charles.' He didn't want her to stop touching his body so he had to comply with her wishes.

After a solid hour of total pleasure they came up for air. Isabella cradled his head on her breasts and told him that he would have to go but she would see him tomorrow at the same time. Dismissed like a naughty puppy, he retrieved his clothes and made a hasty departure, fearing her husband might be on his way home.

Charles laughed at the memories of his first sexual foray, which had driven him to the depths of desire but had rendered him unable to achieve his ultimate goal. In fact, it had been a full week of nightly sessions before Isabella had allowed him to penetrate her. She had instructed him on how to make love to a woman's body with just his fingers, mouth and tongue and until he had reached her high standards he was not getting the prize he desired. He was too innocent to understand that she was teaching him the art of lovemaking, just like his art tutor was teaching him to paint. He had fallen in love with the beautiful Isabella with the innocence of youth. He thought she must have loved him but what he failed to read was that she was instructing him on giving a woman what she wanted before taking his pleasure. He realised that he was indebted to her for her tuition. It would make him a better lover and certainly a better artist. His knowledge of female anatomy and psychology had reached master's level. However, he was yet to know real love.

His lessons continued for six weeks, during which he never told a soul for fear it would get out. He thought Isabella wanted him as a lover to replace his tutor and assumed this was what she had done. However, the penny finally dropped when he was having a landscape lesson down on the beach. They had all selected their preferred spot and he had chosen a position further back than most of his classmates on a rocky headland.

His teacher came over after he had been sketching for about an hour.

'Charles, I have been meaning to have a chat to you about your work. You have improved rapidly over the last three months and now that you have achieved an A grade in biology I expect to see an improvement in your portrait work. You paint horses in great detail because you understand not just their anatomy but their psychology too and that's what you need to do to paint women.' With that he chuckled and moved on to his next pupil.

Charles could still remember how embarrassed he felt and he had wanted to walk out into the sea and drown himself. Obviously, his tutor and his darling Isabella had set the whole thing up as part of his tuition. Like a fool, he hadn't even suspected what was going on. The realisation that he was dismissed by 10 p.m. every night because his tutor was coming round and that Isabella would have been reporting on his performance, filled him with dread even to this day.

He was, however, determined that he was going to put Isabella's lessons on technique to good use to ensure that Marie reaped the rewards. Isabella had at least taught him the difference between love and lust and he was sure many of his female conquests would give him glowing references; certainly he could never be accused of being a selfish lover.

He couldn't remember a woman ending a relationship with him. It had always been him that had ended them, either deliberately or purely by circumstance. Some of his conquests had just been brief dalliances and he had difficulty establishing relationships with women because of his work. He knew he had been guilty of breaking several hearts and for that he was remorseful. He enjoyed his sitters flirting with him but it was rare that he took it further than that. When he did fancy some sexual relief he knew where to find plenty of women in Paris to indulge him, who didn't require payment. He did not spend his limited free time in the bars of Paris; he hadn't the time, money or inclination to do so. He had no time to court women; he had a living to make. Besides, he had never experienced true love until he met Marie and the depth of his emotions since had overwhelmed him on several occasions.

He had never had one of his paramours accuse him of fathering a child but whether that had been luck or down to his careful management was debateable. He had been very careful to ensure he did not risk losing either his own reputation or that of the ladies concerned. All artists were highly volatile and passionate and prone to letting their hearts rule their heads. He had managed to avoid death in the one duel he had been called to fight in, due to his skilful fencing and he had refused to proceed further once he had disarmed his opponent of his sword. He had been lucky to win the call to dictate the weapon of choice. Had it been his opponent's call he may have had to face pistols and he was not as certain of achieving the same outcome.

5

It was almost four weeks before a note arrived from Van Dries saying he had found the perfect sapphire and diamond ring at a very reasonable price of 1500 francs. Marie would be coming in for her lesson in two days' time so he would take her round afterwards, to view the ring. He realised that it may not be a perfect fit and the size may need altering.

The following Tuesday morning, he waited for Marie's carriage to arrive and went down to greet her. After she had alighted, he turned back and told the driver to pick her up at 4 p.m. at the main gate of the Luxembourg Gardens. Before they went up the steps to the main studio he pulled her into his arms and kissed her cheek.

'Marie, after your class I am taking you to Van Dries' office to look at a possible engagement ring.'

Marie replied, 'Oh, really Charles? That will be wonderful.'

They arrived at around 3 p.m. after a pleasant walk through the centre of Paris. Van Dries ushered them into his office and Charles could see by his reaction to Marie that he was captivated by her beauty. He opened the ring box and switched on the light to reveal a square set, deep blue sapphire surrounded by twelve glittering diamonds on a platinum band.

Marie gasped, 'Oh, Charles it is beautiful and will match my sapphire necklace perfectly.'

Charles examined it carefully and was delighted with the depth of blue in the stone. He only hoped it would not be too big for Marie's slender finger and would leave enough room for a wedding band. She tried it on and Van Dries gave her a platinum wedding band to try with it.

Van Dries said, 'It could not look better on your elegant long finger Mademoiselle, and there is plenty of room for the wedding band as well.'

Marie asked, 'Will I be able to take the ring today?'

Charles laughed. 'Well, I don't think you will appreciate waiting any longer sweetheart, so if you go back into the waiting area I will sort out the finances.'

He did a bit of bartering with Van Dries and managed to get the ring for 1200 francs with the promise of purchasing the two wedding rings from him. He left with the ring safely tucked in his inside pocket and as they walked back he changed the route and suggested they walk through the Luxembourg Gardens. He headed to the Medici Fountain area and although there were several people around, he led Marie up to the edge of the fountain. He dropped down on one knee and took her hand.

'Marie, will you do me the honour of becoming

my wife?'

Marie's face was a picture of amazement but she replied, 'Of course I will. I love you more and more each day.'

He stood up and produced the ring box and placed the ring on the third finger of her left hand and then kissed her cheek. To his surprise he received a round of applause from a small group that had stopped to watch when they saw him on his knee in front of the fountain. He took Marie's hand and ushered her over to an empty seat.

'Now my darling, the ring is on your finger and I feel you are a step closer to becoming mine. You do realise that I will have to work non-stop until our wedding day so I won't be able to visit you at weekends as that is when I have my commission portraits to do. I will try to get over when I can but at least I will see you when you come for your weekly lessons. At least the negotiations for leasing the house we saw together are nearly finalised and we should get possession at the end of July. Do not think I am being negligent; you can always send me letters via your father if you want to discuss wedding plans with me. If we are to have a month's honeymoon in Lille together then I need to get some money to pay for it.'

She hugged him close. 'I do understand Charles, but it will be difficult not seeing you nor being able to spend time alone with you, but I appreciate that you are doing it for me and if it means we can have four weeks away together then I will try and bear it.'

He led her towards the main gate entrance and she was surprised to see her carriage ready and waiting. He took her in his arms and kissed her on the lips and he was touched when she blushed. He helped her into the carriage and waved her off.

He made his way back to the studio, full of happiness and determined to work non-stop to achieve his financial goal.

oOo

Charles attended an art exhibition at the Louvre, along with several pupils and had been explaining the techniques of a particular portrait with his pupils gathered round. They were in a large gallery with several people milling around.

Suddenly, a loud male voiced bellowed behind him, 'Don't believe a word he says; he hasn't a clue what he's talking about!'

He turned around quickly, ready to defend his honour. His adversary was none other than Manet.

'Keep your opinions to yourself, Manet, or I'll run you through with a sword!' He was aware of the amused looks of his students and the outraged faces of the people in the gallery.

Manet approached him, laughing with delight, saying, 'I'm sorry, Charles, I could not resist the temptation to embarrass you. Let me take you out for a drink later as recompense?' Charles relaxed as he began to see the funny side of the situation.

'All right then, Edouard, but all the drinks are at your expense, you rogue.'

Manet turned to Charles' pupils. 'I listened to his critique and it wasn't too far off the mark.' Realising that Charles was in danger of punching him he whipped round and set off declaring, 'See you at Café Gerbois from 8 p.m., Charles.'

Later, Charles arrived at the appointed bar to find Manet surrounded by a group of artists and friends. When he saw him he had to face Manet's detailed account of his dishonourable prank on Charles at the Louvre and this caused considerable amusement amongst the assembled crowd.

He had to admit he would probably have done the same in similar circumstances but he vowed he would find a way to return the favour whenever the opportunity arose. He settled back and enjoyed the bonhomie and as promised, Manet refilled his glass.

After about an hour he took the opportunity to join Edouard at the bar as he wanted to speak to him privately. He suggested they went back to his studio for a chat and he readily agreed. They made their excuses and departed.

Both of them were slightly the worse for drink and Edouard could not resist inspecting the portraits in his studio. Charles had been careful to remove the frames he did not want Edouard to see, before he had gone to the bar. The paintings included some of his students' work and he was pleased that Manet came to the same conclusions as he had on their work.

He also commented that he had heard on the grapevine from his students that Charles's temper was escalating and he wondered if this had anything to do with his frustration at not bedding the delectable Marie.

Charles responded in disbelief. 'Edouard, I brought you here with the intention of asking you to be my best man, but after your escapades today I may have to seriously reconsider.'

'Rubbish, Charles, how could you possibly ask anyone else? I was the one who pushed you into asking for her hand and so I am going to see my project through to fruition. Am I to assume you are being the perfect knight and leaving your fair maiden until your wedding? I admire your self-control; I'm afraid I would not have been able to restrain myself. France could not have given the Légion d'Honneur to a more chivalrous man.'

Charles laughed. He could not turn Edouard down; he had a knack of summing up his situation with such clarity, combined with a wicked sense of humour but the ability to ridicule him kindly.

'Did you know that Anne Boleyn made Henry VIII wait eight years to consummate their love and it happened here on French soil when he came over to visit Francis I, to persuade him to join forces against the Spanish? He had already fathered a son to Anne's sister Mary and she kept him at bay until a month before the wedding. She spent her youth here at the French court observing the politics and intrigue. It was obviously well worth it but the only problem was she failed to produce a son and then Henry had to contrive an affair to be rid of her. His only saving grace being that he sent for a French swordsman to cut off her head! However, her daughter Elizabeth was the best queen that England ever had.'

Charles said, 'Edouard, I never had the opportunity to study history. I was painting from the age of eight and living in abject poverty.'

Edouard's reply was, 'Good job it was worthwhile then. How old were you when you had your first sexual encounter? I was a mere uncouth youth of fourteen who couldn't wait to discover the vagaries of the female body.'

There followed over the next hour Edouard's full, unabridged version of his first sexual encounter with one of his family servants, fuelled by another bottle of wine each.

When he had finished, he wanted to hear Charles's version and the wine had sufficiently loosened his tongue enough for him to confess to his encounter with Isabella. This invoked a high level of amusement from Edouard, who had sensed the deception from the very beginning and taunted him mercilessly. Charles's only defence was that he had been an innocent boy at the time. He also cautioned him regarding faithfulness.

'Be careful, Charles. When you become so intimate with a woman in body and soul they have an instinctive ability to know, without any evidence, when you have been unfaithful. A year after I married, my eyes strayed to another woman and Suzanne knew immediately. It was only an inconsequential passing fancy but did I live to regret it. She banished me from her bed for three solid months, flirted outrageously with any man she encountered and drove me to the depths of despair. Eventually, I begged for her forgiveness on my knees as I was terrified of losing her. Suffice to say I am a weak man and have failed her twice since and have lived to regret it.'

Charles could not contemplate ever being unfaithful to Marie.

They reminisced about one of their drinking bouts, which could have resulted in Charles's death. They had been very drunk one night and on returning home had got into a skirmish with two rogues determined to rob them, even though by this time neither of them had more than a franc on them. As both of them were fighting in the street, Edouard had seen in the reflection of a shop window, Charles's opponent pull a dagger from his sleeve. His shout of warning had saved his life and he had disarmed his opponent and then punched him so hard to the head he fell unconscious to the ground. It could have been a disaster but he would be forever in Edouard's debt.

Sleep was beginning to settle on both inebriated men and Manet took his leave to walk the ten minutes to his apartment. Edouard's parting shot was that he hoped that his first encounter with Marie would fulfil all his expectations.

oOo

It was the last Saturday in July and the weather was very warm. Charles was on his way to visit Marie at her home outside Paris and it would be the first time they had been together since their engagement in April. He had seen her at his weekly art class but they had rarely had chance but for the odd kiss before she departed. Marie had corresponded with him, which had kept his spirits up when he had been working hard to get all his commissions completed.

The house lease had been secured and although it came fully furnished, Marie had been busy planning what alterations and decorations she wanted to make before the wedding. He had given her a free hand to do what she wished as it took the responsibility out of his hands, but he had given her a tight budget to work with.

The carriage pulled up to the drive and before it had stopped, Marie was running out of the house down the main steps and pulling the door open. As he stepped out she threw her arms around him and he lifted her off her feet, giving her a big hug and a kiss.

'Someone is pleased to see me then?'

'Charles, you have no idea how much I have missed you over these last three months. I know I have seen you weekly but never alone and it has been so hard. I have thrown myself into planning the changes to the house and I need your approval before I commission the work.'

They went inside the house and he greeted Pierre and Louise and was delighted to find that Henri was home for the weekend too. They went into the dining room for a light lunch and the wedding was the topic of conversation.

After lunch, Marie ushered him into the library and showed him the sketches she had drawn of the rooms in the house she wanted to change. He was fascinated that she had drawn each room with all its furniture and then made a second drawing showing how she wanted to change it, whether by just decorating and re-carpeting, or changing the layout. He was really proud of her efforts. She had transformed the main salon and dining room and also made alterations to their bedroom by incorporating a smaller bedroom into their own bathroom and dressing room. She had also transformed the main entrance hall, stairs and landing.

'Marie, you have excelled yourself in this work and the house will have your elegant feminine touch, which it was sadly lacking. Have you obtained fixed prices from the builder and decorators for this work?'

'Of course I have, Charles, and it all comes within your budget – even the purchase of new salon furniture – plus I have persuaded Mother to let me have one or two essential items from here.'

They had a trip to make to the church to see the priest and Marie would explain how the service would work. They changed into breeches and white shirts and planned to ride over to the church then go down to the sea where he had painted her portrait. They passed Louise on the way out and she tutted disapprovingly at Marie in breeches rather than a riding habit. However, Marie ignored her and they made their escape to the stables.

The head groom offered to tack the horses up for them but Marie insisted they would be fine doing it themselves. She was riding Favorit and Charles was riding one of the hunt horses. They put halters on under the bridle so they would be able to tie them up outside the church. They saddled up and set off to the church. The temperature was very hot and humid.

They went to the church and found a shaded spot to tie the horses up next to a well. They offered them a drink and then left them. The beautiful Norman church was beautifully cool and calm and they sat down in the front pew, waiting for the priest. Charles loved watching the sunlight pour through the stained glass windows, casting a sceptre of colour on the marble pillars leading up to the altar. He felt safe warm and secure in this hallowed church and he was so glad they were marrying here in informality rather than having the service in a grand cathedral. He held Marie's hand as he wanted to share this quiet moment, reflecting with her.

The priest arrived and Marie explained the order of service to both of them and then the priest left them alone. Charles led her up to the altar rail and they knelt and prayed for a few moments in dignified silence. As they stood up he pulled her to him and gave her a passionate kiss on her lips.

'I can't wait for you to be my wife, Marie. You have brought such joy into my life already, I can only wonder at how good life will be when you are by my side.'

'Oh, Charles, you do say the loveliest things to me and I hope I can make you a good wife.'

They walked back out of church into the brilliant sunlight and heat. They mounted up and headed into the coolness of the forest to ride down to the beach. They came out from the trees and down onto the beach and rode along the water's edge until they reached the spot at which he had painted the portraits. They tied the horses up to an overturned boat and took their riding boots off and walked over to the sea to paddle in the cool water, walking slowly, hand in hand.

Marie paused and said, 'Please give me one of your soul-searching kisses, Charles. I have missed you so much, my body aches for you.'

He pulled her to his chest and bent down and put his arms right round her tightly, then sought her lips with his own. Marie responded and put her hand on his cheek. They kissed until they both had to stop for air.

Marie said, 'Tell me what you are thinking, Charles?'

'I am thinking that I would like to carry you out into the sea and undress you and make passionate love to you.'

'Well, what's stopping you, because I want that too?'

'Do not tempt me, Marie. We are not married yet and there will be time for you to learn how to satisfy your body when we are married and I will take great pleasure in showing you.' He pulled her hand and made her walk back towards the horses.

'But Charles, nobody is here and even if someone appears they won't be able to see anything if we are in the water.'

He laughed at her determination to get her own way and shook his head. 'No, you little temptress. I am the boss in this marriage; you will obey my commands.'

Marie was disconcerted but she had another plan up her sleeve, which she would put into action now that this one had failed. They returned to the stables and Henri was there having just exercised his horse. Marie released her Borzois and they sat on the stable wall and chatted until it was time to go and dress for dinner.

They had a wonderful dinner as everyone was discussing the wedding and new house plans. Louise confirmed that Marie's younger sister Sophie, who had remained in St. Petersburg with friends, would not be able to make it to the wedding. She had been cast as the leading lady in a forthcoming play and would be unable to get time off at the end of September as the play would be in full production, daily, until Christmas. Charles enjoyed his chat over port with Henri and Pierre and afterwards, Marie and Louise joined them in the library and they all had a turn playing at the piano and singing along.

Marie was being provocative with her choice of song and he hoped her mother had not seen some of the looks Marie had given him whilst she was singing.

At the end of the evening he went to his room tired, emotional and definitely frustrated... but at least he had not lost control of himself. He knew she was becoming adept at orchestrating time alone for them but he was going to have to put an end to it before he did something he would regret.

He tossed and turned in the bed, first too hot and then too cold. He was dreaming of making passionate love to Marie but his self-control was so used to denying him satisfaction that he kept waking before he had gone too far. This time, he left the covers off in an attempt to cool both his ardour and his body and he felt himself finally drifting off to sleep.

His dreams intensified and he dreamt he was kissing her passionately and she was running her hand down his thigh and when she touched him intimately, he woke to find her lying beside him in the bed. His first reaction was to leap out of bed as if he had been struck by lightning.

'For God's sake, Marie, what are you doing in my bed?'

She was still on the bed, thankfully wearing her chemise, and replied, 'I couldn't sleep and my desire for you was so strong it drove me to seek you out. We only have two months to go before the wedding and I just want you to make love to me now.'

He was on his knees, leaning over the bed in an effort to conceal his nakedness.

'No, Marie, I will absolutely not take you until we are married. You are my gift from God and I will not risk his wrath by taking you before we have taken our vows.' He saw the shock and disappointment on her face. 'I could so easily be tempted but it would be over in minutes and you would not enjoy it. I want to awaken your sexuality slowly and carefully and most of all I want our union to be of heart, body and soul. I promise you that it will be worth waiting for as I will take you on a journey of discovery that you can only dream of. Once we are married my body will be your servant, as it is all I have to give you. Please do not think that I am rejecting you; I just want to do everything to ensure our marriage is a success. What if you got pregnant? How could I look your father in the eye knowing I had taken his daughter before our wedding day?' Marie sat up and slid across to him and sat on the edge of the bed and he put his arms round her, sensing she was close to tears. 'Sweetheart, please don't cry. I'm sorry if I have upset you but we have only a few weeks to go, let's not spoil it.'

He held her close while her sobs subsided and then he realised that she was within inches of him with just a chemise between them and he was stark naked. If he stood up she was going to get more than an eyeful of something an innocent girl should not see. The chair with his drawers and shirt on was about ten feet to his right. He planned to pull her up onto her feet as he rose from his knees and then make a dash to the right, grab his drawers and put them on with his back to her. He executed this move rather too quickly and as he grabbed his drawers and put his left foot inside he caught his toe on the waistband, overbalanced and went flying over the right arm of the chair and ended up sprawled on the floor with his buttocks and other parts totally exposed.

To his horror, Marie started to laugh as he was struggling to get his other foot in the drawers. With one mighty effort he got them on and ran and picked her up, shoving her back into the bed with the covers over her head. He jumped in beside her, telling her to shush as Henri was in the room next door and he was terrified he would have heard the chair falling over and come into his room. He lay there for a couple of minutes and then he turned to her.

'Marie, I need you out of here this minute.'

'All right I am going, but you have got to admit that was extremely funny and serves you right for turning me down.'

'It was not funny for me.' He sat up, grabbed

her wrist and pulled her out of the bed and led her over to the door, carefully opening it just an inch to check that all was quiet. He listened carefully for any sound and heard nothing. He bent and kissed her passionately and then opened the door further and pushed her into the corridor. She had taken two steps and then the bathroom door opened on the opposite side and Henri walked out to go across to his bedroom, directly in front of her. They looked at one another and then Henri smiled and smacked her lightly across the bum as she turned and fled.

He closed the door quickly and leant with his back to it. *What will Henri be thinking of him for having his sister in his bedroom?* It was obvious that he would assume she had come straight from his bed. He would have to try and speak to him in the morning, but would he believe him? He saw her with his own eyes and he would think he was trying to lie to cover up what they had been doing. He threw his drawers off and jumped back into bed. *Oh, why couldn't she have waited patiently another few weeks? How many men would have turned her away from their bed? Did she even think of the danger she was putting herself in if she had she become pregnant as a result? How can you explain a seven-month term baby that looks full term?* Her parents would have been so disappointed in them. He really couldn't work out whether she had just been foolish, precocious or consumed with passion. Either way, this firebrand of a girl was going to need some taming and he knew he was going to have his hands full, just as her mother had predicted.

oOo

The next morning, he went down to breakfast early in the hope of catching Henri alone. His plan was slightly disrupted by Pierre's presence but he followed Henri out after breakfast and took him through the salon and outside. Henri looked slightly puzzled to be bundled out of the door so rapidly.

Henri said, 'Charles if this is about last night, forget it. I saw nothing. What you and Marie choose to do is entirely your own affair; you are an engaged couple and nobody will hear anything from me.'

He interrupted, 'But Henri, it wasn't what you thought it was. I have not in any way dishonoured your sister. She took it upon herself to seek me out and ended up in bed with me whilst I was initially asleep and when I came round, thankfully I realised I was not alone and I absented myself from a very compromising position.'

Henry laughed. 'I do believe you, remember I am her brother and I know only too well how downright naughty and headstrong she can be. If you refused her you deserve a second Légion d'Honneur medal for chivalry. I don't know another man on earth who could have done that. Perhaps she will see the error of her ways now she has had time to consider her unruly behaviour and you may find she will be full of contrition. Marie does not realise her effect on men; she is totally oblivious to her own beauty and sometimes her own safety. She is a tomboy and perhaps had a little too much freedom to flex her muscles when in Russia as she was permitted to study alongside me. She has no idea of her power over men and now all her energy is expended on capturing your heart, she will never have thought of the possible consequences of her actions. She got me into several scrapes as a teenager, from which I managed to disentangle her. And believe me, Russian men are nothing like as chivalrous as you.'

Charles replied, 'I can see I am not going to have an easy ride turning your wild sister into a demure French wife.'

'Probably not Charles, but it will never be boring living with her. She might try your patience to the limit but once you are her husband she will never stray from your side; she is the most loyal person I know and will fight like a lioness to protect her loved ones. The two of you will produce some beautiful and clever children... Let's hope they inherit your temperament rather than hers.'

6

When Charles came down to his studio on the Friday before his wedding there was a lot of activity, especially for 9 a.m. He was surprised to find all his current students in the studio as Friday was usually the quietest day. Antonio announced that he had organised a tutorial on architecture for all of the students and he was taking them out round Paris to teach architectural drawing. Charles was a little mystified but Antonio explained that he had done it because he did not expect Charles to be teaching today as he was leaving for the chateau at 2 p.m. with Manet. He had no objection as it gave him chance to tidy up as he would be missing for a whole month on his honeymoon and he did have one important portrait commission to finish.

Antonio was the only student going to his wedding; he could not invite them all as it was only a small family wedding and as Marie's parents were funding it, he had kept his invitations to a select few. He thought it strange that Antonio only took one large sketch pad and pencils but perhaps he was not intending the students to do any individual drawing. His students wished him well for tomorrow and his long honeymoon but he could detect an undercurrent of excitement and saw some exchanges of glances between them. He could only think that Antonio had probably promised them a study of the bars in Paris rather than the bridges and architecture. He watched them all leave from the window and the group of about fifteen looked more like they were off for a day at the races than a drawing lesson.

He selected the portrait he had been working on of an eminent lawyer and finished off the colouring of his robes. He worked quickly and accurately, reflecting on his wedding day. He had waited six months for this day to arrive and he was so relieved he would finally be able to have his wife by his side. He desperately did not want their first sexual experience to be a failure as the tension of the prolonged wait had built up to boiling point.

He finished the final touching up of the canvas and left it to dry. He wrote Antonio a note, asking him to deliver it to his client next week. He went up into his apartment to pack his suitcase for their honeymoon and made himself a quick snack of bread and cheese. Antonio was moving in whilst he was away, mainly as a security measure but he dreaded to think what state it would be in after a month of him living in his apartment. He would have to hope that any conquests he made would be house-proud as there was no chance with Antonio.

He came back down to the studio, selected a roll

of canvas and packed up his oils, watercolours and crayons in another suitcase with two large sketch pads. His parents would call for these when they returned to Paris to take the train to Lille as he and Marie would be riding down.

At just after 2 p.m. Manet arrived, full of joy and anxious to ensure that he had remembered everything he would need for the wedding day and most importantly, the wedding rings. Charles assured him he had everything necessary just as the carriage from the chateau pulled up outside. Pierre had already been picked up from the Conservatoire as he had been teaching today. He noticed a meaningful glance between Manet and Pierre but had no idea what it was about.

Pierre asked him if he was looking forward to his big day and he assured him that he could not wait for the ceremony tomorrow. He had left the order of service and the hymns to Marie and Pierre as they were better placed to liaise with the church. He had been consulted about the vows and they had both agreed to the full Catholic vows being used. They had decided against having a mass afterwards as this would make a very lengthy service.

Pierre advised that he had attended a church choir practice last week and the choir had been in good voice and been augmented by another local church choir to increase the impact. Marie's arrival in church and procession was to be to Handel's 'Arrival of the Queen of Sheba', which he had picked as he thought it suited Marie and so did Pierre so they had dismissed Wagner's 'Bridal Chorus', which was the usual bridal entrance tune. Their final processional piece was to be to Mendelssohn's 'Wedding March'. The hymns were to be 'Love Divine all Loves Excelling' and 'Ode to Joy' by Beethoven. The choir was doing a special arrangement of 'The Lord's my Shepherd (Psalm 23)' whilst they were signing the register. He assured Philippe that as he was Director of Music at the Conservatoire Paris, he had every faith in him overseeing his wedding service. He noticed a meaningful glance between Manet and Pierre but had no idea what it was about. They had a convivial journey to the chateau.

As the carriage pulled up at the front door Marie flew out. He jumped swiftly from the carriage and she ran into his arms at the bottom of the steps and he embraced her.

Manet commented, 'Is it a case of long time no see then, Marie?'

She blushingly replied, 'Oh yes Edouard, it is nearly two weeks since I last saw Charles.'

They went into the salon and afternoon tea was served. He greeted Louise and thought she looked a little stressed but then, it was rather a special occasion. He knew that Marie had just had her final dress fitting.

He turned to Louise and asked, 'Did the dress fitting go well Madame, and are you delighted with the result?'

Louise smiled and replied, 'As usual Marie had her own ideas about what she wanted as a wedding dress and although I offered to buy her whatever dress she wanted, I was told when we went to Charles Worth's that she was "marrying an artist in her local church" and not "marrying a prince in a cathedral," and she therefore dismissed any gown that did not fit her remit.'

Charles realised there had obviously been some tension. He replied, 'I have great faith in Marie's taste, Madame, and I am certain she will look stunning on her wedding day.'

After tea, Manet was shown up to his room and Charles and Marie managed to escape into the library for a few minutes alone.

Charles said, 'My darling you look the picture of health are you looking forward to tomorrow as much as I am?'

Oh, Charles I can't wait for the ceremony and then to have four weeks honeymoon together will be perfect.'

He pulled her close to his chest and kissed her passionately on the lips. They had a few moments together until he heard footsteps coming towards the library. Her father and Manet appeared and Marie had to leave as her two maids of honour and the flower girl and page boy were due to have a dress fitting at 4:30 p.m.

They had a brandy together and at 5 p.m. the butler showed Gabriel Fauré into the library. He had arrived from his job as an organist in Rennes, Brittany. Charles had met him when he was a student at the Nidermeyer School of Music in Paris and, although he was nine years younger than Charles, they had become good friends. He also knew Pierre through his work and it was Pierre who had invited him to stay with the family during the wedding. Fauré had written his first composition at the age of 19, 'Cantique de Jean Racine', in 1866. Charles asked him if he would perform the piece on the piano for them and he agreed.

It was a beautiful piece of music and although written for the organ and in four part voice sections Fauré sang the tenor section as he played and all of them were overwhelmed by its beauty. Fauré said he was so pleased with its reception that he intended to write a full requiem in the future when he had some time to devote to doing so. Fauré had been a devotee of Charles Gounod when he had been in Paris and he was invited to the wedding too. He would also be able to see Emmanuel Chabrier, a composer who was four years older than him but worked for the Ministry of the Interior in Paris; they met while Fauré was studying at the Nidermeyer. They chatted amicably and then at 6:30 p.m. they all went to change for dinner.

As the family assembled before dinner, Charles sought out Marie to introduce her to Fauré but he found her already engaged in conversation with him. Marie explained she had met him at the

Conservatoire whilst he had been at the Nidermeyer. Henri had made it in time for dinner from his barracks in Paris and was looking fit and well. Marie introduced him to her two maids of honour who were staying overnight and the parents of her flower girl and page boy. He did not enquire about their dresses as Marie's mother was in the group and he did not want to cause any further embarrassment.

Charles' mother and father had also arrived from Lille and dinner was delayed for a quarter of an hour to allow them to change. The train had been delayed coming into Paris. His parents joined them full of apologies for their delay. He was delighted to see them after twenty-five years and they both looked well. His mother was a little overawed at the opulence of the chateau but Marie's parents were wonderful at putting her at ease. He introduced them to Marie and he could tell she had made an impression on his father with her beauty.

At the dinner table he was sat opposite Marie, with his parents on either side. Manet, Fauré and Henri were further down the table with the maids of honour. His mother asked about the timing of the ceremony the following day and he admitted that apart from the bare minimum, Marie's parents had organised the service and reception as they would be the ones coping with the guests. The service was timed to start at 12 p.m. and the reception back at the chateau for 3 p.m. followed by a buffet dinner and dance in the evening. He had to ask Marie how many guests were expected and she said about eighty for the wedding and up to 100 for the evening dance. Charles was surprised as he had no idea who all these guests were, but no doubt he would find out. He had never really thought past the wedding service as to him that had been all that mattered. He just wanted to wed Marie so they could be together at last as he had been waiting for so long.

During the sweet course, Marie told him in a whisper that in keeping with tradition they would not be permitted to see each other again until the wedding ceremony. Her father had already instructed Manet as best man and Henri as groomsman that they were to keep Charles away from her and had to breakfast at 8 a.m. so as to ensure they did not meet in the morning. Marie suggested they meet after everyone had retired and he was quick to dismiss any notion she had in her mind of doing this and assured her that if she needed anything she must send a note via her maid of honour and he would do likewise with Henri. After the last time Marie had been foolish enough to enter his room in the small hours and he had sent her packing; he was not risking anything going wrong at this final stage. All this fuss just because it was considered unlucky for the groom to see the bride before the wedding ceremony? Personally, he couldn't see why but again, he had to bow to tradition.

When it was time for the gentlemen to withdraw he squeezed her hand under the table and as he rose, kissed the nape of her neck. This did not go unnoticed by several of the guests. Manet caught him as they left for the salon.

'Well, have you been told you are under house arrest now so no sneaking off to meet Marie overnight, both me and Henri are in rooms either side of you?'

Charles replied, 'I have no intention of going anywhere near Marie. I have waited six months so one more day is not going to matter.'

Manet replied reflectively, 'I don't honestly know how you have managed to wait this long. I certainly admire your restraint.'

'I love her and if she is my gift from God I would do nothing to risk our marriage failing.'

They had arrived in the salon so any further discussion was untenable.

He sat down next to Henri and he said conspiratorially, 'I gather Manet has told you that you are under house arrest. It seems my father should have put the armed guard on my sister not you?'

Charles just smiled. At least Henri had believed him that when he caught Marie leaving his room, there had been no impropriety on his part.

The discussion over drinks centred mainly on the music scene in Paris as Fauré had been teaching in Brittany for the last year. He was pleased neither he nor the wedding was the main topic of conversation. After dinner, the men retired to the library and his father indicated he wanted a word with him. He showed him into a small salon next to the library so they could speak privately.

Jean said, 'I just wanted to let you know that I have sorted out your accommodation in the small cottage when you get to Lille for your honeymoon. We thought you would rather do that than stay in the main house. Your mother and I will leave you alone to get to know one another as we both appreciate you will have had little time together during your engagement. You will need to take care when you ride down and I have put together a list of suitable places to stay without drawing too much attention to yourselves at various towns or villages on the way. You said Marie was beautiful in your letter but I never thought she would be so exquisite. She will cause quite a stir if she rides with only you as an escort.'

'Don't worry, we are both aware of that and she is insisting on dressing as a boy and riding astride so as not to create any tension.' replied Charles.

'Very wise as you just never know who you might encounter on the way.'

They went back into the library and Manet suggested they have a game of cards as Pierre and Fauré were sat at the piano, playing. He agreed in the hope that it calmed his nerves and left the two of them alone at the end of the room. They played rummy as he was in no mood to risk playing poker with Manet.

Manet chose the opportunity to ask, 'Are you

worried about the wedding night?'

'Why, should I be?' he retorted.

'Well, I think I would be after anticipating the beauty of Marie's body since meeting her. I would be terrified of "over egging the pudding," shall we say, and coming sooner rather than later.'

Charles smiled and replied, 'There are ways of dealing with that particular problem.'

Manet said, 'Well at least she will have the knowledge of what to expect; she's hardly an innocent girl.'

Charles gave him a long, hard stare and growled, 'I think you had better explain exactly what you are insinuating here?'

Manet realised how he could have been misconstrued and was quick to respond, 'Don't misunderstand me Charles, but she is a classical scholar and the Romans and Greeks were just as quick to describe their sex lives on paper as they were their battles. She was also raised in Russia and would have been aware of all the politics, intrigue and sex lives of the Russian court. I am not suggesting for one moment she indulged in it but she would have known what was going on around her.'

Charles calmed down and sighed, 'Well let's hope that I live up to her expectations then.'

Manet sighed, 'I am sure you will, Charles and yours will be a marriage of mind, body and soul.'

The men retired to bed early as everyone had been travelling to get to the chateau and they had a very busy day tomorrow.

Charles was escorted to his room by both Manet and Henri and apart from a joke about Henri being on guard outside his room, he was left alone. He got changed and then checked his uniform over for the next day. He decided his boots were not shiny enough so he gave them a polish. He checked his sword and had visions of tripping up over it going down the aisle or worse still, when they had to kneel at the altar, not remembering to check the angle as he knelt down. *How was he going to get to sleep with all these nightmare scenarios churning round in his brain?* He just hoped everything would go well and they could get off to Lille and have some time to themselves.

7

Charles had deliberately left the curtains open so that he would wake early in the morning and when he checked the clock it was 6:30 a.m. He looked out to check the weather and it was a bright sunny day and it did not look too windy. He could already see activity out in the garden as the gardeners were picking hydrangeas and roses to deck out the inside of the house. A few more were sweeping the entire driveway and he could see across to the stables. The family horses were being turned out into the field to make way for the many carriage horses that would need to be accommodated during the day.

He thought he might walk over to the church and have some solitude and prayer before breakfast. He got washed and dressed and just as he had finished, he heard a knock at his door. He went to open it to find Manet in his robe.

He said, 'I heard you moving about and just thought I would check what your intentions were for this early morning.'

'Well it is such a nice day, I thought I might walk across to the church and have some peaceful prayer time.'

Manet was horrified. 'No Charles, you cannot go near the church; it will be so busy with everybody decorating and preparing for the service. The priest will have a fit if you turn up so early in the morning. He will think you are having second thoughts about the marriage.'

Charles stared at him, incredulous. 'Why ever would he think that?'

Manet replied, 'Why don't we walk down to the beach where you painted the portraits… or you could show me the stables and I would love to see Marie's Borzois?'

Charles was still astonished by Manet's behaviour but he told him to get dressed and he would take him round the stables but he knew the grooms would not be too happy about having them underfoot. Manet went back to his room and Charles thought over their strange conversation. Maybe Manet had been told to keep an eye on him by Pierre, to ensure he had no contact with Marie. Or did he think he was going to leave his beautiful daughter at the altar? Surely Pierre knew him better than that.

Manet returned promptly and they started to go down the main stairs. Manet went in front and made him wait whilst he checked Marie was not in the hallway. They went out through the main doors and all the gardeners wished him 'good morning'. They walked down to the stables and as he entered the main yard the head groom came running over to see what they wanted. He seemed very surprised when Charles assured him he was just showing Manet the horses and had come to see Marie's Borzois. He ushered them over to the kennels and turned them out into a run but made Charles promise he wouldn't take them out as if either of them got away he would be in big trouble. Manet was fussing Lily and Monty and they both welcomed his attention.

They watched as four Percherons were harnessed in the yard and then yoked in couples to the two hay wagons that had bales of straw attached in lines to the sides of the vehicles. They left the Borzois safely in the pen and Charles asked the young lad harnessing up the Percherons where they were going. He said they were going to the station to ferry guests to the church and Charles was bemused at why they were using the hay carts when the carriages would have been more appropriate. The boy said four carriages were also being prepared to go to the station but not until 10 a.m.

They wandered over to the first field, which had the family riding horses in, and he introduced Manet to Favorit and to Henri's chestnut horse, which he had painted him on and then to his new, black cavalry mount that his father had purchased for him when he joined the Hussars. Manet thought the black horse was wonderful as he was galloping about and rearing up, playing with Favorit as he obviously wasn't used to having a field to play in. He was also flirting with Favorit as all the cavalry horses were stallions or geldings and mares were not used. Although he was a gelding he still had eyes for a pretty mare like Favorit.

It was already 7:30 a.m. so it was too late to go down to the beach as they had to breakfast at 8 a.m. They walked slowly back up to the house and into the dining room. The entrance hall and hallway had already been decorated with enormous vases of white roses, blue hydrangeas and red crocosmia. Outside the main double doors, urns of roses had been placed and on each step up to the house a planter of white gladioli had been placed at either end. There was obviously a theme of red, white and blue and he knew the maids of honour were in royal blue and Marie would be in white so maybe the red was for his red uniform and breeches.

Already in the dining room were his parents, Pierre, Henri and Fauré. Pierre looked relieved to see him so maybe he had been worried that he was going to jilt his daughter. Over breakfast, Pierre told them that a small salon at the back of the house had been prepared for the groom and his party so that he would be unable to see the bridal party before they left for church. Pierre said he needed Manet and Fauré for a couple of hours and so Henri would be in charge of him. He was thankful that Henri could help him with his uniform and sash with his Légion d'Honneur but had no idea why Pierre needed Manet.

He asked Manet what it was for and he said just

to go over his best man's speech and Pierre's father of the bride speech. Charles had completely forgotten about the reception speeches although he had made copious notes for his own speech. He wasn't too happy about what Manet might reveal about him and he warned him to keep it very clean and there was to be no mention of any women he may have been seen with in Paris. Manet always jumped to conclusions whenever he was seen with a female pupil as he assumed because he was in the company of women he must be having a relationship with them too. Why hadn't Pierre asked him about his speech? Probably because he knew Manet could be a loose cannon so he was checking it out on his behalf.

After breakfast, he went into the small salon with his parents and Henri, so he would be out of the way while the bridal party had their breakfast. He was beginning to get more nervous as the clock ticked. There was one small window in the salon that had a view of the driveway and he was surprised to see a carriage drive off. He was certain the occupants were Marie, Pierre, Manet and Faure.

At 10 a.m. he went up to his room with Henri to bath and change into his uniform. He washed and brushed his hair till it shone and made an attempt to keep the curls to a minimum. He was glad of Henri's assistance as he was all fingers and thumbs and incapable of fitting the sash or buckling his boots. Whilst he was in the shower, Henri had polished over his boots again. After he was in his boots and had placed his sword by his side Henri found him a back staircase to practise kneeling with his sword without catching it on the steps.

He went with Henri to his room while he got changed as Henri did not want to leave him alone. He was beginning to get paranoid that the family seemed so concerned that he was going to jilt Marie at the altar. He thought about raising this with Henri but decided against it as he knew Henri was well aware of how much he wanted to marry his hot-headed sister.

They went back to the salon where his parents were now assembled, changed and ready for the ceremony. His mother looked elegant but not 'Paris chic' in her navy gown trimmed with white lace buts she had a fashionable hat. He had already agreed with his father that he would pay him for their honeymoon stay as he was keen not to leave them out of pocket and so he made a mental note to add extra to cover their wedding clothes. There was lots of activity in the house and he could hear the flower girl and pageboy being restrained from running around the entrance hall by their parents.

Finally at 11:30 a.m. he made his way to the main entrance with Henri and his parents. Manet was now dressed and ready for the wedding and they exchanged smiles. Charles handed him the leather pouch containing the wedding rings as he felt even Manet could not lose them between the chateau and the church. Pierre was also in the hallway and gave him a warm handshake and complimented him on his uniform.

The carriage and four horses were waiting for them. The horses had white plumes attached to their headpieces and white ribbons tied to either side of their brow bands. He wondered if this had been Marie's idea or was the grooms' touch. He helped his mother into the carriage, followed by his father and then himself and Manet. He had remembered to be aware of his sword as he got in and did not trip up or catch it on anybody's leg as he sat down. As they left the driveway he could hear the church bells ringing and he could feel his stomach churning with nerves. He was in no mood for idle chit chat as he would not have been able to concentrate. As they got closer to the church, the coachman pulled up as he could see in the distance there were already two carriages depositing guests at the gate. He could see there were photographers taking pictures of the guests and knew they must have been from the newspapers as he did not recognise them – he had engaged the official wedding photographer. Finally, the carriage moved off into a brisk trot towards the church. Crowds of locals lined the street and his nerves increased again. A groom appeared at the door before they had even halted and he decided to alight first. Conscious of his sword, he went very carefully and Manet followed him. He offered a hand to his mother and helped her down. She looked surprised by the number of people around. As his father took her hand, the press photographers were taking pictures. The coach departed back to the chateau for the bridal party.

Guests were still arriving and greeting them as they went into the church. The arched doorway was decorated with a wreath of white roses and blue hydrangeas and the perfume of the roses was evident. The choir was milling around the entrance and the choirmaster shook his hand. The priest met him in the vestibule and he handed over the envelope with the money for the church fees. He looked through the open door, up the aisle of the Norman church. It was a mass of flowers and the scent from the many roses was intoxicating. The sun was shining through the stained glass window above the altar and filled the choir stalls and the nave with light.

oOo

The priest approached him and said it was time for him and Manet to take their seats. They followed the priest down the aisle. The church was full and he recognised guests as he walked, but just smiled. The organ was playing Pachebel's 'Canon' and he felt emotional as he took his seat in the front right- hand pew with his mother and father. Manet immediately turned round to chat to the row of eminent composers behind him: Fauré, Gounod and Chabrier. Behind them, in the next row were his eminent artist friends: Gustav Courbet, Henri Fantin-Latour, Zacharie Astruc and James McNeil Whistler.

All of them had been prominent artists when he

returned to Paris. He felt even more humbled that all these men had given up their valuable time to witness his marriage to his darling Marie. He heard noise from outside and assumed the bridal party had arrived and his heart missed a beat.

Suddenly, he heard the first notes of Handel's 'Arrival of the Queen of Sheba' but as well as the organ accompaniment there were strings, woodwind and brass. He could see they were positioned in the back rows of the right hand pews and were being played by an ensemble of teenage musicians. He saw his mother-in-law Louise being escorted by her son Henri down the aisle to the front left hand pew, followed by the clergy and choir. After they had passed he and Manet moved out into the aisle to await the bridal procession. He knew he should remain facing forward but there was no way he was missing his first sight of his bride.

At last, she was framed in the doorway. She was wearing a fitted white silk dress embellished with lace at the sleeves, neckline, bodice and hem. She had a red silk shawl over her shoulders, fastened at the back of her waist. She had a waist length, white silk veil over her shoulders and flowers in her hair. She was carrying a mixed bouquet of white, blue and red flowers. Her maids of honour wore royal blue fitted shift dresses with cowl necklines at the back. The page boy was in a royal blue sailor suit with white shirt and hat and the flower girl was in a white hooped silk dress with a matching red shawl.

He was fighting his emotions as she drew nearer on her father's arm; he faced forward and hastily wiped a tear from his eyes, which Manet and all his friends to the right noticed. His bride was at his side. He watched, enchanted as the maid of honour came forward and pulled the veil back over Marie's head to reveal her beautiful face and although the top of her hair was up, the rest flowed down to her shoulders. She then took her bouquet and the bridal party moved into the left hand pews, leaving Marie and her father with Charles and Manet.

He leant over and whispered to her. 'You look stunning, ma cherie.'

She did not speak but the sparkle of her deep blue eyes and her shy smile proclaimed how she was feeling. The sunlight bathed them in warmth and light and he silently thanked God for his wonderful gift.

The priest started the ceremony and Charles concentrated as hard as he could on the job required of him. When they reached the part of the ceremony asking if there was any objection to the marriage he remembered his recurring nightmare that some Russian count would appear at the church claiming she was legally promised to him. He held his breath in fear as the priest made the announcement. He was terrified that some man would snatch her away from him. Thankfully, only Manet had seen his signals of distress and he smiled encouragingly as the priest continued.

They moved on to the vows and at last, he was able to touch her hand as her father passed it over to the priest and he joined their hands together. He spoke his vows with clarity and true conviction. He had every intention of keeping his vow of faithfulness and he would love and cherish her until the day he died. Marie's responses were spoken quietly but with intensity. They gazed lovingly into each other's eyes as if it was only them and the priest there. Judging by the gasps and sobs of the guests at the front of the church this had not gone unnoticed.

Finally, they exchanged rings and his heartbeat slowed and his breathing steadied. When the priest spoke, saying 'Those whom God has joined together let no man put asunder,' he felt safe at last. They were officially married in the sight of God; they just had to sign the register to make it legal. At last he was commanded to 'kiss the bride'. He resisted the temptation to be overly demonstrative and gave her a lingering kiss on the lips and to his delight she blushed.

They moved to the altar for the blessing and prayers and he remembered to guide his sword as he knelt down beside his bride. Under the stained glass window the sunlight split into a myriad of colours reflecting off the wall, the altar and the marble pillars. He would have loved to have been able to stop and paint this phenomenon but he would have to try and fix it in his memory instead. The blessing over, the priest led them to the vestry to sign the register.

As they got through the door from the back of the altar he stopped her and pulled her close and gave her an urgent kiss on the lips and whispered, 'You have just made me the happiest man on earth, ma cherie.' He saw the tears well up in her eyes as he fought to contain his emotion.

Through the opposite door, both sets of parents, Henri and Manet appeared. He was pleased to note that both women had obviously been crying and he even detected the odd tear in Pierre's eyes. They signed the register with both fathers as witnesses. He could hear the melodic strain of 'The Lord's my Shepherd' being sung by the choir. He shook hands with Pierre, and his father and mother hugged him.

He was expecting the service to be over now and that they would be leaving the church. However, he noticed Marie, Pierre and Manet leave by the altar door as Henri came over to him, smiling.

'You are under my escort yet again, brother, a surprise awaits you. Follow me.' The organ played and Henri escorted him out of the door and back to his pew, followed by his parents and the bride's mother. When he sat down he was astonished to see that seats and music stands had been set out below the altar steps and in the first row of musicians he saw Gounod, Chabrier and Fauré with violins and behind them, the young musicians who had played the Handel piece. To his utter disbelief the first row of singers on the altar's steps consisted of Manet, Courbet, Fantin-Latour, Astruc, Whistler and Marie.

Ranged behind were three rows of his present and former art students including a beaming Antonio and then three rows of mixed choristers whom he did not know. Pierre was obviously conducting the entire performance, including both choirs and the orchestra, from the pulpit.

The first piece was Vivaldi's *Gloria* and he could not take his eyes off his artists' choir, especially Antonio who was revelling in the fact that it was an Italian composition. He vaguely remembered coming back one afternoon and hearing the strains of the *Gloria* being sung as he came up the steps but it had ceased as soon as he had entered the room. Having the church choir as well as the extra voices combined with the orchestra sounded truly triumphant.

The next piece was Mozart's 'Ave Verum', which has a haunting but peaceful melody. It was the exact opposite of the 'Gloria' and showed the skill of the voices to perfection and the composer's artistic ability.

The third piece was Anton Bruckner's 'Ave Maria', which had only been composed by the Austrian in 1861. Charles had not heard it before but he was amazed when Marie came to the front of the assembled orchestra within feet of him. As the music began he was spellbound to find that she was singing the soprano piece as a solo with the remaining alto, tenor and bass parts sung by the choirs. How brave was she to take on this task on her wedding day, especially for him. This was her personal wedding gift to him and he was overwhelmed. There was no stopping the tears falling this time; they came straight from his heart. He had heard her sing at the piano but never a piece of this complexity. He noticed that Henri and his mother were deeply affected by Marie's performance and her father must have been so proud of his daughter even though he suspected he had coached her through the piece individually as well as rehearsed the choirs. At the end, he saw the emotion break as she went back to her place in the choir and tears fell.

The final piece was Fauré's 'Cantique de Jean Racine' and he went to the organ to play the piece. The only other instruments needed were the violins to accompany the four-part harmonies of the choirs. He found it hard to believe that Fauré had only been 19 when he wrote this piece whilst he was still a student. The text was both sublime and romantic and being in French rather than Latin, had a melodic impact. As it came to a close there was a huge wave of clapping and stamping of feet mingled with loud hurrahs and Gounod went round to the organ and escorted Fauré to the front and shook his hand, as did Chabrier. Charles felt as happy for Fauré to be respected by his own peers as he would have been to have a painting accepted in the Salon.

He got to his feet and went to shake Faure's hand and give him a pat on the back. He motioned for Marie to join him as he would be expected to give a speech thanking all the musicians and singers for their performance. He kissed Marie lightly on the cheek as she joined him, to the amusement of the audience.

He took a deep breath and said, 'On behalf of my wife and myself I would like to thank you from the bottom of our hearts for the wonderful performance you have given in honour of our wedding. I suspect my father-in-law Pierre is responsible for staging, rehearsing and directing this concert and I really cannot convey how wonderful and uplifting I have found it as I had no idea this was planned and it has deeply moved me. I duly noted that his programme had a multi-European theme and included pieces composed by an Italian – Vivaldi, Austrians – Bruckner and Mozart and last but by no means least, French – Fauré.' (A huge round of applause erupted from the guests). Charles continued, 'Pierre must also have been responsible for coaching an army of artists, some of whom will have never sung a note before, into a passable choir. Now I understand why Antonio has been taking tutorials in architectural drawing, which appear to have taken place in the Conservatoire, and I can only hope that Pierre worked you as hard at your singing, as I do at your painting. I would also like to thank some of my past students from all over Europe who have bothered to come back to honour their master. I truly appreciate your time and effort and this probably explains why the wedding suddenly switched from August to September so that you could all be back in Paris.

The bridal party assembled in the vestry for the final procession out of church. He noticed that the artists' choir left their seats and moved back down the aisle, except Manet, who joined him in his best man role again. He gave Pierre another hug for his efforts and he managed to give Marie a kiss.

Mendelssohn's 'Wedding March' started playing in the church and he and Marie led the procession down the aisle. They were followed by the flower girl and page boy who been able to partake in a nap during the concert, Manet and Henri with the maids of honour on their arms, his mother and Pierre and finally, his father and Louise. They smiled at the guests they knew personally as they went down the aisle and he could feel a warm glow of contentment around him fuelled by the spectacle he had just witnessed.

As they reached the church door and came out into the bright sunlight they were met by a guard of honour with artists wielding paint brushes instead of swords. They paused so the press photographers could get their cameras into position. They then posed for their own photographer in varying groups and he began to relax now that the formal side of the day had finished. His father was beaming from ear to ear and told him how proud he was of him and his amazement at the wonderful music he had heard at the service. Jean had not realised that his love of music had been so deep.

Finally, with the photos over, they escaped to the

tranquillity of their coach for the ride home. As soon as they were seated he pulled Marie across his body into his arms and gave her a long, passionate kiss and after they paused for breath he said, 'How does it feel to be Madame Duran?'

Marie smiled and said, 'Ask me again in the morning when my transformation from girl to woman will be complete.'

Charles was slightly daunted by her response as this notched up the pressure on his performance that night. He had no real plan of action; he did not think he would need one. After Manet's comments yesterday he had accepted that Marie was more expectant than the average virgin bride of what took place on a wedding night, but he was not sure whether that made his task harder or easier. All he did know was that he would not be rushing as he wanted to savour every curve of her body from every angle before any sexual advances were made.

8

They were the first back at the chateau and were greeted individually by a guard of honour of staff filing down the stone steps at the front door. He took the opportunity to thank them all for their sterling work in organising the wedding. He asked the coachman to convey their thanks to the stable staff for their efficient service.

Marie's parents and Henri and Manet were in the next carriage and Pierre made a point of pulling him to one side for a word.

'Charles, I would just like to convey my congratulations on your marriage to my firebrand of a daughter and I wish you both a long and successful marriage. I would also like to convey my appreciation of how well you have conducted yourself throughout the long engagement. You have been a perfect son-in-law and there has been no hint of any scandal as far as you have been concerned. I heard from my butler that Marie put you in a compromising situation about two months ago but Henri tells me that you sent her packing unfulfilled, for which I am very grateful. I also appreciate how very few men would have had the inclination, chivalry or self-control to do what you did. Do not be afraid of taking a firm hand with Marie; she acts before she considers the consequences and there have been many occasions when I should have given her a severe beating but as her father, I could not. You will understand what I mean when you have a daughter yourself. I do know that you both love each other very deeply and I think you may have a better chance of taming her than I ever did. My tribute to you was organising the concert and I think you appreciated all the effort that everybody put into it, especially your artistic friends.'

'Thank you, sir, for your kind words. I am so relieved that you weren't keeping me under armed guard because you thought I may jilt Marie at the altar. I was overwhelmed by your concert and thank you from the bottom of my heart.'

'I am sorry if it appeared that way but we all wanted to keep it a secret and when you told Manet you wanted to go to the church early this morning when we had a final rehearsal booked at 9 a.m. he nearly had a heart attack.'

The conversation ended then, as more coaches were pulling up at the door. They both went into the hallway to join the reception line to greet the guests as they arrived from church. During the lunch he and Marie were on the top table with both sets of parents, Manet, Henri and the maids of honour so between courses they went round the tables, chatting to all the guests.

They came to the two tables consisting of his past and present pupils and then another containing his artist and composer friends. He introduced Marie to his past pupils and she got waylaid by an American female student; he left her deep in conversation with her. Manet appeared too and he sat down at the artists' table with them. Henri Fantin-Latour and Zacharie Astruc were both smitten by Marie and Gustav Courbet, who had helped him when he first came to Paris, was full of questions.

'Are you going to use her as a model?'

'Possibly, but she is an artist herself not a muse, the decision will be hers alone, not mine.'

'Will you paint her nude?'

'Only for my own personal pleasure but never to exhibit in public.'

'Why ever not? She would win you a medal at the Salon, especially in a religious piece.'

'I would prefer to win one with her fully clothed thank you, she is my wife not my mistress.'

'You mean you will be having a mistress as well?'

Certainly not, you witnessed me take my vows today and I fully intend to keep them.'

'You will never manage it, especially with your clientele. Your high society ladies will expect your undivided attention.'

'My attention to painting their portrait they will receive, but not my body or my heart – it belongs to Marie.'

'Well Charles, I can only wish you well and we will all raise our glasses to you tonight, wouldn't we all like to be in your shoes?'

Manet replied, 'Gustav, leave him alone. He has waited six months for this day and has never strayed since he met Marie. Theirs is a true love marriage that we lesser mortals can never aspire to.'

'Coming from you Manet, who must be one of the biggest sinners in town, that's priceless.'

'I admit I have a total lack of self-control when it comes to women but I admire Charles greatly for his religious moral code and ethics and I will support him wholeheartedly in his marriage.'

Marie finally came over to the table and as Charles introduced her to everybody, he knew instantly that her sheer beauty moved them all and he felt so proud she was finally his wife.

The cutting of the cake ceremony followed the meal and he was amused when his mother-in-law commented that the top tier was for the first child's christening cake and it would be as fresh as a daisy as it would be needed in less than a year. He would be delighted if their first child arrived quickly as he was driven by this desperate desire to become a father, which he could not understand as he had never shown the slightest interest in babies before.

The speeches followed and he remembered to thank everybody who had worked on the wedding planning including the gardeners who had been responsible for growing the masses of roses and hydrangeas. He presented a huge bouquet of flowers to Louise for her part and gave the maids of honour gold lockets, and toys for the two youngest attendants.

Pierre's speech was very complimentary towards him and he was delighted to have such a warm welcome into his new family. However, Pierre did point out that Marie was now his responsibility and he was looking forward to not having to deal with any more of his daughter's escapades.

Manet's speech was next and he held his breath, concerned about exactly what he might say. Thankfully, he did not reveal any personal information that may have embarrassed his wife and father-in-law. Manet even complimented him on his artistic skills and although he made one comment about looking forward to seeing some of his honeymoon sketches he let him off reasonably lightly.

The speeches over, he finally began to relax. He had no formal duties at the following dinner dance and was looking forward to enjoying himself. He knew they should really circulate amongst their guests but he wanted to have some time alone with his wife and wondered if there was a chance they could get some time alone for a while. He suggested to Marie that they go and speak to some of her relatives who were at a table in the corner where they could slip out by a convenient door, possibly without being noticed.

His mission accomplished, they slipped away and

went to the library. Marie had suggested they go to their own room but he was not falling into that trap as he feared the outcome if he was left alone with her. That would have to wait until later.

Marie turned to him and said, 'What's wrong? Why do you want to speak to me?'

'Nothing is wrong, ma cherie, I just wanted a few moments alone with you to reflect on our day so far.'

'It has been wonderful Charles, and I was very moved by your reaction to the concert, especially to my solo.'

'It touched me to the heart, Marie. You really should spend some time on your singing and music. I don't want you to give everything up just because you are married to me. I worry that you will become bored by the life of an artist's wife and I do want to encourage you to continue improving your own artistic skills. I don't want to stifle any of your talents; you are free to pursue them however you desire. Why don't you join the Conservatoire Choir and perform at some of their concerts? If you wish to pursue your academic studies then enrol on a course at any of the teaching establishments. I will support you in any way that I can.'

'You are wonderful Charles, but let's just get your business back into action and prospering and then I will see how much free time I have to devote to myself. I suspect you have motherhood on my agenda sooner rather than later and that will bring a whole new dimension to our lives.'

'I can't deny that I have developed a desperate need to procreate but if you would prefer to wait I shall abide by your wishes.'

'Don't you think we have waited long enough? I just hope I live up to your expectations.' She put her arms round his neck and pulled his head down to kiss her and pushed him back against a marble pillar. He kissed her passionately and the closeness of her body sent his senses into overdrive. His mind was reeling with doubt as to whether he would live up to her expectations tonight.

He decided they had better move on before he went too far or they were discovered, as he knew Pierre would bring guests into the library before dinner. Marie rounded up her maids of honour as they were going to help her change into her ball gown, but he was remaining in his military uniform. He wandered back into the dining room over to the artist's tables to join Manet and company.

They had partaken of the more than generous amount of wine available and were now onto stronger drinks.

Courbet said, 'Ah the groom returns to the fold. We wondered where you had got to. We were just discussing the days when kings had to have courtiers witnessing the consummation of the marriage and we have decided that in your case we think we should all be there to paint the event; imagine the different interpretations we would produce.' A loud roar of laughter exploded and Charles decided to say nothing rather than try to parry Courbet.

Fauré said, 'I would be more than happy to provide the background music for you.'

Manet could not resist. 'Well I wouldn't be capable of holding a paint brush; I wouldn't be able to take my eyes off the bride.'

Charles retorted, 'Fine best man you turned out to be, traitor.'

Fantin-Latour commented, 'No Manet, you wouldn't get a view of the bride, only Duran's backside!'

Zacharie Astruc retorted, 'I think Duran will be too stage struck to perform, he has had to wait too long.'

The laughter and merriment was causing other guests to switch their attention to the group and he was mortified.

Whistler saved the day when he said, 'God you bastard, Frenchmen are merciless; leave the poor man alone. We would not dream of treating a bridegroom like this in the USA. I thought the French were supposed to have impeccable manners and be chivalrous.'

Charles intervened, 'Thanks James, for your support, but I expected there to be some teasing… but at the end of the day I can afford to be generous as they are only jealous that they won't have the opportunity to experience the delights that I will.'

Courbet sighed, 'Well you are right on that point; she is exquisite. No wonder you begged for her hand before she got out into Paris society; she would have been pursued by the aristocracy of Europe.'

Manet retorted, 'Well he had me to thank for pushing him into it; if he hadn't asked when he did, he would not have been marrying her today.'

Henri approached. 'Charles, you are needed to meet and greet the newly arriving guests.' Charles was thankful for an opportunity to escape and he followed Henri, breathing a sigh of relief. He arrived in the hall just as Marie was descending the main staircase wearing the ball gown she had worn at the party. He was delighted and knew exactly why she had chosen to wear it when no doubt her mother had expected her to have the latest style from Worth. He approached her and took her hand, kissed it and bowed.

'Madame, you look spectacular tonight. Your beauty increases day by day.' He was delighted that she blushed at his compliment. They joined her parents as the first guests arrived.

He watched her as she greeted the guests with such confidence and made them feel so welcome. Perhaps she was wasted on him, just a simple artist; she should have married a Russian count but he was eternally grateful she had married him. It was as if he still could not believe that she was finally his wife; he still felt as though someone would snatch her away from him.

After their duty was done they moved into the ballroom together and heads turned as the newly married couple entered. He felt so proud to have her by his side but disappointed that he would have to release her to dance with other men.

He bent down and whispered, 'You will have to tell me what is expected of me tonight. Should I dance with anyone in particular or can I make my own choices; if so, may I dance with you all night, ma cherie?'

Marie laughed. 'No you cannot dance every dance with me. You would be expected to dance with my mother, your mother and the maids of honour. After that you are free to make your own selection. We should perhaps not dance together more than three times throughout the evening.'

'That means then, I have to watch you in other men's arms all evening.'

Marie leant close and whispered, 'But you, my love, will have me in your bed later and will have my undivided attention.'

He gasped as the desire to pick her up and run up two flights of stairs to the honeymoon suite was overwhelming.

Manet joined them and claimed his first dance with the bride. Charles could not help the twinge of jealousy that crept over him but he knew there was nothing to worry about as far as Marie was concerned. He looked round to see if Louise, his mother or the maids of honour were around and finding none of them, went back into the dining room. Louise had just entered the room alone so he made his way towards her to fulfil his duty of dancing with her. As he reached her she turned towards him and said, 'Charles, I wanted to catch you alone for a quiet word.'

He instantly wondered what on earth his mother-in-law was going to say. He hoped he had not already made some dreadful faux pas. They moved over to the edge of the room behind the marble pillars for some privacy.

'Charles, I just wanted you to know that I have not lectured Marie on her duties in the marital bed. I think she is more than aware of what is expected of her. I am certain with your teaching ability she will prove an avid pupil. I know you both have strong feelings towards each other and I can only wish you both a long and happy marriage. One word of warning Charles, do not spoil her or she will take advantage. She can be very impetuous and never considers the consequences of her actions and she will need a firm hand on the reins. Pierre gave her too much freedom and was far too soft on discipline.'

'Madame, I am aware of her weaknesses but she has so many strengths as well. You need never be concerned about her welfare. I will protect her with my life and when she becomes a mother she may calm down.'

'I would not be too sure about that Charles, she has never expressed any maternal instinct as yet but now she is married, hopefully children will be uppermost in her mind.'

'Madame, I was seeking you out to ask if you would dance with me, so perhaps we could return to the ballroom.'

When they entered, he noticed Marie was now dancing with Fauré and he made a mental note to ask her how she knew him as he had been at the Neidermeyer music school, not the Conservatoire. He wasn't overly concerned apart from the fact that Fauré was within two years of her age but as he was teaching in Brittany he would not be on the Paris social scene. He concentrated on his dance with Louise as he did not want to give her any cause for concern. He had been surprised enough at her acceptance of the marriage as he was sure he was not the husband she would have wanted for her daughter.

The rest of the evening flew by and he was finally in the arms of Marie for the last waltz. The pressure was building up in his head for his next debut performance in their marital bed and he prayed it would live up to both their expectations.

oOo

Finally, they were free to escape to their room. Marie had selected a bedroom on the second floor at the far end of the house, overlooking the formal garden. He thought she had deliberately done this to remove herself from her childhood bedroom, to signify her monumental change of status to a married woman. It was elegantly furnished with a large four poster bed with the silk drapes tied at each corner. A white rose and hydrangea garland had been attached to the central canopy and run down the front pillars of the bed and the air was heavy with their scent. Vases had been placed around the room with fresh flowers picked from the garden. The heavy damask curtains had been closed but the room had plenty of wall lights as well as a central chandelier. The room had large dual aspect windows due to being on the corner of the building and there was a small attached bathroom. A tray of food had been left on a chest of drawers along with two bottles of champagne, glasses and a bowl of fruit. He walked over to the bed and spread himself across it to test the softness and pillows. Marie went and sat at the dressing table and began to remove the roses from her hair and unpin her tresses. He could see her directly in the reflection from the mirror. Their eyes met and she tilted her head to one side and smiled.

'Marie, do not remove your clothes, that is my privilege.'

He got up, took off his jacket and opened the wardrobe to find that all his clothes had been transferred from his original room so he undressed quickly and put on his robe, aware that Marie was watching him closely in the mirror as she brushed out her lustrous hair.

He went over to her, stood behind her and leant down and kissed her head and then moved slowly to her right ear and down to her neck. His hands cupped her tiny breasts and he carefully lifted her into a standing position, still with her back to him. He continued to nibble her ear and run his tongue delicately in the nape of her neck. He then led her to the centre of the room, directly under the chandelier, and skilfully unfastened the buttons at the back of her dress whilst kissing her lips very tenderly. As the dress slid to the floor he retrieved it and laid it carefully over the back of a chair.

She was now left in her underwear, which consisted of a white silk and lace embroidered corset cover, silk drawers trimmed at the knee in lace, and her silk stockings. He admired the sight that beheld him and then set to deftly unbuttoning the corset cover, which revealed a lightly boned, lace trimmed silk corset, which he proceeded to slowly undo. The sight of her tiny uplifted breasts was an artist's dream. He unfastened the button of her drawers and they dropped down to her feet and she stepped out of them. He sat her back down on the dressing table seat and removed her stockings. He pulled her back to her feet and positioned her facing him.

He kissed her delicately on the lips and said, 'Don't move, my darling.' He stepped back and let his eyes drink in the exquisite beauty of her naked body. He moved around her to see every angle and his heart missed a beat when he viewed her from behind. The sheer joy he would have painting the woman stood before him and the fact that she was his to savour forever touched his heart. He stood in front of her. She had her head down to avoid eye contact. He touched her chin and raised her head and gave her a brief kiss on the nose.

He moved to the bed, repositioned the pillows, pulled back the covers and looked in the wardrobe and found Marie's silk robe. Conscious of the falling temperature he put it on her then picked her up and carried her to the bed. Lying her carefully on the left hand side he moved to the right, propped himself up on the pillows and then pulled her across his body so that he was cradling her head in his left hand and his right hand was at her waist. He kissed the tip of her nose and then concentrated on her mouth. He took his time to accustom her to his tongue exploring her mouth gently, but she responded with delight. He then moved onto her breasts, caressing the curve of one while sampling the delights of her nipple with his mouth on the other. He was delighted to feel her body shudder with delight at this new experience. He then moved to running his tongue down her chest to her navel.

He then lifted her gently while he manoeuvred his body out from under hers, propped her up on the pillows and knelt at her waist. He bent over and traced his tongue from her waist to the soft down of her pubic hair at the same time as running his finger down the inside of her left thigh. The effect on Marie was electric; she grabbed his hair and guided his mouth down into the depths of glory. At the same time he was resisting Marie's attempts to pull him over to straddle her body as he knew in that position, all his self-control would be lost.

He whispered to her, 'Not yet.' The sudden realisation that he had spoken in Spanish shocked him. However, Marie was too immersed in her own feelings to have even noticed his slip of tongue. She reached out with her left hand to touch his thigh and he removed her hand away from his body, pinning it under her hip. After she had reached the point of no return he slid down beside her, turned her on her side and removed her robe and then his own. He threw them to the floor, rearranged the pillows, snuggled down beside her and pulled the covers over them.

When Marie realised that apart from his hand resting lightly on her right breast he was not continuing with his attention, she twisted round to face him and said, 'But Charles you are surely not intending to just go to sleep now?'

He smiled at her anger and replied, 'Marie I have waited six months for this moment. Surely you can wait till morning, I can assure you that you will have my undivided attention and you won't be disappointed.'

Her look of pure shock touched him to his core; an angry Marie was infinitely as exciting as a sexually charged one and he very nearly took her there and then but he patiently turned her back to him and hugged her. He kissed the back of her neck and whispered, 'Good night, my angel.'

As he moved his hand back to her breast she

moved it up to her mouth and instead of kissing it she sank her teeth into the flesh of his palm and bit him. After the shock he said,

'You little vixen, behave yourself and go to sleep and you will pay for that in the morning.' Realising that Charles had her pinned down and was now holding both her hands, she knew would have to do as she was told. She nestled as close as she could to his body and fell asleep, anticipating the delights to come.

oOo

Charles awoke around dawn and his joy at having his new wife curled up beside him was overwhelming. He slipped quietly out of the bed, donned his gown and went to the bathroom. On his way back he quietly opened the curtains. Dawn was just breaking. He pulled a chair up close to the bed so he could study her face. He poured himself a glass of wine and ate a chicken leg and an apple.

He examined the teeth marks on his right hand and traced the outline of her teeth on the fleshy part of his hand. He also inspected his wedding ring, turning the shiny platinum band around his finger several times. He offered a silent prayer that their marriage would be a long and happy one and he vowed he would try never to give Marie any cause to regret her choice of husband. Maybe Marie was going to be more spirited than he had anticipated. He remembered her mother's warning that she was headstrong, and the time she had stamped on the toes of the lecher who danced with her. However, the prospect of taming this wild spirit and finally possessing her exquisite body thrilled him.

Slowly, she began to stir and her eyes opened. She saw him there and she looked at him while her body woke up. Finally she spoke.

'So, my neglectful husband, are you going to consummate our marriage before I die from unfulfilled desire?'

With that he flung off his robe and dived back into the warm bed, straight into the arms of his ardent wife. Mindful of Isabella's lessons, he took them both to the peak of physical desire. When they had sated their desire several times, they lay in each other arms, watching the sunlight flicker through the window onto the carpet. When Marie had recovered her strength he felt her hands move to his thigh and her fingers stroking him gently. He rolled over onto his back and allowed Marie to explore his body. He kicked off the covers so he could have the extra pleasure of watching her naked body at work. What had transpired between them had exceeded his expectations and he truly felt that Marie was indeed a gift from God.

9

After their early morning passion they decided to join the family for breakfast. They could not decide whether they were expected to be there or not and so they decided to avoid any embarrassment, they would. Charles was mindful of keeping his hand out of Manet's sight as he might otherwise jump to the wrong conclusion and think he had forced Marie to do something she did not want to, which was so far from the truth.

When they arrived down at breakfast, already in the dining room were his and Marie's parents and various members of Marie's family but thankfully, no Manet. They sat down at a table with both sets of parents. Louise caught Marie's eye and flashed her a knowing smile. To his delight, Marie blushed. There was no hiding Marie's obvious contentment; her cheeks were flushed and her eyes were as bright as buttons.

Realising that he was being watched (he saw his mother studying him carefully), he instinctively removed his left hand from the table. She gave him a reflective look but refrained from speaking.

Pierre could not resist a teasing remark, 'Well, I didn't expect to see you two down for breakfast. I would have thought you had better things to do!'

The plan for the day had been that the men would go down to the beach for a picnic lunch and then have a ride out if they wished. The ladies were going to spend the morning in the salon gossiping about the wedding and inspecting the display of wedding presents. Marie had already complained that she wanted to join the men and knowing how resourceful she was, he expected she probably would. Most of the guests were due to leave by around 5 p.m. that evening.

They were due to meet on the driveway at noon but Charles, knowing how much his father was dying to see the horses, took him down to the stables with Henri for a guided tour an hour earlier. Jean was in his element checking each horse over in his usual horse dealer's manner. His preferred horse on conformation was Marie's horse, Favorit as her beauty and elegance appealed to his eye. However, he loved Henri's new dark bay cavalry mount that his father had recently purchased for him because of his noble head, generous ears, eyes and calm temperament. He told Henri that he was a lucky man to have such a great horse to ride into battle with as he was certain he would be more than up to the task. Carefully, he examined the two horses selected for Marie and Charles to use on their long journey to Lille and was pleased with the soundness of their limbs and feet.

He loved the Percherons for their strong, compact, workmanlike conformation. He helped the head groom harness a young gelding to the hay cart to bring down the picnic to the beach and chatted happily with him about the work the horses did on the land. Finally, he met Marie's Borzois and Charles was surprised to see the dogs' enthusiastic greeting of Jean. He had only ever seen them as effusive with Marie but they jumped up at his father, vying for attention like two puppies. He had always considered them rather aloof but they had sensed Jean's love of dogs immediately and responded. The dogs were joining them on their trip to the beach.

The grooms were busy so they tacked up their own horses and headed round to the drive. He was leading Manet's horse so he was careful to make sure he had his gloves on. Manet appeared looking slightly the worse for wear and threw himself stiffly into the saddle. Marie had managed to slip away from the ladies just to see them off. Charles bent down and kissed her and noted the longing look on her face. He wasn't quite sure if it was meant for him or the fact that she was disappointed about being unable to join them. The group of ten men including two grooms were finally all aboard and set off slowly down the drive.

They rode out into the wood and assembled in double file due to the narrow paths. Manet seemed rather quieter than usual. Charles had expected a tirade of teasing comments about his wedding night but they weren't forthcoming. Perhaps he had over indulged last night and had a bad head this morning. Charles was pleased that Pierre was in front with Jean at his side, and appreciated the effort he had made to make his parents feel at home.

They got down to the beach and the hay cart was already there with two servants setting up the picnic. The Percheron youngster was behaving impeccably. This was the spot he had used for his paintings of Marie and Henri. He looked out to the sea, savouring his memories of their first kiss.

After he had eaten a genial lunch, Manet asked if he could have a private word with him. They moved to some rocks further down the beach. He couldn't imagine what he wanted but whatever it was probably explained his dull demeanour. Manet proceeded to inform him that he had got himself into a bit of trouble over a woman again and her husband had demanded a duel. His second had come to the chateau late last night with the challenge. It was due to take place tomorrow morning at 7 a.m. in the woods next to the chateau. Finally, he asked Charles to be his second. The first thought that hit him was, what a cheek his friend had to ask him this on his honeymoon. They would be preparing to leave for Lille tomorrow. Charles assumed it was probably just a sword duel that would only go to "first blood" and then cease. However, Edouard told him that the selected weapon was pistols and this threw a whole different light on the situation.

Charles asked him how he was going to deal with this problem and Manet's reply was, 'Well, I don't think he is going to accept a grovelling apology and anyway I denied it because I never touched her, so I will have to face the consequences.'

Charles looked at him closely. 'Are you really prepared to die for something as trivial as this? Yes, I will be your second Manet but not a word to anyone, especially Marie.'

Edouard turned to him and said, 'Thanks Charles, to be honest death by duel may be a better option than facing Suzanne alive afterwards. She can inflict harsher punishments than death.'

Charles replied, 'Well you do need something to stop this behaviour; this time you may not be so lucky.' This was the end of their conversation as the party was mounting back up as Pierre had suggested that they put the hounds into the wood to see if they could find any game.

They all followed into the wood and the head groom released the two Borzois; they immediately picked up a scent and were off through the woods at full pelt. They had an exhilarating canter through the woods, avoiding the low branches and uneven surface. They came to a sharp, narrow incline that was only wide enough for two horses as there was a six foot drop to a rocky ditch below. The head groom was in front, followed by Pierre and Jean then Henri and Manet, with himself behind. Suddenly, from their left a deer had been disturbed and was running directly towards the path. Henri's horse swerved violently to the right and cannoned into Manet's horse's shoulder, shoving him over the edge of the path. There was the sound of sliding earth and an ominous thud as they hit the ground. Henri was the first to dismount and look over the path. Horse and rider were strewn separately on a rocky terrain. The horse was winded but Manet was definitely unconscious and thankfully not under the horse… but its back legs were too close to his body for comfort.

Henri scrambled down the banking, shouting for a rope. His father was next to go over the edge and he went straight to the horse and talking gently to him, slid his body across the horse's neck and shoulder and lay across him in an effort to keep him down while Henri dragged Manet away from the horse. He scrambled down to help Henri and noticed blood on the rock where Manet's head had landed. He was still out cold. Pierre shouted from above that he would go back down the path and find a way into the ditch. Henri was checking Manet's pulse and eyes. Thankfully, his eyes flickered open and he groaned.

Charles said, 'Keep calm, Edouard, and come round slowly. Where do you hurt most?' Edouard sat up with Henri's support and winced at his elbow and head.

'I have a mighty headache and my right elbow is sore but my biggest problem is I can't see at all out of my right eye and my left is not focussing properly.'

Henri replied, 'It's probably the effects of concussion. Just stay where you are and don't attempt to get up yet.'

By now, his father had helped the horse stand although it was shaking violently, and was deftly running his hands over its body and legs to check the damage. There was some blood on his offside which looked like relatively minor surface scratches and he was obviously shocked and shaking his head repeatedly… probably suffering the same effects Manet was experiencing. Jean walked him a few paces and he did not appear initially unsound but was definitely stiff and unsettled. Pierre and the head groom appeared, leading all their abandoned horses.

Pierre said, 'We are not going to be able to get a cart up here. Is Manet fit enough to get back on his horse?'

Jean replied, 'Put Manet up on my horse and I will take this poor fellow back and if necessary, dismount and lead him. He's too shocked to risk Manet on him.'

Manet said, 'I will be alright if someone leads me but I cannot see well enough to cope with the terrain.' His first attempt to stand was very unsteady and he soon had to sit back down as his legs were like jelly. Between them, Henri and Charles got him mounted on Jean's horse and Charles threw the reins over the horse's head, mounted his own horse and led him quietly back down the ditch.

They set off in a slow walk back to the chateau and

after ten minutes he noticed Edouard was shivering and very white.

'Don't worry, Edouard. It's probably shock; it often occurs after a trauma, we will be back soon.'

Pierre had ridden at speed back to the chateau to call a doctor and when the party arrived at the front door, Marie was the first to greet them. Henri helped Manet down from the horse. His elbow was starting to swell along with the bump on his head. He and Henri supported him into the house into a small salon off the main hall. They settled him on a chaise longue and Marie fetched pillows and a blanket. She was going to give him a drink of coffee but Henri advised no fluids until the doctor had seen him.

The doctor arrived and he and Henri took him through to see Manet. After a careful examination he declared that he had concussion and would recommend he went to the hospital on his return to Paris to check his elbow but he didn't think it was broken, just badly bruised. His sight should return to normal slowly as the concussion subsided but it could take up to three days before he resumed full vision. He suggested that Manet be left to sleep if he could but stressed he must be checked on every two hours to ensure he did not fall unconscious. He could have hot drinks and minimal food but no alcohol whatsoever. He may take a week to feel fully recovered.

Whilst the doctor had been examining Edouard, Charles suddenly remembered the duel. Etiquette required that the second had to take the place of the challenged party should they not be fit or fail to turn up to fight. Surely this duel would have to be postponed until Manet recovered. A creeping sense of unease started to envelope him and he gasped at the prospect of having to take Edouard's place, especially with pistols as the chosen weapon. The prospect of dying didn't occur to him but the prospect of leaving Marie did. *What in God's name was he going to do if he had to fight?* Pistols were not his chosen weapon – he would have much preferred swords – and to fight to "first blood" only would have given himself and his opponent a fair chance of living.

Henri showed the doctor out and he took the opportunity to follow as he wanted to speak to Henri about his dilemma and seek his advice. The doctor left and he ushered Henri outside into the garden.

'I need to speak to you privately Henri, I need your advice. What do you know about duelling?'

Henri looked shocked but said, 'Quite a lot as we talk about it back in the barracks frequently. I haven't experienced it personally yet but I thought you already had. You must also know that legally since 1837, duelling has been classified as "an attempt at murder", which is punishable as a criminal offence, but as we both know many get described as hunting accidents and even if people are prosecuted, they are acquitted.'

Charles responded, 'Yes, but it was a mere skirmish and I was able to disarm my opponent in less than a minute, nick his cheek and there it ended. What's happened now is that Manet has been called to a duel by a hapless husband and I am his nominated second and it takes place at 7 a.m. tomorrow in the woods here. He is going to be in no state to fight with limited vision and a sprained right arm.'

Henri retorted, 'Charles, you are not seriously thinking of standing in for him? Surely you can negotiate a stay of execution until Manet recovers. This husband has no reason to want to harm you.'

'Possibly I can reason with him to wait, but if he insists, I shall have no alternative but to fight. I won't be accused of being cowardly even though I have no wish to die.'

Henri said, 'Look, it's only 4 p.m... Let's go back inside. I will fetch my father's duelling pistols from the gun safe and we'll go over into the woods and I will give you the benefit of the experience of one of my commanding officers who has fought six duels and survived. I will bring two swords as well because if you have to fight you may be able to choose your own weapon. You go and offer to stay with Manet while Marie says goodbye to the house guests and we'll sneak out the back and over into the woods. Don't say a word to Marie or anyone else; there's every chance we may be able to postpone this bout and there is no point in giving the whole family unnecessary stress.'

Charles was relieved at Henri's suggestion as he was going to need all the advice he could get if this fight was going to take place. He went back to Manet's room where Marie was reading as Manet appeared to be sleeping. He persuaded her to go and join her parents whilst he stayed with Manet and carried out the doctor's instructions. He could hear the carriages coming up the drive and so Marie left him. Within two minutes, Henri appeared with a bag containing the weapons. He checked Manet and he seemed to be in a contented sleep so they both slipped out of the room and made their way to a little used back door and walked over into the woods. They selected a suitable spot and Henri marked out twenty paces from an oak tree using his sword as a marker.

'First of all, let me go through my assessment of the situation. You are going to be far quicker and more flexible in your wrist and movement than your opponent. Your boxing, fencing and even painting activities will ensure that. You have to be the first to turn then you stand in a fencing position and fire at your opponent, aiming straight between his eyes. Do not stand head on to him as you are exposing your whole body as a target and you need to keep your heart out of his direct sight line. So many duellists are killed because they give their opponent a full target area to shoot. As soon as you have fired you must move immediately either three paces to the left or right. Even if you have beaten him to the draw he may have fired his weapon and you must not get caught in the crossfire. Do not for one second think you can risk aiming for his arm or shoulder in the hope of wounding him rather than killing him because you will be the one that ends up dead. He will be aiming to kill you and so you must do the same. The problem is, pistols are not a very accurate weapon. They are completely different to rifles and shot guns. We did an experiment on the shooting range using a target firing pistols from a twenty yard distance and not one of us got within six inches of the centre spot.'

Charles replied, 'But I am not a murderer and I have no wish to kill for the sake of someone else's honour!'

Henri responded quickly. 'Charles, don't you think I felt the same before I joined the cavalry? I shared my fear with my commanding officer and he told me that in the heat of battle the will to stay alive conquers the desire to preserve life. It really is a case of "kill or be killed" and I hope when the time comes, I will be up to the job.'

Charles said, 'Henri you have changed from the young innocent boy that joined up to a wise honourable man in less than a year. You will be a credit to your family and country whatever befalls you and I pray that you live to enjoy a happy and fulfilling life.'

Henri replied, 'If you want to live a full and happy life with Marie then you have to do what I told you in the duel. We have to try to get this duel postponed and I insist as acting as your second so I can take part in the negotiations. Now let's see how quick your response and aim are by shooting at that face I have drawn on the oak tree.'

Charles did as instructed and he did manage to hit the target face on all three attempts. Henri shouted at him for not moving away quickly enough after he fired the pistol at the first attempt, but at least he felt a little more in control should he have to face the inevitable. They returned to the chateau to check on Manet and change for dinner.

10

Over dinner there was much consternation over Manet's accident and so it covered the fact that Charles was quieter than usual. Manet had woken and been sent a tray so Charles excused himself from the after dinner port and went to find him.

Charles confessed that he had told Henri about the duel but Manet was insistent that he would be more than capable of fighting by morning. His sight was returning slowly to his right eye and his left was near normal, but his elbow was swelling and would be worse still by morning. He would have no hope of beating his opponent to the draw and even less hope of hitting the target.

Henri joined them later and they discussed their tactics for tomorrow. The main aim was to postpone the match and if that failed, get the weapon changed to sword with a "first blood" end. If that failed then Charles insisted he fight rather than be accused of cowardice. Manet, however, would not agree to let him fight in his place but until they met the other side there was no way of knowing the outcome. Manet insisted he would be capable of riding with them in the morning so they all retired to their rooms to try and get an early night. Henri said he would have the horses waiting for them behind the house at 6 a.m. and nobody else was to be told of the duel.

Charles went to find Marie in the salon and excuse them but until he had said it he didn't realise that it could be construed that he wanted an early night to spend longer with his new wife. Marie blushed as she left the salon and both sets of parents looked highly amused at his faux pas. He was expected to see his parents off in the morning to the station after breakfast and the possibility that he may not even be alive by then made the hair stand up at the back of his neck.

He undressed quickly, leaving his riding clothes out on the chair so they would be to hand in the morning. He tried to banish all thoughts about what tomorrow held, from his head and to concentrate on his beautiful wife.

Marie was in an exploratory mood and so he let her take the lead and indulge her fantasies. She soon had him in raptures but as he tried to take the initiative she rolled on top of him and proceeded to dictate the pace. He was more than happy to just lie back and enjoy the experience. Charles was intoxicated with the depth of passion that was erupting within his body, the likes of which he had never experienced before. His mind was blown apart, all the vivid colours of the rainbow were exploding in his head and he was powerless. It reminded him of the colours cast by the sun shining through the stained glass window in the church. He was a slave to the powers of sexual pleasure that were consuming every morsel of his body and soul. For the first time in his life he was under the spell of a woman's erotic powers. His head sunk deeper into the soft pillows. He accepted that he was no longer in control. He was powerless, but by God it was amazing.

After he and Marie came together in the most awe consuming crescendo of passionate climax he lay exhausted and motionless, drained of all his energy, his body glistening with sweat and his mouth dry. He finally realised that this was truly a match of heart, body and soul. Tears welled up in his eyes and he quickly turned her on to her side away from him, fearful she would see his overflowing emotion. He let the tears flow into her lustrous hair and held her tightly against his body, nuzzling into it, absorbing her scent. He lay quietly beside her, reflecting on his worst fears of losing her so soon when he had finally discovered the meaning of real love.

He slept fitfully, dreaming of the duel. Every time he reached the point of death, he awoke dripping in sweat. At 5:30 a.m. he slipped quietly out of the bed, gently kissing her stray hand that had been lying across him. He knew he had to get out without waking her so he was as quiet as possible while dressing and then he went down to the second floor to wake Manet.

Manet was already partially dressed but as he put

his shirt on Charles saw the bruising and swelling forming on his elbow, shoulder and cheekbones. His right eye was already going black around the edges. He saw him wince as he lifted the shirt over his head and knew there was no way he could fight a duel. He whispered quietly and asked him about his sight. Manet looked out of the window pretending he could see, but Charles knew he couldn't as *he* could see Henri approaching from the stables leading one horse and another figure on a second horse, leading a fourth. *Who the hell was that?*

They moved quietly down the corridor to the servants' staircase. Charles took Manet's right arm and guided him but at one point Manet nearly lost his balance and he was obviously in pain on his right side. There was no doubt he must have a badly bruised hip and knee from his fall as well as his head injuries.

They ran across to where Henri was waiting at the entrance to the wood. He had assumed that Henri had commandeered a groom maybe, to see to the horses during the duel, and so he was shocked to see his father.

Henri said, 'I am sorry Charles but Jean was already at the stables checking Manet's horse for injuries when I got there and I could hardly concoct some tale as he could tell by my face I wasn't going out on a hack, especially when I was tacking up three horses.'

Jean spoke directly to Charles. 'I am here to try

to prevent this duel happening; you cannot throw your life away for this ridiculous cause. This has to be stopped.'

Charles continued giving Manet a leg up on his horse and despite Manet's best efforts, he could not stop himself gasping when he had to throw his right leg over the saddle. He offered to lead him but Manet would have none of it. They rode off in silence. He noted that Henri had got the bag of weapons and he looked longingly at a protruding sword handle, praying that if he had to fight, it would be with a sword.

They were the first to arrive at the clearing where the duel was to be fought. They talked over their options and when the discussion became heated between his father and Manet, Charles walked away and went over to a low wall, craving solitude and when Henri attempted to come over he saw that Charles was in deep thought so decided to leave him alone.

They could hear the approaching horses coming through the wood. There were four riders and it was immediately obvious to Charles who the challenger was. He was in his forties, over 6ft tall and was wearing a woollen cloak and riding an Anglo Norman horse. He had all the trappings of aristocracy and no doubt the breeding and education but without the manners. They all dismounted and Manet introduced his party and then Monsieur Beauchamp introduced his and he was relieved to hear that one of the parties was a doctor. The second looked a more amenable man to deal with and he hoped he would be able to control Beauchamp's already rising temper.

Manet was quick to explain what had happened yesterday and requested a postponement of at least a week. Beauchamp was having none of it and insisted that Manet fight. Charles intervened saying that if he did not believe him then he could get his doctor to check Manet over. Thankfully, the doctor did not wait for Beauchamp's permission. He helped Manet remove his jacket and checked over his right arm, carefully examining his swollen elbow and wrist. He asked Manet if he could check his hip and knee joints and Manet agreed, undoing his breeches. His right hip was already going purple and his knee was the same. Charles wondered how on earth he had managed to ride over to the wood. Lastly, the doctor checked his right eye and tested his vision. When his left eye was covered Manet could hardly see the doctor's finger two feet from his eye never mind the distance of a duel. The doctor had no hesitation in declaring Manet unfit to fight a duel.

Beauchamp exploded in anger shouting, 'Then his second will have to stand in!'

Beauchamp's second retorted, 'Jean-Paul you cannot expect his second to risk his life; your argument is with Manet not Duran.'

Charles breathed a sigh of relief and he saw the relief on the faces of Manet, Henri and his father.

However, Beauchamp countered with, 'Why he is

just another bloody artist; they are all the same, the scum of the earth!'

Charles whirled round and advanced menacingly on Beauchamp.

'That's it then, you bastard. Get your miserable arse over there and I will take great pleasure in blowing your head off!'

Henri pushed himself between the two irate men saying, 'I am Charles's second and I demand he has the choice of weapon.'

Beauchamp laughed. 'Oh, so he would prefer the sword then. Well the answer is no!'

His second intervened. 'Jean-Paul, under the circumstances I think he has every right to call the weapon of choice.'

Beauchamp sneered, 'Well he's obviously a better swordsman than a shot so I deny him the choice.'

There followed a heated discussion in which all parties agreed that Charles had the right to choose the weapon but Beauchamp was not backing down.

Charles had been observing the weather and noticed that although it was cloudy, the sun was starting to break through the deep cloud. He calculated that if he selected the right-hand side of the pitch there was a small chance that he would benefit by the shade if the sun came out, as his opponent would be in full sun. He had made his decision.

'Right, I have had enough. I will proceed with pistols and I need to get on with this now; I have better things to do with my time. If the idiot wants to die then let's get on with it.'

He had to smile at the look of horror on Henri's face. Then Manet begged, 'No Charles, I want to be the one to send this piece of shit to hell, not you!'

Charles retorted, 'Well you heard the doctor. You're not fit to fight! Henri, check the pistols over and I demand the right-hand side of the pitch.' With that he took off his jacket, rolled up his sleeves and handed his jacket to his father and strolled confidently out to the pitch.

Henri and Beauchamp's second checked and loaded the pistols. They placed a small stick in the centre, paced out the distance together and plunged the swords into the ground at either end.

Henri came over to him and he drew him close. 'Promise me if that bastard moves an inch to turn round you will shout and if he kills me and I haven't killed him, you will do it for me later.'

Henri patted him on his shoulder. 'Of course I will and if I shout you must move out of the way in case he's fired and then take your shot. I understand why you have taken this side but I hope to God that you get the light when you need it.'

Charles laughed, 'Don't worry Henri I have already asked God for divine intervention last night. I just hope he wasn't asleep. Tell my darling wife that I love and worship her and am desolate at the thought of losing her.'

They walked back to the start line and Beauchamp

approached with his second who read out the duelling rules and spoke directly to Beauchamp when it came to the rules of foul play. Obviously, even he was concerned about Beauchamp pulling a stunt. He looked across to his father who acknowledged with a smile and Manet made one more plea for him to stop, but he shook his head. The second said he was going to call every stride so as to control the pace as he obviously feared Beauchamp would attempt to turn early. He asked them both if they would reconsider their position and they replied with an emphatic 'No'.

They moved back to the centre point and just before they turned into a back-to-back position, Charles saw the sun breaking through the clouds, directing strong rays of light through the dawn mist and reflecting off the sword at Beauchamp's end.

He took a deep breath as the second declared, 'Ready,' and then called the first step. He moved forward step by step with every fibre of his body strained and alert. They got to 18, 19, and on 20 he reeled around into a sideways position, already raising the pistol. Beauchamp was still turning but the sunlight lit his body like a lamp and Charles steadied his aim and before he was facing him full on he had fired the gun directly at his left eye. He then leapt five feet to the right, seconds before Beauchamp discharged his gun. He saw Beauchamp's knees buckle and the pistol fall from his hand as he was propelled backwards by the force of the shot. He felt a searing pain in the flesh of his left shoulder but he kept his eyes trained on his opponent. Realising he wasn't getting up, he turned to focus on the moving image to his left and saw Marie running across the grass towards him but collapsing on her knees when the second shot rang out.

He ran towards her; she was prostrate on the ground, sobbing and screaming his name. He dropped to his knees, scooped her into this arms and the look on her face seared into his soul. Aware that a copious amount of blood was streaming down his left arm he held her close to his chest and murmured, 'God, Marie, I was so afraid I would lose you just as I had found you.'

She then wriggled free from him, stood in front of him and shouted, 'How dare you risk your life and my happiness for a stupid duel that had nothing to do with you!' With that she swung a punch, which caught him on his left eye and sent him reeling backwards into unconsciousness. When she realised what she had done she threw herself of top of him, sobbing relentlessly.

Henri and the doctor were with him in seconds. Henri pulled Marie off him shouting, 'For God's sake, Marie, he's injured. Let the doctor see to him!'

The doctor bent down, checking the pulse in his neck and then he ripped the sleeve down off his left shoulder exposing a hole where the bullet had gone right through the fleshy part of his shoulder and out the other side, missing the bone by a fraction of an inch.

'Thank God it's just a flesh wound; the bleeding has nearly stopped. He's just out cold due to the force of the blow to his eye and temple from this young madame, whom I assume is his new wife.'

Manet and his father were now around him and Marie turned her anger on Manet. 'How dare you stand as best man at my husband's wedding and then twenty-four hours later let him stand in for you in a duel!' With that she reached up and administered a resounding slap across Manet's left cheek. He grabbed both hands behind her back and pulled her close to his chest as her anger subsided into sobs. Manet replied gently,

'Marie I'm so sorry. I never meant this to happen. I begged him to let me fight and he wouldn't hear of it.'

Charles was starting to come round whilst supported by Henri and while his fuddled brain attempted to make sense of what had happened his eyes were riveted to Marie in Manet's arms.

Henri saw the direction of his gaze. 'Don't worry, Charles, she has just slapped him across the face and he was just restraining her from doing any further damage. Although the punch she gave you would have felled a charging bull, never mind an injured man!'

Charles called out to her. 'Marie!' She spun round from Manet and ran to Charles and helped him sit upright. Her eyes surveyed the damage to his eye and forehead and already it was swelling at an alarming rate.

Henri helped pull Charles to his feet and said, 'Beauchamp is dead but his second and the doctor will sign a sworn statement that he taunted you into a fight and you were not to blame for your actions.'

Beauchamp's second had loaded the body onto his horse and leaving it with the doctor, mounted his own horse and rode over.

'The doctor says you have just a flesh wound, thank God. I do apologise for Beauchamp's behaviour and I will sign a statement confirming that you had no option but to defend yourself under the circumstances. I don't know why he wouldn't leave it till another day; I'm just thankful you were the victor.'

Jean headed over with their horses and gave Charles a hug saying, 'Thank God you are back on your feet. I thought he may have hit your head.' Jean held his horse while he mounted and then lifted Marie up as well, in front of him. 'I suggest you let Marie steer the horse as your eyes don't appear to be focusing yet.' Henri retrieved the weapons and Charles's jacket and they all rode at a slow walk back to the chateau.

Charles asked Marie how she had known about the duel and apparently a young groom had overheard Jean and Henri talking and had gone up to the house kitchen and told Jeanette, Marie's maid and she had come and told her and she had run straight into the woods to find him.

They got back to the house and Pierre was waiting at the door. He took a long, measured look at Charles and breathed a sigh of relief that his injuries were only minor.

'Charles, you really were extremely rash to put your life in such peril within hours of marrying my daughter. You promised me and God you would love and cherish her "till death do you part", but within twenty-four hours you could so easily have broken your promise.'

Charles lifted Marie down and attempted to dismount and said, 'I do beg your forgiveness. I will…' At which point his knees buckled and he fainted head first onto the gravel drive.

Marie screamed and threw herself to her knees beside him, cradling his head. Henri was the first to reach them and he assured her, 'Don't worry; he has just fainted due to lack of food and loss of blood. We just need to get him in, feed him and get some brandy down him and he'll be fine.' Henri lifted him up and carried him into the house and along to the small salon where Manet had been yesterday. He laid him on the chaise longue and Marie covered him in a blanket and put a pillow under his head. She went down to the kitchen to arrange some food for them.

11

Charles had come round but with a blinding headache, pain in his shoulder and his left eye half closed and swelling from the blow Marie dealt. He saw Manet come in limping and settle himself down in a large armchair and put a footstool under his left leg.

He murmured, 'God, it's starting to look like a military hospital in here.'

Manet smiled. 'Well at least you have retained your sense of humour after that blow to your head from Marie. My head was already throbbing and sore from yesterday's fall and now I have got the imprint of your wives' fingers across my left cheek to add to my troubles.'

Henri came in with two bottles of his father's best cognac. 'I think we will all feel better after a glass or two of this.' He filled three glasses and passed them round. 'Charles. I suggest you leave your wound open to drain until bedtime and then I'll clean you up and strap your shoulder so you can get some rest tonight.'

The door opened and his mother and father

arrived. His mother ran to him and knelt beside him.

'Oh Charles, you hothead, did you never think of the risks you were taking? Your father told me what happened at the duel but I can't understand why you were fighting in the first place?'

'Don't worry, I'm fine; it was just a flesh wound and I am well aware of what a fool I was. I did try to avoid the confrontation but when he insulted me as well as Manet I really didn't have a choice.'

He turned towards his father and said, 'Aren't you supposed to be on the train back to Lille now?'

His father replied, 'What, leave you straight after a duel? We thought we would postpone our return until you are better and hoped you would both come back with us on the train as you're not going to be fit enough to ride down after this.'

Charles considered this and he thought it would be a good idea as they could always return on horseback when his wound had healed as they had intended to honeymoon for four weeks. He knew he needed to get away with Marie as they needed to get to know each other away from his working life and discuss their future plans. His parents left to eat and he said he would talk it over with Marie.

Marie arrived, followed by two servants bearing trays of food. She fussed around and then turned to Henri. 'Will you promise to get Charles to eat as I have to go to lunch as Papa has guests coming?' She then knelt beside Charles and said, 'Do you think we will be able to get off on honeymoon tomorrow?'

Charles laughed. 'Honeymoon, Madame? I don't think so! I am sending you back to Henri's barracks with him. You will be a credit to the cavalry with your fighting skills. I have only been married to you a mere forty-eight hours and so far you have bitten a chunk out of my hand, given me a black eye and knocked me out cold.' Henri and Manet roared with laughter.

Marie went bright red and said, 'Perhaps we can talk about it later.' She beat a hasty retreat from the room, avoiding making eye contact with Henri or Manet.

Henri laughed and said, 'I think you will have to reconsider that idea, Charles. How am I supposed to defend her honour from a hundred sex starved soldiers! I'd better go and greet my father's guests but I will be back to ensure you have eaten… but don't dare drink all the cognac.'

After Henri's departure, Manet got up unsteadily to help himself to some food and passed a plate to Charles. He asked him,

'So, your delectable wife is perhaps not the quiet filly you expected to bed then? Now you have awoken her sexuality you have found that you are no longer in control – she is. Just relax and enjoy it, Charles. With a beauty like her in your bed you are the luckiest man in the world and she has eyes only for you. I saw the look you gave me when you came round and saw her in my arms. I may succumb to weakness of the flesh when it comes to women, but I do assure you that deep in this heart I have some French honour and chivalry concealed within. Besides, she would tear any man to shreds and spit the bones out if they laid a finger on her. Don't let jealousy start to eat you up; she can't help it that she is so beautiful that men desire her. Just laugh it off and be proud that she is your wife and you get to keep her at your side every night whilst we lesser men can only dream of ever possessing such an angel.'

Charles did see Manet's point as he had certainly felt pangs of jealousy but it was more a morbid fear of losing her and the fact he didn't feel he was good enough to be her husband, rather than pure jealousy, that was eating away at his mind. Edouard went on, 'Don't ever waste a minute regretting you killed Beauchamp. He was an evil, wicked bastard; you have freed his wife from a life of pure hell. She was a frightened virgin of 18 when Beauchamp married her only five months ago. When he brought her to my studio for her first sitting she was like a terrified mouse. He had dictated the dress she wore and believe me, bright red and black looked horrific against her pale complexion, blue eyes and blonde hair. The dress was meant for a matron complete with a bustle and went right up to her neck. She looked dreadful; it completely drowned her. Thankfully, he went off to his club and said he would be back in three hours. What could I do? I know you like to approve what your sitters wear before you start to paint them but there was no arguing with that ogre. He even insisted on overseeing the position she was to be painted in. He wanted her standing and painted in profile. Why? With that dress there was not one curve of her body visible and her breasts were completely swamped by the fussy bodice. I started to paint what I was looking at but I hated what I saw. I tried to engage her in conversation but she would not speak. I may as well have been painting a terrified deer.'

Charles said, 'Well how did you manage to entice her into your bed?'

Edouard replied, 'On her third and final sitting she came alone; he was otherwise engaged. I had gone closer to paint her head and neck and noticed tears running down her face and her eyes had the most haunted look. I put my arms round her without any sexual intention at all. I just wanted to comfort her but she actually kissed me and told me to remove her dress. I wasn't going to turn that invitation down but nothing prepared me for what I was to witness and it will haunt me for life. When I finally got her free from that damnable dress and restrictive underwear I recoiled in utter shock. Her neck and breasts were covered in bite marks and bruising. Some were new and others fading. Her left hip had a gouge mark of six inches or so and severe bruising. When I looked closely I realised what it was. God, Charles, he had taken her fully clothed with his sword by his side.'

Charles groaned. 'God forbid!'

Manet continued, 'I knelt down and gently examined her stomach and inner thighs and again, she was covered in bite marks and I dread to think of what damage he had inflicted on her internally. Worst of all, her waist was thickening and she was in the early stages of pregnancy. I picked her up, wrapped her in a sheet and laid her on the sofa, cradled her in my arms and wept. That poor girl had been raped every time that bastard had taken her. She had never known what it felt like to be touched and caressed and driven to ecstasy by someone who really loved her. The fact that any man could do that to any woman especially his own wife is incomprehensible, but to continue to do so when she was carrying his child is just unbelievable. Believe me, I never touched her sexually. I still have the portrait and when I get back to Paris I am going to slash it to pieces.' Charles could not believe what he had heard and he wondered what he would have done in his place.

Marie and Henri came into the room and Marie said, 'How are the invalids? Have you both eaten?'

Charles said, 'I am feeling much improved. I need some fresh air; In fact I have a desire to walk to church.'

'Church?' Marie interrupted.

He caught the look of shock on both Henri and Manet's faces.

'Yes, I have reason to thank God for helping me stay alive and I also need absolution for killing a man. Marie, would you mind fetching me a clean shirt? Henri, would you strap up my shoulder? I think it has stopped bleeding now.'

He and Marie set off walking the half mile to the church they had been married in only two days before. He held her right hand and when they took a shortcut through the woods, he pulled her over to a fallen tree trunk and sat her down.

'Marie, if I ever hurt you when I am consumed by passion you will tell me, won't you.'

'Charles, whatever brought that on? No woman could have been as fortunate as I was to lose their virginity to a more gentle, caring and considerate lover than you. It's me that has inflicted hurt on you with my vicious temper.' She caressed his blackening eye with the tips of her fingers and gently kissed his swollen nose.

Satisfied with her reply, they walked on to the church. He opened the door to the beautiful Norman church and he was pleased to find it empty. He revelled in its silence and the feeling of warmth that enveloped him. He went up to the centre of the altar rail and knelt on the thick embroidered kneeler on the top step, directly opposite the altar with a round stained glass window behind. To his delight, a shaft of sunlight came through a side window illuminating the stained glass window and the altar below. Marie had stayed back at the first pew in the nave to give him some privacy.

This was the third time that sunlight had broken through cloud and influenced his life. The first time was on the beach when he had been plucking up the courage to ask for Marie's hand in marriage, the second in this church on his wedding day and then yesterday when he had fought the duel. Was it a sign or just his furtive imagination? Light was hugely important in his working life as an artist as he used it to bring life to his subjects. Had God helped him in the duel by blinding Beauchamp and allowing him a clear first shot? Did God know what a wicked man Beauchamp was and use him to end his life? Who knows whether the outcome would have been the same without the extra light? He would have been quicker to draw than Beauchamp, certainly, but the extra light had given him a clearer view of his face and a moment longer to aim and fire. Had Manet fought him, would he have killed him too? Surely, Manet would have killed him, especially with the benefit of knowing the evil torture Beauchamp had inflicted on his poor wife.

He rested his arms on the altar rail and put his chin on his hands and prayed. He asked for absolution for killing a man but he felt no qualms of conscience for ending Beauchamp's reign of terror on that poor innocent girl. He thanked God for his life and allowing him to return in one piece to his beautiful wife whom he considered his "gift from God", and prayed they would be fruitful.

He then turned to Marie and asked her to join him for a moment. She knelt beside him and he took her right hand, raising it to the altar and then lightly kissing it and placing it back on the altar rail. They knelt in silence for a few moments and then he helped her back to her feet. He paused at one of the altar vases and selected the head of a white rose and gently placed it in her hair, behind her ear. He remembered the beauty of the Sistine Chapel in Rome and vowed he would take her to see Michelangelo's frescoes one day.

They left the church and discussed their honeymoon on the way back. He was desperate to get away and have her all to himself and he wanted to paint her exquisite body before it changed from the virginal girl to a pregnant woman. Now that he had possessed her body he wanted to know her mind too.

He suggested they return to Lille with his parents by train tomorrow and then spend three weeks or so there and ride back to Paris, stopping at leisure on their return. He remembered Manet's suggestion that if her father refused her hand he should kidnap her and hole up somewhere with her until he had got her pregnant. He couldn't think of a more idyllic pastime than making non-stop love to his new wife. Where this desire to reproduce had come from, he had no idea. He really wasn't overly fond of children and had never experienced being around babies and he wasn't sure he would like his peace disturbed by a rabble of children... but the fact that they would be his children was what mattered.

12

They left for Lille the next day by train, with his parents. He had slipped back to his studio to pack a travelling case with his oils and watercolours, selected three canvasses and a new sketch pad. Marie had raised her eyebrow when he came back to the station with the canvasses under his arm. He reassured her that he just wanted to do some relaxing landscapes of his homeland; he was not intending to do any serious work. He could tell by her measured look that she knew he was lying but he could say nothing more with his parents present.

He settled down with Émile Zola's book, *Thérèse Raquin,* which Manet had given him before he left. He had been given it by Paul *Cézanne*, another artist who was also a mutual friend of Zola, who was emerging as a talented writer in Paris. After a few minutes he realised he wasn't reading it, his thoughts had turned to planning what they would do in Lille.

He was thrilled that they would be occupying the small cottage across the yard from the main house; it would allow them much more freedom than being with his parents. He would take pleasure in showing her the countryside and he planned to go to Lille Academy, where he had started his career, to see if any of his colleagues or tutors were in residence. He wanted to show her off to his sister and brothers who all lived in the area and had children. He had not seen any of them since he left home at 11. She would enjoy watching his father work with his young horses. He was surprised that he felt as tired as he did but the last few days were beginning to take their toll on his body and he needed to recoup his strength.

Marie was chatting amicably with his parents and he vowed he would find some time to talk privately with his mother and reassure her about his future. He also craved her opinion of Marie, which he knew would be difficult for her as Marie was maybe not the wife that she would have envisaged for her son. Marie was more forceful and better educated than him and had lived in Russia, which would be an alien concept to his mother who had never left Lille until she came to Paris for his wedding.

They arrived at the farm at around 7 p.m. and he was filled with emotion as he entered his childhood home for the first time in twenty-five years. It seemed smaller than he remembered but the farmhouse had not changed, structurally. However, there was now a large barn and a set of ten loose boxes built on the west side of the house, indicating his father's success at horse dealing. To his surprise, he employed two grooms now, to assist him as he was getting too old to take the constant knocks of dealing with young horses or retraining damaged ones.

They were met by a mixed pack of dogs including terriers, hounds, sheepdogs and a massive St, Bernard, which headed straight for Marie and demanded her attention. Marie's eyes lit up at this gentle giant of a dog who was in danger of knocking her over with his enthusiasm. From that moment, Caesar became Marie's shadow and followed her everywhere. Charles did draw the line in the bedroom for fear the dog may think he was molesting her and would proceed to savage him, but Caesar did not like being confined to the kitchen and he had a huge voice of disapproval so he would spend many nights going back downstairs to let the dog up so they could all sleep in peace.

The cottage was small but adequate, consisting of a galley kitchen, pantry, small lounge with open fireplace, one large bedroom and a second small bedroom, which had been divided to make a bathroom. He was worried that Marie might find it a bit austere compared to her sumptuous chateau, but she thought it was like a miniature doll's house. He knew cooking was probably not on her list of talents so now was her chance to start learning as he had no intention of eating with his parents in the farmhouse and his cooking skills were non-existent – hence he had nearly starved on his return to Paris.

They had eaten dinner on the train so they didn't have to worry about food tonight. A fire had been laid in the grate so they settled down together on the sofa with a bottle of wine. She took his shirt off to check his shoulder wound and as there were no signs of blood, left the bandage in place that Henri had expertly put on. It was still giving him some pain, mainly from the bone that had been skimmed as the bullet had passed through his arm. She traced her finger down the inside of his damaged arm and then across his chest to his nipple. She leant across and ran her tongue over his right nipple and then down his chest to his navel. Sensing his arousal, she got on her knees between his legs and unfastened his trousers and using just her mouth and tongue, sent him into sheer joy and oblivion.

When his breathing had calmed down he looked at her saying, 'God, you brazen little hussy, that was incredible!' Realising that she had done all that without him laying a finger on her, he pulled her back onto the sofa. He got onto his knees, hitched her skirt up, removed her drawers and gave her exactly the same treatment in return.

Afterwards, she remonstrated with him, 'You could have removed my dress and underwear before you ravished me.'

He looked her in the eye and wagged his finger at her. 'Right, Madame, let me make this absolutely clear. Whilst you are in the house you are banned from wearing any under garments except your chemise or nightdress. I am sick of having to remove all these damn pieces of frippery, especially stockings. You may wear a dress for decency's sake during the day, but nothing else.'

Marie responded quickly. 'Is that a command, husband? Because I will only do it provided the same rules apply to you. I expect you to remove your drawers from under your breeches and be bare chested as much as decency allows.'

He roared with laughter and said, 'God, I have met my match with you, woman. I will never win a duel of words against you will I?'

Marie said, 'Charles, the sooner you realise that you are a slave to my commands, the easier your role of husband will become.'

He realised that she was probably right so he would just have to get used to being the subordinate. They went up to bed and Charles attempted to show her that when it came to her body he was in charge and if she wanted to fulfil her pleasure, she had better leave it to him.

oOo

He woke early as the sun rose the next morning to find Marie's head lying across his chest. The tenderness he felt for her was indescribable. He slid her off his body and slipped out of bed and fetched his robe from the bathroom. He quietly found his sketch pad and pencils and pulled the armchair up to the bed. He pulled the covers back to expose her head, neck and upper body and tucked the bedclothes over her hip.

He started to sketch her outline and he was

overjoyed to be united with his sketch pad and at last be able to commit her body to paper. He worked furiously and quickly to draw the outline of her body and had got as far as her hip before she started to stir. When she saw what he was doing, she blushed.

He dropped to his knees and leant over the bed. 'Marie, don't ever be embarrassed about your beautiful body, it's what nature gave you. You, above all must know that I have to draw you because as an artist, seeing perfection means I have to capture it on paper. I promise you these sketches or portraits will never be released in the public domain; they are for my pleasure only.' With that he pulled the covers away from her and drew from her hip to her toes. He then realised she was feeling the cold so he got into bed with her and covered them both up. He held her to his chest and wrapped his arms round her to warm her up with his body heat.

oOo

He got dressed and smiled when he remembered he would have to leave his drawers off, but it was too cold to go downstairs without his shirt. Marie was already down in the kitchen, crashing about with pots and pans, attempting to make some coffee. She had found some bread and cheese in the pantry and some jam his mother had made. As she got the bread knife out of the drawer it caught on the handle and fell to the floor. She bent down to pick it up and quick as lightning, Charles pulled her skirt up and checked she wasn't wearing any drawers, and pinched her bottom.

She whipped round. 'How dare you touch me without my permission?'

Charles grabbed her from behind, twisted the knife out of her hand and it fell to the floor, lifted her skirt, bent her over the kitchen table and took her with no foreplay. She screeched with rage and he felt her shift her weight and attempt to kick him but he skilfully deflected her blow to his shin and smacked her soundly across her right buttock. He heard her gasp in shock but he was too far gone to stop now. He felt her body relax under him and he hoped she was enjoying it as much as he was.

Exhausted as he was, he knew to be very careful as he was well aware how dangerous she could be. He kissed the nape of her neck and she twisted onto her side but he still had her pinned to the table and as an extra precaution had hold of both hands. Her face was within inches of him and she looked flushed and her eyes were angry. He waited with bated breath for her to speak.

'Bastard, but I loved it. Now do it again!'

He released her and pulled her up into a standing position, creased with laughter and said, 'No, I am dying of starvation here and if you want me to keep up this sort of pace for four weeks you are going to have to feed me.' He plonked a gentle kiss on her nose and took the boiling water pan off the stove to make his own coffee.

After breakfast, he suggested they go and look round the stables. They went outside and were instantly surrounded by the pack of excited dogs. Caesar was fussing around Marie but an elegant deerhound seemed to be rather partial to him so he gave her a good patting and rubbed her ears. His father was out in the paddock behind the stables with a young, well bred grey filly, along with his groom. The groom had her on the lunge and his father was just putting the saddle on her back and girthing it up very gently. The groom sent her forward into trot and then she realised that she had something rigid on her back and round her belly. Suddenly, she put her head down and set off bucking like mad, first one side and then the other. The groom kept her going forward into a circle around the small paddock. The force of her bucking escapades had shifted the saddle further down her back and now the girth was acting as a real bucking strap. She set off again, trying her hardest to shift it but then stopped dead, her neck and chest lathered in sweat and her body shaking. Unknown to him, Marie had already unlatched the gate and was on her way over to the mare. *Oh God, what if she got on in her dress and the mare threw her? She could end up on the ground with her buttocks exposed, right at his father's feet.*

He ran after her shouting, 'Marie, you need to go and change into breeches if you are going to handle the horse; you will get your dress filthy. You know how dangerous unbroken horses can be, do be careful.'

She totally ignored him and stood stock still about three feet from the filly. She deliberately avoided eye contact but talked soothingly to her and held her hand out. The filly whickered at her and walked up to her outstretched hand and smelt her. Marie then stroked her neck and moved to her shoulder, quietly talking to her, and skilfully checked the girth. She put her left foot in the stirrup and leant over the mare's back, still stroking and talking to her. He held his breath because he knew what might happen when she felt Marie's weight. She didn't flinch so Marie lifted her right leg over the saddle and gently sat down. She unclipped the reins that were attached to the saddle and used her voice to ask the filly to walk on. The filly did exactly what she asked after a little pressure from her legs and Marie continued to talk quietly to her and the filly's ears twitched back and forward, listening to her melodic voice as they walked on. She then leant forward and unclipped the lunge line, loosely took up the reins and asked her to trot. She trotted on as if she had been carrying a rider for years, totally relaxed and willing and after about three laps she halted and slid out of the saddle.

His father was clapping and shouting 'Bravo!' and Marie finally acknowledged Charles' presence and gave him the cheekiest grin and giggled. He bent down to her ear and said, 'Did you not hear my warning that you had no drawers on? You could have so easily ended up on the ground with your buttocks exposed at my father's feet.'

'Of course I hadn't forgotten but I knew the filly would succumb to my charms but if she hadn't and I had ended up on the ground it would have served you right for taking advantage of me before breakfast.' Charles gasped in amazement. He obviously had a lot to learn about women – she was as calculating as a wily fox. She had risked her neck at the throw of a dice just to teach him another lesson.

His father was overjoyed with Marie and full of admiration for her skill and expertise and asked her where she had learned to handle horses like that.

'In Russia they use the same approach because if you get them to trust you early on they will do your bidding for life. How else can you get a cavalry charger to keep returning to the battlefield time after time knowing he is staring death in the face? They do it for love, nothing else. If you show them love at the beginning, just like a dog they will be faithful to man forever.'

Charles hadn't realised that his mother had been watching the whole scene from the other side of the paddock and their eyes met.

'Charles, may I have a word?'

Oh God, by the look on her face she did not approve of her daughter-in -law's antics. Jean had wandered back to the stables with Marie so Charles told the groom to tell them he was going back to the farmhouse with his mother. He went over to his mother, held her hand and they walked back to the house. After they had got inside she made them both a coffee and they sat at the kitchen table. Finally, after a bit of idle chat, she said what she had obviously been thinking.

'Charles, Marie is rather headstrong and unconventional. She is hardly the French aristocratic lady I pictured when you wrote and told me of your engagement. She is I admit, extremely beautiful but in a rather Bohemian way.'

He refrained from laughing at her description because she had summed her up well.

'Mother, you have to remember Marie was born and raised in Russia for fifteen years in a liberal family. Women there are obviously more outspoken and have a little more freedom in their upbringing than French girls and her father treated her no different than Henri. She is very well educated, speaks five languages, sings like a lark, plays the piano as well as any woman I have heard, is a skilled artist and a competent horsewoman. I admit that due to her rich upbringing she may lack cooking, sewing and housekeeping skills as she has never had to do them but she is a very quick learner.'

His mother smiled and said, 'And you, my son, are totally besotted with her.'

'Yes, Mother, I am afraid so madly, passionately, deeply, head over heels enraptured by her.'

His mother replied, 'And she has you twisted round her little finger in only five days of marriage.'

'Yes, I am aware of that and she is a firebrand

when she is thwarted but I will try to keep her temper under control, there is no malice in her. She does love me as deeply as I love her and I can't wait to have children with her.'

'Children Charles, you have never spoken of wanting children in your life before, why now? Marie has plenty of childbearing years ahead of her. I'd have thought you would have wanted to settle down and have some time together first.'

'I know that would have been the sensible thing to do but I don't know where this desperate urge has come from to want to father a child.'

'Charles, you're finally totally in love with a woman and it's perfectly natural. It's what keeps the population growing; it's nature at its best.' She patted his hand and said gently, 'Enjoy it while you can; when babies come along you won't get the time to yourselves, especially with your painting. Your father was saying only yesterday what beautiful children you will produce between you.'

'Oh great, now I am to be assessed as potential stallion material am I?'

'Well your father is right, she is exquisitely beautiful and maybe she will calm down a bit with a foal at foot, eh? As Marie's kitchen skills are a bit limited, do you want me to prepare your evening meal and you can send Marie up for it about 7 p.m. each evening? Don't worry; we will keep out of your way. You had better go and find her; she might be on another horse by now, knowing your father.' *God, and what if she had fallen off?* He left the house and walked quickly back up to the stables.

He retrieved Marie from the stables and suggested they go for a walk. He had no intention of telling Marie about his conversation with his mother other than they had, had a friendly discussion about the wedding. He set off in search of some of his childhood haunts and after a few moments he heard a noise behind and out of the hedgerow appeared Caesar.

'Oh, so we are going to have him tagging along behind us are we?'

Marie laughed and said, 'Leave him be, he's just being friendly.'

oOo

That evening he was delighted to eat the casserole prepared by his mother and then they settled by a roaring fire on the sofa in the lounge. Marie threw off her dress and just had her chemise on. She pulled at his sleeve and indicated he had to remove his shirt, so he obliged. She snuggled down next to him and began caressing his chest.

Charles, you know you were telling me about "realist painters" only painting what they see rather than the old masters who painted what they thought you should see?' He was astonished that she was suddenly asking him questions about art.

'Yes darling, that's right. Michaelangelo painted most of his paintings using models but he altered their features if they didn't portray the image he wanted. That's why all his murals of angels have beautiful faces like yours.'

'Did he paint the horses too?'

'No he didn't, he used other artists, skilled in portraying animals. He did have a whole ceiling to paint, not just a canvas. He couldn't be expected to do it all on his own. It took nearly two years to complete as it was. I promise I will take you to Rome to see the Sistine Chapel, perhaps next year.'

'So, do you as a realist, always paint the truth even with your portrait work when some of the women you paint may be ugly?'

'Well you can usually find one outstanding feature such as their hair, eyes or figure that will help outshine the lesser features such as a big nose or wobbly chin. So I may be guilty of a little misrepresentation on some occasions but when someone is paying highly for your work you have to be a little careful – they don't want to see an exact picture of themselves, especially if they are ugly.'

'Oh Charles, you mean you would compromise your art for money? You do disappoint me. Are you going to sketch me again in the morning?

'Well yes, I thought we would ride over to a place called Houplines where there is a secluded waterfall and if I take my watercolours then I could paint you as well. '

Marie replied, 'In the nude?

'Well, only if there is nobody around. I'd love to

paint you nude. You are suddenly getting very brave about exposing your body aren't you?'

Marie retorted, 'Only if it is for your eyes and you promise to paint me exactly as you see me.'

'Of course darling, there is nothing that any artist would want to change about your perfect body.'

'Are you sure about that, Charles? You wouldn't compromise your realist mind to hide the truth?'

'Never, why?

Marie got up from the sofa and faced him while she undid her chemise and let if fall to her feet. His heart fluttered at the sight of her body.

'Then Charles, I expect you to paint my bottom exactly how you see it now.' She slowly turned her back to him and to his horror he saw the red imprint of his hand and fingers across her right buttock.

'Oh Marie, you little witch. Now I know why you have been questioning my principles. I will ensure I do it exactly as it is and then I can treasure it forever and remember the reason I thrashed you, when I am in my dotage.' He pulled her back onto the sofa and kissed her gently and inspected the handprint on her buttock. 'I'm sorry darling, I hope I didn't hurt you but I didn't want a broken leg as I know how hard you can punch and kick.'

13

They were going to visit Houplines, an area he remembered as a child that had parts of secluded forest with natural waterfalls, which could provide a suitable place for him to paint. His mother had provided them with sandwiches for lunch and his father had selected suitable steady horses for them to ride.

Caesar sensed activity and was shadowing Marie closely. Charles asked one of the grooms to shut him in a stable as he didn't want Caesar joining them on the trip, especially when he was intending to paint her nude, as he knew that one thing would inevitably lead to another. He realised the dog sensed him as a rival and if he thought for one minute he was harming her, he knew Caesar could be capable of ripping him to pieces. He put his watercolours and sketch pad in a second saddle bag with Marie's cloak and buckled it to Marie's horse's saddle.

Just before they set off, he asked his mother to remove the bandage on his arm and check his wound. It had been giving him some discomfort but there had been no further bleeding, but he was acutely aware of infection being his biggest danger. He winced when the bandage was removed but heaved a sigh of relief when the wound appeared to be free from infection. He gritted his teeth while his mother bathed it in brandy to clean it and then despatched Marie to the stables to get some of the horse wound powder his father used to treat his horses' injuries.

Finally, they mounted up and set off, listening to the mournful cries of Caesar's howling receding in the distance as his devoted Marie left the farm. He teased her about the dog's devotion towards her and told her in no uncertain terms that he would not consider Caesar returning to Paris with them. The thought of the damage that massive dog could do in his studio filled him with dread.

As the terrain became more rugged and isolated, he was grateful his father had picked these two draught horse crosses as they were safe conveyances. They entered the forest and experienced the dark and stillness closing in on them. Marie paused to put her woollen cloak on over her shirt and breeches to keep her warm as the temperature had dropped by at least ten degrees now they were shielded from the sun's rays. In the distance they could hear the sound of water and headed towards it. They came out of the woods into a grassy clearing where the sun flooded through and highlighted a waterfall, which cascaded from the rocks above into a pool of deep blue water. This would be a perfect setting for his painting.

They dismounted and he was grateful his father

had thought of everything and put halters underneath the bridles of both horses so he could tie them up securely when they reached their destination. They unsaddled them both to make them more comfortable, led them to the edge of the pool for a drink and then brought them back and tied them to two suitable trees, next to each other.

Marie had wandered back to the water's edge and leant over to dip her hand in the water. Quickly, Charles moved to stand directly behind her and when she raised her upper body he put his arms round her, nuzzling the nape of her neck. She turned round and gave him a slow, sensual kiss at the same time as caressing his ear with her left hand. He deftly unclipped her hair and relished watching it cascade down to her shoulders. He unbuttoned her shirt and removed it, followed closely by her breeches and drawers. She then started removing his shirt, pausing briefly to caress his nipples with her fingers and then had his breeches and drawers removed in seconds. He moved back from her, just to wonder at the sight of her perfect body, and then swept her up into his arms and carried her into the clear blue water. They both gasped at the freezing temperature. He walked towards the waterfall and was pleased to find the water level rising up to his chest. He released her from his arms and she gasped as she was engulfed by the water, and swam away from him. He followed her and they swam towards the base of the waterfall where the water was swirling and frothing. They retreated to a quieter spot behind the waterfall so they were not directly under its flow and he found he could stand. They then encountered their first sexual experience in water, which he found an absolute delight.

They emerged from the water, their fingers and feet numb from the cold but their bodies alive with their exhilarating experience. They picked up their discarded clothes and ran over to where the horses were tethered and he retrieved Marie's cloak and laid it over the grass. They clung together for warmth while the sun gradually awoke their numb bodies. He lay there imagining he was in the Garden of Eden, lying with the delectable Eve at his side. The sound of cascading water was like music to his ears. *Could life get any better?* He felt as though a huge sand hole had swallowed him up and to escape he'd had to swim to the other side and pull himself out of it. His life had gone from darkness to light and with Marie by his side he felt capable of conquering the world.

The sun was high in the sky and he realised he had better get on with his sketching while Marie had the warmth of the sun on her naked body. He put his clothes back on, wrapped Marie back up in the cloak and led her back to the water's edge. He surveyed the scene before him; with the sun coming from the east he positioned Marie just to the right of the waterfall but still on the water's edge. He thought about drawing her emerging from the water but decided that he would get the rear view that Marie had demanded last night. He turned her horizontally to the shoreline and released the cloak from her shoulders; it fell in a folded outline behind her. He decided to leave it where it was as it gave the indication that she was just about to walk into the water. He moved back about six feet and, with no easel to use, he sat on the ground with his knees up and the sketch pad supported against his legs.

He sketched her rear outline quickly and fluently in pencil, admiring the curve of her bottom. His hand mark was clearly visible on her right buttock, as it was now turning purple. He didn't speak to her as he needed to concentrate but he told her he was going to sketch her back view now and then she could put the cloak back on to warm herself if she was cold. He worked hard on the outline and the angle of the waterfall in the background, with the sun's rays reflecting on the waterfall. More detailed work could be done on Marie's back view later. He gave her a rest and wrapped the cloak back around her and held her close, kissing the tip of her nose to check how cold she was. He called her his little water nymph and kissed her passionately.

She wandered back towards the horses for a sit down while he worked on the scenery. He had marked the spot where she had stood with a small stone. When he was satisfied that he had drawn enough of the elements of the pool and grassy bank of the waterfall, he went over to join her and they ate their lunch. He thought about the best way of presenting his picture as he needed it to represent his view of nature at its best... A scene of perfect harmony between life and nature, co-existing. The last thing he wanted was to make it an erotic portrait of a woman. His aim was to represent love, not lust. He also decided he would draw her in profile from the front and came up with an ingenious way of using the cloak to frame her body. He retrieved two of the hairpins he had put in his pocket when he had let her hair loose. He led her back into position but turned her facing away from the shoreline and, measuring the angle of the sun across the waterfall, turned her at an angle of 45-degrees to the shoreline. He left the cloak fastened around her neck but pulled it back over her shoulders and secured the two sides with the pins to stop them falling back.

Marie laughed. 'My husband the perfectionist, what am I going to do with you?'

The effect was stunning – the cloak hung in a perfect line from her shoulder blade through to her hip and knee. The black cloak emphasised the curve of her left breast and provided an exquisite contrast to her porcelain skin. He had to commit this image on canvas but he used a new sheet of paper as he had decided that this painting could only be executed in oils back in his studio in Paris. He needed time to do justice to this scene. He would decide later which portrait of Marie would grace the frame. He worked quickly and fluently with his pencil, just like he had when he had been a boy drawing horses out in the field. He drew her outline only, knowing he could position her in the studio to perfect the finer details and draw her face in profile.

Conscious that her feet must be freezing on the wet grass, he picked her up and carried her back over to the horses. She got dressed and he remembered her hair had been up in a chignon so he expertly redid it. He had often rearranged the hairstyles of his sitters as loose hair gave a far different effect in a portrait than coiffed hair.

They made their way back through the forest at a walk but cantered on when they had a clear path across fields. About a mile from home they came round the corner of the track and his horse shied and veered off to the right as a large animal came bounding over the wall to his left. It was of course none other than Caesar, who must have known instinctively that they were on their way back and come to greet them.

When they got back to the stables his father came out and he told him about the dog's appearance. He laughed and said, 'Charles, these mountain type dogs are "people" dogs, not "dog" dogs. They have been selectively bred as companions to humans for centuries. They have no interest in scenting prey, flushing game or chasing sheep. Their prime instinct is to love and protect their master and family. These dogs are the closest you can get to soulmates. They have been used to protect sheep on mountains from both prey and theft. They are capable of living out in the coldest of temperatures, watching over your livestock and property but if you let them into your home they are in their element. They are content to leave you to get on with your work without interference but they want to be within sight of you at all times if possible. They crave attention but do not demand it. They understand your moods and will come and put that enormous head on your knee if they think you need comforting. You can train them to a point but they are used to assessing the situation and acting on their own initiative. They are not aggressive dogs naturally but if you harm their owners they would be more than a match for anyone. You wait and see Caesar with children; he is the perfect nanny. For all his huge size, enormous paws and gigantic teeth he is the gentlest of dogs with a child. I would trust no other breed of dog to be left alone with a child. Your brother and his wife and child are coming over on Sunday and I promise you will understand how this dog ticks when you see him react to Louis. Caesar has no children at home to guard now so he has taken over the role of personal protector to Marie because he instinctively knows what a special woman she is. He is as devoted to her as you are but he will respect your authority… but probably only in the bedroom.'

They went back to the cottage and Charles was glad to have a rest to ease his aching shoulder. He fell asleep with Marie at his side, dreaming of the perfect day they had just had. When he came round from a deep sleep he woke to Marie tracing the outline of his face and gently kissing his nose and lips. As he stirred, Marie said,

'That's the first time I have woken before you and been able to return the favour. It gives me such a warm feeling when you are touching me gently when I am still half asleep. I feel so safe and secure when you do that to me.'

oOo

On Sunday, he was awake bright and early and he glanced over to Marie who was spread out, her arms and legs all over the bed, whilst he was delicately balanced at one side, practically falling out of the bed. She was the most restless sleeper – she would toss and turn and thrash about and one night, had inadvertently kicked him right out of the bed. Unfortunately, he had fallen on top of Caesar who had been lying at his side of the bed. For one awful moment he feared that Caesar would attack him as his face was within inches of those massive teeth. Remarkably, he growled at him but got up and left him with all his extremities intact.

He could hear movement across in the stables and buckets being banged around. As the sun was shining he decided to get up and go and help his father, as the grooms did not work on Sundays. He left Marie spread-eagled across the bed and dressed quietly. To his surprise, Caesar followed him downstairs and up to the stables, the rest of the pack bounding around him. His father was leaning over the stable door of one of his brood mares. Charles joined him and observed that she was a young mare, probably only three or four years old, and she had an enormous belly. You could actually see the movement of the foal.

Jean said, 'She's not far off now; she should foal within the next three days. I'm just fearful there may be more than one in there.'

Charles replied, 'I hope not; you won't get two foals out of this maiden mare. There's bound to be problems if she's carrying twins.'

'I know. I could end up losing all three of them if its twins. Some experienced mares do manage to bear twins successfully but it is not ideal – they never make good horses if they do survive. They are always weaker and prone to problems. You have to supplementary feed them on a maiden – she wouldn't have enough milk to sustain two foals and besides, one is always weaker than the other.'

'What stallion did you put her to?'

'A friend of mine had a young colt he bred from a saddle horse mare and put to an Arab stallion. He was full of quality with no heaviness about him in either his limbs or conformation. He was bright bay with dapples in his coat showing his Arab genes. I thought he would be perfect for her, especially as he was barely sixteen hands at three years old.'

'I saw these pure Arabs in Spain; they have a

floating gait and are as tough as nails, even over the hardest terrain. They cross them with their Lusitanos to introduce more refinement and speed. I have never had the pleasure of riding one though. Is the mare 3 or 4 years old?'

'She's 4 now. I don't breed off any of my stock until they are 3; they are not mature enough to cope with pregnancy and grow at the same time.'

Charles said, 'You must tell us when she starts in labour. Marie has never seen a foal born.'

Jean laughed. 'Nay son, it may put her off for life if this mare is carrying twins. If there are twins inside and they get their legs tangled on the way out and I can't reposition them I could end up having to shoot her.'

Charles asked, 'Have you ever thought about doing a caesarean on her?'

'I have heard of it being done but I would be terrified of attempting it for fear of cutting some vital organ and I don't want to be left with a dead mare and possibly two foals. We will just have to wait and see and let nature take its course.'

They moved on and he helped his father lead the mares out to the field. The young mare screamed in protest about being left in her stable and he went to talk to her; eventually she calmed down. His father said he would put her in the paddock for a stretch later but he wasn't risking taking her out with the others while she was so close to foaling.

He asked his father about Gustav, who had been

a baby in the cradle when he had left home at 11. His father told him that Gustav was doing well at the bank in Lille and he had met Freya two years ago and they married very quickly after meeting. He could tell that his father was suspicious of his quick marriage. He told him that Freya was the daughter of a Norwegian sailor and French mother and was very beautiful. She was tall, blonde, blue eyed and with athletic limbs. Charles suddenly became intrigued about Freya, as he had never really encountered a Viking descendant before. One of his pupils had been to Denmark and he had raved about the beauty of Scandinavian women.

He helped his father muck out the empty stables and between them they had it done in half an hour. He went back to the cottage and it was around 8 a.m. Marie was still in bed but just coming round. He leant down and kissed her trailing hand.

She turned to face him and said, 'Where have you been? I don't like waking up to an empty bed. Then the smell of the horses hit her nose and she said, 'Oh God, Charles. I know where you have been; don't you dare come near me until you have had a bath.'

He pulled back the covers and contemplated his next move. Marie was screaming at him to keep away from her and so he decided he would take the bath first and then Marie afterwards. He instructed her to stay in bed whilst he had a bath.

14

Gustav and Freya arrived on horseback at 11 a.m. He had taken Marie up to the stables to show her the mare and he had heard the approaching hoof beats followed by the welcome barking of the dog pack. He saw them cantering up the drive and as they got closer, he watched his brother approach. He gasped in surprise, as did Marie, when he realised he was looking at a mirror image of himself. Gustav had the same colour eyes, nose and mouth as him. His hair was a fraction lighter brown with some sunny streaks through it and he had a moustache rather than a beard. Gustav unbuttoned his coat and to his delight, he saw a sleepy little boy with blonde curls and blue eyes nestled against his father on the front of the saddle.

Gustav gently lifted Louis up into his arms, proffered him a kiss and said,

'Hello brother, would you mind taking your nephew while I get down?'

Charles was shocked as he hadn't a clue about babies. He reached up and took Louis in his arms. He was, by now, waking up and wriggling around.

Thankfully, Marie stepped in and took Louis from him as Charles moved back to greet Freya.

He couldn't believe what his eyes were seeing. She was riding astride, not side saddle, wearing a turquoise silk dress, not a habit. She had thick, long blonde plaits carefully pinned round her head and the deepest blue eyes he had ever seen, a medium size nose and full lips. As she dismounted he saw the beautiful, lithe body of this Viking princess and was rooted to the spot.

Gustav shouted, 'Charles, are you going to take Freya's horse off her and put it in the stable while the ladies go down to the farm with Louis? We will do the formal introductions later.'

His legs were not moving as he was still drinking in the image of his brother's wife. He took the horse from her and she flashed him a grateful smile and thanked him. He led her horse away and put it in the next stable to Gustav's. He untacked the mare and went to the tack room to put the saddle and bridle away.

Once they had stored the tack, Gustav turned to Charles and said, 'Well big brother, how are you doing? Is painting at last reaping you some reward? Are all the women in Paris as beautiful as your wife?'

'No, there aren't many women as beautiful as Marie in Europe, never mind Paris, but tell me how you found your beautiful wife in Lille, of all places?'

Gustav smiled. 'I could tell you had noticed. She has that effect on most men. The first time I laid eyes on her was in the bank as she came with her mistress to collect some money. She was in charge of the baby and she worked for a very rich shipping merchant who lived just outside Lille.'

'So if she lived with them, how did you manage to meet her?

'I cleverly arranged to take the paperwork he needed to his home one evening and just as I was leaving she was also in the hall, preparing to go back home for the weekend to see her family… so I offered her a lift back to Lille on my horse.'

The family were all in the kitchen and as they walked in, his father stepped forward to give Gustav a hefty pat on the back and he gave his mother a kiss and hug. He saw the adoring look in his mother's eyes and knew straight away who her favourite child was.

Gustav fetched Freya over to him, having handed Louis to his mother and said, 'Charles, may I present my wife Freya.'

Charles kissed her on both cheeks and got a swift glance into those hypnotic blue eyes. He collected Marie and presented her to Gustav and he reciprocated, taking just a fraction longer than necessary over the second kiss. *What on earth was up with him?* He was feeling jealous of his brother kissing his wife and yet equally, he was coveting his brother's wife.

They all dispersed to the lounge, with his father charged with rounding up all the dogs and shutting them outside. His mother had already left some toys for Louis to play with and he set off crawling towards them. At this point his father appeared with Caesar, who bounded straight over to Louis and licked him on the face. Louis promptly sat down and babbled away to Caesar. He searched through all that hair and found his leather collar and he hauled himself to his feet and set off in a wobbly gait, using Caesar as a support. When he toppled over Caesar stopped and lay down and Louis crawled over the dog's shoulder and sat behind his head, laughing and crowing. Charles watched in amazement as this massive dog lay still and let Louis bounce on his back, pretending he was a horse.

Marie was so enchanted she went off to find his sketch pad so she could draw some of the action. If Louis got too close to Caesar's eyes or put his hand in his mouth, the dog gently used a paw to push him away. When Louis crawled away, attracted by the fire, Caesar deliberately sat between Louis and the fire. His mother had already erected a temporary barricade to keep Louis away. However, when Louis got within three feet, Caesar gently got hold of his shirt and literally picked him up and took him to the far corner of the room. Charles was astonished and grateful that Marie had arrived back just in time to see it. Louis put his head on Caesar's chest and was obviously feeling tired again and within minutes he was fast asleep, lying on his back across the dog's chest and shoulder. Caesar lay as still as a mouse so as not to disturb the sleeping baby.

His father laughed and said, 'You see, Charles? I told you he was the perfect nanny. That dog did that purely off his own initiative – no training whatsoever.'

Charles got up and suggested Gustav accompany him to check on the mare back up at the stables, as he wanted to talk to him. Gustav was happy to join him and they headed off. The mare seemed calm enough so he led her into the paddock and let her have a good roll and a fling about. They went back to outside the dairy and sat on a convenient low wall so that he could keep his eye on the mare.

He chatted to Gustav about his job and what he had done at school and why he had chosen banking as a career. He asked about his sister Narcisse who had married a cloth merchant living just across the border in Belgium. Narcisse was a skilled lace maker and she combined this at home while raising her two children.

He then started to ask more about him meeting Freya and Gustav confessed that he had fallen in love with her the minute he had laid eyes on her. *Indeed, who wouldn't?* Her parents were an amiable couple and he persuaded them to let him have their daughter's hand within a month of their first meeting. He had already rented a small house close to the centre of Lille within walking distance of the bank, so there was no real reason to wait. The family Freya worked for was so desperate not to lose her that they allowed her to come to care for their daughter daily, rather than live in. Of course when she got pregnant and had Louis, she had stopped working.

Charles asked him, 'Did you wait honourably until you had wedded her before you took her virginity?

Gustav laughed and said, 'Not quite. I got carried away one evening and the deed was done. That's another reason we married quickly – in case there were any repercussions.'

Charles said, 'And is she everything you ever dreamt of as the perfect wife?'

'Well to be honest, we didn't have the best start as she wasn't over-enamoured with my early advances.'

Charles quickly jumped in, 'Why not, Gustav? How much sexual experience had you prior to your marriage?'

The shock on Gustav's face was a picture. 'Well I certainly wasn't a virgin if that's what you are implying?'

Charles responded knowing he was pushing his luck, 'How long would you say you take making love to your wife?'

Gustav's mouth was wide open with shock. 'Well, about ten minutes or so?

Charles could not stop himself. 'Ten minutes? Do you mean just to satisfy yourself? What about Freya?

'What do you mean, Charles?'

Charles took a deep breath, knowing he could insult his brother and said, 'Have you ever pleasured her to a climax without physically taking her?'

Gustav gasped, 'But why would I do that? She's my wife, not my mistress.'

'Gustav, she is entitled to more of your care and attention because she is your wife. You promised on your wedding day to love and cherish her before God. Have you invited her to make love to you?

Gustav exploded, 'For Christ's sake, Charles, she's not a strumpet. How would a virgin even know where to start?'

Charles countered, 'Exactly, so it's your job to teach her.'

'But we had only been married a month and then she fell pregnant and suffered the most appalling sickness all day every day for five months. She lost so much weight and became so dehydrated, she was bedridden. I could hardly consider touching her sexually when I feared for her life.'

'Of course not Gustav, but didn't you nurse her and comfort her? You were responsible for her condition and it was your child she was carrying.'

Gustav replied, 'No, she had her mother to nurse her. I moved into the spare room and by the time she stopped being sick I was too terrified to touch her and besides, I didn't like the changes in her body.'

'What changes?'

'Her thickened waist, heavy breasts and stretch marks on her stomach; they turned me off completely.'

'She was carrying your son, did you never think of just lying with her and holding her close to comfort her? What happened at the birth?'

Gustav replied, 'It was horrendous and I kept out of the way. That's women's work – she had her mother and a local woman. I knew there would be problems; she was tiny down there and I couldn't imagine how a baby was going to get out. She was in labour for two days and the baby was stuck and eventually she had to be cut. Louis was born but apparently he was blue on delivery and struggled to breathe afterwards. I could so nearly have lost them both.'

Charles said quietly, 'So you left her alone throughout her entire labour when she needed you most. Do you love Freya, Gustav? Because you are not giving her – or me – any indication that you do.'

Gustav shouted, 'What the hell has it got to do with you anyway? Of course I love her; she is beautiful.'

Charles replied quietly, 'Well you need to show her how much you love her and not reject her. She is very beautiful but she needs you to connect with her mind as well as her body. It's not just your pleasure that matters; it's hers too.'

Gustav turned on him. 'What makes you such an expert on women then?

'I could sense there was something wrong between you. She has the most beautiful deep blue eyes but when I looked at them I could only feel the pain she was suffering. There was no sexual chemistry between you. Your eyes never followed her and even though Marie and I are only newly married, neither of us can keep our hands off each other. You touched Louis with more affection than you touched her. Gustav, if you really love Freya these rifts can be healed with a lot of time and patience but first of all you need to get down on your knees and beg her forgiveness for abandoning her throughout her difficult pregnancy. If you don't you will lose her to the first man that offers her the attention she craves. You could have such a brilliant marriage to her if only you worked at it.'

Gustav smiled. 'Charles, I thought you were an artist, not a psychologist.'

'But it's because I am an artist that I can sense when something is wrong with the women I paint. I spend most of my working day around them. I paint nude women but I don't ravish them. It's my job to find out what makes each woman tick so I can represent that in how I paint them. I admit I took my pleasure when I felt the need, prior to marriage, but now I have Marie I wouldn't dream of touching another woman sexually.'

His mother appeared at the farmhouse door, shouting and waving them in for lunch. He waved back, indicating they were coming.

He put the mare back in her stable and fetched her some hay. He had an idea and turned to Gustav.

'Why don't you leave Freya and Louis here for a couple of days? I would love to paint her for you and it would give us a chance to get to know Louis. Since I have been wed I have had a desperate urge to become a father, but have none of the parenting skills. If you think it will help I will talk to Freya about what happened, because all you did was run away from the situation out of fear not malice, but each time you did it you made matters worse in Freya's eyes. You are not a cruel man, Gustav, just a frightened, sexually inexperienced one.'

'Would you really paint her for me?'

'Of course I would, as long as you allow me free rein to paint her as I see her. By that I don't mean in the nude – much as I would love to do it. I assure you that when I show it to you; you will see your wife in a completely different light and understand her more.' He gave Gustav a pat on the back as he knew he had put him through the mill, emotionally.

They went into the dining room and Marie gave him a quizzical look. He realised that she must have seen his interest in Freya and he was sure she would be feeling uncertain of his motives but he would have to wait until after lunch to calm her down. Louis was apparently asleep in a chair in the lounge with the devoted Caesar guarding him. He would be in to tell them the minute Louis woke up.

He took the opportunity to catch his mother when he cleared the soup plates back into the kitchen. He told her that he had asked Gustav to leave Freya and Louis with them as he wanted to paint them.

His mother looked at him suspiciously. 'Charles, what are you planning? Surely you are not coveting your brother's wife? You have only been married to Marie for two weeks.'

He was horrified. 'Mother, how dare you even think it? If you want to see your beloved son happy in his marriage then you had better hope I can salvage the mess he has made of it so far.' With that, he stormed out.

He made it through the rest of the meal by avoiding his mother's eyes completely. He could feel Marie's tension and he felt the friction between Gustav and Freya. He had never been so attuned to an atmosphere before he was married, so why did he suddenly feel like this?

Just as they had eaten pudding, there was a mournful wail and an agitated Caesar came bounding into the room, went straight up to Freya and practically pulled her off the chair. It did at least lighten the tension in the room. Freya left to go and rescue Louis and Gustav followed but signalled for him to come too. They were out of earshot of Freya in the lounge when Gustav suggested that after Freya had fed Louis, he wanted to take her for a walk and talk over some of the issues he had raised – so would he and Marie look after Louis for a while? Charles found himself agreeing but his full concentration was on Freya. Louis had been crying when Freya reached him but as soon as she touched him and picked him up, he went silent. He was rubbing his eyes and as she sat him on her knee his little hands scrabbled at her bodice to get to the treasure within. Freya was struggling with one hand undoing her chemise and the other arm holding Louis, who was by now frantic for his lunch. Finally, she had undone her chemise and Louis pulled her dress down over her left breast and helped himself.

Just at this moment, his mother walked into the room to see him staring intently at Freya feeding the baby and she uttered, 'For goodness' sake allow the girl some peace to feed her child – get out, the pair of you!'

The look his mother gave him reminded him of the time he had stolen an apple pie that was cooling by the windowsill and she had found him in a stable, consuming it. She had taken him over her knee and given him a good thrashing, which he thoroughly deserved. However, this was far worse; his mother thought he was lusting after her darling Gustav's wife.

He turned to Gustav, 'Please promise me you will talk to Mother about what has happened between you and Freya because she thinks I am lusting after her and I promise you I am not. You could have talked to her, Gustav. She would have understood how Freya must have been feeling.'

Gustav chuckled. 'I could hardly discuss my sexual performance with my mother but I am glad that you had the guts to raise it with me today. Don't worry; I will put her mind at rest.'

He was horrified to admit that he had watched Freya's every move. He wasn't sexually aroused by it, just fascinated by seeing nature in action. Freya came out to them with Louis and Gustav suggested she leave him with Charles while they go for a short walk. Reticently, she handed Louis to Charles and suddenly he had a squirming ten-month-old baby in his arms, which was certainly a first. He practically ran back inside to find Marie, who was helping his mother wash up. They both turned round as he entered the kitchen as Louis, realising he was with a stranger, let out an angry wail.

He announced to them both, 'Gustav just wanted some time alone with Freya so I volunteered to look after Louis. There was a resounding smash as his mother dropped the plate she was holding and thankfully, the noise stopped Louis' cries as well. They stared at him incredulously as he went on, 'I thought we could take Louis back to the cottage and amuse him until they come back. He's fed and changed.'

His mother turned to him, 'You had better leave the child with me. What do you know about babies?'

He felt panic at the prospect of looking after Louis but anger that his mother mistrusted him so much.

'No Mother, Gustav left him in my charge and unless I have chance to be with a baby I am never going to learn. Marie, would you join me please.'

He stepped back and turned to the door to find Caesar standing about three feet behind him, eyeing him suspiciously. He pushed past the dog, praying he would follow him, and stormed back to the cottage with Marie and the dog trotting behind.

When they got safely inside the cottage Marie said,

'For God's sake Charles, what is going on here?' She took Louis out of his arms and sat on the sofa with him on her knee, with Caesar covering him in sloppy kisses, to his great delight. He poured himself a large brandy and sat on the chair. He knew he would have to tell her every single detail that he and Gustav had discussed. He could not risk holding anything back as, if she found out something at a later date, she could misinterpret his intentions.

After he had told her every detail she said, 'Charles, you are a very sensitive man and I love you for it. I don't know how you dared tackle your brother on such a difficult matter when you haven't set eyes on each other for twenty-five years. He could have really taken offence and never spoken to you again. It does show, though, that he does love Freya deep down – he just isn't any good at showing it. Freya must have had a dreadful time throughout the pregnancy and the childbirth. It has certainly frightened the hell out of me.'

'Marie, that's the last thing I wanted to do. Remember, you will have me by your side every step of the way from conception to birth. I want to be involved in the whole process from start to finish.'

Marie interjected, 'Even at the birth, Charles? Men should be spared the trauma of childbirth and you might never want me sexually again.'

'Why, for God's sake? It's men that get you pregnant in the first place; surely we should be there to suffer it with you? You can rest assured that no thickened waist, large breasts, stretch marks or watching you give birth are going to put me off. I would hope it would bring us closer together as it is what God intended marriage to be.'

Louis had now escaped from Marie's knee, had grabbed hold of Caesar's collar and was heading in his direction. He held his arms out towards him and Louis wobbled over to him and then he picked the child up and plonked him on his knee. Charles inspected Louis with his finger as if he was a sitter for a life class. He had a round face with blue eyes, a button nose, a firm, dimpled chin and a mass of tightly curled, ash blond hair to his shoulders. Charles ran his fingers through the delicate strands. He lifted his arms above his head and Louis scrambled into a standing position on his knee. He traced his outline with his finger, from neck to toe. He took a sock off and gently traced his toes, talking to him in a quiet tone as if he was a foal or a puppy. Surprisingly, Louis responded and started to investigate Charles's face with his chubby little fingers.

Marie looked on, transfixed. She had seen Charles behave like this with her when they had lain exhausted and ravaged in bed but she had never expected to see him exhibit such tenderness to a child. Perhaps the irascible artist could make the perfect father as well? She began to understand why he had suddenly developed the desire to become a father.

There came a knock at the door and she ran to let Gustav and Freya in. Freya went anxiously through to the lounge to see if her son was still alive and stopped dead when she saw him climbing all over Charles and stroking his hair and nose. Gustav followed her in and he was surprised to see his brother so natural and relaxed with his son. Even he could feel the emotion between them and he began to realise what Charles meant when he had said he needed to connect emotionally with Freya. Charles had a natural empathy with people and nature that unfortunately, had been missed in him. Louis turned round to see his mother and uttered a sound very like 'Mama'. Charles lifted him up into Freya's welcoming arms and he looked deep into Freya's eyes and he felt she was calmer and less anxious than earlier.

He managed to get a few moments alone with Gustav before they went back to the farmhouse. He said he had apologised to Freya and they had both cried in each other's arms. Gustav gave him permission to talk to Freya about what had happened in an effort to help him make amends for his behaviour.

All three of them stayed the night at the farm and then Gustav left early for Lille and the bank. He was coming back on Wednesday after work, to escort them home. Charles prayed that Gustav would leave Freya alone that night and not force her into any physical activity. Gustav needed to regain her trust slowly and gently before he took her intimately again.

15

Charles and Marie ate in the cottage that evening because he wanted to prepare for painting Freya the next morning. He wondered what his mother was thinking about his unusual behaviour but as Gustav and family were there she probably never gave him another thought. He realised he was feeling unduly bothered by Gustav being his mother's favourite. Why did it worry him? He left home at 11 and never went back so it was obvious that his mother would have a far greater emotional attachment to Gustav. Suddenly, he was becoming overwhelmed by all these deep emotional feelings: wanting to become a father, playing with Louis, Freya's inner turmoil… What exactly was going on in his mind?

Marie asked him how he was going to paint Freya and how he would convince Gustav to change his pattern of rejection. To be truthful, he hadn't a clue at the moment. The first step had at least been taken in that Gustav had recognised what he had done. How this would be reconciled by Freya, he didn't really know.

He turned to Marie and said, 'If I tell you what

comes into my mind when I look at Freya, please do not misinterpret my words. I am not comparing her to you and I do not like her more than you. I am just trying to help her find a way out of her predicament. My first impression when she arrived in the yard was of a beautiful Viking princess. Her eyes are like deep blue pools and her face is very pretty. Her hair is her outstanding feature and I need to get that undone and flowing down her back. I think it will be at least waist length, possibly longer. The colour is so unusual as there are at least three different colours running through each strand. It will be a challenge to paint, as each strand will have to be done individually and I am going to make it even harder by wanting the sun going through it. She is very tall for a woman and must have a long length from her hip to knee and I would expect her to have very shapely thighs and calves.'

Marie said, 'Where are you thinking of painting her and in what form?'

'It has to be outside but I want to do a full length portrait with no background. This picture is going to be all about her – no distractions whatsoever.'

'What is she going to wear?'

'It will have to be a very simple dress and of a soft colour, not to distract from her complexion and eyes. It cannot be blue – I don't want to portray her as a Madonna – I want to show her as a Viking warrior. Do you think she will be prepared to have no underwear on? She doesn't understand what I am trying to do and she may be horrified at the prospect.'

'No she won't, Charles. You can tell she doesn't like the restrictions of undergarments anyway. She can only be wearing a simple chemise now as she's feeding Louis. I assume you want her barefoot? I think I may have a dress that might do the job; I will go and put it on for you.' She ran upstairs to find the dress.

She bounced back into the room wearing a very simple, pale lilac, silk shift dress. She had nothing on underneath and it clung to her body, outlining every curve and contour. The bodice was low and empire line, just delicately embroidered with lace on the neckline. The only problem was that it had sleeves.

'I think the colour will be fine as it will just warm up her fair complexion but until we see it against her face we won't know for sure. She may need a touch of makeup to contrast with her marble skin but you can deal with that. The sleeves will have to go as her arms will be as lithe as her legs and need to be exposed. If I could, I would slash the dress from her thigh at one side to her knee at the other, both back and front. I want some small white roses braided into her hair to promote a virginal look.'

Marie interrupted, 'But she's not a virgin, Charles.'

'Oh yes she is, maybe not in the physical sense but she is still untouched by love. Remember, I have to get Gustav to see her as pure and to want to nurture and cherish her, not just possess her body but her mind too. He needs to banish his selfishness and learn to worship her, not just take her because he's her husband. How difficult is that going to be for him? He has lost his connection to nature and even religion and he has shown no empathy for her during her pregnancy. I really don't know whether he will be up to the task because he doesn't know what real love is yet. If he can do it he will be transformed and if she can release her feelings that she has trapped in a little black box in her brain due to the trauma of the pregnancy and birth that will be the key. When I first saw her I thought her icy ethereal quality was due to calmness and serenity but it's not. She has shut down all feeling for Gustav because he betrayed her when she needed him most.'

Marie said, 'It's only 8 p.m. Shall I go back to the farmhouse and see her and talk it over with her to ease the path? Shall I ask her to leave her hair unbraided tonight so that it won't have any wrinkles in it tomorrow? You can cut the hem off the dress tomorrow, as you need to check the length. I will go and change back into my dress and see you later.'

'Yes, that would be a good idea, darling. I will check over my paints. I could do it in watercolours for ease but I won't get the definition I could if I were to use oils. I just hope I have enough paint for all that blonde hair.'

Marie hurried off, worried they might have retired already. He poured himself a brandy and thought through his challenge for tomorrow. He needed to find a suitable tree with high branches as he didn't want to have to paint leaves but it would all depend on the sun and whether it would penetrate enough to reflect off her hair.

oOo

The next morning he woke up with Marie wrapped around him, perilously close to falling out of bed. He rearranged her and snuggled up to her on his side, with her back to him. He traced her outline from the nape of her neck, shoulder, waist and buttock and reflected on his imminent task. Really, the two women were polar opposites. Marie had her French looks, athletic body and fiery temperament whilst Freya had her beautiful Nordic looks combined with a feeling of pure strength and an icy heart, which he had to try and unlock for Gustav. He heard Gustav ride off from the stables back to Lille and he sighed, hoping he was going to succeed with his endeavour.

Marie stirred, turned over to face him and kissed him gently on his nose. She moved down to his chest with her mouth and traced her fingers down his left-hand side. He smiled, knowing exactly what she was doing. She probably didn't realise it but she was obviously feeling a little jealous of his attention to Freya and so she was claiming his body in an attempt to enforce her superiority. She was basically warning him to dismiss any sexual thoughts he may have for Freya because he belonged to her. Well she need not have any worries. He rolled over onto this back and let Marie have her way.

They rose at about 7:30 a.m. and Marie went to look for some white flowers in his mother's garden while he made the breakfast. She returned with a basket of white roses and some fallen heads, which she thought he could sprinkle around her feet. She found some hairpins, a comb, white ribbon, needle, thread and scissors and added them to the basket.

Marie had seen Freya last night and told her what Charles had planned for her. She was a little apprehensive when she suggested no undergarments but she reassured her that she would be with her all the time and no unseemly part of her body would be exposed. His mother was looking after Louis until lunchtime and then would bring him to wherever they were sitting, along with some sandwiches. Marie took her woollen cloak to wrap round Freya in case the weather turned cool and windy.

Freya came to the cottage and Marie took her upstairs to try on the lilac dress. She had tied her hair at the nape of her neck with a white ribbon but it was unplaited. Marie had unpicked the sleeves on the dress last night so it was ready in advance.

When Marie and Freya came back downstairs they went out into the little cottage garden so that Charles could check the dress. The colour suited her skin tone and in the sunlight would reflect back a rosy glow onto her skin. The bodice was a fraction too tight as her breasts were larger than Marie's due to her nursing. They could probably unbutton the top buttons when she was in place. He advised

Marie to bring her makeup just in case he needed to highlight her cheeks and eyebrows. He had packed up all his materials and so they set off in search of a suitable spot. They went into one of the empty fields where there was a copse of trees in one corner. He found an old oak tree, which was positioned away from other trees. It had a lovely gnarled trunk with roots protruding from the base. This would be perfect provided the sun's rays could penetrate the upper branches to illuminate her face. The clouds were beginning to disperse and he reckoned the sun would be high enough in the sky in about an hour's time.

He apologised to Freya before he started to cut the hem of the dress. He wanted to paint her head-on, but with her body at a 30-degree angle and with her feet placed one in front of the other to elongate her leg. He decided to cut the dress from right thigh to left knee leaving a triangular shape to the hem. He felt her tremble slightly as he started to cut from about two inches below her upper thigh. He was careful to avoid touching her bare skin but he was on his knees and very close to her body. The length of her marble white thigh and her muscular calf were all he had anticipated. When he was satisfied with the hem of the dress, Marie started on her hair. She released the bow and it cascaded over her shoulders like ripe corn in a field; he had to contain a gasp of appreciation. It was just so beautiful, it touched his heart. He and Marie discussed the flowers and decided to try lightly braiding the front sections on both sides of her face with the rose heads. Marie skilfully weaved them into her locks and then fastened them with needle and thread and then twisted the side sections and pinned them to the back of her head. He moved her into position with her back as close to the tree trunk as possible and Marie scattered the rose head petals in a circle around her feet.

He spoke quietly to Freya, 'I want you to imagine that you are a Viking princess back in Norway looking out across the sea, watching a small boat being rowed by Gustav into the shore… and you have been parted for six months. You need to raise your head slightly.' He lifted her chin slightly to the right and looked deep into those ice blue eyes. There was the faintest flicker of recognition and he prayed that the ice would start melting. He pulled her hair back behind her shoulders and ran his hands through the thick lustre of gold. He examined a strand in fine detail and he knew he was going to have a massive job on his hands to recreate the shades as the top was nearly silver, the middle like corn and then lower down was burnished gold.

Marie had prepared his palette and he moved into position about three feet away from her, which was very close for a portrait. He drew the outline swiftly so that if she moved he would be able to recreate her positon. The raising of her chin had exposed the length of her elegant neck and emphasised her prominent cheekbones. As his eyes moved down her body he saw the pull of the silk across her breasts. He put down his brush, went over to her and leaned round to her back to undo the top two buttons. For one brief moment his chest was actually pressed close to her breast and he had to restrain himself from touching her. He realised he should have asked Marie to do it as he could feel her eyes boring into the back of his neck.

He returned to his position, flashed Marie a smile and carried on. He needed to get the dress outline fixed first and then draw her lower body. Her thigh was marble in colour and as muscular as an athlete's, running down to a neat calf and foot. She looked as though she could run effortlessly for miles and he pictured her with a sword at her side. Finally, she was beginning to relax and as the sun rose higher; its rays filtered down through the leaves and cast shadows on that hair of burnished gold. He worked quickly to finish her lower body and then he suggested she have a rest and sit down. Marie fetched her cloak over so Freya could sit on the grass. She came over to him.

'You have no idea what it feels like to watch you paint someone as beautiful as her; I feel so vulnerable.'

He wrapped his arms round her and kissed her slowly and reverently. 'Marie, you are my wife. I only have eyes for you.' He whispered in her ear, 'I think I have been very well behaved and I admit that had I been a single man I would have had difficulty keeping my hands off her, but she is "ice" whereas as you are "fire" and I know which I would rather have in my bed at night.'

They reassembled and he guided Freya back into position and told her he would be working on her upper body and arms next. The time passed quickly for him as he was working at speed. He had noticed the dress was slightly off-centre and had gone over to Freya, bent down and readjusted the dress. He felt eyes glaring at the back of his head and assumed it was Marie but to his horror, he heard Marie talking to his mother. *Oh no, not again!* He had been caught in a compromising position by his mother who must by now be thinking her son was a sexual deviant.

Louis was crawling towards them at a fierce rate and when he got close, Charles lifted him up and then threw him up in the air and caught him. Louis giggled with delight at this new game. He put him over his shoulder and motioned Freya over to an overturned tree stump. By now, Louis was wriggling and shouting 'Mama' so he released him into Freya's arms. She sat him on her knee and asked Charles to undo the buttons at the back of her dress. He leant over and undid another two, by which time a hungry Louis had pulled the dress down and was tucking into his lunch with delight. He moved out of the way quickly, but he knew that both women would have seen what had taken place. He went back to his portrait, too afraid to go near to his mother – he would rather starve than face her anger.

He picked up his sketch book and found a new

page and quickly started to capture the scene of Freya and Louis. He knew he was taking a risk as Marie might think he was doing it from a sexual viewpoint but he honestly did not feel that way. He was just so fascinated by the interaction between mother and child. Louis reminded him of a spring lamb suckling its mother and he could imagine if he had a little tail he would be wagging it profusely. Freya put Louis back on the ground while she tied her hair back as Louis had been trying to reach the roses in her hair. Louis was extremely cross to have had his lunch interrupted and was scrabbling at her knee to get back to her breast. She pulled up the left side of the bodice of the dress and then exposed her right side. By now, Louis was screaming in anger and when she did pick him up he grabbed Freya's nipple with his hand with such force he saw her flinch. Deftly removing his hand, she allowed him to suckle.

Charles carried on with his drawing, realising he would have to ignore the fact that she had changed sides with Louis. His brain had to sketch a mirror image and he hadn't had to practise that for a while; it took a lot of concentration. Marie and his mother went over to Freya and thankfully, didn't block his view so he carried on as fast as he could, knowing that it would all be over very soon.

When Freya had finished feeding Louis, Marie brought him over a sandwich and said, 'Your mother is really mad about you painting Freya, especially with her dress slashed and no undergarments on.'

'Well I trust you defended me, Marie. Of course she would be shocked –she has no idea about the work we do as artists – she has never been off the farm. She already thinks I am lusting after Freya and I hope you put her mind at rest. Would you mind setting up my palette now? I need to start on her hair; I will need to mix several pale colours to match that hair.'

He went and brought Freya back to her position, much to his mother's disgust, as he had to manoeuvre her into the original pose. The sun was now at its height and the effect of the light and shadow caused by the leaves was spectacular. Marie brought him his palette and he used his knife to put the basecoat of silver across the top of her head, then he mixed the colours to produce the corn and then the gold effect. He took his brush and blended them in, strand by strand, and then took another brush to paint the shadow from the leaves. Finally, where the sun's rays were visible, he changed the colour yet again to capture the light. Marie stayed quietly at his side, fascinated by his technique.

He worked non-stop for three solid hours, labouring over her hair. The life and movement sprang out from the canvas and where the sun caught it her hair looked like lightning was shining through it. Freya had a break but he carried on working as the complexity of colours on the palette meant he had to keep going before they dried out.

They returned to the farmhouse at about 3:30

p.m. and Freya went to get changed. His mother had invited them up to the house for dinner tonight as Freya was there. He went upstairs for a lie down and rest and to ease his aching left shoulder before dinner. He was completely exhausted by his work today. He brought the pencil sketch of Freya and Louis and hid it with the sketches he had of Marie in the woods. He had a couple of hours' sleep but Marie had not joined him as she had gone up to the stables to see the brood mare as his father reckoned she was getting close to foaling.

At dinner, he could feel an atmosphere between himself and his mother but he was too tired to do anything about it. Thankfully, Marie and Freya were in a chatty mood so he was content to just listen. Freya told Marie that Louis's full name was Louis Odin Auguste Durand. Odin was a Norse god and his name meant "furious" in French. Charles smiled to himself; so his little nephew had to live up to the reputation of sixteen "Louis" French kings – the last one they had beheaded had ended 1000 years of continuous French monarchy – and a Norse God. Auguste was a Durand family name. Having seen his tantrum at having his lunch interrupted, he thought he was well on his way, for only ten months old.

16

The next morning he was awake bright and early and left Marie asleep while he went downstairs to study his canvas. He went over every inch deciding whether he should make changes and for once he could have done with Manet, as his eye would have picked out any flaws he hadn't seen. He decided he needed to revisit her left leg as there wasn't enough definition on the calf. He had yet to start on her face and he considered how he was going to paint those ice blue eyes depicting the deep blue turbulent sea he could feel within her soul.

He heard Marie stir upstairs and she came down looking for him with that wonderful half awake and half asleep demeanour that he was coming to love.

She said, 'I hate waking up alone. I'm going to ban you from leaving the bed before me.'

'I don't think so, Madame, but you can sit here next to me for a good morning kiss provided you keep your hands off my body.'

'Spoil sport.' She snuggled up next to him on the sofa and he wrapped her in his arms and gave her a long, slow, lingering kiss. As her hands strayed to banned parts of his body he pinned them behind her back.

'Charles, considering I am going to have to bear another day of you looking at Freya, the least you could do is make me feel loved and wanted.'

'What did I say to you yesterday, my little firebrand?'

Marie said, 'I know but tell me truthfully, are you tempted to touch her?'

'I wouldn't be a man if the thought had not crossed my mind but she's not my wife, you are. I would not wish to sacrifice the relationship we have together just for the pleasure of the flesh. Besides, I would be in fear of my life because I know you would sense the betrayal the next time I touched you. We are so in tune mentally and physically already that you would detect the slightest change in my behaviour. Go and get dressed now; we have work to do.'

Satisfied, she went back upstairs to change. He did have some sympathy for her plight because if it had been her painting a man he would have been faced with the same scenario.

They waved Louis goodbye and as he was rolling in the grass with his nanny Caesar, he didn't seem unduly worried that they were leaving him. To be honest, he had learned a lot from the wily Caesar and his interaction with Louis. If he, a giant male dog, could show such tenderness and emotion with Louis then why shouldn't he be able to do the same? Caesar had given him the confidence to reach out to the child and he was delighted with the response he had received from Louis.

The weather was being kind and the sun was already making a prominent appearance through the clouds. Marie expertly wove the roses back into Freya's hair and it didn't matter too much that they were showing signs of dropping as he had captured them well yesterday. Freya was confident enough to joke with Marie about having no undergarments on and how free it made her feel. She even managed a smile when he told Marie not to bother with any makeup on her cheeks as she had signs of colour in her face today.

He set to, trying to reproduce that divine face on canvas and capture the marble-like quality of her skin and the depth of those blue eyes. Marie watched him work, conscious that she mustn't disturb him or break his concentration. She marvelled at the detail he captured, even down to the crease in the lobe of her ear. She could see the icy sea through Freya's eyes, looking out on a snowy landscape, which must be very similar to Russia. As Charles paused to change paint colours she kissed his cheek and whispered, 'Her eyes are perfect. I don't know how you do it.'

Charles touched her cheek. 'Wait until I paint the sunlight across her face; then she will transform into a living being.'

Charles had told Freya that she couldn't look at the portrait until he had finished, so on hearing their conversation, she blushed. As it faded; it just gave her that touch of rosy hue to her cheekbones and he worked fast to capture the image.

After three hours painting her face, he stopped for a short break. He sat on the grass and lay back, enjoying the sun warming his body. He had promised to speak to Freya about Gustav's behaviour and so he began to prepare what he was going to say to her as he must not make it look as though he was condoning his behaviour, because he, too was shocked that Gustav had abandoned her when she needed him most. He supposed his reaction had been a combination of fear and helplessness and like most men he had stepped back rather than come forward. *Why can't men follow their instincts when they have to deal with huge emotional upheaval?* He supposed it was as a result of centuries of being conditioned that to show emotion was weak and made you vulnerable to your enemies. He was sure that the Vikings had never felt that way. They brought their wives over to Britain with them when they came to conquer it. The Romans hadn't bothered taking their wives and eventually, they lost the battle.

Back to work he went, redefining her left calf and knee. Whilst he was doing her skin he checked out her arms and chest for any flaws. He sighed as just at that moment, he would have given anything to see her naked to see if her body lived up to his expectations. However, the approach in the distance of his mother and Louis soon banished any further thoughts on that subject.

Freya fed Louis and he had remembered to put his previous sketch into his pad this morning. He checked his original sketch over and was happy with the drawing he had done yesterday. He overheard Freya telling Marie that now Louis was on solid food she would be cutting back the frequency of his feeds. Watching how much his Viking nephew was enjoying his lunch he thought she might find her son had some objection to that proposal.

They carried on until 3 p.m. and by then he was satisfied that he had done the best he could under the circumstances in which he had been working. He would have liked to have taken it back to Paris but he didn't know when he would next see Gustav and Freya and it was vital that Gustav had the portrait in his possession.

They wandered back down to the farmhouse and he had arranged with Marie to ask Freya to join him in the cottage when she had changed as he wanted to speak to her and reveal the painting to her alone. Marie went up to the stables to check on the brood mare.

He took the canvas up to his bedroom where it was lighter due to the bigger windows. He appraised it from every angle and he knew that if he submitted it for exhibition at the Salon he would undoubtedly win a medal with it. The French judging panel would not have been able to fault his technique or skill at bringing to life this beautiful Viking princess. Her raw earthy strength was shown in every sinew of the muscles on her legs and arms. Even the most hardened man could not fail to be moved by those hypnotic blue eyes and her hair was the crowning glory. As the sun streamed through the window, lifting the sunlit parts of her hair even further, he had to admit this was one of his best portraits so far. Could he recreate it again from his original sketches back in Paris? It would be a huge task, particularly with the depiction of the sun and the shade of the leaves above. Perhaps Gustav might let him have the portrait back to exhibit in a year or so.

He heard a knock at the door and he went downstairs to greet Freya. She came in rather hesitantly as she knew he had asked to see her in private. Charles offered her a glass of wine, which she declined, and he poured himself a brandy.

'Freya, my brother has given me permission to speak to you, having confided in me the unfortunate details of your pregnancy and birth. Please accept my apologies if you consider this an intrusion into your privacy or offensive in any way but I assure you that I am only trying to be of help. I recognised in your eyes a deep sorrow and isolation and when I questioned Gustav, he told me of your problems. I am in no way defending my brother's behaviour and have told him that I think his actions in his lack of support during your early sickness and his absence from the birth of Louis was, in my opinion, tantamount to cruelty. I would stress, however, that it is customary in France that the majority of men do not attend their wives in childbirth. I don't personally agree with this as I consider having created life within the sanctity of marriage, why would you wish to be absent from the birth? I can also appreciate that behaviour such as this may be regarded with some astonishment in Norway. Gustav does love you very much Freya, but he has been incapable of showing you his love, both from fear of losing you and Louis and due to his emotional instability. He is not a cruel man; he just ran away from a situation he could not deal with at the time. I'm afraid many men are guilty of this, especially when they have had little experience of women. I told him to get down on his knees and beg your forgiveness for his actions. I know you have now both briefly spoken about this and I hope you will find it within you to forgive him. I think you can both work at this marriage and you could be very happy and content. I have warned him that if his indifferent behaviour continues that the first time another man shows you kindness and attention you could be likely to respond. Believe me, he doesn't want that to happen and I do think he will do his best to make amends. You will have to take the lead in helping him unlock his emotions, which I know he has because I have witnessed his tenderness towards Louis.'

He stopped as he saw tears falling from those beautiful blue eyes. He went over to her, knelt at her feet and took her hand.

'Please don't be upset, Freya. I hope I haven't

offended you.'

She looked at him and smiled. 'No Charles, I just could not believe that a man could have even been aware of the torment I had suffered. You are a very astute, kind and rare man with a purity of soul. Marie is so lucky to have a husband like you.' She put her arms round him and kissed his cheek.

'Now before I show you your portrait, I want you to know why I painted you like I did. I need to connect Gustav with your soul so I have done it in the way that I see you. You are a very strong woman Freya, and I thank you for your patience as my sitter. You must have wondered what on earth this mad artist was doing but I think both of you will appreciate the end result. It is in my bedroom, as I was checking it over in the better daylight.'

He saw a look of hesitation flicker in her eyes and then he realised why. 'Oh Freya, I am not doing the classic artist joke of asking you to come and see my paintings with any intention of trying to get you in my bed.' They both laughed and he said, 'Oh God, I do hope my mother doesn't find out as she already thinks I covet my brother's wife.' He led her upstairs, praying the sun would be still shining through the window. 'I want you to tell me what you see, Freya.'

Her eyes lit up when she saw it and she gasped, 'Charles that is surely not me, my hair and eyes are not that exquisite. I feel you have painted my Nordic heritage so perfectly. I cannot thank you enough.' She dissolved into tears again so he hugged her and said,

'I just hope Gustav can see it too.'

Just at this point, they both saw through the window, Gustav riding into the stable yard and handing his horse to a groom. Marie and his father came out from the mare's stable to greet him.

'Freya, when you and Louis have had some time together would you send Gustav to see me here. I need to speak to him too and I want to be alone with him when I reveal your portrait.'

Gustav arrived about twenty minutes later, looking a bit apprehensive.

'Freya says you want a word with me, although with you Charles, I can't see one word ever being enough.'

'How very astute of you brother,' he replied, pouring them both a brandy.

Gustav continued, 'Well you have certainly made an impression on Freya; she can't sing your praises highly enough.'

'Well as a matter of fact I have a true story to tell you about my first initiation into sex at the tender age of 18.'

He then related his story of Isabella in an effort to give his brother some guidance on how to improve his performance in the bedroom.

'Well that's maybe alright if you are dealing with a prostitute but I would not want to behave like that towards my wife or expect her to behave like that with me,' said Gustav.

Charles's anger flared. 'For God's sake, stop being so bloody pompous and downright French. You haven't a clue what the joys of real love can bring to your life. It isn't just about the sex; you have to connect to Freya and learn to worship her for the beautiful, pure person she is. Gustav, most men would die to have a wife like yours. You need to open up and talk to her about your feelings. If you think she's beautiful then tell her so. She's the mother of Louis, your own flesh and blood, she put her life on the line to bear him for you and what did you do? You rejected her. Now I am going to show you the painting and I want you to tell me exactly what you see and what you feel, however bizarre it may be.'

He marched him up the stairs, praying the sun would still be on the window and reflecting on the canvas. He positioned himself with his back to the wall about six feet to the left of the portrait so that he could see Gustav's reaction.

Gustav stopped about three feet from the portrait and his face visibly drained. 'Oh God Charles, she is so beautiful. How on earth have you produced such a lifelike vision of her?' He moved closer and touched her hair. 'How did you capture all the colours in her hair?'

Charles replied, 'With great skill and technique and hours of work. Now tell me what you feel.'

There was silence from Gustav and he watched him touch Freya's cheek and when he looked at his face, silent tears were pouring down his cheeks. Charles moved towards him with his arms outstretched.

'Hallelujah, finally I have touched your heart and soul.' With that, he put his arms round him and gave him a hug of comfort.

When Gustav had recovered emotionally he said, 'I just thought painters splashed a bit of paint on a canvas. I never knew you could paint like that, Charles. What an extraordinary talent you have.'

Charles responded, 'I am only doing the same as great writers, actors, composers, musicians and singers have been doing for generations – painting a picture that moves your heart and connects with your soul.'

He heard Marie and Freya come into the cottage and he shouted for them to come upstairs. Freya came hesitantly, wondering what Gustav thought of the painting. Gustav led her over to it, put his arms round her and whispered something in her ear and for the first time Charles could see a hint of sexual chemistry between the couple.

Gustav had taken some leave from the bank to spend some time at the farm and to get to know his brother a little better so they were staying until Sunday. His mother had made dinner for all of them so they went up to the house and had an enjoyable meal.

When they came back to the cottage they decided to go straight to bed as the mare was close to foaling and his father had promised to come for Marie so that she could be with her when she foaled, which could be at any time during the night.

Marie was the first to go upstairs and he heard her shout. From the urgency in her voice, he ran up to the bedroom quickly. The light switch for the room was over the bed and so when Marie had come upstairs she'd had to cross the room to switch the light on. The painting was where he had left it on top of the dresser but now the moon had filtered through the window and illuminated the whole canvas and Freya's hair was reflected in a myriad of gold highlights and it looked as if she was alive. Marie did not bother switching on the light.

Marie said, 'Oh Charles, that is stunning; she looks like an angel with such an ethereal natural beauty.'

Charles said, 'I really have achieved my brief of conveying the ice theme. I would love to paint you both together nude so I could depict "fire" and "ice".'

Marie laughed, 'I don't think Gustav would be too pleased as you can't expect him to understand how an artist's mind works. I would certainly be happy to do it and perhaps Freya would as she has a natural affinity with nature and she had no concerns about feeding Louis in front of you. Imagine your mother's face if she found out though!'

He groaned at the prospect. 'I think she would have me locked up as a sexual deviant if I proposed that idea.'

Marie said, 'By the way, where is it?'

'What?' he said, surprised.

'Charles, do you honestly think I didn't notice that you were sketching Freya while she was feeding Louis? I know you weren't doing it from an erotic sense, in fact I was enamoured by the whole scene, just as you were.'

Not saying anything to Marie made it feel wrong but he hadn't wanted to make her feel the slightest pang of jealousy over his fascination with Freya. He went to the wardrobe and fetched the sketch he had done. Marie examined it carefully.

'Charles, it's a perfectly natural scene but if you are going to use it commercially you will have to obtain their consent. You would also have to create a backdrop for it.'

Charles replied, 'Yes, I know. I hadn't really made any plans for it other than to finish it back in Paris. I could easily make it into a religious scene but I don't want to depict Freya as a Madonna and child.'

He put the sketch back and they got ready for bed. He had a good look in the mirror at his shoulder injury and it seemed to be healing well. His shoulder blade and upper arm were bruised and sore but he could live with that as time would be the best healer. Infection would have been a far worse outcome.

They settled down to sleep with Marie tucked in back-to-back with him and apart from a goodnight kiss they both refrained from any further activity.

He was awoken from his sleep when he heard Caesar barking and his father's voice shouting for Marie. The mare was showing definite signs of discomfort and foaling was imminent. It was about 5 a.m. She suggested he stay and sleep but it had been a long time since he had seen a foal being born and he wanted to be there.

17

When they got up to the stables, the mare that Marie had now named Eloise was starting to sweat and she was obviously starting to feel contractions. Dressed in breeches, a shirt and a jacket, Marie walked straight up to her and stroked her nose, talking quietly to her. He was about to warn her to be careful as the mare could be very unpredictable but he knew it was a waste of time as she would do what she wanted anyway. The bed had been dug up and his father was shaking the straw up and replacing the bedding back up the walls. He decided he would stay out of the stable and leave them to it. The mare paced the stable, her eyes rolling with fear. One moment she was digging the bed up and the next she was rubbing herself against the wall.

His father came to join him as he watched over the stable door. He said, 'Marie is convinced there is only one foal in her and it's a colt. I just hope she is right.'

Charles asked him, 'Do they normally get this sweated up?'

'No, not usually but the more highly strung ones

seem to feel the pain more than your cold-blooded draught mares. They foal with a minimum of fuss and don't appear to be in pain at all. However, she is a maiden mare and has no idea what's happening to her as she's never experienced it before.' He moved quickly and pulled Marie to one side as the mare threw herself on the newly bedded straw. She rolled and thrashed around a few times and then stood up, shaking the straw off, and stood trembling. Marie went back to her head and slowly stroked her all down her neck. The sweat was now starting to froth into white foam and her eyes were wide with fear.

His father fetched a head collar and put it on her. They could see movement in her belly as the foal moved into position and she groaned with a mixture of pain and fear. She started to dig the straw up furiously with her front leg as a contraction was visible through her belly. She stopped moving when the contraction subsided. His father told Marie to hold onto her while he had a look under her tail but nothing was visible yet. He told Marie to come and stand over by the door. Within two minutes she was digging up the straw as the next contraction travelled through her body and she dropped to her knees and lay down, groaning. Nature was now in full control of her body and she had to submit to its great force.

His father checked his watch and said, 'Right, she has only got thirty minutes to get this foal out as these contractions can only last that long and if the foal isn't born by then, she is in big trouble.'

She was straining and pushing and then she suddenly stood up and leant against the wall to steady herself. His father moved straight behind her and put his hand inside her and with a sigh of relief announced, 'Thank God, I can feel one foot.'

She threw herself down on her other side and lay pushing and panting, waves of the contraction rippling through her body.

Marie asked, 'Why does she keep getting up and down?'

His father responded, 'The foal's shoulders have got to pass through her pelvis and they can't go through both at once. The repositioning allows the mare to get the right shoulder through the pelvis first and then she stands up and when she goes down again she can push the left shoulder through.' At this point she stood up panting heavily and his father checked her internally again. The first foot was visible now and his father said he could feel the second foot and a nose was tucked in about three inches higher up.

Marie said, 'Can she foal standing up?'

Jean replied, 'Well, I have seen one born like that but it's safer if they deliver on the straw. I think she's presenting normally as sometimes the second foot gets caught on the pelvis and then they get stuck. You then have to battle against these massive contractions, which are so strong they can break your arm and push the foal back, to get the second front leg into the right position.

The mare flung herself back onto the straw. Both

front feet and the nose were visible. She pushed and strained with the next contraction. Charles' father was right behind her and he waited patiently for her to get first one and then the other shoulder out. He then burst the amniotic sac and cleared the foal's mouth. The mare gave one enormous last effort and the foal's hips were born. He instructed Marie to get down and stroke her to keep her down while the final blood ran through the cord from the mare to the foal.

The mare suddenly whickered as she knew she had given birth but could not physically see her offspring, and the foal responded faintly. His father dragged the foal round within reach of the mare's head and she whickered again and then started licking his nose. The cord had broken when the foal was moved and his father now turned his attention to the mare as the afterbirth was still to be delivered. He warned Marie that she may attempt to get up straight away and to be careful, but some mares stayed down as they were so exhausted by the birth.

She got up within five minutes, whickering to her baby and as she licked him clean, he tried to get up. His first attempts at trying to gain control over his four legs were very wobbly. Charles was fascinated when his father showed him a thin layer of extra hoof, which covered the inside of each foot to prevent any puncturing of the amniotic sac whilst in the womb from the foal's feet. The foal had managed to get his bottom up but wobbled and fell forward on his nose as his mother kept licking him and pushing him over. Jean warned them to stay back as it was essential that mother and foal bonded without any interference unless it was necessary.

Finally, the foal stood up and teetered on his long legs and took his first step. His mother whickered encouragement at him as he touched her chest with his nose. His coat was now drying and he was dark bay on his body with a black mane and tail. His head was bay with a white star in the centre and one white teardrop patch of white over his right nostril. He had the dished head from his Arab father. His long legs were impeding his movement as he appeared to be tottering on his toes.

Jean said, 'His pasterns need to let down so he can walk properly; it is just that they have been rigid in the womb and they need to flex and let down now he is moving. It will correct itself within a couple of days.'

The mare delivered the afterbirth and his father removed it to the back of the stable. Laying it out in the shape of the foal he carefully checked that it was all intact saying, 'You have to check there are no tears and the whole sac has been delivered; if she retains any afterbirth she could get infected.'

The foal was steadily moving down the side of the mare, instinct guiding him towards his mother's udder. Suddenly, she squealed and pushed the foal away, knocking him back down into the straw. He got up again but the mare was now showing signs of restlessness and unease.

Marie said, 'What's the matter with her?'

Charles' father replied, 'Remember, she is a maiden mare and she doesn't know exactly what to do. Her udder will be very tight and sore so she doesn't want him near it. Charles, can you come in here and put a lead rope on her and stand her up against the wall. You hold her left pastern up to her knee to stop her moving and I will guide the foal to the udder. Marie, you get back behind the door as she may start barging about and could turn nasty. Charles, watch her head as she may attempt to bite you to get her leg free, or she may try to rear up. Do not let go of that front leg or it gives her the opportunity to kick me or the foal with her hind legs. If she won't accept him the first time, I will have to milk her to relieve the pressure but I don't want to lose any of the precious colostrum if I can avoid it as it so vital for the foal. Once he is suckling, she may be fine.'

Charles did as he was bid, slightly reluctantly, as he was concerned about what she might do… but at least his father had warned him. The mare eyed him suspiciously as he clipped the rope onto her head collar but he talked quietly to her, running his left hand down her neck. He walked her round the box as his father held the foal to keep him from moving. He lined her up against the wall and carefully ran his hand down her fetlock, lifted the hair in her heel with his left hand and thankfully, she lifted her foot off the ground. His father manoeuvred the foal to the side of him, facing her back legs. As the foal's mouth got near her udder she squealed and tried to snatch her leg back from his grasp. He clung on for dear life, watching her head carefully and pushing her into the wall. His father tried again and he released the pressure on one teat before running the milk over the foal's mouth. The mare voiced her disapproval but Charles had her shoulder pinned against the wall and his father had her hip. Thankfully, this did the trick and he could hear the foal suckling and as the pressure in her tight udder was released, she relaxed.

His father moved back away from the foal and then Charles carefully let go of her leg. She twisted round and nibbled the bottom of her foal but she did not attempt to move or push him away. His father told him to leave her as she needed to be left alone to suckle her baby. Charles unclipped the head collar and went back to Marie, pleased that he had done the job perfectly. Marie gave him a kiss on his cheek for his efforts.

Mother and foal were doing fine. The foal reminded him of Louis suckling his mother, and he looked to see if his tail was wagging but it wasn't – *maybe that was only lambs and puppies.*

oOo

They made their way back to the cottage hand in hand, both moved by the scene they had witnessed, again showing nature at its very best.

They undressed and climbed back into bed and he enquired of Marie, 'I hope that didn't put you off childbirth?'

'No,' she replied. 'I just couldn't believe the strength of those contractions; the poor mare must have been terrified and in agony as she didn't know what was going on.'

Charles laughed and said, 'Well at least I know what to do if you won't let my son suckle.'

Marie propped herself up in bed and leant over him. 'Son, Charles? What if I have a daughter?'

Charles looked up at her. 'Well I shall be just as delighted.'

'But Charles, I will need to get back to work with you soon after any baby is born. Perhaps I would stay at home with him for the first six months but I thought we could get a wet nurse...'

He sat up as rage tore through him and he pushed her back onto the bed. 'Wet nurse! Now listen to me very carefully, Madame. God gave you two perfect vessels with which to suckle your own child. There will be no wet nurse anywhere near my child, as he needs his mother. If it means I have to lock you in the nursery every day then make no mistake Marie, I will do it. You have not yet felt the maternal instinct and the power of the bond with your own child and that is the only reason I am prepared to forgive what you just said.'

He realised that he had overreacted when tears fell from her sorrowful eyes and she sobbed, 'Oh

Charles, please forgive me. I have never seen you so angry before.'

He scooped her into his arms and hugged her. 'Marie, it is me who should be sorry. I've been unable to control this overwhelming desire for a child since we married and the thought that you would abandon him just made me see red. Please forgive me.'

'But Charles, what if I cannot produce the son you want?

'In God's name why not, Marie?

'Well I was very late starting with my courses, in fact I was 14 and they have never been regular; I have sometimes gone as long as three months without one.'

'Marie, you have many long years ahead of you to produce children and we just need to keep practising and let nature take its course. You are only 18 now. When you have produced your first ten offspring then I will consider your job done and find another young filly to continue breeding.'

He saw the flash of anger in her eyes and she pushed him on his back on the bed. 'Ten children, my lord! Well you will find the bedroom door locked and bolted after the first four and if your eyes stray to another woman you will find you haven't the means to reproduce when I have finished with my knife.'

'I love you, my little firebrand. Now when did you last have a course?'

'About two weeks before the wedding.'

'Perfect, darling, and now I have a desperate desire

to ravish you.'

oOo

The next morning, he woke before Marie and after retrieving her from nearly falling out of bed he sat up and just looked down at her magnificent body and reflected on what a very lucky man he was. If God had given him his painting talent then he must also have gifted him this beautiful woman to be his wife.

Marie stirred and opened her eyes for the first time and said, 'Can any woman be as lucky as me to wake up to see my husband appreciating my body with such love and tenderness? Are all women as lucky as me?'

Charles replied, 'I very much doubt it. Some men are incapable of appreciating the female form at all; they just want it to appease their sexual appetite. They have no knowledge of the joys of true union between men and women.'

Marie smiled. 'You are wasted as a painter; you should have been a philosopher, doctor or priest.' She suddenly giggled. 'No, you couldn't have been a priest, celibacy would not have been your strongpoint; you love the female form too much.'

Charles laughed. 'Exactly, celibacy is one doctrine of the Catholic Church I do not comprehend. How can a priest be expected to care for his flock when he has no understanding of women who make up half of it. It's the same with the confessional. It portrays to people that they can do anything they like including murder, rape or theft and it will be forgiven. They should not be encouraged by the church to do it in the first place and repent later. I know I am guilty of murder and it does worry my soul that I took another man's life for a fight that was not even mine. But when faced with the possibility of losing you, I chose you and so his death had to be pursued.'

Marie said, 'Would you have ever wanted to be a cavalry officer?'

Charles reflected, 'I would willingly do it to protect my country and family from invasion but I am not a natural killer. I admit I am a natural horseman so I would turn to the cavalry rather than be a foot soldier. War is ugly; it brings out the worst in men. There are acts committed that you wouldn't believe possible under the auspices of war. I don't think Napoleon would want me by his side; I am afraid I would argue over his tactics.'

Marie replied, 'I know all about them; my history teacher in Russia saw to that. He took great pleasure in detailing what brutal acts rape, pillage and murder were.'

'God, how old were you then?'

'Probably 12 or 13, I think he saw it as a game. He just wanted to see me frightened and I wouldn't give him the pleasure.'

'Evil bastard, your father would have been horrified if he had known.'

'Charles, you can't wipe history out of the textbooks just because it may offend the senses of women. You do women a huge disservice – we need to know what happened so we can try and prevent it recurring. Do you think there would have been as many wars if all the crown heads of Europe were women instead of men?

Charles laughed, 'I very much doubt it darling, that would make a wonderful subject for a painting with all the queens sat round the negotiating table, dividing each country up. Trouble is, I would end up beheaded and a target for every king so I don't think I dare paint it. Imagine what Paris would say if I submitted it for a medal, never mind what Napoleon and his government would have to say. '

'Do you think Henri would take part in raping women? I do hope not.'

'Your brother has the same gentle, pure soul as you Marie, and we both know that he would never harm a woman normally but you forget he will be a disciplined soldier acting under orders and in battle conditions. Would you expect him to disobey orders in the heat of battle for his own principles? He would be ridiculed and tormented by his own comrades who would have no scruples about turning on someone they considered a coward. His own life would be as much at risk as the enemy's. Let us both hope that he doesn't have to face such a choice as well as risking his life in battle.'

'The prospect of war is terrifying. I do hope Henri doesn't have to experience the full horrors of war.'

'So do I, darling.' He could only pray to God that

Henri's life would be spared but he was also a realist at heart.

18

It was soon time for Gustav and family to leave so he had a quick word with his brother and told him to go carefully with Freya and spend more time getting to know her as a person. If he needed help he only had to write to him but he hoped he would come up to Paris at Christmas. Gustav said he hoped that they would find Marie pregnant when they came. *Well it certainly wouldn't be for lack of trying on his part if she wasn't.* He gave Louis a hug and kiss and told him he would teach him how to paint when he came to Paris as he knew Gustav wouldn't bother. He told Gustav to get Louis signed up for fencing lessons as he could hardly have a kingly name like Louis and not be able to sword fight. Gustav said he would have to wait until Louis was walking properly before he started fencing. He would, however, ensure that he learned to ride as early as possible. Gustav had also spoken to his mother and assured her that Charles was not coveting his sister-in-law.

He took Freya to one side and she thanked him for all his help and said she thought they could now get back on track as both of them had made mistakes.

Charles was sad that his Viking princess was leaving, and his nephew too. They all waved them off and he and Marie returned to the cottage.

oOo

The next day, they were having a rest day as on Tuesday they would be going to Lille Academy for Charles to do a masterclass with the art students and Marie was to sit for them. They had a leisurely breakfast discussing the project ahead. Marie asked what he wanted her to wear and he said a simple figure hugging dress with no corset as he wanted her to look as natural as possible. She asked if red would be suitable and he thought it would reveal more of her fiery temper. He said he proposed telling them a bit about Marie's background and heritage and then he would assign them the task of either painting her portrait or painting her in a setting that the students imagined she came from. Marie thought that might be a little hard and that only the most artistic would be capable of attempting such a brief. Charles assured her that he was looking to see if there was an exceptionally talented student as he had a mind to offer to bring him to Paris and tutor him himself and if possible, with other artists to give him a thorough art education.

Of course, Marie could not resist teasing him, saying that there might be an exceptional female student. To which he replied, that would be better still as he would then have two females in his household to satisfy his sexual appetite. This caused Marie to rise to the bait and she flung him back against the kitchen wall and had her hands round his neck, attempting to strangle him. She really was so sexually attractive when she was angry and his passion took over and he pinned her hands behind her back and pushed her away from the wall and forced her backwards over the kitchen table, sending plates and cups flying onto the floor. Thankfully, Marie was abiding by the house rules and had no underwear on so he had no problems finding his target. He was just cautioning her to keep still or the breakfast dishes would be on the floor when to his utter horror, his mother walked through the open kitchen door with an envelope in her hand. Their eyes met and he saw her taking in Marie, prone on the table but thankfully with her back to her, and him standing there with Marie's dress round his thighs and no way of hiding exactly what he was doing. She put her hand to her mouth indicating him to say nothing, smiled, turned away, left the letter on the dresser and quickly departed.

He was rooted to the spot, unable to move or say anything while the full horror of what his mother had witnessed filtered through his brain. Sensing a lull in activity, Marie sat up and announced,

'Charles what's wrong? I was enjoying that.'

'My mother just walked in and saw exactly what I was doing.'

Marie laughed. 'Oh Charles, you forget she was young and in love once.'

'But I doubt she ever experienced sex on the kitchen table with my father. Oh God, she already thinks I am a sexual deviant and now she has the proof.'

'Charles, we are married and on our honeymoon and we did both wait until we were married before we indulged, so it's not as though we have done anything wrong.'

'I'm sorry Marie, but I cannot resume our activities. It is the first time I have failed you, but no man would be able to perform after having been caught "in flagrante" by his mother.' He kissed her gently, lifted her off the table, tidied her dress and adjusted his breeches.

He went over to the dresser, intrigued about the letter she had brought in. It was addressed to him at the farm and when he opened it he saw it was from Manet. *Oh God, was he facing charges over the duel?* He read the letter.

Dear Charles,

I thought I would put your mind at rest regarding the duel; you can rest assured that you won't be facing any legal challenge on your return to Paris. Beauchamp's second, who turns out to be Monsieur Henri Fouquier, a prominent Paris lawyer, called at my studio on Friday. Beauchamp, by the way, is actually the "Duc de Beauchamp," which I wasn't aware of when he commissioned me to paint his wife or I would have charged him more. We had an interesting meeting and it would seem that the family have agreed to his death being classed as a hunting accident. His funeral takes place on Monday and I have been warned to keep well out of the way.

My concern was ensuring that his wife (who by the way is called Angelique) is adequately maintained. Thankfully, as he was the eldest son she should maintain her right to live at the family home and inherit a considerable chunk of his estate in her own right. However, this will depend upon her successful delivery of the child she is already carrying. Should she lose the child, or indeed produce a female child then the outcome may be very different. Without a direct son and heir, the title will pass to his younger brother Gilles. In order to secure her future, Monsieur Fouquier is trying to reach an agreement between the Duchesse and her-brother-in law whose character is thankfully, the opposite of his brother. However, his young wife has tuberculosis and has not produced any children so the possibility of issue from her is unlikely.

It may well be that the Duchesse would prefer to move away completely from the family estate in the event she does not produce an heir or has a daughter, as why would she wish to remain there after all the unhappiness she has encountered? Her health is, as you are aware, in a delicate state, and Monsieur Fouquier is rightly concerned. He thinks the Duchesse would prefer to leave Paris altogether and await her confinement in peace. There are other properties owned by the Duc where she may be able to reside. Should she not produce an heir, she may be able to keep one as part of her settlement but unfortunately, she will lose her title and land. Fouquier thinks she will have no problem in receiving further marriage proposals in view of her tender age, but both you and I know that she may not wish to remarry at all.

It is proving rather a dilemma and one which only time will be able to resolve. She has requested Fouquier to ask you and your wife to contact her on your return from honeymoon as she wishes to thank you and apologise to Marie for ruining her wedding. I think Marie would prove an excellent friend to her as I doubt she will have much care from the Beauchamp family.

Paris is full of gossip and scandal as always and I had to take some ridicule at Marie's handprint across my face when I returned. I was discreet as always to protect her identity, but rumour abounds. You have become a hero and I doubt you will need to pay for a drink until after Christmas due to the number of people who have been seeking you out to congratulate you for disposing of Beauchamp. There really is nobody who has a good word to say of him.

I must also report that your wretched Italian student Antonio, whom you left in my charge, has driven me to distraction. His incessant chatter in full speed Italian to nobody at all caused me to gag him for an afternoon so that I could concentrate on my own painting. My knowledge of Italian was from a textbook and I have no idea what he is gabbling on about half the time. I have set him various painting assignments, only to discover that he adds extra items to his canvas.

I left him to do a simple portrait of Suzanne and he painted her with a poodle on her lap when there was no dog in the studio! His excuse being that he thought "she looked lonely and in need of a friend". I told him he was never to put anything on a canvas that he couldn't see! I thought I would teach him a lesson and confine him to still life drawing and set him up with a simple bowl of fruit and he painted it with an extra apple in the bowl!! When I remonstrated with him he told me that "it needed an extra apple to make it balance!" I then set him up with a vase of five pink roses and he proceeded to paint the vase with five roses but added a white lily in the centre and not only that, he changed the table from wooden, to an ornate gilt one from Louis XIV's era. By this time I was apoplectic!

The next day I gave him Velasquez's "Maids of Honour" to copy in the hope that he would not dare violate a master's work. To my utter horror he painted it but removed the female dwarf in the portrait and replaced her with an Italian cherub claiming "she was too ugly to paint and ruined the scene". I told him that you would be so angry that you would send him back to Italy in disgrace on your return. I then tried to get him to copy Da Vinci's "Last Supper," assuming he would not dare to ridicule his own master and defy his own religion but what did he do? Yes, you guessed it – added an extra disciple! The fact I did not run him through with a sword or knock him out cold was entirely due to Suzanne's timely intervention and what made matters worse, when she saw the Da Vinci copy she roared with laughter and then had me in stitches. He was lucky to escape with his life but I did manage to make contact with his head by flinging a jug after him before he made it down the stairs.

That night, Paul Cézanne was in the café and I told him of my trials and tribulations with your wretched Italian pupil. He also seemed to think it was incredibly amusing but agreed that the honour of France was at stake and we had to bring this wretched Italian youth to heel. He offered to have him under his wing the next day and he would set him an assignment and if he carried it out without one extra brushstroke we would consider him thwarted. Of course, I was to ensure that Antonio knew of Cézanne's reputation for violent temper tantrums and black moods (which make our outbursts mere child's play). I was to particularly highlight the incident when he had smashed his entire studio up because he couldn't find his favourite colour. I was to leave Paul to decide on his assignment.

The next day, after telling him that I was washing my hands of him and handing him over to Cézanne to tame, I marched him round to his studio and threw him into the lion's den. I hadn't realised that Paul was fluent in Italian and it obviously came as a bolt out of the blue to Antonio. Cézanne's acting skills would probably bring him in as much money as his painting skills, were he to consider switching professions. Even I was terrified of him and the look on Antonio's face when Cézanne marched him out of his studio would have made the Blessed Virgin weep. He took him to the Louvre and for one dreadful moment I thought he was going to have him copying inside the Louvre and dreaded the scene, which may unfold. However, Cezanne tasked him to paint the Louvre building itself, directly outside the main entrance from the bottom of the steps. Antonio had no option but to get started. We settled down on a bench about twenty feet away from Antonio's easel in case he tried to escape. Cézanne reckoned that the ornate architecture of the façade on the Louvre could be too difficult a task if he had never drawn buildings before. He also said it would be easier to check the painting afterwards for errors. We studied the building and both had a wager. I was convinced he would change one of the gargoyles into an angel. Paul settled for him adding an extra *window.*

It took Antonio seven hours to complete his work but I have to give him full marks for his execution. He may only be 18 but his mastery of drawing the façade was outstanding. This boy must have drawn buildings from the cradle to have perfected that technique. However, our inspection of his canvas was thorough. He sat on the Louvre steps and had the pleasure of watching us check every aspect of the painting. He hadn't added a window or changed a gargoyle and he watched with glee while I counted the sections of railings around the front entrance. Paul went through every figure he had painted walking up and down the steps. He was very nearly in the clear when Cézanne found it. He had put in an extra step from the entrance to the street level.

Cézanne shouted at him and was obviously swearing at him in Italian at the top of his voice and I think he said he was going to hang, draw and quarter him on the steps of the Louvre. Antonio begged his forgiveness and apologised for going a "step too far" and proclaimed he was only carrying out his "master's orders".

Then Cézanne let out a great bellow of laughter and pointed at me saying, 'Manet, you have been had for a fool by this talented boy and his "master" Duran.'

Oh Charles, you bastard, you set him up to taunt me in revenge for that incident in the Louvre last year. Well, bravo. I fell for it like a lamb to the slaughter. Not only had he added the extra step, he had painted you holding open the door of the Louvre.

I concede that I have ridiculed you in public on a few occasions but this time you excelled yourself. I am keeping all his paintings because they are such a delight and one day Antonio may become famous and I can reap my rewards. I will never be able to look at Da Vinci's revered "Last Supper" again as the vision of Antonio's 13th disciple is imprinted on my brain. You have also put me off teaching for life. How you do it I will never know; you must have the patience of a saint.

Give my regards to your beautiful wife and I can only imagine what a delightful time you are having! You are a very lucky man to have found your soulmate, cherish her with care.

Best wishes from your much maligned fellow artist and friend Manet.

Charles was hysterical by the time he had finished the letter and as Marie was getting anxious, he read it out loud to her and she was as delighted as he was by Antonio's behaviour. He had set him up to taunt Manet in revenge for his debacle in the Louvre last year. He had promised he would bide his time and when the opportunity of sending Antonio to Manet came up he could not resist. Obviously, Antonio had carried out his instructions in his typical, flamboyant

Italian style. He was pleased that Cézanne and Manet had witnessed Antonio's skill for drawing architecture, which he had recognised very early on. Antonio just needed to improve his portrait work and learn to control his flamboyant Italian style. How he would have loved to have been there when he was painting the Louvre and of all the places for Cézanne to pick, it could not have been better.

He now realised that he would have to tell Marie the full story of Madame Beauchamp and Manet, which would prove harrowing for her as no woman would want to hear of the torture inflicted on her by her own husband. It hardly showed the male species in a very good light and to him this sort of behaviour was inconceivable. Still, it was better done now as once they got back to Paris he would have to throw himself back into his work to make some money to cover his four-week honeymoon.

He asked Marie to come into the lounge as he wanted to explain the circumstances behind Manet's duel challenge. They sat on the sofa and he put his arm round her and told her exactly what had happened. He also emphasised before he started that he had not known the full truth when he had fought Beauchamp in the duel.

Marie was horrified when he described the wounds on Madame Beauchamp's body, particularly where the sword imprint had been on her hip. Silent tears ran down her face as she listened as she just could not imagine why anyone would do that.

Marie said, 'But if she hadn't been pregnant she would have been free after his death.'

'Free maybe but without any financial support and we don't know what her family circumstances were. She may not have been able to return to them.'

'So if she produces a boy then she will have a home and some land in her own right and could maybe move away?'

'It depends on her brother-in-law; he may not allow her to rear the Beauchamp heir on her own. He may insist she stays where she is. If his wife is unlikely to produce an heir then unless he remarries after her death, he is not going to produce one either.'

'Why do you think Beauchamp reacted to her like that?'

'Oh darling, I have thought about this long and hard and I can only surmise at the reason. Someone does not inflict such pain on another human being without there being some traumatic incident in their own life. Maybe his father was a bully or a drunkard and he witnessed him beating his own mother. Maybe he was beaten or bullied as a child by a teacher or servant.'

'You mean he could have been sexually abused himself.'

'Possibly, it may not have even been someone in his family.'

Marie said, 'Could he have been homosexual?'

Charles was horrified. 'Marie, in God's name, how do you even know about such things? Please do not speak to me on this subject. I can hardly bear to know that you are aware of such behaviour. I am going to show Manet's letter to my father to set his mind at rest. If we don't go outside soon my mother will think we are still romping on the kitchen table!'

He found his father up at the stables, supervising one of his grooms as he put the harness on a young draught horse for the first time. He watched and waited patiently until the horse's first lesson was finished. Marie wandered off to see Eloise and Shadow, out in the field with the other mares and foals.

He showed Manet's letter to Jean, who was delighted to hear that he would not be facing any charges on his return to Paris. He roared with laughter at Antonio's antics and agreed that he could not have taken better revenge on Manet.

Charles asked him if they could have two horses for tomorrow to go into Lille and his father said he could have the usual two that they had ridden so far. They talked about what he intended to do if he found a student worth pursuing and offering training back in Paris. His father was delighted as without the scholarship and help Charles had received from the academy, he would never have gone to Spain. They discussed when he would be leaving and whether he intended to ride back to Paris. He hesitated as it had been surfacing at the back of his mind that it may not be the best idea.

His father intervened and said, 'Well, Charles,

you gave Marie the same concentrated look when she walked over to the field that I would give my broodmares when I think they may be in foal. Is that what's worrying you?'

Charles replied hesitantly. 'Well, I have absolutely no evidence at all but I just feel there is something different about her… but if you asked me to define it, I couldn't.'

His father laughed. 'Well you have certainly spent the last four weeks devoting your entire attention to covering that young filly at every opportunity so there's every chance you may well have succeeded. Your mother tells me you couldn't get through breakfast this morning without ravishing her over the kitchen table.'

Charles blushed. 'I am sorry. My mother must really think I am some sort of pervert, especially as she suspects I was lusting after Freya when I painted her, but I honestly had no designs on her whatsoever.'

'I think you will find that Gustav has reassured her about your motives and she has said she will speak to you about it. I am not criticising your passion for Marie at all, you should consider yourself extremely lucky to have her as your wife and I can understand your sudden desire to procreate. It's a natural animal reaction – you just want to make sure that she is yours – and the quickest way of ensuring no other creature can touch her is to breed with her.'

'Really? I suppose I hadn't thought of it like that but you may well be right. I have gone from never wanting any children to being desperate for one, especially after having Louis around.'

'I am pleased to hear it, son. You will make a good father and it will curtail Marie's exuberance a little when she has her own child to care for. You certainly should produce some exceptional offspring between you.'

Marie appeared at the gate and Charles said, 'Say nothing please, I may well be wrong and Marie hasn't shown any classic signs like sickness and there are no indications externally yet, I just sense it in my head. I don't want to risk riding back to Paris just in case something happens. Look at what happened to Manet – it doesn't have to be her horse that is the problem. If we were attacked by thieves and she lost the child I would be totally bereft. I just don't want to put her at any risk whatsoever. I will discuss it with her later and suggest we have more time here and go back by train.'

They left the yard and walked back down to the farmhouse with Caesar in attendance. The old boy had been moping about since Louis left; he was obviously missing his charge. He decided to go and seek out his mother and make his peace, so Marie stayed in the cottage.

Charles' mother was in the kitchen and when she saw him she poured them both a coffee. She had her peace to make with him.

She held his hand and said, 'My son, I owe you an apology. I understand you had no intention of coveting your brother's wife and I misinterpreted your interest in her altogether. I believe you were only trying to heal the deep rift that had occurred between Gustav and Freya, which you alone detected as you are such a sensitive, caring soul.' With that she put her arms round him and hugged him tight.

'I know it may have looked bad but I just had to paint her as the warrior princess I could see in her. Her heart was frozen towards Gustav because he let her down badly.'

'Charles, never have I seen a painting as beautiful as that. Her hair was incredible. You brought her to life and it did reach out to Gustav. I hope he can repair the damage he has done. Tell me how you painted her picture so beautifully.'

'I can only say it would be like painting one of your roses in the garden. It would be so exquisite and lifelike that even though it was your rose you would not dream of picking it because you would destroy its beauty. That's why, although Freya appealed to my senses, I would not dream of stealing her from Gustav. Besides, I have my own firebrand to contend with, who would know in an instant if I had been unfaithful in either thought or deed.'

'Ah, you mean the one you were indulging over the kitchen table this morning. May I give you some relationship advice for a change?'

'Certainly, Mother. I hold your opinion in high regard but I daresay I won't like what I am going to hear?'

'I only wanted to say… just give Marie a bit of space sometimes. You have a tendency to let your love and tenderness towards her cloud your judgement and you overprotect her. You can't lock your little bird in a cage forever, Charles; she needs to fly free and if you can do that she will never let you down. Stifle her and restrict her and you will risk losing her; she will only ever have eyes for you so don't let jealousy invade your soul.'

'I didn't expect that and if I am giving out those signals then I must learn to control those feelings. I had my first row with her when she had the audacity to suggest that she returns to work at my studio within a few months of the birth and leaves my child with a wet nurse.'

His mother roared with laughter. 'For heaven's sake she's not even pregnant yet. You need have no fear of that – when her maternal instinct kicks in nobody will be allowed near her child and she certainly won't allow another woman to breastfeed her baby. I would have thought your fascination with Freya feeding Louis would have given you some idea of how the mother and child bond works. It's nature at its very best and you need have no fear about Marie; she will be a very good mother. Stop being so desperate to have a child and let nature take its course.'

'I wish I could but I think I may already have achieved my desire.'

'Then for heaven's sake, leave Marie to come to

terms with it in her own way. Don't crowd her; she is still only 18. She will calm down when the birth is imminent. I expect you will be attending her in labour, unlike your brother? Just be warned that there is a happy medium and some women do not take kindly to having the man responsible for their pain in the same room. I think I would have taken a horsewhip to your father had he been around at your birth. It can be a very fraught time and some women fear their husbands will never want them sexually again after the birth. However, I imagine in your case that would be impossible as you can barely keep your hands off her. But don't expect that she will be as receptive to you in the latter stage of pregnancy – she may even want nothing to do with you.'

'Mother, please do not mention to Marie that I think she may be pregnant. I have no evidence that this is the case, just intuition, and I don't want to raise any expectations to find that I am wrong.'

'Of course I won't but she will know soon enough; if she is pregnant the signs will soon become obvious. I think you may have been wiser to leave having children until your married life had become more settled. You are asking an awful lot of Marie to go from single girl, to married woman and then to mother in under a year. Mind you, patience has never been one of your virtues has it, Charles? You couldn't wait to get started on your career as young as 8 so why should you be any different when it comes to having children? I am just thankful you are going to have a family as I feared you would sacrifice that for your career. I am very proud of you, son. You have become an honourable man in both your work and private life and you have retained a deep love and connection to nature that shows in your work.'

Charles was shocked to hear such a glowing report from his mother. Maybe he had misjudged her and she was wiser than he had given her credit for. He gave her a hug and kisses and thanked her for making them so welcome at home. He did feel totally rejuvenated and he was anxious to get back to Paris and finish some of the sketches he had done whilst there, particularly the one of Marie and the waterfall. He also needed to get some income to pay for their new house, and surprisingly, he did miss his teaching. He loved to see his pupils improve and he had received many enquiries for pupils wishing to study with him. At least Marie could take the paperwork, finance and organisation off him and he could get on with his teaching.

oOo

After dinner, they relaxed in the lounge with a bottle of wine and talked about the teaching side of his business. Marie was full of ideas for tidying up his studio and having some wooden drawers made to store complete canvasses so he wasn't forever falling over them. He was sure she would relish organising his pupils' schedules and had offered to use her multi-lingual talents to teach French to those who did not have French as their first language, as soon as they arrived.

She scolded him, 'Sometimes you expect too much of your pupils as you lecture in French most of the time but you have pupils from Italy, Spain and England who must find it hard to understand your technique sessions in French. Can't you sometimes switch to their languages in order to help them get a better understanding of technique?'

'I suppose I could. I hadn't actually thought about that, how perceptive of you ma cherie. It will prove a challenge but I promise to swat up on my English and rusty Spanish when I get back. However, Antonio needs no encouragement to jabber in Italian any more than he already does. As Manet says, he needs gagging when he is working so the rest of us can get on with our own work.'

'What are you going to do with Antonio when you get back, workwise?'

'He is proving skilled at painting people but he is not getting faces right yet – they are too flat and he is not defining light on the canvas. I think I need to push him into the limelight more – perhaps if he had a commission with money as an incentive, it might improve his work. Certainly, if I get outside portrait commissions with a building as a backdrop I shall take Antonio with me as I admit he is far better than me at getting building perspective correct and both Manet and Cézanne have confirmed my opinion. However, he has not had time to pursue horse portrait work so I might see if I can get him drawing horses at Henri's barracks… although I am sure he will drive them to distraction with his incessant banter.'

'What about the letter you received from America requesting you go over for a portrait tour?'

'I really can't see me having time to do something like that in the next couple of years. It would be very risky financially and if I didn't receive enough commissions, it would be very expensive. Besides, I don't want to leave you and travelling by sea when you're pregnant would not be a sound idea. If I get more recognition and medals for my portrait work then perhaps it would be worthwhile.'

Marie showed him some of the sketches she had done of the mare and foal, which were very good. He suggested she turn them into watercolours when they got back to Paris.

They retired early as they would have to be up and away to Lille in the morning. He took the opportunity to carry out a careful inspection of Marie's body to see if he could find any hint of pregnancy, but nothing confirmed his suspicions. If she had conceived on their wedding night she would only be four weeks pregnant at most. He would just have to wait patiently for nature to take its course.

He reflected on his mother's advice and realised she did have a point about rushing Marie from wife to mother too quickly, and about giving her a bit more space. He realised that once he was back at work he would have to make that his first priority and restrict his sex life to more manageable levels and he would ban her from making approaches to him in the studio and vice versa because he just knew that, however careful they were, somebody would inevitably catch them. *Imagine if they were caught in a comprising position by one of his pupils. They would be the talk of Paris and he would die of shame.*

He intended to keep his home life completely separate from his working life. He was determined not to paint at home and to do all his artwork at the studio. He would try and ensure that Sunday was a rest day and they enjoyed life together before their first baby arrived. He would make time to take Marie to Italy within the next twelve months, but only for a holiday.

19

They set off for Lille at 8:30 a.m. to allow plenty of time to be at the academy for 10 a.m. Marie was wearing the red dress with her woollen cloak and had chosen to ride astride rather than side-saddle, for the journey. He looked at her face and she had certainly caught the sun and had a healthy colour and bloom to her face. Both of them had noticed they had put on a little weight, which he was pleased about as he was fighting to keep himself fit and healthy since his long illness. Their relationship had blossomed and they were now totally at ease with each other and felt they could discuss anything. For once in his life he felt totally content and ready to face the future with his soulmate by his side. He had brought Freya's portrait with him as a fine example of his work, to show the pupils.

Back in March, he had contacted Lille Academy to say he would be coming to visit family in September and would like to visit the art school and meet some of the tutors and pupils. To his delight, the art director was one of the pupils he had studied with at Lille when he had attended, Philippe Cabachon.

He had replied enthusiastically and asked him if he would do a masterclass with his most gifted students to give them a new learning experience. He had been honoured to be asked and this had set him off on his quest to offer a teaching opportunity with him in Paris if there was a student worthy of promoting. He had discussed it with Marie as it would mean providing accommodation at their house and he needed her to agree as it would affect her life as much as his. Depending on the age of the pupil selected, he appreciated that he might have to provide education in other subjects, which Marie would also be left to co-ordinate. She had been enthusiastic and had already offered to help with the language tuition and had obtained her father's support should any music tuition be required.

They arrived in good time and a groom came to take their horses into the stables for the day. Philippe Cabachon met them at the front entrance and made them feel very welcome. He remembered him from his time at Lille but Philippe only joined the Academy at 16 so they had not known each for long. He showed them round the academy, which had been extended considerably since his time. Now, they taught many more subjects including all the arts: English, Drama, Dance, Sport as well as Art. All pupils also completed a course of academic subjects from 11-18.

There was a gallery of paintings in the main hall, which included work from past pupils and a small section of current students' work, and three of them took his eye. He promised Phillipe he would send him a portrait so that the school had one to add to their collection. The first student portrait he had liked was a scene of a stately home and a carriage drawn up at the bottom of the main entrance steps and a young couple walking up the steps holding hands. From their clothes, it was obvious they were a bride and groom. Philippe told him this had been done by François de Steuben, who was 18 years old. He had painted this scene of his sister's wedding. Charles said he particularly liked his skill at painting the horses, the carriage and the front of the building but he needed to work on the portraits of his main characters as they did not stand out enough. Phillipe said François was a very confident young man and did not take criticism well.

The second painting of the market square in Lille was done by a young boy called Jacques Lansac, in his first year at Lille, who was the son of a doctor and was a gifted boy in most subjects. He was proving to be exceptional in both art and music but was a talented writer and poet. He applied himself well to all his subjects but his father was hoping he would become a doctor. Philippe wasn't sure whether that would be achieved as he was a sensitive boy and although he was good in maths and science, his talents were definitely towards the arts and languages.

The third painting was of a simple vase of flowers set in a windowsill looking out into a garden. This had been done by 14-year-old Armand Richelieu who was a farmer's son and lived about 20 miles from Lille; he was a boarder at the Academy. Charles had been immediately struck by this painting as it showed talent in its technique. He knew that this boy was homesick by the way he had executed each flower with such detail, and he was certain this was a scene from his home.

He asked Marie which she liked best and was pleased she favoured Armand's, although she recognised the potential in Jacques as he had taken on such a variety of subjects in his picture and executed them all well.

Phillipe took them for a coffee and introduced them to another art tutor, Nicolas Froment. Charles asked him his opinion of the three boys and he said that François was a typical rich, arrogant and spoilt youth who undeniably had talent in art but only when he wished to apply himself. Jacques was a shy, sensitive boy whose artistic talent was undeniable but he was a deep thinker and he thought his talents in writing would be his chosen vocation. Armand was totally at one with nature and his drawings reflected that, but in areas that he had never encountered, he was struggling as he did not have a natural talent.

They discussed the assignment and both Phillipe and Nicolas were delighted with his suggestion. It would certainly give them all something to work on. Nicolas suggested that using Marie as the sitter may throw some of the adolescent boys into a spin as they would never have seen a woman as beautiful as her before and they may become overawed at the prospect. Charles said they would have to overcome their personal feelings if they were intending to do portrait work. They had picked twelve of their best students and they hoped they would carry out the assignment to the best of their ability.

The first part of the workshop was an introduction from Charles of his career so far, and then he would explain their assignment. They were shown into a small classroom and they were introduced to each student individually. He met François first and he was indeed as Nicolas had described – both cocky and arrogant – but he was certainly full of confidence. Jacques was shy and overawed at meeting him but his eyes were riveted to Marie and he knew that the boy was totally smitten with her. He prayed it would not prevent him from producing a good portrait. Armand was also shy and nervous but Charles put him at ease by explaining that he had been brought up on a farm, and the boy visibly relaxed.

He gave his talk and then revealed their assignment and he heard a few gasps when he said they could paint Marie in any scenario they wished or do a life portrait of her. However, he did give them a brief outline of Marie's background, explaining she was an expert horsewoman and had hunted bears in Russia with her own hounds. She was gifted in music and singing and an artist in her own right. He also explained they had only been married a month. He volunteered to help them with the execution of their work if they required it, but not the composition. He would do the life drawing of Marie at the same time as them and they were welcome to ask questions on his technique if they wished. Nicolas would be overseeing the session and they could also ask for his assistance on technique if they wished.

They were given ten minutes to consider how they were going to compose their work. There was much scratching of heads and he thought back to his student days and wondered which option he would have taken. The safe option was to paint Marie exactly as she was. The harder option would be to set her in a scene as they would have to be able to draw on experience to get their backgrounds correct and it would prove a much greater risk. After the ten minutes were up, Nicolas asked them to raise their hands if they were going to do the portrait of Marie and seven boys raised their hands. One of these was Armand and he suspected that it was purely lack of confidence that made him take this road. In the remaining group of five were Jacques and François. He was delighted and full of anticipation to see how they would approach their task.

They went through to the studio and Nicolas suggested that the first two rows of easels were delegated to the portrait artists and the back two rows to the freestylers. He inspected the raised dais and there were props available to use. Above the dais was a row of lights so he picked a plain background of black velvet. There were some fake statues and marble pillars and he suggested they use a marble plinth in the foreground with Marie placing her left hand on the plinth. He positioned her at an angle of 45-degrees so that to the majority of the class, she would be in profile but to those on the right-hand side she would be head on. He told Nicolas to put Armand on the right-hand side front easel and save him the same position in the second row. He gave Marie a kiss and apologised that she would be standing rather than sitting but would ensure she got plenty of rests. She looked a little anxious as this was unusual territory for her.

He went to his easel and then realised Marie's hair was pinned in a chignon. He leapt back up onto the dais, unpinned her hair and released it down her back. He combed it through with his fingers, leant down and kissed the top of her head and surveyed the room and was delighted with the reaction by some of the students to her loosened hair.

He went back to his easel and started to sketch her outline in charcoal. He thought he had better get on with it quickly in case he was asked for help by any students. He felt happy to be back in a studio atmosphere doing the job he loved. About an hour into the session he was aware of some gasps and talking going on at the back of the room. Nicolas was having an altercation with François over his easel. Quietly, he moved to the back of the room and went up to the two of them unobserved, as they were having a heated discussion. François's charcoal sketch of a horse was well executed but then he saw what all the fuss was about. He had drawn Marie astride the horse with no saddle, but she was naked. He tried to keep any sign of amusement out of his eyes. There was complete silence in the room and every student had stopped painting, instead watching and listening intently to the scene.

Nicolas said, 'My apologies Monsieur Duran, but it would appear François has overstepped the mark on the composition of his painting.'

He replied, 'I gave the students free rein as to their composition and if that's how François wishes to portray my wife then he had better make absolutely sure that it matches reality. Fortunately, only I know the truth so François will have a hard task to ensure his portrayal is correct.'

He moved two easels to the left, where Jacques was looking decidedly uneasy. Charles was captivated by the scene on his canvas; he had attempted to draw a scene with Marie on horseback, galloping after hounds, bear hunting in Russia. It was still in sketch outline but it had masses of potential.

'Jacques, would you like my wife to help you with the bear outline? She is more au fait with their characteristics than I am.'

Jacques could only manage a nod of his head as he was probably so worried that he was going to pick his canvas to pieces. Charles returned to the dais and asked Marie to go and help Jacques but warned her to totally ignore François's nude painting of her.

Nicolas came over and apologised again for François's arrogant behaviour and lack of respect. Charles smiled and said he had to admit François had shown a lot of daring and courage so he had forced him into coming up with the goods.

At 1 p.m. they broke for lunch and after the boys had all left he walked round all the easels, checking their work with Marie and Nicolas. Armand had produced an accurate sketch of Marie's body but he worried about her facial features. He decided he would give him some help when he came, to draw her face. His was the best of the portraits so far. Marie had been delighted with Jacques's work and had quickly sketched him a picture of a bear running so he could copy it onto his easel.

They all looked long and hard at François's canvas and agreed his horse sketch was good and that the likeness of the rider was a good attempt. However, the skill would be in the oil painting of the subject, so that was all in François's hand. Marie commented that she was delighted with the generous chest he had given her, which exceeded reality by some degree.

They were invited to join Philippe for a private lunch in his office, so they went upstairs to join him. He was furious when he heard of François's project and was all for dragging him into his office and sending him home with a strong letter to his father. Charles would not hear of it as he had now challenged him to make a credible effort and he would enjoy watching him work under the pressure. They enjoyed a pleasant lunch and he told Philippe of his time in Spain and Italy. Charles retrieved the portrait of Freya that he had left in Philippe's office, which he was going to use to help his demonstration of face painting. Philippe asked to see it and was so amazed by it, he insisted on joining them for the talk.

They returned to the studio after half an hour and were surprised to find that François was already back at his easel, working away. Charles exchanged glances with Nicolas and Philippe and they all hoped François would be capable of performing a miracle.

Charles started his talk on face painting and explained how important the light had to be to ensure the features looked alive. Equally important, however, was the fact that light always produced shade and often the skill was in producing the shaded areas. Generally, hairstyles and hats would always cast a shadow over the face along with the effect of the sun or artificial light. Sometimes, there may be an added complication with the background setting eg. trees or buildings. At this point he took the cover off Freya's portrait and was met by gasps of admiration from the students. He was delighted that it prompted Jacques to move himself from the back to get closer to the portrait, and even cocky François came closer to inspect what all the fuss was about. He explained that even though the leaves of the tree were not visible on the canvas, the light had still filtered through and cast dappled shadows across Freya's hair. As he finished his talk, the boys returned to their canvasses… all except Jacques, who came nearer and touched Freya's hair. He seemed fascinated by the leaf patterns Charles had depicted across the width of her hair.

He jumped down off the dais and said to him, 'Jacques, tell me what you see in this painting?'

Jacques paused to think and then replied, 'I see a beautiful woman with deep blue eyes, which are frozen in ice, and the most wonderful blonde hair I have ever seen with three distinct shades running through it. She is very tall and athletic so she can't be French; is she Russian?'

Charles smiled. 'She is from Norway and I commend you for sensing her ice-cold heart; that's very intuitive for a boy of 11. Come over here with me now and I will show you how to paint Marie's face in oils.'

He shepherded him to his canvas and leant forward and invited Armand to join them. He layered the first skin colour on his palette knife and spread it across her face then drew round the pre-sketched outline of her eyes, nose and mouth. He mixed the paint for her eyes and then turning to Armand, he gave him the brush and told him to fill in her eyes. He hesitated but as he had already attempted it on his own canvas, he completed his task. He then mixed the colour for her lips and invited Jacques to fill them in. He did a credible job and then he asked them both what other features on the face were required. Armand pointed out that the eyebrows needed doing but Jacques picked up on the colour in her cheeks and the shadow under her eyelids and her nose. Pleased with their observation and efforts, he sent them back to their own canvasses. He had not missed the fact that François had been close behind, watching him teach the boys.

At 4:30 p.m. Nicolas called a halt to their work and the boys were sent back into the classroom while their paintings were examined. He, Marie, Nicolas and Philippe wandered down each line of canvasses, assessing the paintings silently. Charles looked carefully at each one and selected his top three. Nicolas set up three easels on the dais under the lights. Philippe invited Charles and Marie to select their top three.

Without any hesitation they selected François's, Jacques's and Armand's and placed them on the dais for detailed inspection. He evaluated Francois's first.

'There is no doubt he has talent, a huge amount of self-confidence and a good deal of courage. His execution and technique are good and I think under my wing I could make him a good portrait painter. Whether he would be willing to take criticism and learn is another matter. He may also have another career to follow, depending on his family circumstances.'

He turned to Armand's portrait. 'This boy has a great feel for nature so had he been confident enough to risk painting freestyle using a countryside scene, there is no doubt he would have done a good job. However, his portrait is still superior to the other six paintings and with good coaching this boy has talent… maybe in several areas.'

He then turned to Jacques's portrait. 'He is only 11 and yet he took on a huge project by doing this scene as he was not even familiar with the landscape setting. However, his detailing of the snowy background, terrain and the horse and hounds are way beyond his years. With a little help from Marie, he got the bear right. He watched, listened and carried out my instructions on painting her face and he revealed Marie's spirit through her eyes.'

Nicolas and Phillipe nodded in agreement with his summing up.

Phillipe turned to him. 'My only concern is that Jacques is also exceptionally good at writing and music. His academic subjects are way above average and his father is hoping he will follow his career path. Art has just been relaxation for him and so what you are seeing is raw natural talent; it is not down to the tuition he has received here as we have only had him nine months.

Nicolas went to recall all three students as Charles had promised to speak to each of them about their work. Phillipe agreed to arrange a meeting at the academy with Jacques' father and Charles to discuss whether he would allow him to go to Paris to study. Charles pointed out that he would have contacts to push him with his art, writing and music but that he had no wish to push the boy into specialising in art at such an early age. If he was so talented then it would be up to Jacques to decide which career path he wanted to take.

Nicolas returned with François and Charles moved to his canvas. He was pleased that he looked a little afraid about what he was going to say to him and just for once, he saw a flash of vulnerability in this outwardly confident young man.

'Francois, I congratulate you on your work; you have obviously studied the anatomy and physiology of horses and show an excellent technique. You have also painted my wife admirably, which indicates you have studied human anatomy with the same zeal. You need to take more notice of light and shade as you have not followed the sun's rays across your canvas. Are you intending to consider a career as an artist?'

François replied, 'I would like to pursue a career as an artist but my father would prefer me to join the cavalry when I am 21.'

Charles said, 'If your father would allow you to study in Paris I would welcome you as a paying student in my studio. You would do well to consider Spain and Italy as well, and I have contacts there and would be willing to use them for your benefit if required.'

François replied, 'Thank you, Monsieur Duran, I will speak with my father about your kind offer. I do hope I have not offended you or your wife with my painting but I have never seen such a beautiful woman before and I was so infatuated with her that I let my imagination run away with me.'

Nicolas ushered him out and returned with a nervous looking Armand. Charles looked over at Marie and indicated she should make the first move. Marie took his hand and led him over to his canvas.

'Armand, you have made the best portrait of me out of the seven paintings. The likeness is very good and you listened to Charles's instructions on face painting. Did you draw when you were a boy?'

Armand smiled at her and said, 'Yes, I was always drawing the farm animals and dogs and cats and getting into trouble with my father for doing it instead of cleaning out the barn or doing other chores.'

Charles asked him, 'Would you prefer to be a farmer or an artist, Armand?'

He hesitated and said, 'Well, I don't think farming will be an option for me as I have two older brothers so I would like to think I would be good enough to make painting a career.'

Charles said, 'You have a lot of talent Armand, you just need to believe in yourself more and have the courage to push your boundaries. I am sure that if you continue to work hard at your studies here you will improve significantly and I will keep in touch with your tutors and will offer you a place to study with me when you are older.'

Armand said, 'Thank you sir, and Madame Duran,

for your encouragement and kind words and I will work hard to impress you.'

Nicolas ushered him out and returned with Jacques, who was looking equally as nervous as Armand had been.

Charles addressed him, 'Jacques, you have considerable talent and flair and if you want to become an artist, the world awaits you. You took on a huge task today in composing a scene you were totally unfamiliar with but you did it with great skill. I know that you also have many talents in other areas and at this young age it would be unwise to specialise so soon. Tell me what appeals to you about painting compared to your other studies.'

Jacques replied, 'I love the freedom of expression painting gives me and I can escape from my surroundings and concentrate on producing an image to the best of my ability. I have not studied Russian history or geography but I knew it was a bitterly cold country and so I drew it from my imagination. I thank Madame Duran for her help with the bear as I had no idea what one even looked like.'

Charles replied, 'Jacques, if I could convince your father that I would ensure you continued your academic subjects but promoted your writing, music and art talents do you think he would allow you to come to Paris?'

Jacques looked thunderstruck. 'Monsieur Duran, I would love to pursue writing, music and art in Paris and I will do my utmost to persuade my father to allow me to go. He does want me to follow his career but I do not think I would make a good doctor.'

'I understand, Jacques and I will do my best to persuade him to let you have this opportunity.'

Nicolas ushered Jacques out of the room and on his return said, 'Jacques is completely stunned by your offer, Charles, and I think it would be a wonderful opportunity. I just hope his father appreciates what an amazing son he has and would be prepared to forego his hopes of him going into medicine.'

Charles had arranged to return to the academy in two days and hoped that a meeting could be arranged with Jacques's father. He remembered Freya's painting and they made their way to the main door. He was delighted to find Armand was holding his horse and he could sense that he was a natural horseman by the way he handled him.

They rode back to the farm, both exhausted after their long day. They had a delicious casserole made by his mother waiting for them on their return, and they ate it with relish. They went straight up to bed after their meal as they were both tired.

As they snuggled up together, he asked Marie if he had selected the right boy and she agreed with him. She agreed that Armand needed more time to learn the basics before he came to them. It would be a shame if Jacques was denied his opportunity but that depended on his father. Charles said he was going to ask Jean to have Armand over for a weekend once a month to relieve his homesickness for the countryside and he hoped it would benefit the pair of them. Marie was delighted at the prospect as it would give Armand a break from the academy and a chance to get to know the horses and dogs he so missed the companionship of.

She turned over and kissed him. 'You are a thoughtful man; nobody else would have thought of doing that but you. I am sure your father would welcome some help at the weekends as there are no grooms on Sundays and he is probably a bit lonely now there are no children on the farm.'

Charles replied, 'Then we had better start producing the next generation so my father can have a grandchild to teach how to ride.'

Marie laughed. 'All in good time, my love!'

oOo

On Friday, they both returned to Lille Academy. Nicolas had arranged a meeting with Jacques's father. He arrived at 12 p.m. and was ushered into Nicolas's study and introduced to them. He was in his early forties, tall and thin and dark haired with startling green eyes. Charles noticed his long appraisal of Marie and knew he admired her, instantly.

Charles explained what he had in mind for Jacques and said he would ensure that he received tuition in academic subjects as well as art and music. His father explained that he had hoped that Jacques would follow his career path but he appreciated that his son would have to make up his own mind about his future. Marie explained that her father Pierre was Musical Director at the Conservatoire and would supervise his music studies. She would teach him languages, of which Italian and English were the priority, but she assured him that he would still study Latin and Greek. Marie confirmed that he would live with them as family and join Charles's art students at his studio.

His father asked what would happen to his place at Lille and Nicholas confirmed that it would remain open should he wish to return at any time. They agreed that Jacques would join them in January and they would all see how the arrangement worked and keep an open mind.

They all shook hands and Marie assured him that his son would be in good safe hands under their guidance. She would write to Jacques and confirm the arrangements for his travel to Paris in January.

After lunch, they joined the students in an art class and had a private meeting with Jacques and outlined their study programme. He was delighted and excited at the prospect of a new life in Paris. He thanked them both for offering him such an opportunity to study all the subjects that he loved and he assured them he would make sure he was worthy of their support.

They rode back to the farm and on a steep hill overlooking Lille they halted and took in the scenery. Charles promised Marie that they would spend time visiting his family during the forthcoming years. He was delighted by how close he felt to nature, being back home, and he wanted to just enjoy the countryside. Next time he came back he would paint some landscape watercolours of the area.

oOo

On Saturday morning, Jean drove them by carriage to Lille station, to return to Paris. Tears were shed by both of his parents as they boarded the carriage to leave the farm, as it had been such a long time since he had been home. He promised they would be back soon. Jean hugged him on the platform and whispered to him that he thought Marie was pregnant too… and wished him well.

20

On the train back to Paris, they discussed their plans for their married life in their new home. They had minimal staff consisting of Jeanette, who had been Marie's maid at home but was now to take on the role of housekeeper at their house in Paris. They also had a cook, housemaid and groom/gardener and they had the back-up option of borrowing staff from Marie's parents should they need extra staff at peak times. Marie would continue her role as administrator at his atelier, sorting out his commissions and co-ordinating the teaching of his pupils. This would continue until she became a mother, although she was determined she would continue in the role after that.

He had left Antonio in charge of the studio during their honeymoon and had delayed the start of his teaching until his return. He was looking forward to getting back behind the easel although he was now fully aware of his responsibilities as a husband and knew he would have to devote more time to family life. He considered turning one of the bedrooms into a studio at home so that he could do some of his commission work from home at weekends as his teaching duties were increasing.

Marie had not said anything to him about whether she might be pregnant as she had no real way of knowing as her courses were very unpredictable anyway. He had noticed she was becoming tired more easily and her sleep pattern had altered but there was no sickness as yet. He was fairly sure she was pregnant but he would have to wait until her body told her itself that a new life was being created. He was well aware he was asking an awful lot of Marie at the age of 18, to become a wife and mother so quickly, and financially he would have liked to have had more money saved before they started a family… but he was 33 now and since finding his soulmate he wanted to create a family unit.

They had the carriage to themselves and so they were able to talk privately. He took Marie's hand and kissed it.

'Are you looking forward to becoming Madame Carolus-Duran and managing our household and studio?'

Marie smiled and replied, 'Of course I am, but I am more tentative about running the house… more so than the studio… but at least I will have Jeanette to guide me. You will have twelve students joining us this term so we must make a general course plan for them all, as well as finding an individual timetable to suit them. This will prove quite a daunting task, Charles, and you will have to allow your students to assist with some of your portrait commissions as your time is going to be veering towards too much teaching. You also have a mix of nationalities and languages and you promised you would teach in English and Italian as well.'

'I promise I will teach in all three languages but you will have to bring the English and American students up to speed in French when they arrive. I liked your idea of using other artists to give lectures too and I think they should all do sculpting sessions to improve their drawing skills. I will ask Rodin if he would be willing to teach occasionally.'

They went to the restaurant car to have lunch and when they returned to their carriage he pulled her into his arms and gave her a long lingering kiss.

Marie giggled and said, 'What was that for, Charles?'

'Just to let you know that my desire for your body is as strong as ever and I promise to ensure that when we get into our daily working routine I will not forget you need loving and cherishing.'

She stood on her tiptoes and kissed his nose. 'Don't worry; I won't let you neglect your marital duties.'

He groaned and replied, 'I think I need to get back to my fencing and boxing to keep fit for all the demands you are going to be making of my body.'

When the train pulled into the Gare du Nord he suggested they call at the studio, as he was desperate to ensure it was still standing after Antonio had lived in the flat for a month. He carried their two suitcases and Marie carried his canvasses, pads and paint boxes. They would take a hansom cab to their house from the studio.

On their arrival, Antonio was working alone in the studio and he was delighted to see them. Marie realised it would need a good clean as Antonio had not bothered about cleaning it since they left. He presented Charles with an armful of post and he sat down to go through it while Marie persuaded Antonio to show her the flat so she could see what state it was in.

Antonio chattered incessantly while she surveyed the flat. It was obvious Antonio had, had some female company as the flat was relatively clean and tidy and well stocked with food. She asked him who his latest girlfriend was and he admitted that she had stayed over on several occasions and that she worked as a milliner for one of the Paris fashion houses. Antonio complimented Marie on her bronzed skin and rosy cheeks and commented that Charles looked better than he had ever seen him, both physically and mentally. Marie confirmed that for once, Charles had relaxed and completely unwound from his incessant pursuit of painting and had immersed himself in nature.

Antonio said, 'I am glad for both of you. Charles needs a woman in his life to keep him grounded.'

Marie replied, 'I think Charles has discovered that there are other things in life besides painting and I think he genuinely wants to settle down and have a family.'

Antonio clapped his hands and said, 'What beautiful children you will produce between you. Do you think you may be pregnant already?'

Marie gasped as the thought had not crossed her mind, as she had assumed getting pregnant would take time. Although why she would think that she had no idea, as they had certainly been vigorous in their lovemaking during their honeymoon and she knew Charles was desperate to have a child.

She laughed and said, 'I don't know yet, we certainly have been busy practising but I have lots of work to do and I have plenty of time for rearing a family.'

They both returned to the studio and Charles had opened the mail and he thrust a gold embossed invitation into Marie's hand, which was from Emperor Napoleon and Empress Eugenie, inviting "Monsieur and Madame Carolus-Duran to an Arts' Ball at the Tuileries Palace on November 25th."

Marie jumped up and down in excitement. 'Oh Charles, I am so delighted to be invited to court as your wife. I will have to buy a new dress from Worth.'

Charles grinned. 'I shall be so proud to show you off to the world as my beautiful wife. I am also sure this will give me some credibility in your mother's eyes at least.'

He handed her another invitation – to spend a weekend with the Duchesse de Beauchamp in

October.

Marie said, 'Will it just be us or will Manet be invited?'

Charles replied, 'Well, I would expect him to be.'

Charles gave Marie a batch of letters from art students requesting a place at his studio and some letters asking for him to paint commissions.

'We will have to deal with these promptly, so let's take them home for now.'

Charles asked Antonio to go and find them a hansom cab. As soon as he had gone downstairs Charles put the canvasses and drawing pads into a large drawer, locked it and hid the key. These were his unfinished sketches of Marie on their honeymoon and some unfinished landscapes in watercolour.

He said to Marie, 'There they are, safely under lock and key now and I do intend to finish them as well as recreate Freya's portrait. I would love to paint both of you in a "fire and ice" scene.'

Antonio came back upstairs and picked up their suitcases and they went down to the carriage. They were home within ten minutes and when they arrived at the house, Jeanette and their groom André appeared as the carriage pulled up. The groom dealt with their cases and they went up the steps to greet Jeanette at the door.

Charles pulled Marie back from entering and said, 'I believe it is customary for the groom to carry the bride over the threshold of their new home.' He swept Marie up into his arms and walked into the hallway where he deposited a lingering kiss on her lips whispering, 'Welcome home, my darling wife.' Marie was pleasantly surprised that he had even heard of this tradition but pleased that he had been so effusive.

Jeanette bowed a curtsy and welcomed them and accompanied them on a tour of the house as most of the decoration had been completed whilst they were away on their honeymoon.

After their inspection, Marie and Jeanette went to the master bedroom, as Marie wanted to change. Jeanette had supervised bringing all her clothes from her parents' chateau over to their house.

Jeanette said, 'Oh Madame, you look really well and glowing in health. I can see married life suits you both and sir looks so relaxed and happy.'

Marie laughed and said, 'Oh Jeanette, we have had such a wonderful time and Charles has been such an attentive husband. I could not have asked for more. We have had four weeks just getting to know each other and he has surprised me with his tenderness and sensitivity and I have seen a side to his character that I had not seen before. He really is desperate to start a family so I hope I can fulfil my obligations in bearing him a son.'

'Madame, a young girl as healthy as you should have no problem in filling the nursery with a brood of children in no time at all.'

'We have been invited by the Emperor to a dinner dance at the Tuileries in honour of the Arts and I have to find the perfect dress… and we have been invited for a weekend with the Duchesse de Beauchamp and I will need to know what sort of clothes to take.'

'How exciting for you, your mother will be delighted you are being feted by high society.'

Jeanette helped her change into a day dress and then Marie returned to the lounge with Charles while Jeanette unpacked her clothes.

oOo

That evening, they dined together in the dining room, feeling slightly lost at the big table, which could accommodate up to twelve people. Marie had also been daunted in the nursery wing, which had small individual bedrooms for four children as well as a nursery bedroom. These rooms had been decorated but not furnished and she felt slightly overwhelmed by the prospect of being expected to produce and rear four children with no wet nurse or nanny. Remembering Charles's outburst whilst they were on honeymoon she realised that any thoughts of passing the rearing onto someone else was not something her husband intended. *Heaven forbid what her mother would have to say about it all.*

After dinner, they retired to bed, both tired by the journey and as she sat at her dressing table in her chemise, Charles unpinned her hair and brushed it through for her. He loved the auburn colour, which ranged from mahogany to chestnut and he ran his fingers through the curls. He kissed the nape of her neck and his hand undid the bow at the front of her chemise and he exposed her breasts, all the while observing in the mirror.

'You, ma cherie, are just irresistible. I have never known such happiness and I will worship your body forever.' He gently picked her up and carried her to the bed, pulled the covers back and laid her on the right-hand side pillows. He divested himself of his wrap, got into the bed and knelt beside her. He pulled her chemise over her head and gazed down at her exquisite body.

'Marie, tell me how you think I have been as your lover. Has what you have learned enhanced your life?'

She reached up to his face with her hand stroking his cheek. 'Charles, no woman could have a better lover than you. Your whole concern has been to satisfy me and you have done it with such love and tenderness, you have melted my heart. You have taught me so much about my own body but also about your body and its intricacies. You have never forced or frightened me and you have awoken my sexual desire so gently that I am uninhibited in my responses.'

He leant over and tenderly kissed her full on the lips and then made his way down over every part of her body, kissing and caressing with his mouth and tongue until she was screaming for him to make love to her – and then he obliged.

The next morning was Sunday and their last day

of freedom. Marie had suggested that they take a ride around the area and investigate their surroundings. Charles woke at around 7 a.m. to discover Marie lying on her stomach horizontally across the bed, trapping him with her legs and in danger of falling out of bed. He repositioned her onto her side, tucked in with her back to him and his right hand lying lightly on her right breast.

He reflected on the answers she had given last night when he had asked her what she thought of him as a lover. He had been especially proud that she had recognised that he had awakened her sexuality slowly and carefully and was as concerned that she enjoyed the whole experience just as much as he did.

He stroked her nipple and then ran his hand down to her waist and stomach. Was his child already stirring within her? Had she conceived within forty-eight hours of their wedding, on the night after the duel? *Oh, how he wished it could be so.* There was no evidence yet on her body but her sleeping pattern had altered and she was showing fatigue in the evenings, which was also another early indication. He would not tell Marie of his suspicions yet, as he did not want to tempt fate and he wanted her to discover for herself that her body was changing. He calculated that at the Arts' Ball she would be around eight weeks pregnant and by then should be showing slight changes in her breasts and waistline… not enough to spoil the fit of her dress, but by Christmas there would be no hiding the pregnancy. The baby would be born next June and he was not bothered whether it was a girl or a boy as long as it was fit and healthy. He resolved to do some research on pregnancy and childbirth so he would know whether everything appeared normal.

She stirred in his arms and turned over to face him.

'What are you thinking, my husband?'

Charles was not prepared to reveal that he was hoping she was pregnant so he answered, 'I am admiring your beautiful body and thanking God for it.'

She put her arms round his neck and kissed his lips tenderly. 'Now I am going to make love to you and you will obey my every command. Do you understand, husband?'

'I am yours to command Madame, you may do what you wish to me.'

There followed one of the best sexual experiences of his life where she used every move he had taught her and some inventions of her own besides, to drive him to the most exhilarating climax he had ever had. His feelings were so intense that tears were pouring down his face afterwards and he lay with his head on her chest, sobbing like a baby while she just stroked his face and ran her fingers through his hair until he calmed down.

He finally said to her, 'Marie, I never knew that sex could feel this good when it is with someone you love so intensely both in body and soul. You have changed me from an irascible man who only loved his work, into the happiest man on earth who is madly in love and devoted to you.'

oOo

After a leisurely breakfast he went down to the stables to tack up their horses as Sunday was their groom's day off. Marie had gone to change into a habit as she would have to revert to being a lady again and riding side-saddle. It would be inappropriate for her to be seen riding astride in Paris.

Favorit her mare whinnied as he came close to the stables as she was anticipating being turned out into the field with her companions. He collected her tack from the harness room and hoped she would let him tack her up without having to tie her up first. He removed the light rug from her and her bay coat shone like mahogany and she was fit and well-muscled. He carefully put the side saddle into position and gently did the girth and balancing strap up. He put her bridle on gently and she was full of anticipation and raring to go. He looped her reins under the saddle to keep her quiet whilst he tacked up his mount. He was slightly concerned that she could prove a handful as she would not have been ridden for over a month.

Henri had presented them with two black ex-cavalry horses as a wedding present. They were both around eight years old but had been retired from the cavalry with minor defects. The gelding

302

with the white star on his forehead and two white socks had been caught in wire at the knee and had a deep swollen scar that was fully healed but could limit his soundness in the future should he remain in service. The other black gelding had developed a recurring abscess in his near fore which had now healed successfully and he was sound. Both horses were trained in battle drill and both had been driven in harness. Henri had bought them as a pair to drive the carriage or be used as riding horses. He picked the gelding with the white star who Henri said was called Merlin, as he was the lighter bodied of the two and looked to have a little Spanish blood in him. He also had a gleaming black coat and was very well mannered, standing stock still whilst he tacked him up.

Marie arrived and proceeded to chat to Favorit, who seemed delighted to see her mistress once again. Marie came over to Merlin's stable and she patted and admired him. Charles led Favorit out and cupped his hands together to give Marie a leg up. He told her that he was concerned that Favorit may be a little fresh and to be careful, but the look that Marie gave him confirmed he was wasting his breath. He pulled Merlin out and mounted and as he walked close to Favorit she squealed at Merlin and laid her ears back threateningly. He suggested they had ten minutes in the outdoor paddock, but Marie once again silenced him with a dagger-like look. He was concerned that if Marie fell off Favorit she might lose the baby but as she did not know she was pregnant, he could hardly argue the point. They left the driveway and headed towards the river, exploring their new territory. Favorit was dancing on the spot, desperate to stretch her legs, but Marie kept her under control although within ten minutes, sweat was showing on her neck and shoulders.

Thankfully, when they reached the river, the grassy bank was flat and wide and could take them both side by side. Merlin was a delight to ride; he had a very soft mouth and required little contact in the hand but responded equally well to Charles' legs and any shift of balance. Charles was reluctant to increase the pace when he did not know the terrain well, in case they encountered more difficult terrain. They came to some woods where the path narrowed and he suggested he take the lead so Merlin would block Favorit if she took flight. As they came out of the wood they followed a marked path through some fields and Marie insisted they have a canter. Charles insisted on taking the lead and controlling the pace, concerned about Favorit. However, apart from a few squeals and the odd buck as she cantered, she soon settled down and relaxed.

The track was rising steeply to the top of a hill and he let Merlin canter on at a leisurely pace while Favorit's energy was sapped by the sharp incline. At the top of the hill they stopped and surveyed the view of Paris below them. Now Favorit had settled down, he manoeuvred Merlin close to her and leant over and kissed Marie.

'You look radiant today ma cherie, quite the aristocratic French lady. You should have married a prince or a king, not a mere artist.'

Marie smiled at him and touched his face. 'No king or prince could make me as content as you do, my love.'

He was touched by her words and the memory of the passion she had conveyed last night. Had he finally tamed his little firebrand and would she welcome the challenge of parenthood as much as he did? He suspected not but hopefully with his guidance, she would learn to become as good a mother as she was a lover.

'Well if we fall on hard times you may have to sell your body to make ends meet. Plenty of men would pay a handsome price for a night with you in their bed.'

Marie gasped in shock and instantly blushed. 'How dare you suggest I would even contemplate another man in my bed. I am your wife not your harlot and expect to be treated with respect.' She spun Favorit round and cantered down the hill.

Charles realised she had not taken this in jest, as he had intended. He cantered after her. He caught her up on the flat and forced Merlin to draw level with Favorit and he grabbed her rein to halt her.

'Marie, I was only joking I did not wish to dishonour you in any way. Please forgive my foolish tongue. I had not realised how shocking the idea would sound to a young lady.'

Marie smiled. 'In one respect, I am pleased that you consider me accomplished enough to entertain such a thought but in another way horrified that you would contemplate me being with another man.'

'Darling, I would never want that to happen; you are my precious wife whom I want to protect forever.'

21

It was the end of the working day at his studio and he found himself alone. Marie had gone to see her father at the Conservatoire and he had said he would stay on until she came back and they would go home together. He went to the locked drawer where he had stored his drawings and canvasses that he had painted on honeymoon. He looked at the sketch of Marie that he had done by the waterfall, realising how lucky he was that she was his wife. He was about to prepare his palette when he heard the door open downstairs. He quickly put the sketch back and locked the drawer. Manet appeared at the top of the stairs.

'Charles, here you are returned from your honeymoon, looking better I might say than you have in years. Marriage obviously suits you!

He strode over to Manet, hugged him and patted him on the back and said, 'Yes, you see a very different man from the irascible lonely artist you knew before. Marie has changed my life completely. I have never known such contentment.' He fetched two glasses and a bottle of wine and they sat down while he poured the first glass.

Manet laughed and said, 'Well have you accomplished what I told you to do and got her pregnant on your month long honeymoon? I shall be so disappointed if you haven't.'

'I hope so; it happened very soon after the wedding, possibly the night after the duel, but it could have been any time within that first week – we certainly put in many hours discovering the delight of each other's bodies. However, it is as if she has opened up my emotions to such a high degree I can feel other people's emotions and I have somehow reconnected with nature. Marie doesn't realise she is pregnant yet, so say nothing when she returns. I want her to realise for herself that her body is changing.

Manet replied, 'Well then, she has transformed you both physically and mentally. You really do look well... and with a suntan, too. You can't have spent all day in bed. Neither can I believe you haven't drawn her, so come clean and show me what you have done?'

Charles gasped. 'Where is it written that the best man has the right to see pictures of the bride on honeymoon?'

'When her husband and the best man are both skilled artists and revere the female body,' retorted Manet.

Charles laughed and went to the drawer, accompanied by Manet, and gave him the sketch of the waterfall with Marie standing in profile on the water's edge.

'Oh Charles, she is more stunning than I imagined, and to use the cloak to frame her outline was inspired.'

Charles gave him the second sketch of her back view and related why the hand mark was on Marie's right buttock and the questioning she had put him through to establish his "realist" artistic principles. Manet was highly amused and urged him to paint both of these in oils. Charles confirmed he had no intention of exhibiting either of these pictures as they were for his eyes only.

He then showed Manet the working sketches of Freya's portrait and he was captivated by her beauty. He told him how he had instinctively recognised Freya's inner turmoil over her feelings for Gustav after the birth.

Manet commented, 'Freya is beautiful. How did you keep your hands off her?'

'Quite easily, my wife was watching my every move and occasionally my mother, who thought I was coveting my brother's wife, as it was. I did paint it in oils for them and Gustav loved it and I think it helped break the ice that had formed in Freya's heart. I have asked if they would object if I submitted it to the Salon but I would love to do one of both Freya and Marie depicting "fire and ice" as that is how I see them.'

'That's a brilliant idea; it would look spectacular with the waterfall background,' said Manet with excitement.

'I also intend to do a self-portrait of the wedding day. It was such a spectacular day both spiritually and musically. I still can't get over the sound of a choir of artists singing Verdi's 'Gloria' and Fauré's 'Jean Racine'. How much practice did you all do for that – it must have been several sessions?

Manet laughed. 'Well, you know Pierre, he is used to teaching the best choirs and so he was not satisfied until we were note perfect. We must have had between 10-12 rehearsals. That was why I panicked when you wanted to go to the church early on the wedding day as we were due to rehearse at 10 a.m.'

Charles relayed the scene when his mother delivered Manet's letter and caught both of them passionately indulging over the kitchen table. Manet was delighted he had caused such chaos and they discussed Antonio's prank in detail, which he wished he had been able to see. Manet thought Antonio had promise and his talent for drawing architecture was indisputable.

Charles groaned. 'I know, but I have to get him to paint people with the same accuracy and detail. I shall use him on external portraits although he will never paint horses as well as I do.'

Charles topped up the drinks and then carefully put the sketches back and locked them away as Marie would be back soon. They discussed the invitation from the Duchesse de Beauchamp and Manet said Suzanne had declined to go to that weekend or to the Arts' Ball with Napoleon as she hated these social outings. Charles said he was delighted to get a chance to show Marie off at such a prestigious occasion although he worried about Napoleon's obsession with beautiful women. He was also mindful of how pleased his mother-in-law would be as she had been quick to condemn his lowly station compared to the status of the preferred husband she had wanted for her daughter.

Manet confirmed he had done some research on Beauchamp and had heard from several sources that he had been homosexual and this may have been the cause of his brutal attack on his wife. They both agreed that unless the Duchess referred to it, they would not bring it up at the meeting unless she herself raised the subject. They decided he would have to advise Marie of Beauchamp's homosexuality prior to the visit as it might be that the Duchesse would choose to confide in Marie. Charles realised he would have to raise this issue tactfully with Marie.

Marie returned at 7 p.m. and was welcomed by Manet with a kiss and some bawdy comments on how well marriage was suiting both of them.

As they were on their way home, Marie advised that they had been invited to lunch next Sunday and Henri was due back on leave. Charles was delighted that he would be able to inform Louise of the Arts' Ball. Marie was going to the House of Worth to look for a dress on Friday. She had asked if he would approve her final choice, which flattered him immensely but he did have a flair for style and colour and particularly what suited each individual.

Surprisingly, the next day he received a hand delivered letter from the Tuileries Palace advising that they would be sat at the top table next to Empress Eugenie, and Marie next to Napoleon. His first reaction was concern over Napoleon's fascination with women and whether Marie could cope with his advances at such a young age. Then he remembered that she was no aristocratic French lady and would not be daunted by Napoleon. In fact her tongue was more likely to get her thrown in prison, especially if he propositioned her and she slapped his face.

Antonio had answered the door to the messenger and he was concerned as he watched Charles read the letter.

'Is everything OK Charles? You look rather perturbed.'

Charles replied, 'I have just been advised that at the Arts' Ball we will be sitting next to Napoleon and his wife and dancing with them. His reputation for flirting with young women is well known.'

'Surely you don't think Marie will be flattered by his attention? He is old enough to be her grandfather.'

'No, I am more concerned about her slapping him across the face if he says anything inappropriate to her and you well know it could happen with her fiery temper.'

Antonio roared with laughter. 'You can hardly challenge Napoleon to a duel!'

'Precisely, as I would end up rotting in jail whilst he turns my wife into his mistress! I am going round to see if Manet's at his studio, to seek his advice. Marie will need a very expensive dress from Worth for this occasion!'

Antonio chuckled at his obvious distress as he left the studio at speed.

Thankfully, Manet was in and alone when he arrived and seemed surprised at his obvious distress.

Charles said, 'Have you had a letter from the Tuileries about the Arts' Ball?'

Manet replied, 'Yes, it was hand delivered this morning. It appears that you, I and Monet are sitting on the top table with the Emperor. Can't imagine why he has picked me over Renoir, Cézanne, Gaugan, Degas or Courbet, although they have all been invited, even Whistler and he is American.'

'Really? My letter just mentions that Marie and I will be sat next to both of them and will dance the first dance with them. You know Napoleon's reputation with women – he flirts outrageously – and neither you nor Monet will be accompanied by wives unless Monet married Camille after she gave birth to their first child last year?'

'No, they are not married yet to my knowledge.'

'Well that leaves Marie as the only woman in our group and if he says anything inappropriate to her he will end up with one of her famous slapped faces.'

Manet laughed, 'And I thought you were panicking with jealousy because he would be bound to find her attractive. It appears you are more concerned for his personal safety.'

'Well you saw her stamp on that cavalry officer's toes after he held her too close at her brother's party. I can't challenge him to a duel or I will be thrown in jail while he pursues her for his mistress.'

'Charles, you do your wife a disservice; she is more than capable of putting him in his place if he transgresses her moral code. She only has eyes for you as it is and she knows how to behave in these situations. He will be attracted to her beauty and her mind, she is hardly an airhead and he will be intrigued by her time in Russia. You need to polish up on your Spanish if you want to make a favourable impression on the Empress. I believe she is extremely learned and a delight to socialise with.'

'I was sending Marie to Worth tomorrow to find a dress but she is going to have to look sensational now and will need expensive jewellery to complement her outfit. The Empress has been using Worth for her state dresses for years. This will cost me a fortune; thank God I will be in dress uniform!'

'Charles, you only need to have a word in Worth's ear and he will give you a huge discount on the dress. The ball will be covered by the world's press and make his business even more money, provided you inform them where her dress came from. You surely have contacts in the gem world to get the jewellery on loan rather than buy it. Marie could do a lot of good for the art world if she handles Napoleon carefully.'

'Who else do you know that is going?'

'Well from the music world there is Gounod, Chabrier and Fauré representing composers and several outstanding musicians. The writers who have been invited include Guy de Maupassant, Gustave Flaubert, Alexandre Dumas, Victor Hugo, Jules Verne and of course Émile Zola who can't quite believe it as he has been so outspoken about Napoleon. As for the actors, I have not a clue. Our artistic friends, Henri Fantin-Latour and Zacharie Astruc are also going.'

'Sounds like it will be quite a night with so much artistic talent together in one room. I just hope Marie does not develop any sickness symptoms as she should be around eight weeks pregnant by then, although she still has not noticed any changes herself yet. I had better tip Worth off and suggest a final fitting as late as possible in case she puts on weight.'

'Charles, don't panic her over Napoleon; she is no fool and she will keep her temper under control with the world watching her every move. You had better polish up your dancing before then and remember with a shortage of women at the ball, Marie will be sought after for every dance.'

'There's one thing I won't be doing a lot of and that is drinking. I will need to keep a very clear head and keep a watchful eye on my wife.'

They chatted for a while and he promised he would have a night out with Manet in the next few weeks and then he returned to the studio as he had a client coming at 2 p.m.

He informed Marie of the letter from the Palace over dinner and she was speechless at first.

When she had had enough time to digest the implication of the task ahead he said, 'Well my love, do you think you can cope with dining and dancing with Napoleon? He is renowned for his flirtations with beautiful women even though he is 60 now and has had several mistresses. Will you be able to control your fiery temper and resist slapping him if he says anything inappropriate?'

Marie laughed. 'Oh, don't you worry about me, Charles. I can match him with my sharp tongue just as easily as with a slap across the face. I will not do anything to ruin my reputation, or yours for that matter, while the world's press are watching. I am sure I can keep the old wolf at bay for one night only. My mother will be so impressed she will be beside herself. It does mean I will have to have an exquisite dress to carry this off.'

'Of course my darling; you just go to Worth tomorrow and select whatever dress you like, regardless of the cost as I am sure I can get a huge discount if we assure him the press will know who the dress designer is. I believe the Empress has been using him for some time now. Just explain to him that you are to be sat next to Napoleon as principal guest and you are representing the French art world and he will be sure to come up with the perfect gown. Would you like me to come with you from the start or are you just going to summon me when you have decided on a shortlist?'

Marie replied, 'I think I would rather go alone to start with and then when I have got it down to my favourites I will send the carriage to pick you up from the studio.'

'That's fine by me dear, and don't worry about jewellery. I have an idea for borrowing whatever is necessary to compliment the outfit.'

When they retired that evening as she sat at her dressing table, he went over and unpinned her hair and brushed it through for her and then, overcome with desire, he carried her to the bed and they made passionate love.

oOo

The next morning, Marie took great care over her appearance in preparation for her visit to Worth. She contemplated whether to take Jeanette to help her with trying on the gowns but decided that Worth would have more than enough assistants to help her. She selected a low necked silk corset to take with her for the fitting but was sure Worth would have the underwear needed if she had to purchase it.

She arrived promptly at 11 a.m. for the pre-arranged fitting and as she entered the salon, Charles Worth himself came to greet her.

'Madame Duran you are enchanting. I will have no problem in finding you the perfect ball gown for the Arts' Ball. Tell me, how old are you? I suspect still a teenager and if so we don't want you dressed like a matron.'

Marie replied, 'Just 18, Monsieur Worth and as you know my husband wishes to cast his eye over my dress as he has such style and flair for colour as he advises his clients on what to wear for their portraits.'

Worth replied, 'Madame, this is going to be an honour. With your beautiful lithe body, blue eyes, porcelain complexion and lustrous auburn hair we will have no problem. I have prepared my models ready to show you some gowns and we can discuss them together and then proceed to a fitting.'

He led her to a luxurious blue and gold Louis XIV settee, sat down next to her and clapped his hands and the first model appeared on the catwalk. She was dazzled by the opulence of the gowns both in fabric, colour and design. A maid brought in fresh coffee and poured it for them both.

Nearly all had crinoline skirts and she ventured to ask Worth, 'I do prefer a more fitted style rather than a crinoline skirt. Would I be able to get away without a crinoline at the ball?'

Worth replied, 'No, Madame. A crinoline skirt is still required for ball gowns, particularly for an important event such as this. Fashion styles are becoming more fitted and for a night at the opera or private dinner dance you could get away without a full skirt. It would not be appropriate for the Arts' Ball. Now tell me which styles you liked and we will look at them in detail?'

She selected a rose pink silk gown trimmed with gold lace, a deep red velvet dress trimmed in ivory lace over the bodice and back, a coffee silk dress overlaid in black lace on the bodice and skirt and a champagne silk taffeta dress with fluted waist, bodice and puffed sleeves with a waist sash edged in green linen trim.

Worth replied, 'Well Madame, all excellent choices but shall we see what they look like on you?'

She was ushered into a large changing room and had two women to help her change. She tried them all on for Worth's inspection but said nothing until she had tried all four of them.

She then faced Worth wearing the champagne silk taffeta dress with a crinoline skirt and trimmed waist sash.

'Well Madame, what do you think?'

'Monsieur Worth, I love this one most and the coffee silk dress overlaid in black lace next.'

'Perfect, Madame – absolutely right and I would confirm that with your youthful beauty it is too soon for you to wear black just yet. Shall I send your carriage for your husband, Madame? I know how anxious he is to oversee the decision. Perhaps Anna could adjust your corset and tighten the bodice and waist a little whilst you are waiting.'

Charles arrived within fifteen minutes and she stayed in the fitting room whilst Worth ushered him into the studio. She was soon summoned to the runway. The crinoline skirt was the fullest she had tried on and the bone underskirt was so light she knew it would look stunning while she was dancing. She watched Charles's face carefully as she stepped out onto the runway and he beamed in delight as she sashayed down the catwalk and then turned to show off the back and trailing sash.

She tried the other one on as an alternative and then waited for his decision.

'My darling, you look radiant in both, but for impact alone and for such a prestigious occasion, the champagne and green stands out a mile. We have just been discussing how an emerald and diamond necklace, tiara, earrings and bracelet will finish it off perfectly. I would also like the back of your hair loose but the top and sides up and Worth thinks you can get away with it due to your age. Indulge me and try it on again please.'

'Oh Charles, I love it. I'm so pleased that you do too.'

As she went, Charles turned to Worth. 'May I suggest she has a final fitting a week before the ball as I suspect she may be pregnant but I don't think she has realised yet? It would only make her eight weeks anyway.'

He replied, 'Well there's no problem if she increases up the top and she is tiny around the waist anyway. She is stunning Charles; you are a very lucky man to have her as your wife. Word got around after your wedding and you were both the talk of the salons; Marie for her beauty and her singing ability and you for the duel. Word will have reached Napoleon and I am sure that's another reason you were chosen to represent the art fraternity… not that I am insinuating your contribution to art is not well renowned.'

Charles laughed. 'Well you know the Empress well and I will have to entertain her so tell me what she is like and interested in.'

'Eugenie is a delight and far too refined for Napoleon as she was a Spanish princess at birth. She is too devout, educated, devoted to her duty and a perfect mother for young Louis, but she deplores her husband's philandering. She was born in Granada although educated in Paris and she promotes the rights of women to become doctors and lawyers and has fought to get them entry into medical and law school. She is an avid horse rider and breeds racehorses. I am sure she will prefer your company to her husband's at the ball and she will approve of your wife. I am sure Marie is capable of coping with Napoleon's flirtation although he will be an admirer of her spirit and individuality. He likes strong, spirited women who know their own mind.'

'Ah, but that's the problem. She is quick tempered and has hands as quick as any sword if she is thwarted.'

'Yes, I understand Manet sported her handprint across his face after your wedding for risking your life in a duel.'

'He was lucky, she gave me such a right hook after I had been wounded in the shoulder in the duel that it knocked me out cold.'

'Oh, tell her to divulge what happened, to Napoleon; it might keep his hands off her stunning body. Seriously, if she ever fancies modelling just tell her to get in touch.'

'How much is this design of yours going to cost me?'

'Let's just say I will do the dress at cost price as I think your wife will do it more than justice at the ball and should get me some press coverage. I have just finished Eugenie's dress and she is due for a fitting next week. Of course, age wise, she cannot compete with Marie but she is still a beautiful woman to dress. I cannot understand why she hasn't taken any lovers.'

'I can – if she is a devout Catholic then she will remain faithful. I spent three years in Spain and in many ways their devotion to their religion far exceeds that of the Italians or French.'

Marie returned from the dressing room and they made their departure. In the carriage Marie turned and kissed him passionately.

'I do love the dress, Charles, it is beautiful. Can you really afford it?'

'Sweetheart, I don't have any choice; you have to look stunning if we are to be principal guests and sat next to Napoleon. You will just have to think carefully before you speak to him and I just pray he behaves. I think we should have some dancing lessons as well, to polish our repertoire.'

22

On Sunday they rode over to the chateau for lunch with Marie's family. Marie insisted on riding side-saddle on a sharp and fit Favorit and Charles was anxious to keep her calm as the prospect of a fall at this early stage of her pregnancy worried him considerably. Marie thoroughly enjoyed the ride and the freedom to gallop across country again. Merlin proved a valuable asset as a riding horse but he also calmed the impetuous Favorit, which pleased him.

On arrival he was pleased to receive a delightful reception from his mother-in-law, Louise. Marie had told Pierre about the Arts' Ball when she had met him at the Conservatoire and for once he felt genuine admiration from Louise. Henri was on leave from the cavalry after a heavy fall when his mount had caught a foot in a rabbit hole and he had sustained damage to his right hip. He was enjoying his time in the cavalry and his shooting and sword skills had improved.

After lunch, Charles joined Henri and Pierre in the library and they chatted about the honeymoon and he told them about offering Jacques a scholarship and regaled them with the story of Francois painting Marie nude on horseback. They both found it highly amusing and a very daring thing to do, especially with Charles being a new husband. Pierre asked if they had enjoyed Lille and he told them it had been perfect and having the cottage to themselves had given them some privacy. Pierre joked that he expected to see the end result of their extended honeymoon in nine months' time but Charles gleefully kept his news to himself.

Later on in the afternoon, while Marie was with Louise discussing the ball, he and Henri slipped away to the stables for a look at the horses and to have a private talk. He thanked him again for Merlin and the other cavalry mount as wedding presents.

Henri said, 'Marie looks content and well Charles, I sense she may be with child. Am I right?'

'Ah Henri, it is too soon to be certain yet and I want Marie to recognise it herself but there are tiny signs of change, which I can only hope means that a child may be on the way.'

'I hope so Charles, but Marie has always been a lover of animals with four feet and a tail – not babies. I do hope she transforms into a good mother because she has not had the best role model in our own mother. She was always distant and self-absorbed and not the closest mother one would have wished for as a child.'

'I am sure that with me by her side we can make

good parents. She doesn't know yet that she is pregnant so don't say anything to her or to anyone else.

'I think you will make a great father and perhaps Marie will finally settle down to a domesticated life.'

Charles laughed. 'We can only hope so but I wouldn't put money on it; Marie seems to court adventure more than domesticity. I don't expect her to remain in the nursery long once the baby arrives; she still intends to supervise my studio and to be fair, she will be a tremendous asset. Her organisational and financial skills are already evident.'

Henri laughed. 'She can be dangerous if she loses her temper but I think she will be more than able to manage Napoleon. He would not dare to do anything outrageous, especially in front of his wife. He does still love and respect Eugenie even though they live separate lives. You will have no problem entertaining Eugenie; you are both admirers of Velazquez and she has some of his pictures at the Tuileries.'

All three of them left the chateau at 4 p.m. and had an enjoyable ride back to Paris. He was able to show Henri how good and obedient Merlin was. However, Marie did insist on having a short race on Favorit and both of them were able to appear to chase her without causing any danger, while ensuring Marie won.

oOo

They had arranged private dancing lessons after work

for the next two weeks to ensure they were both foot perfect for the ball. Their tutor Monsieur Martell was well versed in the latest dances and tutored them personally. Charles was terrified of stepping on the Empress's toes but his tutor was pleased with his lightness of movement, helped by his return to his fencing and boxing classes.

After the class they went to the Café Gerbois for a meal and several of the artistic community came in during the evening. He introduced Marie to Cézanne and they heard his version of Antonio's Louvre painting story and it thoroughly amused Cézanne who was renowned for his moods and bad temper. He was also bowled over by Marie's beauty and her knowledge of art.

Just as they were about to leave, Whistler and Courbet arrived so they stayed for a couple more drinks and discussed the Arts' Ball with them. Courbet joked about their role as principal artists at the ball and also teased him that Napoleon would find Marie irresistible and dance her out of the ballroom, into his bedroom. Marie carelessly mentioned their dancing lessons and Courbet gave them even more jesting. However, Whistler repaid him with a derogatory comment suggesting that they could hardly have had Courbet stamping on the Empresses' feet as he could hardly dance at all. Courbet retaliated by questioning why Whistler, a mere American, had been invited and suggested he must have influence in high places.

That evening when they returned home, they went straight to their room and Marie told him she felt shattered but could not understand why; she could only describe it as feeling as though she wanted to hibernate. He avoided the issue as he knew exactly what was wrong with her. As much as he would have liked to have had sex, he resisted and cuddled up behind her and within minutes, Marie was fast asleep.

He woke at 2 a.m. to discover Marie missing from the bed. There were no lights on and the bedroom door was closed. He assumed she may have gone to the bathroom but there was no sound of her returning. He knew how her sleep patterns had changed since their honeymoon so he got up, found his wrap and set out to find her. He assumed she may have gone downstairs for some food but there was no light shining downstairs. A slight noise made him look up the staircase and he could see a beam of light on the second floor. He mounted the stairs quietly and followed the light, which was coming from the main nursery. The door was open and he saw Marie sitting in the big rocking chair in her nightie, gently rocking to and fro. He suspected she might be sleep walking so he entered quietly and she registered his presence. He moved slowly towards her and knelt in front of the chair, which had ceased rocking. He took her hand and said,

'Darling, what's the matter? Are you not well?'

Suddenly, Marie pulled him close to her chest and sobbed, 'Charles, I think I am pregnant and I am so frightened that I won't be a good mother and yet I desperately want to give you the children you want. I am terrified of my body changing and the pain of labour and breastfeeding and that I might not get my figure back and I have no idea how to raise a baby.'

Charles gathered her in his arms and kissed the tears running down her face.

'Marie, you are just frightened of the unknown. It won't be a difficult labour and I will be beside you every step of the way. I told you I had no intention of leaving your bed and we will get through this pregnancy together and your beauty will increase as the pregnancy progresses as you become a mature woman. Come Marie, you are not a vain girl obsessed by your looks, you are just frightened of the changes your body will go through. I will see no harm befalls you and that you have sufficient knowledge and help to cope with the baby after it is born. I think we should engage an experienced nursemaid once the baby comes so that you can recover and resume your work.'

'Does that mean I can have a wet nurse too?'

'No, you know my feelings on that point; you need to build a close relationship with the baby and breastfeeding is the best way of doing that. Remember your feelings will change after having the baby and you may find you enjoy feeding our baby.'

Marie groaned. 'I woke up feeling sick and I have thrown up twice since.'

Charles patted her hand and said, 'Well it was probably the alcohol so you are going to have to give that up for a while. The sickness won't last throughout the pregnancy but it would be safer to avoid alcohol anyway.'

'Oh God, Charles. What about the Arts' Ball? I cannot decline alcohol sat next to Napoleon.'

'I will have a word with the serving staff beforehand and you will have to do the toasts with water, although you could just sip the champagne in the toasts – it won't be as potent as drinking wine. Now come back to bed before you catch cold and tomorrow we shall go to Notre Dame and thank God for his precious gift.' He held her hand and pulled her up from the chair and led her back to bed.

He pulled her close to his chest and wrapped his arms round her, kissing her gently and stroking her hair. She fell asleep relatively quickly and he lay there pondering her fears and feeling slightly guilty that he may have rushed her into pregnancy too soon. However, he was delighted that she now knew she was pregnant and he vowed to take good care of her and see she continued to eat well. He would have to watch she did not cut back on eating in order to prevent putting on weight.

The next morning, he woke at 7 a.m. and quietly extracted himself from Marie. He ran downstairs in his nightgown to the kitchen and frightened cook to death. Finding a bucket in the pantry, he took it back upstairs to the bedroom. Marie was still fast asleep so he went to the bathroom in the hope she wouldn't wake until he got back.

When he returned she was just stirring and he knelt beside the bed and gently kissed her lips.

'Good morning, my beautiful pregnant wife; are you ready to get up?'

She sat up in bed and shook her head saying her head ached and told him not to kiss her. She pulled the covers aside and sat on the edge of the bed with her head in her hands. She slowly stood up and then walked a few steps and as she suddenly started to run he caught her and produced the bucket from behind his back. She stopped dead, grabbed it and threw up. He guided her to a chair and then gathered up her luxurious auburn hair and pinned it up as she continued to throw up.

After a few moments she said, 'A husband should never see his wife in this demeaning position!'

'Why not? I am the cause of the sickness. I made you pregnant in the first place. I'm just thankful you aren't attempting to run me through with a sword.'

'Don't tempt me Charles; I will do, if this continues for the next few months, I promise you.'

He removed the bucket and went to the bathroom to get washed and empty the bucket and when he came back, Marie was laying out her clothes, looking slightly less pale. She went to wash herself and he got dressed and went down to breakfast.

Jeanette, Marie's maid served them breakfast and she asked if Marie was well but he could tell from her face that Cook had told her about the bucket. He took the opportunity to speak to her privately.

'Jeanette, Marie is pregnant and is suffering from morning sickness and I want to enlist your help in keeping a watchful eye on her. Please let me know if you think the sickness is serious and do tell me if Marie isn't eating because of it. She needs to keep eating to nourish the baby and she does have a tendency to stop eating if her stomach is upset.'

'Oh sir, I am delighted for you both. I did suspect she might be but I didn't say anything. I will keep a close eye on her at home and let you know if anything untoward occurs. May I offer my congratulations on your welcome news?'

'You go up to Marie and ask her if she would like me to go to the studio alone – she could join me later if she feels unwell. I can manage breakfast on my own if you need to stay with her.'

Jeanette left to go up to Marie and he helped himself to croissants and coffee and welcomed the chance to read *Le Figaro* at the table.

About ten minutes later, Marie appeared fully dressed and he asked her if she wanted to go to the studio with him or follow on later. She agreed to accompany him now so he sent Jeanette to tell the groom he would require the carriage to take them. Marie managed to eat some bread and fruit so he did not push her any further.

He would take Marie with him to visit his friend Monsieur Van Dries who was the gem dealer he had bought her sapphire engagement ring from. He had promised to find him a set of emeralds that he could hire for the Arts' Ball. He had sent him a message to say he had found something suitable if he wanted to come and inspect it. They could also visit Notre Dame together and then Marie could return by carriage afterwards if she was tired.

On the journey to work he suggested that they stay overnight at the Hotel de Ville after the ball as it would be a long day and night and would save them having to come back to the house. Marie welcomed the idea with relief as she would be able to rest there before the ball and ask Worth to deliver the dress to her room and hopefully send a fitter who could help her get dressed.

They arrived at the studio and Marie checked the diary and as Charles had no students today and no commission sitters booked they set off to the gem dealers at 10 a.m. by carriage. He had refrained from asking how she was feeling but she seemed to be considerably better when they had been out in the fresh air.

Monsieur Van Dries' office was on the left bank of the Seine and he welcomed them both enthusiastically and was very complimentary towards Marie.

'Madam Duran, you are exquisite. No wonder they chose you as guest of honour from the Arts to sit next to the Emperor; someone must have told him of your beauty. I only hope the emeralds will do you justice. I can see why Charles wanted a deep blue sapphire for your engagement ring, to match your beautiful eyes.'

He lay a piece of black velvet on the table and then produced a jewellery box from the safe. He switched on a small bright light and opened the box. It contained an emerald and diamond necklace, a small tiara with a central emerald encrusted with diamonds, a bracelet and set of earrings. The necklace was set on a thick gold chain and had six small emeralds on either side of a very big square-set emerald, surrounded by diamonds. The earrings had a square emerald with droplets of small diamonds and the bracelet echoed the style of the necklace.

Marie gasped when she saw them and said, 'Oh Monsieur Van Dries, they are beautiful pieces and such a deep emerald green.'

Monsieur Van Dries replied, 'I am glad you like them, Madame. When is your final dress fitting with Worth? I shall bring them round to his salon and we can make sure the necklace is the correct length for your dress.'

Marie replied, 'I am having my final fitting on November 15th at 2 p.m.'

Charles commented, 'That is very good of you Erik. We have decided to stay at the Hotel de Ville on the night of the ball on November 25th so they can be delivered there and can be locked in their safe overnight. They really are stunning. I dread to think what they would cost to buy.'

'I purchased them through an English contact so I believe they have been in England most of their life and have hardly been worn. They are in exquisite condition.'

As they set off in the carriage, Marie hugged him and said, 'Oh Charles, they were beautiful. I will feel like a princess wearing them on the night. Nobody could fail to see the quality of the stones; they could never be classed as paste. How much is he charging you to hire them?'

Charles kissed her hand and said, 'That is between him and me; you just enjoy wearing them on the night. I know how you can repay me. I want to do a self-portrait in oils of us both on our wedding day so we have something permanent to remember our special day. We need to do it quickly before you start to show so I will paint it at home this weekend, so you will have to sit quietly for me as I will have to do it with the help of a mirror.'

'Oh Charles, you are wonderful. No man but you would have thought of doing something so romantic. I don't deserve you for a husband, especially now I am going to be so irritated by my pregnancy and the restrictions it will induce.'

'Why should it restrict you, darling? I don't intend to stop you doing anything. I just want you to be particularly careful about riding and not take any unnecessary risks. I don't expect you to go into confinement and take to your bed; I think it is important you keep up your fitness as long as you can.'

The carriage pulled up at the Notre Dame cathedral and they made their way to the small chapel where they could kneel together at the altar and be blessed. When it was their turn they approached the altar rail holding hands, and he told the priest that they were celebrating an impending birth. They knelt and Charles placed his hand over her right hand, on top of the altar rail. The priest blessed them both and then they had five minutes of prayer together.

They decided to go to the confessional and whilst they were waiting he sat back in the pew and took a detailed look around the magnificent cathedral. He could feel the historic atmosphere pervading his senses, wrapping him in a band of warmth and peace. He was in awe of the changes marriage had made to his life. He was bursting with happiness and grateful for achieving his desire to produce a child. Marie meant everything to him and he prayed for a safe delivery of their child and he vowed to protect her for the rest of his life.

After they had both made their confessions they moved back towards the main aisle and heading in their direction, was Gabriel Fauré. He recognised them at exactly the same time as they spotted him.

'Charles, Marie, how well you look. I am back for the half term week in Paris and I hear you are the principal guests of Napoleon at the Arts' Ball. I shall be attending as well. Charles, will you be going to

Café Gerbois tonight? I would love to have a drink and a chat. I am playing here for the Sunday morning mass and doing an organ recital afterwards.'

Charles turned to Marie. 'Would you mind if I went out tonight? I need to speak to Monet and Manet about the ball.'

'Of course not, Charles. You go and enjoy yourself; I was going to suggest that the carriage takes me home after we drop you at your studio.'

He left his studio at around 6 p.m. intending to have some dinner before the majority of customers arrived. He had just finished his sweet course when Manet and Zola arrived and came straight over.

'Charles, delighted to see you, have you come just to eat or to meet someone?'

'Well I was hoping to catch you and Monet and I met Fauré today and agreed to meet him here for a drink. I am pleased to see you here, Émile. I assume you will be present on the writers' table? Do sit down.'

'Probably, under sufferance. I don't think Hugo and Dumas are fans of my writing; I think I am too young and radical for them. I was surprised to be invited as I haven't been very kind to our esteemed Emperor in print.'

Manet chipped in, 'Neither have I been a particular devotee, but I do have considerable respect for Empress Eugenie.'

Charles replied, 'Good, I am relying on you talking and dancing with her to take some of the pressure off me.'

Manet replied, 'Oh Charles, you will have plenty to chat to Eugenie about with your time in Spain.'

Charles answered, 'I am more concerned that as you and Monet will have no female companions, my wife is going to be on her own, fending off Napoleon.'

Zola laughed. 'But Napoleon is 60 now, old enough to be your wife's grandfather. Surely you don't think he will make a pass at her?'

Charles countered, 'His reputation for flirting with women is on a par with Louix XIV. My fear is that if he oversteps the line with Marie she will end up slapping his face and both myself and Manet have been victims of that plight.'

Zola laughed. 'From what I hear of your firebrand of a wife Duran she will be more than capable of keeping Napoleon at bay and he adores clever and independent women.'

Charles paid for his meal and moved into the bar with Manet and Zola and as he looked round, he observed Monet was at the bar with Camille Pissaro. He excused himself from Manet and Zola and went over to Monet. Claude Monet held out his hand and also embraced him.

'Duran, I haven't seen you since your wedding but it looks to be agreeing with you. I am looking forward to meeting your wife at the ball; the salon gossip assures me she is a sight to behold. Allow me to introduce you to Camille Pissaro. I don't think you have actually met.'

Charles shook Pissaro's hand and replied, 'I am always delighted to meet a fellow "en plein air" (painting outdoors) artist.'

Having purchased their drinks, Manet and Zola came over and they all sat chatting. They discussed one of Napoleon's greatest achievements in the art world. Back in 1863, the Paris Salon jury refused two thirds of the paintings presented for exhibition including works from Courbet, Manet, Pissaro and Whistler. They complained bitterly in the press and word reached Napoleon. He agreed that the public should be the judges and set up the Salon des Refusés. More than a thousand visitors a day attended the first exhibition and Manet's painting, *The Luncheon on the Grass,* which featured two nude women and had been heavily criticised by the judges and deemed indecent when submitted to the Paris Salon, was well received by the public thanks to an effusive review by Émile Zola. James Whistler's *Symphony in White* was also acclaimed by the public having been turned down by both the Royal Academy in London and the Paris Salon. The art critic Theo Thoré-Bürger claimed it followed the tradition of Velazquez and Goya.

More artists and students were arriving and Cézanne and Degas joined them and contributed to their lively discussion. Cézanne told them of his encounter with Antonio and this provided an hour's entertainment while the whole story was related by Manet to the rapt audience. Charles bought them all drinks followed by several other patrons who were intent on hearing the full story.

Around 9 p.m. Fauré arrived and Charles detached himself from the group and went to greet him and buy him a drink. They settled at a quiet table for two in the bar and chatted about music for an hour. Fauré sought his opinion about his career and it appeared he was missing the buzz of Paris now he was teaching in Brittany, but he admitted he needed a job as composing, like painting, does not pay the bills.

Charles soothed Fauré, telling him to be patient – he was only 23 now. He compared composers to artists, whose work was never respected until after their death.

'Use your time in Brittany to compose. You do have the school holidays to return to Paris to do other projects to keep you in the public eye.'

Fauré reflected, 'I intend to write a Requiem which will be very different from anything we have heard before. I want it to be joyous, not morbid; if you are going to meet your maker then it should be a beautiful experience, not horrendous.'

Charles laughed. 'But I suppose it depends whether St. Peter allows you through the gates of heaven or condemns you to hell?'

'I don't believe there is such a place as hell. I think we are already living in hell and when we die there is only heaven. I believe in the afterlife too and that some spirits do come back.'

'Be careful you keep these views to yourself Fauré; the Catholic Church would not be pleased to hear such opinions from a principal organist, teacher and composer. Remember, you rely on them to make a living and one careless opinion could cause your downfall. Personally, I have serious doubts about some of the teachings of the Catholic Church but I don't voice them in public.'

'I am well aware of that Charles, but I know I can trust you with my innermost thoughts. I am going to compose a Requiem in the same romantic composition as you artists do.'

'Well, I can't wait to hear it then, get on with it!'

'Do you think I would get away with writing it in French instead of Latin?'

Charles laughed. 'No, probably not. Look what wrath and derision Manet faced when he painted two nudes in his *The Luncheon on the Grass*. That may be a step too far and you don't want to alienate your audience. Remember writers, composers and artists are the real historians; we document the present and then will be judged in the future.'

'I see your point, perhaps one day Manet's nude painting will be revered throughout the world.'

'I believe Manet is an outstanding artist and I think the artists of today, working in Paris, are the best the world will ever see. The talent here will, over the next twenty years, far exceed that of the Italian Renaissance period. That is why I am honoured to be representing them at the Arts' Ball.'

'How does Marie feel about the ball?'

'She is both excited and nervous. I have ensured she will be the belle of the ball and there is no doubt that Napoleon will be delighted with her. I just hope he behaves; she won't have him compromise her.'

'She has a beautiful voice, Charles. She sang Bruckner's 'Ave Maria' at your wedding, perfectly. I have been commissioned to direct some Christmas concerts at Notre Dame. Do you think she will agree to be a soprano soloist for me?'

'By all means ask her. I have suggested she join the Conservatoire choir already but she wants to make sure my studio is running well before she commits time to other projects. However, I have already given her another role, which may take up some of her valuable time.'

'Oh Charles, is she with child already? Congratulations! I didn't get the impression you were into children; not many artists are.'

'I confess until Marie came along I had never contemplated being a father but she has opened up my life so much and suddenly I was consumed by the desire to become a father. I suppose that was what God intended for us, but I assure you I approach it with some trepidation. Keep this to yourself for a while until the pregnancy is established – you know the risks involved in pregnancy.'

'You will make a great father. You have endless patience with your art students… something I find difficult with my music students.'

'Don't worry, Fauré. Wisdom increases with age and you will become more tolerant of their weaknesses.'

Manet approached and asked him if he wanted to accompany him home. He declined to stay the night at Manet's as he wanted to get back to Marie, but he walked back with him and then took a hansom cab home.

Marie stirred when he entered the bedroom and he tried to be as quiet as possible. He slipped into bed beside her and he thought he had not disturbed her until suddenly she put her arms around him and said,

'Ah, my errant husband returns smelling of wine and cigar smoke.'

'Well at least it proves I have been out drinking in male company, not in another lady's boudoir.'

Marie quickly grabbed him round the throat and said, 'Don't even say that in jest, my husband, or I will kill you. Make passionate love to me Charles, but don't force me out of bed or I will be violently sick.'

Charles was overjoyed at her request and delighted that pregnancy was increasing her sexual appetite, despite her sickness. He couldn't quite believe his luck and ensured that he performed to the best of his ability – and judging by the avid response from Marie, it met with her approval.

23

The next morning, Charles woke early before Marie and planned his painting of their wedding day. He had brought the entire equipment home earlier in the week and he laid thinking of the best position to set up the self-portrait. He decided to use the chaise longue in their bedroom and have Marie lying down and he would kneel down behind the chaise longue, gather her into his arms and then kiss her. As only his upper body would be visible he could get away with only wearing his jacket and shirt from the wedding day. Marie's bouquet was still available but he would have to recreate the flowers, either from memory or lithograph.

Marie stirred beside him and she touched his face and ran her fingers through his hair. He leant on his elbow and traced the features of her face and said,

'Now, my angel, are you ready to recreate our wedding day on canvas?'

'I daren't put my wedding dress on until I am certain I have finished with my morning sickness; you will have to be very patient with me.'

'Don't worry, you can have a bucket next to the

chaise longue. I am going to paint it here in the bedroom. Shall I go and bring some breakfast up here for us while you take your first steps and see how you feel? You were magnificent last night; I was not expecting such a welcome home. Pregnancy seems to be improving your sex drive rather than reducing it.'

She gave him one of her stern looks. 'Don't count on it lasting for nine months; it may be that I decide to banish you from my bed long before the birth.'

'You seemed to miss me in just a few hours Madame, I don't think you want to sleep alone.'

He fetched her wrap and put on his own then made sure the bucket was within arm's reach and went downstairs to the kitchen. It was the weekend so no servants were in attendance, so he could make their breakfast in peace. He knew Marie wouldn't be able to manage more than fruit and dry bread but he put some cheese on her plate. He made some fried bacon and eggs for himself and then went back upstairs with a laden tray.

Marie had made it to the bathroom and for the first time had not been sick, however when he came into the room and the smell of the bacon reached her, she ran straight back. He settled down to eat his cooked breakfast with lashings of croissants and butter and a steaming mug of black coffee. When Marie returned she ate some cherries and chopped up an apple and sipped the hot black coffee.

'Who did you meet last night in the Café Gerbois?'

'Well with it being a Friday night, many of the

artists were there. I managed to get my meal in peace and then Manet and Zola joined me for a while. Afterwards we went into the bar and amazingly, Monet was in with Pissaro so we discussed the Arts' Ball until Cézanne came in and joined us and mentioned Antonio's trials as his student for the day. This resulted in the full tale being told to everyone in the bar and caused much amusement with the other artists. Several praised Antonio for his daring but Antonio was probably unaware of how bad Cézanne's temper can be. Thankfully, he seemed to find the whole thing highly amusing but he did say he could never teach anyone as he would end up killing them.

Then Fauré appeared and we moved somewhere quieter and had a chat. He seems to be missing the cultural life of Paris at his teaching post in Brittany and was asking my advice about his future. He is only 23 and desperate to stamp his name in lights. He told me he was going to compose a Requiem in the style of a romantic painting and suggested he might do it in French rather than Latin. I suggested he leave well alone if he wanted it to become as famous as Mozart's. He asked if you would be willing to sing in some concerts he is directing at Notre Dame before Christmas?'

'I would love to, provided I am not still feeling this sick.'

'He will be at the ball so you can tell him then; I might even let you have a dance with him.'

'Fauré is an attractive young man, Charles. I have to admit he is good looking, dashing and not unlike you in many ways. He has so much energy and loves his work. I would be honoured to sing for him or even better, sing with him; he has a beautiful tenor voice too.'

'Did you think I hadn't noticed that Fauré was enamoured with you?'

'Charles, there was nothing in it just a mutual appreciation of each other's talents. Don't feel insecure; we are just good friends and will never be more.'

She went to the wardrobe and found her wedding dress and turned back to him. 'You will have to help me with the sash and my hair.'

'Of course my dear, with pleasure.'

He undid the bodice of her nightgown and let it fall to the floor. She was directly in front of a full length mirror hung on the wall. He moved her closer to the mirror and then turned her in profile, standing behind her.

'What an exquisite body you have, ma cherie.' He ran his hands down her stomach and remarked, 'And here we have the first hint of our baby. There is just the slightest touch of a tiny increase in your waistline and breasts. He knelt in front of her and put his arms round her waist and kissed her stomach.

'I am going to enjoy watching your body change week by week.'

Marie retorted, 'Well you might but I am not! I

already feel like one of your father's brood mares!'

Charles chuckled and said, 'Now let's get your basque, drawers and chemise on before you catch cold.'

He dressed her gently and carefully and proved to her that she had increased slightly in waist size as he could not do the basque up in the same hole as he had six weeks ago. He also had to release the chemise ribbons slightly over her breasts. With all the movement, she suddenly felt sick but he had made sure the bucket was in reach. He made her sit down and recover for a few moments before he placed the dress over her head. He then made her sit at the dressing table while he brushed through her hair and recreated the hairstyle she had worn on the day, including fresh roses in her hair. He adjusted the red shawl and then led her over to the chaise longue where he had set up his easel and placed a mirror against the wall.

'Now all you have to do is lie back on the chaise longue and relax.' He moved behind it, knelt down and then gathered her into his arms and using his right hand to prop her up, placed his left hand trailing lightly over her left breast, bent down and kissed her gently on the lips. He could see the overall effect in the mirror and after he had kissed her they both looked at the mirror image. She put her right hand round his neck, drawing him closer to her.

'Do you think it may be considered inappropriate to be kissing?'

'Surely on her wedding day a man can kiss his wife? You're not naked, much as I would like you to be… now that would be considered shocking!'

He went to his easel and started sketching the outline of her shape on the canvas, which he had already painted entirely black. Any colour would be laid over the black canvas. After he had outlined her body he went back to her to start drawing himself into the frame from the reflection in the mirror. This required huge concentration as his brain had to convert the mirror image correctly.

He bent down and resumed his position and as he started kissing her she responded ardently.

She whispered in his ear, 'Make love to me, darling!'

'What! You are in your wedding dress and supposed to be feeling sick! I am not disturbing the dress or your hair now.'

She countered, 'But you have only a shirt and drawers on under your wrap and if you move round to the front you will only have to lift my skirt up and remove my drawers.'

'Marie, you are such a temptress. You're supposed to be an artist and appreciate how difficult it is to get a portrait right, instead of encouraging me to ravish you. What if all my sitters behaved in such a seductive way?'

She laughed and said, 'I would have to kill them all one by one and take a knife to your precious tool.' She forced his head down to kiss her again and he kissed her passionately.

'You dare be sick over me, or this dress and I will thrash you severely.'

He moved round to the front of the chaise longue, undid his wrap and drawers and then pulled her into a sitting position and carefully pulled the dress up to her waist, pulled her drawers down and did as she asked.

After a few moments of wild passion, once the storm had passed, she said, 'You see? You can't resist my body, can you?'

'No never, my darling. you are too beautiful to resist. No man could leave you unfulfilled. But please behave now and let me get on with the drawing or I will never get it finished.'

'Oh Charles, I do love you. I never thought you had this erotic, passionate side to your nature. I thought you were far too serious and proper to be so uninhibited.'

'Well Madame, I thought I had stolen a beautiful Russian princess for my bride, not knowing that you were really Jezebel in disguise. Imagine what your mother would have to say about your behaviour if she could see you now.'

'My mother is not the perfect French lady you think, Charles. Where do you think my selfish independent streak comes from? It is certainly not my father.'

He decided not to pursue this conversation any further as there was obviously something in his mother-in-law's past that Marie was aware of, but now was not the right time to pursue it.

He returned to his easel and concentrated on painting the dress, ensuring every fold of the sleeves of the silk dress was correct and that her arm showed through the silk. As the picture was in close up, he really only had the bodice to do. However, getting the position of the red silk shawl correct was quite a task as in places, the white dress showed through the folds of the shawl.

Marie enquired how he proposed to draw his own figure into the frame. Thankfully, over the years he had acquired a photographic memory and he could fix the picture in his mind and then reproduce it in graphic detail. This had been essential when he was learning to draw moving horses. Capturing the position of every leg whilst a horse was moving was required. He could tell in seconds whether a painter understood the movement of a horse, when he observed their work. In gallop there was a point when the horse was suspended in mid-air and then only had one foot on the ground followed by three feet in the next sequence of movement. So many artists got this wrong when drawing horses. Just as many tried to draw the horse by standing opposite the centre point of the horse, and failed to get the correct picture as the only way to draw them in true form was to stand level with the hip bone to get the correct balance.

They had a break at around 1 p.m. and thankfully,

Marie's sickness had eased off. He went and made them some meat, bread and coffee and brought it back up to the bedroom as he did not want Marie to get her dress dirty.

oOo

The next day at around 5 p.m. when all his students had left except Antonio and Marie was working on the accounts, Manet appeared.

'What brings you to my door today?' said Charles.

'I appear to have been appointed Hermes the messenger and have news for you. I have had a letter from the Duchess de Beauchamp informing us that there will be deer hunting on the Saturday morning when we go next week.'

Marie replied with delight. 'Oh, how wonderful. I haven't been hunting for so long; it will be wonderful to get out in the fresh air for a few hours.'

Charles hesitated. 'But Marie, the Duchess won't be riding as she must be nearly five months pregnant by now and her sister-in-law is an invalid, so perhaps they only intend for the men to hunt.'

Marie shouted, 'Charles, you said you would not ban me from riding and I am not missing a day's sport just to stay behind with the ladies.'

Charles reflected, knowing that a compromise was going to have to be made as she was determined to partake in the sport.

'Marie, I meant riding from A to B, not hunting. You know the risks involved; your horse only has to trip in a rabbit hole and fall. I know you are a competent rider but look what happened to Manet only a few months ago. It was another horse that shied and cannoned into his and pushed it over the cliff. Even you could not have stopped that; it happened in seconds.'

Manet chuckled. 'Oh dear, has Hermes caused the first Duran marital row?'

Charles turned on him. 'No, this is just a slight differing of opinions and we have to find a compromise to ensure the safety of our child.'

Suddenly, Antonio appeared from behind his canvas and ran towards them. 'Does this mean Madame is with child? Are we going to have a baby in the studio? Oh well done, Charles. I thought you weren't interested in sex anymore.'

Manet surveyed Charles's face with his mouth wide open, and the look of shock on Marie's face, and roared with laughter.

Charles grabbed Antonio by the collar and shouted, 'Just what exactly did you mean with that remark, you little Italian rat?'

Antonio's face was a picture when he realised exactly what he had implied.

'No sir, I didn't mean anything wrong but I haven't seen you show any interest in a woman for a long time.'

Manet fell about laughing. 'Well Marie, you heard it from the apprentice's own big mouth. You can rest assured that your fiancé behaved impeccably during your long betrothal.'

Marie was laughing too at Charles's fury and poor Antonio's predicament.

Charles shouted at Antonio. 'There will be no babies in my studio; it is a place of work not a nursery!'

Antonio replied, 'But sir, you know how I love to paint cherubs and I could learn such a lot by painting your beautiful son or daughter.'

Charles sighed in frustration. 'Antonio, don't you have a lot of paint brushes to wash up in the kitchen? Keep your big mouth shut about a baby until Marie gets further into the pregnancy.'

Antonio shot off at speed towards the kitchen and then had to run back to collect all the paint brushes, which caused Manet to collapse into laughter yet again.

Charles addressed Marie. 'Sweetheart, I don't want to argue with you over the hunting but I must insist on two conditions if you wish to do so. You must promise me you will not take any unnecessary risks and you will ride Merlin, who I know I can trust to take care of you. I don't want you riding an unknown horse.'

Marie ran and kissed him. 'Oh yes, Charles. I promise to be careful!'

Manet clapped. 'Bravo Charles, a brilliant compromise; you should have become a politician, not an artist. You could hardly deny Diana, the goddess of hunting, her role. However, Hermes has not imparted all his news yet. I still have more.'

Charles retorted, 'Well, it had better not cause as much controversy as the last piece of news did.'

Manet replied, 'I hope not but I have had a letter from *Le Figaro* asking if they can interview you, Marie, Monet and me before the Arts' Ball. Apparently, they want to interview all the principal guests to do a full feature after the ball. They are organising a suite at the Hotel de Ville and they want to take informal pictures of us as well.'

Charles replied, 'We would have to be very careful with that we said as these journalists have a habit of twisting words. If we said anything derogatory about the government or another artist, we could be in trouble. We would have to tread carefully on the subject of the Salon de Refusés as if we offend the judges of the Paris Salon, we could be ostracised for life.'

Manet replied, 'I see what you mean but I think this is more intended to be about our personal lifestyles rather than a political article. I don't think we can refuse as that may offend the Emperor. I will collar Monet next week but in the meantime I had better reply in the affirmative.'

Marie said, 'Oh, I hope it won't be first thing in the morning when I feel so sick. What on earth am I going to wear? It will have to be fashionable.'

Charles replied, 'I am sure Charles Worth will have something perfect that you can make a statement in. Just remember to tell the press that your ball gown is from his salon as well as the daywear.'

24

They departed for the Duchess's chateau after lunch on Friday, by carriage as they had Manet to pick up as well. Marie was extremely grateful that her morning sickness had not been as bad that morning as she had been concerned that the rocking carriage would make her sick. To be on the safe side, a bucket was hidden under the seat. They drove into Montmartre to collect Manet, who was packed and waiting for them.

After about an hour's drive to the west of the city, deep in the countryside, they drove through the gates of Château Nemois and could not even see the house when entering the gates. The drive was very long, winding through pristine fields with young horses grazing contentedly. At their first glimpse of the chateau, Marie gasped and proclaimed how beautiful it was. As their carriage pulled up, grooms appeared from nowhere to attend to the horses. The head of staff had the door open before they had alighted from the carriage and servants unpacked their luggage from the carriage.

The Duchess appeared in the doorway and

welcomed them to the chateau. Manet introduced Charles and Marie and then they were escorted into the main salon. Awaiting them were the new Duc and Duchesse de Beauchamp, having succeeded to the title on the death of his brother. Gilles André Beauchamp was tall, around 30, dark-haired and very good looking but had none of the arrogance or haughtiness of his brother. He welcomed both Manet and Charles with genuine warmth and admitted he was an art lover and was delighted to meet them. There was no animosity towards Charles, especially considering he had been his brother's killer. He was genuinely struck by Marie's beauty, as Charles thought he paused a fraction too long over kissing her hand, but then most men were taken aback by his wife's beauty so he could not blame him for that. Gilles was protective and courteous towards his sister-in-law Angelique, and they were obviously very close. Angelique was showing her pregnancy now but looked healthy and happy.

His wife Sylvie Amelie was in her late 20's, blonde, pretty but very thin and although she greeted them standing, she soon had to sit down. The ravages of tuberculosis were evident through her body but despite this she was cheerful and animated.

Gilles said, 'I want you to know that I had no idea of the problems Angelique was encountering with my brother. He was a very difficult person to understand and I was devastated when I found out. I don't have any issues with you for what you did;

my brother deserved his fate as he was obviously not of sound mind to do what he did. We were very different people and I can assure you that Angelique's future welfare is my top priority.'

Angelique replied, 'Gilles and Sylvie have been incredibly supportive of me since Jean-Paul's death. Until we know the sex of the baby we cannot make future plans but I do not fear being homeless, should I have a daughter, as Gilles has assured me he will support me financially should I wish to move away and set up my own home.'

Charles replied, 'I am delighted to hear that Madame, as none of this was your fault and to be widowed at such a young age in such circumstances must have been extremely difficult.'

Angelique replied, 'Now that I have had time to come to terms with it I have realised that I should look at the situation positively and it allows me the freedom to choose my future.'

Marie said, 'But you are so young, surely you will remarry in the future?'

She responded, 'At this stage Marie, I really cannot envisage ever wanting to marry again, but who knows what the future holds and what God has planned for us? Now I should be apologising to you for spoiling your wedding. I would have been devastated had your husband died defending me.'

Marie replied, 'Oh don't worry Madame, both Charles and Edouard suffered at my hands for their stupidity. I was so angry when I reached Charles that

I hit him and knocked him out and Edouard had the imprint of my hand across his face for quite some time. Neither of them went unpunished, I can assure you.'

Gilles said, 'It appears you have quite a temper, Madame. I would not wish to get on the wrong side of you in battle.'

Charles laughed. 'Her brother serves in the hussars and I suggested he take her back with him to his barracks after the wedding, as she would be a formidable adversary in battle, especially with her riding skills.'

Gilles said, 'Do you have a passion for horses then, Marie? I share it too. I inherited my father's racehorse stud and have had some success on the track too. I also breed a few hunters for sport. I shall look forward to seeing you out tomorrow.'

Marie's face lit up. 'Sir, I was reared in Russia and spent my childhood with horses and have a deep understanding of them. Charles's father also breeds horses in Lille and we spent our honeymoon there. I was delighted to receive your invitation to go hunting and have been looking forward to it.'

Servants appeared with afternoon tea and they sat down to partake. Charles was fascinated by a portrait of a former family member that was hanging over the vast fireplace and went to look closely at it, followed by Manet. Gilles followed them.

'Do you like my great grandfather's portrait on horseback, Charles?'

Charles replied, 'It is a beautiful work but there is no signature. Who painted it?'

Gilles said, 'I really don't know but I can soon find out; my father and grandfather built up an extensive art collection which includes works by Botticelli, Raphael, Titian, Rubens, Goya, Delacroix and Fragonard.'

Charles and Manet gasped in surprise and Charles stuttered, 'What, here in the house you have paintings by all of them?'

Gilles laughed at their faces and replied, 'Yes, I suppose you would like to see them. The majority are in the ballroom but the masters hang on the stairs to the first floor and along the gallery so nobody can easily remove them. Do you think your wife would like to see them or would she prefer to stay with the ladies?'

Charles responded, 'My wife is an artist herself, Gilles and she would be furious if she was excluded.'

Gilles led them out into the corridor towards the main hall. The limestone-clad hall had a double sweeping staircase leading to a first floor landing. They climbed the left-hand staircase and halfway up hung a portrait by Fragonard of a young girl, reading. At the top of the stairs was a painting by Delacroix, of an Arab saddling his horse. On the landing, the centrepiece was Rubens – *Daniel in the Lion's Den* – and on either side was Botticelli's *Portrait of a Young Woman* and Raphael's *Madonna of the Meadow*. On the right-hand side at the top of the stairs, hung Goya's *Woman with a Fan* and six feet lower down the stairs hung Goya's *Maria Teresa de Vallabriga on horseback.* At the bottom of the stairs hung Titian's *Man with a Glove.* They studied each painting in turn. Marie's favourite was Fragonard's, Charles loved the Goya horse portrait and Manet favoured Titian's *Man with a Glove.*

They moved on to the ballroom, which had family portraits on most of the high walls and ceiling frescoes as well. Some artwork by Gilles's grandfather was also hung on one of the walls. Charles begged Gilles to leave him and Manet to study them for a while and escort Marie back to the ladies.

Gilles was delighted to have the opportunity to talk to Marie alone and he showed her the stables from a first floor window and promised to give her a tour.

He said, 'Madame Duran, what were your parents doing in Russia if you were born there?'

'Both Henri and I were born in Russia as my father held the post of Director of Music in St. Petersburg. My parents were not aristocracy so I have no royal heritage. I was educated in Russia and can speak Russian, Italian, English and Spanish and I studied music courtesy of my father and can play the violin and piano. I also studied ballet, singing and art but my first love has always been horses and dogs. In Russia I was able to hunt deer, wild boar and bears and I loved it. The landscape in Russia is very open and you can ride for miles without seeing any signs of civilisation. Unfortunately, it is extremely cold in the winter but then you get around on sleighs wrapped up in layers of furs.'

'It sounds an idyllic childhood for a young lady. So where did you meet your husband?'

'I came back to France when I was 17 and my brother was 21. My parents commissioned Charles to paint portraits of both of us and after only a week I was head over heels in love with him. I persuaded my father to let him paint me on horseback as he had Henri, rather than a posed indoor portrait, and I was smitten. We had organised a ball to celebrate Henri's birthday and with a little gentle pushing, Charles asked me to marry him at the ball. We never thought my parents would consent because they had high hopes of a wealthy marriage for me and Charles thought they would not consider him a suitable match.'

Gilles said, 'I could well understand that, Marie. You could have married into any of the European royal families with your stunning looks and charm. Do you find the life of an artist's wife to your liking when you could have been a princess?'

'Oh, yes – Charles is a wonderful husband and you must remember I am an artist too. I specialise in miniatures and I do pastel work too. However, my husband teaches and has several fulltime students so I help him organise the workload and keep the finances in order.'

They returned to the salon to find that Sylvie

had retired for a rest before dinner so Gilles excused himself and left Marie and Angelique alone. Angelique guided Marie to a large sofa and they sat together.

'Marie, I do really apologise for what happened. You could have lost your new husband in such tragic circumstances.'

'Oh, I know but thankfully, God protected him and we did not lose each other. It made us both realise how much we loved each other and that night we had the most exhilarating union. It was possible that I conceived then and I am in the first few weeks of pregnancy now. I have been sick daily for the last two weeks.'

'I am so pleased for you both. Are you looking forward to the birth?'

'I can't say I am relishing the thought of losing my figure, or the birth, and I really am not the maternal sort and neither was my mother so I am worried about how I will cope with the responsibility of a child. Charles will not contemplate me having a wet nurse so it will rather impede my work in his studio.'

'Marie, the sickness should settle down soon and your figure will bounce back after the birth, regardless of you breastfeeding.'

'Angelique, can I ask you what sex you think the baby is and what you intend to do afterwards?'

'I really am unsure, Marie. In many ways having a daughter would be easier as that would leave Gilles as Duc anyway and I could make my own life. If I have a boy then he will become the Duc and my place will be here by his side but that makes things very complicated for Gilles and it doesn't look as if he and Sylvie will be able to have their own children. I am a little worried that a boy may have more of his father's character and I am not quite sure I would be able to deal with that.'

'Oh yes, I can completely understand your concerns on that score. I really don't know how you cope so well with the prospect of being alone and raising a child.'

'But I don't need to rear it alone as Gilles and Sylvie will be here to help me. It's only if I decide I want to move away, and even then I can go and live at one of the other properties. We are leaving for Spain this week where we have a Spanish villa near Cadiz on the Atlantic Coast, as Sylvie cannot cope with harsh winter weather.'

'It must be really difficult for you, as you and I are at opposite ends of the spectrum when it comes to sex lives. I have only ever known intense pleasure from Charles, whereas you endured intense pain.'

'The worst aspect of it Marie, was that in order to have sex at all Jean-Paul had to resort to sadistic violence to be able to perform, which made it even worse. He should never have married me but he thought he could overcome his homosexual leanings in an effort to produce an heir, but in reality he could not do it.'

'Angelique, I can fully understand why you would

never wish to have a relationship again but it seems such a dreadful shame that you should remain alone for the rest of your life. Believe me, not all men are like him I am sure you will meet a good man who will love and support you and your child. Please do not dismiss the idea completely.'

Manet and Charles returned to the salon, exhilarated by their chance to study the paintings in the gallery together. They all went to change for dinner and Marie managed a short nap while Charles was having a bath. They enjoyed a wonderful dinner with the family and afterwards, the men retired to the library.

After looking around the bookshelves and admiring some more paintings they settled down in comfortable armchairs with their port. Gilles asked if Manet would truthfully tell him exactly what happened between him and Angelique as he had not felt able to tackle her on the subject. Manet described the state she had been in when she had revealed her body to him. Gilles visibly flinched as Manet described the sword mark on her hip and the bites on her body. Charles asked whether he had known of his brother's homosexuality and he had said he had suspected it but they had never been very close as they were so completely opposite in character. He knew that Jean-Luc had a sadistic streak in him as he had witnessed episodes of cruelty with animals that had appalled him and once, when he had tried to intervene, his brother had nearly killed him with a sword. He blamed himself for not being there for Angelique when she had married Jean-Paul and moved in. He explained that during the breeding season he slept up at the stables so he would be on call for the mares' foaling. Sylvie had a nurse available in the next room should she need anything during the night and he had moved up to the stables rather than frequently disturb her. However, Jean-Paul's rooms where at the opposite side of the building to his and even if he had been there he would not necessarily have been aware of what was going on. He could not understand why Jean-Paul had been so cruel to Angelique but Manet said he thought it might have been the only way Jean-Paul could perform – by inflicting pain.

Gilles asked Charles if he had known about Angelique's physical state when he fought the duel. He confirmed Manet had not told him until afterwards and to be fair, although Manet proclaimed his innocence, he had wondered whether he had been lying as this was not the first duel Manet had been involved in for his indiscretion with another man's wife. Gilles suggested that Jean-Paul's refusal to wait until Manet was fit to fight him had been because he wanted to end his own life.

They discussed the options for Angelique, dependent on her producing a boy or girl. Gilles seemed adamant that he wanted her to remain part of the family regardless of the sex of the child. She would be free to do whatever she wished but he appreciated that if she had a boy, it would make moving away difficult. Gilles told them they were going to their villa in Cadiz for the winter months but would be back in March to ensure the child was born in France. Sylvie could not cope with extreme cold weather and it was vital for her health that she was living in a warm climate.

Gilles outlined the plans for deer hunting the next day and said that some of the hunt members would be joining them for dinner in the evening. Charles asked that Marie ride Merlin and explained that she was pregnant and he wanted to ensure her safety. Gilles was disappointed as he had intended to put Marie on one of his hunter stallions but he fully appreciated Charles's good intentions.

25

Charles woke early the next morning as the sun was streaming through the window and shining directly on his face. Marie was strewn across the bed but still in a deep sleep as he carefully extracted himself from the bed. He visited the bathroom and then put on his breeches and white shirt and left the bedroom. The call of the gallery, with its exquisite paintings, was tempting him to go and study them further.

His room was not far from the central gallery and the sun was streaming in through the tall windows and highlighting some of the canvasses. He compared the two horses painted by Goya and Delacroix and concluded that Delacroix's was the most accurate. He had met Delacroix a few times but as he was considerably older than him, had not been part of his intimate circle. He admired his technique and awareness of light although Goya had the edge as he had studied Velazquez and the light on the face of the girl was exquisite. He then spent some time dissecting the Botticelli portrait and had to admit it was very good. Ruben's *Daniel in the Lion's Den* was so accurate he felt like he could walk into the scene on the canvas. Titian's *Man with a Glove* gave him an idea to try this concept with a woman, using the symbolic language of the glove to portray the image. A similar statement was made by Goya in his *Woman with a Fan.*

He was sat at the top of the stairs when Gilles came up, having been across to the stables as he was dressed in his breeches.

'I am delighted my paintings are giving you such pleasure, Charles.'

Charles replied, 'Well as they are in your private collection it is so nice to be able to examine them so closely – otherwise I would never have seen them in the flesh.'

'I imagine you examine them like I do my horses and your ultimate aim is to produce perfection.'

Gilles moved on to his private rooms and Charles reluctantly went back to his room to find Marie just stirring in bed. He knelt down and gently kissed her cheek.

As she opened her eyes she noted he was dressed and said, 'I don't think you will have been down to the stables yet but I suspect you have been examining the paintings in the gallery.'

'Of course I have, darling. It's not often I get the chance to study such celebrated artists' work. Now you had better get moving and see whether you are going to be afflicted with sickness. Do you think you can manage breakfast downstairs or will the smell be too offensive?'

Marie replied, 'It really would be rude to miss breakfast and I am going to have to eat something before riding so I will try but I won't put on my riding habit until afterwards.'

He pulled back the covers and helped her stand up and she went slowly to the bathroom. He thought he had better keep close to her while out hunting in case she had a dizzy spell or worse, was sick. He finished dressing and put his riding jacket on and then Marie came back and put a simple day dress on to go down.

Marie forced herself to eat some breakfast as she knew she would need the energy to keep going out hunting – she didn't want to have to cut short her participation.

She ran back upstairs to change into her habit and Charles went with her to put his leather boots on and help Marie with hers as bending down would not help her nausea. She was wearing the same black velvet habit she had worn when he had painted her; she looked stunning. He dressed and pinned her hair up to go under her top hat and he selected a red carnation from a vase of flowers in the room and pinned it in the buttonhole of her fitted jacket.

'My darling, you look so beautiful. Please be careful today and stay with me. Do not go chasing after hounds jumping walls you cannot see over.'

She kissed his cheek and replied, 'Don't worry, my darling. I will not put our baby at risk.'

They went down to the hall where Manet and

Gilles were ready and waiting. As they came down the stairs, Charles saw the gasp of admiration Gilles gave when he saw Marie. They could hear the horses approaching and the footman opened the double doors and outside, grooms were holding their horses. Gilles' horse was a stunning, young, black middleweight stallion with a white blaze down the length of his nose and he was alert and on his toes. Charles and Manet had two older bay geldings with a large amount of Thoroughbred blood in them.

A groom ushered Marie towards Merlin who was beautifully turned out and carrying her own side saddle. The groom cupped his hand and legged her up and even Merlin knew something exciting was about to happen. Then they heard the sound of horses and hounds approaching up the drive and the excitement caused Gilles's stallion to half rear and Manet's horse to pirouette and buck. Both of them were soon back under control although the stallion was shivering in excitement and starting to sweat.

Servants appeared and soon the whole group was sipping brandy in the traditional stirrup cup. Charles's horse was slightly unnerved when hounds came too close, but did nothing wrong. Merlin stood as solid as a rock, surveying the scene calmly, for which Charles was thankful. In total there were about thirty riders and hunt servants and Charles was pleased to see that two of Gilles's grooms were mounting up to accompany them. They would be useful if anything went wrong or if Marie became ill. They set off back down the drive at a slow trot and this gave Charles a chance to study his horse. He was very well schooled and responded to both his leg and hand. He did not pull or try to overtake any of the other horses and yet he could feel the power and speed beneath him. Manet's horse was a little overexcited and raring to go but he was more than capable of coping. Gilles's stallion was beautiful and had such light movement and although anxious to canter, obeyed his master and stayed in trot.

They went across the grassland acres of the chateau and within minutes, hounds had picked up a trail and were off. The huntsman followed and when they flew into canter, Gilles's stallion gave several bucks of glee. Merlin behaved beautifully, sensing he was intended to look after his mistress, who was behaving and keeping him back. They approached hunt hedges, which had been carefully cut to a height of approximately four feet to ensure there were no protruding branches. They were now at full gallop and Gilles was in danger of overriding the master so he turned away from the hedge and made his horse drop back and he lined up with Marie to take the hedge. They jumped it together and Gilles was obviously impressed with Marie's style and finesse riding side-saddle. Charles's horse gave an enthusiastic leap over the hedge but it did not unseat him. Manet's horse bucked on landing and attempted to snatch the reins and take off but he was more than ready for him and had him back under control in seconds.

They must have jumped over six hedges and hounds were at least two fields in front of them when the stag veered into a wood for cover. This required them all to slow down and gave the horses the opportunity to catch their breath. They halted while the hounds searched. Charles got close to Marie and he could see by her bright red cheeks and flashing blue eyes that she was enjoying every minute of it.

Soon, the hounds had flushed the stag out of cover but he headed deeper into the wood for safety. This meant they would have to follow at a trot and the track only allowed two horses' width. Charles made sure he stayed close to Marie, and Gilles had to settle for riding next to Manet. Within fifteen minutes, hounds had cornered the stag at bay and the huntsman had despatched him.

They went back out of the wood and moved onto grassland. Hounds soon found another trail and they had another exhilarating hunt jumping fences, walls and ditches but there were no casualties. This impressed Charles as the going was fairly deep but nobody fell, even at the awkward ditches.

The field paused while hounds searched a wooded copse and Charles managed to get close to Marie and steal a quick kiss whilst out of sight behind some trees. However, when he looked back Gilles had not missed it. Manet was delighted with his horse, which had now calmed down but was still raring to go.

They finished for the day at around 2 p.m. and returned to the chateau for a cold buffet lunch accompanied by tureens of hot chicken soup and bread. Marie tucked in and was delighted she had not felt sick during the entire hunting experience. She had been the belle of the hunt as although there were some elegant ladies out, her beauty and riding ability exceeded them all. They went upstairs to change and his desire for her was intense, he could hardly get her undressed quickly enough.

Marie laughed and said, 'No gentle warm up from you today, my husband. You have obviously been anticipating this while we were out hunting!'

'I am sorry, darling. I just wanted you so badly! For two pins I would have taken you out in the field, I was so desperate.'

Marie roared with laughter. 'That would have caused a stir in front of the entire hunt.'

'I apologise profusely for my boorishness and will now take you with a little more gentility and decorum.' He covered her mouth in kisses and then moved down her body, very slowly kissing her gently all the way down.

After their second passionate encounter Marie fell asleep and he decided he had better make an appearance or the family would think they were impolite.

He found them in the salon and apologised for Marie's absence by explaining the fresh air and excitement had overwhelmed her and she just needed to take a short nap before dinner.

Gilles commented, 'Marie was outstanding today. She has natural empathy with her horse and is an accomplished rider.'

Charles replied, 'There is no doubt that she is happiest when in the saddle and she loves the thrill of the chase. In Russia she went bear hunting and that must have been even more exciting.'

Manet said, 'Gilles, that horse I rode was outstanding. He had all the speed and stamina to stay all day and never pulled for his head or forgot his manners.'

Gilles replied, 'Well I do introduce the hunters carefully to their job and ride them all on their first outing if I can. If you instil manners and confidence in them at their first attempt, they generally behave. Some can find it very exciting and go off the rails after they have been a few times because they get overexcited, but I do not let them forget their manners. I try to get the right balance of Thoroughbred blood without getting them too sharp and fast. A pure Thoroughbred would be too hot and fast to hunt as he would just be wanting to race the whole time.'

oOo

They had a wonderful weekend at the chateau and on Sunday morning before they left, Gilles gave them a tour of the stables. The three stallion's quarters were very impressive and positioned away from the busy yard. The stables had limestone walls and the floors were covered in terracotta tiles and measured twenty feet square… and at the back there was a door leading to a small grass paddock that was fenced up to ten feet in height. This meant the three neighbouring stallions could see and sniff each other without any risk of them fighting. Marie was delighted with their palatial stables and all three of them recognised her empathy and knowledge and made a huge fuss of her.

oOo

Charles and Marie walked from the studio round to the Hotel de Ville for their press conference. She was wearing the navy blue and gold day dress that she had purchased from Worth, feeling slightly nervous about the questions she may be asked.

Monet and Manet were already there and enjoying their first drink. Manet greeted her with his usual kiss on both cheeks and Monet kissed her hand. She wandered off to the cloakroom to leave her cloak and noted yet again that she appeared to be the only woman in the room so far. The bottom half of the large salon had been set up as a background for some photographs and a large settee appeared to be the main prop. She made her way back to Charles and they were ushered down to the bottom of the room. They were put into the row behind the sofa, along with the writers' representatives. Marie was in the middle with Charles on one side and a writer on the other.

He turned to her, took her hand and said, 'Gustave Flaubert, writer at your service, Madame.'

Marie responded, 'Pleased to meet you. I am Marie Carolus-Duran, the artist's wife.'

They were then chivvied into line whilst the actors' representatives sorted out their seating order on the sofa. Marie noticed one very pretty woman but had no idea who she was.

After the group photo they were ushered into small groups with their own reporter. The art reporter asked various questions about how they saw the current state of art in Paris and each of them answered in turn. Charles said it was becoming the teaching centre of Europe now, rather than Italy. He praised the work of women artists, particularly Rosa Bonheur, who he claimed was the best painter of animals he had ever seen. She could produce anything from lions to birds in near perfect form. He also praised the American women who had trained there and had stayed on to work, in particular Mary Cassatt, whose studio was on the same street as his own.

Marie explained how women artists did not get the coverage they deserved as French society did not accept that being an artist was a suitable job for a woman. Women were only expected to paint for pleasure and stick to flowers, babies and watercolours to amuse themselves rather than as a money-making objective.

They all contributed to the discussion on the

latest painting form of "en plein air" and gave their own personal reasons for using it. Charles gave them the final word when he said,

'Love glory more than money, art more than glory and nature more than art.'

After the art reporter had finished, a young female journalist asked if she could do an interview with Marie to obtain more details about her background and work. Charles asked her whether she wanted him in attendance as he knew Marie was often outspoken and very honest. She declined his assistance and agreed to do the interview alone. However, she was well aware of the need for privacy. The young girl asked her about her background, time in Russia and how she had met Charles. She answered the questions carefully, ensuring she did not reveal anything that could be seized upon by the press. She did discuss her role as administrator and language tutor for the students who attended Charles's art classes and confirmed she did not intend to give up her work when babies came along. She was careful to give no hint of her current state of being *enceinte*. She explained that she was also an artist in her own right and was currently studying miniatures.

With the interview over, they were treated to a wonderful afternoon tea and they had the opportunity to meet some of the other principal guests at the ball. Manet introduced her to Émile Zola who she had been intrigued about for a while. Manet had told them about the many outrageous antics Zola had got up to and his criticism of the current Emperor – he had been amazed when the invitation had arrived.

26

Finally, the day of the ball dawned and Charles woke very early with an unusual nervous feeling, which he had only previously encountered on his wedding day. He thought it must be similar to Marie's morning sickness. Today was a hugely important day for him and he reminisced about his childhood. Who would have thought that the boy of 8 who used to sketch horses out in the field, would be dining with Napoleon III and his wife as a principal representative of the French art movement with his beautiful new wife at his side, tonight? He could not quite believe it himself but he knew that should he put one foot wrong, his career could be over in a flash. He offered a silent prayer that everything would go well and that he would not trip on the dance floor with Empress Eugenie… and that Marie would not slap the face of Napoleon III.

Marie stirred and he wrapped her in his arms and kissed her eyes, nose and mouth tenderly. She responded by running her hand through his thick black hair.

'Surely, you are not demanding my body at 6:30

a.m. on the morning of this special day?'

Charles laughed. 'You know very well I want your body any time of day or night. I still wake and cannot believe that you are by my side. I honestly never thought of marrying until I fell madly in love with you. What a transformation you have made to my introverted, secular life. Today is another huge step towards the future for both of us with you now carrying our child. What happiness you have brought me, Marie, over the last year; let's hope we can enjoy every year together so much.'

Marie kissed his face and licked away the tears of joy running down his cheeks.

'Oh Charles, you do say some wonderful words to me; there can't be many women who have husbands as devoted to them as I do.'

'No they probably won't have, as such endearments are usually told to their mistresses, not their wives.'

'As long as you don't think you will ever be allowed a mistress, Charles, I will ignore that comment. If you ever leave my bed and take another woman I will kill both of you.'

Charles laughed. 'I wouldn't dare because I know you are quite capable of carrying out your threat... but why would I leave the goddess Diana for another woman? You fulfil all my desires and more; I would never stray. Come on now, darling; let's arise. I will resist ravishing you so early – I don't want to make you feel sick.'

Marie went to the bathroom and had a quick wash.

She intended to have a bath at the Hôtel de Ville before she started dressing for the ball. She did feel excited and slightly concerned about the task before her. She would have to think before she spoke for fear of upsetting Napoleon, but she was becoming adept at dealing with amorous men who desired her and she could not envisage Napoleon misbehaving at such an important event.

At her final fitting for the ball, Worth had loaned her a beautiful green velvet cloak edged in ermine to wear on her way to the ball, which cleverly fastened low across her breasts to reveal the emerald and diamond necklace. He had given her shoes made from champagne silk and edged in green, with the toes encrusted in sequins. She had been wearing them around the house to make them comfortable for dancing. She had applied herself to the dancing instruction and the court etiquette session they had been given on how to address their Imperial Majesties. She and Charles had practised the different bows and curtsies required and she was looking forward to Napoleon leading her out on the dance floor and then bowing to her; she was expected to curtsey very low and not move until he took her hand and kissed it, and she had to keep her eyes down. She knew every eye in the room would be on her as well as on Charles bowing low to the Empress and kissing her hand. What a shame her mother would not be there to witness it.

When she returned to the bedroom, Charles was

half dressed but he led her over to the mirror and undid her nightgown and let it fall at her feet. He then turned her in profile to the mirror.

'Oh, darling, you look wonderful; your breasts have increased slightly in both size and shape and there is a small increase in your waist. Nobody but me will be able to tell you are *enceinte* yet, but I know and that's what matters most to me. I have produced a baby with the most beautiful woman I have ever laid eyes on and you are both mine. You have no idea how good it makes me feel to know that every man there tonight will covet you, but you are mine.' He pulled her into his arms and kissed her cheek then took a final look in the mirror and gave a long sigh.

oOo

They set off for the Hôtel de Ville by their own carriage at midday and they had packed an overnight case. Charles had sent his dress uniform to the cleaners and it would be delivered to the hotel. Marie's dress was being delivered by one of Worth's seamstresses and a hair stylist was booked for 5:00 p.m. As they arrived in the massive reception, it was full of people coming and going. Several guests had decided to stay there and they met Gabriel Fauré and Charles Gounod in reception. They were shown to their suite of rooms by the manager himself and they were both overwhelmed by the opulence of the rooms. They had a lounge, a bathroom with sunken bath, a dressing room and a large bedroom with mirrored walls.

Charles chuckled and said, 'Well my darling, you had better get some sleep this afternoon as you won't get much tonight, I can assure you. All those mirrors will give me the added pleasure of being able to see your body from every angle while I make passionate love to you.'

Marie blushed and murmured, 'Charles, you are wicked!'

He grabbed her and twirled her in a waltz around the bedroom and she laughed with glee.

They went back downstairs in search of a light lunch and Fauré insisted they join him and Gounod at their table. He took the opportunity to ask her to sing soprano solos in two of his Christmas concerts at Notre Dame. Marie agreed provided they sang a duet together and Fauré agreed to find the right song for them. He asked after her health and she told him that the morning sickness was decreasing slightly now and she would not be obviously pregnant in December. Charles Gounod congratulated them both on their happy news and commented on what beautiful children they would have.

More guests for the ball were arriving and Marie was slightly disappointed that she had to go to her room for an afternoon nap before tonight's big performance and she reluctantly left Charles in the reception chatting to other artists, writers and composers. She really would have liked the chance to talk to Émile Zola as he always defended the artists against criticism. He was another good-looking young man who had many female admirers. She could tell he was also rather smitten by her but as she went up the stairs she saw Manet wagging his finger at Zola and pointing out Charles, who was still talking to Gounod and Fauré.

Marie managed an hour's nap and then ran herself a frothy bath in the beautifully appointed bathroom. She then showered and washed her luxurious auburn hair. She put her chemise on under the wrap, as she would need help to put on the underwear for her dress, so she would wait until the dresser arrived. Promptly, the ball gown arrived, safely concealed in a black dress cover. The girl who brought it was called Marianne and she hung the dress in the bedroom while she helped Marie on with her basque, chemise, crinoline hoops, drawers and silk stockings in the dressing room.

Marie heard Charles come in and he shouted that he was going to get a bath and he had an enjoyable forty minutes splashing around and singing at the top of his voice – much to the amusement of both Marie and Marianne. Charles appeared in his wrap and went through to the dressing room to put on his uniform. The only way for Marie to get into the dress was to have it put over her head and she would never have managed it without the help of the dresser. Finally, it was all in place and the crinoline was hanging correctly, supporting the layers of champagne silk. Marianne put her shoes on for her and finally, she was fully dressed.

Charles came out from the dressing room at that moment and even he gasped at the figure before him.

'Oh, Marie, you look absolutely stunning and when your hair is done and the jewels are on you will look like a queen.'

As Marianne left the room, the hotel manager appeared with the jewellery. Charles took great pleasure in fastening the necklace around her neck. It had been slightly altered to make it sit perfectly on her collarbone, just above the rise of her breasts. Charles was tempted to ravish her there and then but there was another knock at the door and the hairdresser arrived. He left them at the dressing table and went into the dressing room to put his sword belt and sash on over his pristine, new, white silk shirt.

As Marie's hair was nearly complete, he stepped in and supervised the placing of the tiara to ensure it was visible, and helped with the pinning of her hair. Her abundant hair at the back was left in loose curls draping onto her shoulders and displayed her creamy complexion against the glittering emerald and diamond necklace, to full advantage.

The hairdresser left and they were finally alone and he turned to Marie and said, 'You look sensational darling, and I am so proud that you are my wife.'

Marie laughed. 'You don't look bad yourself Charles, now get your boots and sword on, we are meeting Manet and Monet in reception in ten minutes.'

As Charles came back, Marie had taken the velvet cloak off the hanger and he took it from her and stood her in front of a mirror and carefully draped the cloak around her and fastened the buckle just above the bodice of the dress. The cloak covered the long crinoline skirt perfectly.

They set off to walk down the huge main staircase to the busy reception and front entrance. As they came to the top of the first landing and started the descent into the hallway, several people below gasped as they saw the vision of Marie in the green velvet cloak and by the time they reached the hall there was complete silence and everybody just stopped and stared and then a wave of clapping started. Both of them blushed and Manet and Monet approached them and both in turn gave full bows to Marie and kissed her hand.

Monet had not met Marie before and he just stared at her and said, 'God, are those real emeralds and diamonds?'

Manet said, 'Of course they are; look how they sparkle in the light. Marie, you have exceeded all expectations tonight. You look sensational.'

Charles said, 'Oh God, you don't think she is going to eclipse the Empress, do you?'

Manet laughed. 'For God's sake Charles, Eugenie is 24 years older than Marie. You cannot compare them; Marie is 18 years old and looks perfect for her age. The Empress will look perfect for her age and I'm sure she will be wearing more jewellery than Marie.'

The hotel porter approached and said to Charles, 'Sir, the press seem to have gathered round the hotel entrance, waiting for guests to leave. I must warn you that they have cameras all set up. Allow me to ensure your wife's safety among the melee outside.'

27

A huge crowd was outside with photographers' cameras set up at the bottom of the steps. They were calling for them to stand for photographs.

Charles jumped into action immediately and stood Marie in profile with the hem of her dress just draped over the top step. He moved Manet and Monet about twelve inches from Marie's waist, directly behind her crinoline, facing forward and he faced Marie, bowing and kissing her hand. The photographers went wild to get the picture and as they moved off down the street to the Tuileries, several reporters pursued them. They posed again at the entrance to the palace, where more photographers were waiting. They caused a queue to form as the press would not let them go and were trying to engage Manet and Monet in conversation.

Alexandre Dumas was waiting to come up the steps and remarked, 'These bloody artists have all the fun and also seem to attract the most beautiful women. Look at her, she is stunning, who is the mystery lady in green?'

Several voices could be heard muttering, 'Madame

Duran'.

As they moved into the palace, Charles held Marie's hand and asked her if she was alright as nobody had expected them to receive so much press attention and he was worried that Marie would be concerned for her safety. She reassured him that she was fine and then she went to the cloakroom to deposit her cloak and check her hair.

The principal guests for each art were to be received last in the line-up and then proceed through to the grand hall with Napoleon and Eugenie and take their seats at the top table. Marie returned, revealing her gown for the first time, and there were gasps of admiration as she returned to Charles' side and people stopped talking and turned to look at them.

Manet said, 'Well Marie, you do seem to have had a profound effect on the guests as well as the press. How do you feel about all the attention?'

Marie replied, 'Frankly terrified, Edouard. I wasn't born into this sort of lifestyle so I have no knowledge of what is right or wrong behaviour in the French court.'

Monet patted her hand. 'Madame, you are doing fine. You are such a natural beauty that it is no wonder everyone is clamouring to see you.'

Just as he said that, they were ushered into place for the official photographs. They adopted the same pose as before and Manet whispered to Monet that Charles was deliberately ensuring Charles Worth got the publicity he wanted for his creation.

Monet replied that although he had heard rumours of Marie's beauty, none did her justice.

Manet said, 'Marie is a reincarnation of Diana, the hunting goddess. Believe me I have seen her out hunting and she rides like a Valkyrie and horses instantly submit to her authority and she has the lightest hands I have ever seen yet she could ride bareback with the greatest of ease.'

Monet laughed. 'Sounds like you are smitten by her Edouard; I hope you're not planning to add her to your list of conquests?'

'Certainly not; I am in total awe of the pair of them, theirs is a marriage made in heaven, a union of mind, body and soul and there is no way anyone should come between them.'

The photographs completed, they made their way to the gradually receding line of guests for their introduction to Napoleon and Eugenie. Manet went first and gave a perfunctory bow to Napoleon but gave Eugenie a much more elaborate bow. Monet did likewise and then it was their turn. Charles was acutely aware that the moment Marie had entered the room and Napoleon had laid eyes on her, he too had gasped at her beauty. He bowed to Napoleon who shook his hand quickly as he was anxious to move him on so he could greet Marie. He gave Eugenie an elegant bow and kissed her hand. The room of over 120 guests fell silent and all eyes were upon them.

The Empress gave him a smile and nod of the

head and said, 'Monsieur Duran, I am delighted to meet you.'

Charles saw Marie drop into a low curtsy and, keeping her eyes fixed on the floor, she held her hand out while Napoleon gave her the most exaggerated bow.

He said, 'Madame Duran, your youth and beauty eclipses the moon.' He took her hand and took longer than necessary to kiss it. He helped Marie to her feet and then took her hand and led her through the hall with guests bowing on either side, and out into the Grand Hall. Charles followed suit with Eugenie and had to admit he felt like a king but his eyes were fixed on Napoleon and his wife.

He fussed, pulling the chair out for Eugenie to sit down, and for the first time he looked at her with his artist's eye. She was now in her 40's but her startlingly thick, shiny black hair was her star feature. Her complexion was fairer than he had expected for her Spanish heritage but she also had beautiful green eyes. Her white dress was encrusted with diamonds and pearls on the fitted bodice and skirt and displayed her tiny waist. She had a royal blue sash over her left shoulder and although only around five feet tall, she looked every inch an Empress. After grace was said by the Emperor they all sat down and he turned to Eugenie, addressing her in Spanish, and she looked slightly shocked.

'Monsieur Duran, how very polite of you to speak to me in my native tongue. You have obviously spent some time in Spain; do please tell me about it.'

Charles chatted away, telling her of his time in Toledo and Madrid studying Velazquez when he was just 18. Out of the corner of his eye he could see Napoleon had also taken note but he was too interested in Marie to worry about him.

Napoleon's first question of Marie was, 'Where has such a beautiful girl like you been hiding? Look at all these men watching you; they cannot believe what their eyes are revealing.'

Marie laughed and said, 'Your Majesty, I was born and lived in Russia for 15 years so that's why you have not seen me in Paris society. I met Charles when he was commissioned to paint my brother and I when we returned to Paris last year and we fell in love within a week.'

Napoleon leant forward and looked closely into her eyes. 'A week Madame, did he just fall into the deep lagoon in those sapphire blue eyes and drown? It would only have taken me hours to do the same, not a week.'

Marie replied, 'I really don't know; you will have to ask him. I know when I saw him in his uniform wearing the Légion d'honneur that you had bestowed on him, that was when I knew I wanted to be by his side forever.'

Napoleon smiled at her. 'How enchanting, ma cherie, that you think I am responsible for uniting Venus with a mere artist when she should have become the wife of a king.'

'Sire, I have no aristocratic heritage. I am the daughter of a talented French musician who taught at the St. Petersburg Conservatoire. My only claim to fame was that I was educated in Russia by the same teachers as the fallen aristocracy had been. My husband thinks I resemble Diana rather than Venus but he has seen me out hunting.'

'Tell me Madame, what do you think of the Russians?'

Marie paused and spoke carefully. 'Sire, life is cheap in Russia and men only crave money and power. They will fight for money not glory and will transfer their loyalty to whoever is winning or pays the best price. It is a country of extremes both in weather and terrain and its poorest people are no better off now than they were under the monarchy. As you well know, power corrupts.'

Napoleon threw back his head and laughed. 'Madame, are you accusing me of also being corrupt?'

Charles had caught some of the conversation whilst he had been chatting to Eugenie and Manet heard the last sentence. Charles choked on his soup and turned to look at Marie, his heart missing a beat.

Marie replied, 'No Sire, you were elected by the people of France to carry out their mandate.'

Napoleon laughed. 'Madame Duran, you should have been a politician. When I need counselling in the future I should appoint you to my cabinet. With a mind as sharp as yours combined with the courage of a lion, you would be an outstanding politician.'

Charles and Manet started to breathe again and exchanged worried glances.

Eugenie said, 'Monsieur Duran, your wife seems to have captivated my husband both with her beauty and her intellect.'

'It would appear so your Majesty, but she can be very outspoken at times and although extremely honest she doesn't always think before she speaks.'

'Ah, the exuberance and spontaneity of youth; don't we all wish we were 18 again? Now tell me about your wedding. I believe you fought a duel the day after, on behalf of Monsieur Manet. I don't expect your new wife was too pleased?'

Charles told her the bare details of the duel and made no reference to the Duchesse de Beauchamp. He was delighted that Marie and Napoleon were discussing horses, which was a much safer subject than war or politics. Manet had Marie on one side and Émile Zola on the other side of him and they were chatting amicably. Monet was on Charles's other side and had been listening to his conversation with Eugenie, Napoleon and Marie.

Eugenie asked both Charles and Monet why there were so few wives at the artists' table.

Charles answered truthfully. 'Well your Majesty, artists do not make good husbands; they are too involved in their work to have time for a family. I never expected to marry until I found Marie.'

Monet laughed. 'He is right – it can't be much fun for the wife of an artist – they have to be prepared to rear children on their own. I have just become a father and am amazed at the amount of work involved with such a small child. I would not be able to concentrate on my painting with a baby around.'

Eugenie replied, 'But have you not considered marrying the mother of your child?'

'Yes, of course but we both want to be sure that we will be together before we move on to marriage.'

Charles replied, 'If you look around at the artists here we are relatively young and we don't become established in our careers until well into our 30's and 40's and can't afford to consider raising a family. Some of us will not be recognised until long after we are dead. In the meantime we are judged by our peers who do not welcome new techniques and changes in composition.'

Eugenie replied, 'But don't you all fall in love with the women you paint, especially those willing to remove their clothes?'

Monet and Charles looked at each other and Charles answered, 'As artists we do have an eye for beauty and our work does give us the opportunity to get close to our models. But that doesn't mean we ravish every woman who sits for us. I would have no clients, ma'am, if I had that sort of reputation. We are reliant on men paying us to paint their wives, so we would hardly take liberties with them.'

Eugenie replied, 'Yes I see your point, Monsieur Duran. I now understand why Monsieur Manet was criticised for his painting of nudes in the park.'

Monet answered, 'Precisely, ma'am – if his painting had been on a religious theme he could have used as many nudes as he liked and it would have been acceptable to the Salon judges.'

Charles turned to see what Marie and Napoleon were discussing and it was the subject of women artists, with Marie championing their right to be accepted on the same terms as men... a sound principle but one he did not expect to become reality in his lifetime.

He raised the subject with Eugenie, who had moved mountains to allow women to study science and law on equal terms with men.

The sweet course was now being served and the speeches were due before the coffee was served. Charles gave a short speech thanking Napoleon on behalf of all the guests, then Napoleon gave an interesting speech thanking them for promoting their work and making Paris the arts centre of Europe.

Marie had avoided drinking any wine but had sipped champagne during the toasts. This had not gone unnoticed by Napoleon.

'Madame Duran, do you not drink alcohol or is my wine not to your liking?'

She blushed at the thought of offending the Emperor so gave him an honest answer. 'Sire, I do not wish to offend you at all, but I am avoiding alcohol for two reasons. One is that my husband was concerned about what I may say should I get a little tipsy and secondly, I am *enceinte* and still suffering from sickness.'

Napoleon roared with laughter. 'Madame Duran, you are so delightful and completely untouched by court etiquette. You are a breath of fresh air sweeping through the Tulieries. If only I was forty years younger and could have you as my mistress, what a contented man I would be.'

Marie shot back at him instantly, 'But Sire, you assume that I would be willing to accept such an imposition and become your mistress, which I can assure you would not be the case.'

Napoleon looked shocked. 'But Madame, now is the best time for you to indulge with whichever man takes your eye. You have done your duty as a wife and now you can have some fun.'

Marie was fuming and she said quietly through gritted teeth, 'The fact that I vowed before God to remain faithful to my husband, the man whom I love truly and deeply and would never offend, has not even occurred to you?'

'My humble apologies Madame, if I offend you; consider it the desires of a selfish old man who has been too long at court. I am delighted that you have shown such affection for your husband; he is a very lucky man.'

Charles had sensed something was wrong with Marie by her tense body language and he prayed she would not cause a scene. Eugenie had also sensed that something was wrong and suspected Napoleon had offended Marie.

She turned to Charles, 'I apologise if my husband has upset your wife, Monsieur Duran; he cannot resist assuming that all beautiful women are his for the taking. It appears that we Spanish queens have to tolerate errant husbands. Catherine of Aragon agreed to divorce Henry VIII after a long battle and Marie-Therese had to tolerate Louis XIV's open indiscretions and unfortunately, I have the same cross to bear. There was a time when we were both deeply in love with each other but age and difficult childbirth seem to have been my misfortune.'

Charles was openly shocked as he detected a profound sadness in her that touched him deeply.

'Ma'am I do have great sympathy for your plight and am saddened that you have nobody to confide in.'

'As you know being a staunch Catholic, I could not be unfaithful so I have learned to live with the situation as many other women have before me. I concentrate on my work and help promote women to achieve whatever dreams they have rather than remain repressed by male dominance. One day women will achieve their potential and be represented in all workplaces.'

The orchestra was warming up for the start of the ball and Marie and Eugenie left the table to prepare for the forthcoming dance. Eugenie chatted to her and found her intelligent and articulate but best of all, devoted to her husband. She was delighted as Charles had made a good impression on her as a very caring man. Marie told her she was in the early stages of pregnancy and admitted that rather than offend Napoleon, she had told him of her state. Eugenie resisted informing her that a lady should never discuss her condition with a man, especially at the dinner table. She did however, tell her she was very lucky to have a husband like Charles, and wished her a successful birth.

Marie was getting nervous about the dance but as she returned to her seat Charles stood to move back her chair and as he bent down he whispered in her ear, 'Don't worry ma cherie, you look stunning, simply the belle of the ball, and I am so proud of you.'

At his kind words she instantly felt braver and she was determined to rise for her starring role as principal guest at the ball. Napoleon stood and offered her his arm to go onto the dance floor. She took a deep breath and held her head high and walked regally at his side, the emeralds of her necklace shimmering in the light from the chandeliers. Charles followed with Eugenie on his arm. As they reached the floor, the orchestra played a slow waltz and Napoleon took Marie's hand and bowed low to kiss it as she swept into a very low curtsy. Charles followed suit with Eugenie but surprisingly she also curtsied to him, which he had been told she would not do. There was a ripple of applause from the guests and then both couples set off around the dance floor. After the usual pause, other dancers joined them on the floor.

Napoleon was captivated by Marie. 'Madame, you dance like a ballerina – so light, agile and with such grace.'

'And you Sire are also well versed in the art of dance.'

But of course ma cherie, I spent my exile in London and thoroughly enjoyed the London social scene.'

Charles was more relaxed now they were dancing and Eugenie said, 'Don't worry; your delightful wife looks as though she has been dancing on the Paris scene for years, as do you Monsieur Duran.'

He smiled at her and said, 'Well thankfully, all my boxing and fencing lessons keep me light on my feet but I do confess we both took dancing lessons to ensure we were up to scratch before we came here.'

'Then I commend you both for your hard work.'

After dancing two dances with the Empress, he returned to the top table. Marie had been collared by Courbet as she had been on her way back to her seat as Napoleon had stopped to speak to an actor at another table. As he passed the table he saw Renoir being introduced to Marie by Courbet and as he ushered the Empress back to her seat, he noticed that Renoir was leading Marie out to the dance floor. As they reached the table, Manet asked the Empress to dance and as Monet was chatting at the artists' table he took the opportunity to go over for a chat too.

Courbet collared him and congratulated him and said Marie looked outstanding and that young

Renoir had waltzed off with her.

He laughed and said, 'I have no doubt Marie will keep him in his place.'

Marie had never met Renoir as at 27 he was new on the art scene but had been a student of Charles Gleyre in Paris where he had met Monet, Pissaro and Sisley. Like Charles he had come from a humble background as the son of a tailor and had started as a ceramic artist before he attended the École des Beaux-Arts.

As they walked onto the floor he said, 'They said Duran had married the most beautiful girl in Paris but I didn't believe them until I set eyes on you tonight, Madame.'

Marie smiled as they took up their positions for a gavotte. 'I really do not consider myself a beauty in any shape or form and to be honest I am a little intimidated by the reaction I have encountered tonight. Charles knew it would happen but I have no idea what all the fuss is about.'

Renoir smiled and said, 'That's what makes you so attractive to men, Madame; you have an inner beauty of mystery and exude a strong connection with nature. Manet described you as a reincarnation of Diana the huntress and he was absolutely right.'

The music started and they danced around the dance floor. Marie noticed Manet was dancing with Eugenie and they seemed to be enjoying themselves. After three laps of the floor Marie started to feel lightheaded. Fearing she may faint and cause a scene she asked Renoir if they could slip off the dance floor so she could have a short rest.

Renoir manoeuvred them to the bottom of the hall and they slipped out into the next door salon where he put his arm round her and guided her to the nearest seat. Thankfully, people were only passing through, so nobody saw them.

'Madame, I will fetch you a glass of water but I don't want to leave you if you are feeling faint.'

No, I'm fine Monsieur Renoir, but I would like some water.'

He went back into the bar in the ballroom and asked a servant to bring him two glasses of water to the salon. He returned quickly to Marie. He contemplated fetching her husband but decided not to at this stage. He sat down next to her on the settee and the waiter appeared with the water and sliced lemon.

Marie said, 'Thank you for being so attentive, Monsieur Renoir. I'm afraid the dizziness was probably due to my condition.'

'Please Madame, call me Auguste and tell me, where did you meet your husband?'

Marie laughed. 'The same way all painters meet their match. He painted me on horseback when my father commissioned him to paint my 21-year-old brother Henri before he took up his post in the cavalry, and me. My mother intended me to wear the ball gown purchased for Henri's birthday party but when Charles saw me on horseback he persuaded my father I should be painted outside too.'

'What made you fall in love with Duran?'

'Many things – his good looks, skill as an artist, his generosity and caring attitude, his morals… and he makes me feel so safe and secure. Since we married I have discovered a whole new hidden side to his character and I could not be a happier woman and now I am having his child. I feel better now; we had better get back before I am missed.'

They returned to the ballroom and as Napoleon and Eugenie were both dancing with other guests, she joined Monet and Charles at the artists' table.

Courbet commented, 'Renoir, trust you to be the first artist to have the pleasure of dancing with Madame Duran. I trust he behaved himself Marie, and didn't tread on your delicate toes. You look exquisite tonight; we have all commented on how we would like to paint you dancing with Napoleon.'

'Gustave, I can assure you that Monsieur Renoir behaved like a perfect gentleman, which is more than can be said for some of the Emperor's conversation this evening.'

Gustave roared with laughter and said, 'Did the old goat proposition you, Marie? At least he still has excellent taste in women even though he is 60 now. I am sure you put him in his place but I don't see your hand mark across his face.'

Charles took her hand and said, 'I think I deserve to dance with my wife now before any of you whisk her away.'

As they left, Manet asked Renoir if he could have a private word with him. They moved over to a small table on the far side of the bar in the corner of the room.

Renoir could feel the animosity emanating from Manet, but had no idea what he had done to offend him.

As they sat down, Manet opened with, 'Rather than beating about the bush I am just going to get straight to the point. Back off from Marie Duran, Renoir!'

'I have done nothing wrong; you just heard her say I behaved like a perfect gentleman. And who are you to lecture me when you have a record for seducing other men's wives?'

'Why did you take her off the dance floor?'

'Because she asked me to, as she was feeling dizzy in the gavotte, so I quietly whisked her into the salon next door and instructed a waiter to fetch her some water. For God's sake Manet, you can't think I was flirting with her or behaving inappropriately in any way. What does it matter to you? She's Duran's wife, after all.'

'I am just her friend and protector and I don't wish to see anyone try to break their marriage up. Remember, I was the best man who nearly got her husband killed in a duel the day after she married him. I could never have forgiven myself if Charles had been killed. Those two have a marriage made in heaven; they are bound in heart, body and soul.

Charles thinks she is a gift from God and the more I see of them together, the more I believe it. He worships the ground she walks on and she loves him. The sexual chemistry between them is electric. Of course Charles knows that every man is besotted with her and it amuses him to see it, knowing that it is in his bed she lays.'

'Edouard, believe me, I had no designs on Marie Duran at all. I appreciate she is stunning and has an inner beauty and mystery and exudes a strong connection with nature, but I would never proposition her.'

'Well Auguste, if you can recognise that, then you will make a better artist than I gave you credit for. It seems I have jumped to the wrong conclusion and I beg your forgiveness.'

'Apology accepted Edouard, but you need to examine your feelings for Marie Duran because you have just proved to me that you are in love with her, whatever you say.'

'Perhaps, but it will remain an unrequited love as I have messed up so many women's lives; I will not ruin hers. Let's say I worship her from afar as the goddess Diana. You haven't seen her on a horse. She needs no saddle or bridle; she could ride bareback in total balance with the horse, who would jump the moon for her. The portraits Charles did of her and her brother were exceptional. When he showed me into the library and I first laid eyes on them I honestly felt like the horses were in the room. It was me who pushed him to ask for her hand in marriage, as he never thought he would be considered good enough for her. On their wedding day as they went up to the altar to be blessed, a shaft of sunlight came through the window and bathed them in an arc of light and reflected off the marble pillars in a myriad of colours. When he was in the duel the clouds parted and a shaft of sunlight lit his opponent and he shot him through the left eye. If God really had a hand in that, then I will do my best to keep them together.'

'Don't worry Edouard, your secret is safe with me.'

'You should have gone to Duran for six months rather than wasted a year at art college. He persuaded me to go to Spain to study Velazquez and his technique for drawing light. Most of Duran's portraits are drawn on a black canvas and the colour overlaid. He draws spectacular faces and he always manages to portray the spirit of his sitter as well as their image.'

'I would have loved to go to him but I couldn't afford it.'

'Not all his pupils pay for his tuition. If you have talent, he will help you. He is one of the best teachers of art I have come across.'

'Manet, were you guilty of seducing the woman whom Duran fought in the duel?'

'I never touched her. I don't expect you to believe me but it is true.'

They walked back over to the artists' table and

Charles collared Manet.

'What have you been up to with Renoir? I didn't know you knew him that well.'

'We were just having a difference of opinion as I misunderstood him. In fact, I was telling him he should have come to you instead of wasting a year at the École des Beaux-Arts. I have painted with him at Monet's and he is good, with a natural talent for composition.'

Charles laughed. 'He must be good if you say so. In fact he will probably do better than you because you will have had all the crap thrown at you for being too "avant garde" and he will reap the benefits.'

Manet threw his hands in the air. 'C'est la vie!'

Marie returned to the table on the arm of Degas and Charles was amused as he had never met him yet here was Marie making a favourable impression on them all.

She collapsed beside him and he whispered in her ear, 'Are you alright my darling? Don't over exert yourself; I have plans for you later.'

She blushed and said, 'Well, I think I had better sit this one out as I have promised to dance with Paul Gauguin, Émile Zola, Fauré and Guy de Maupassant.'

Charles spluttered, 'Guy de Maupassant is younger than you, Marie and only here as Gustave Flaubert's protégé; he had a cheek even asking you.'

Marie fluttered her eyes at him and said, 'But he has such puppy dog eyes and he was brave enough to ask me in front of Dumas, Hugo and Zola so his bravery should be rewarded.'

Charles laughed. 'Well don't blame me if he tramples over your toes as he is obviously besotted with you and probably won't be able to dance a step with you in his arms.'

Manet exclaimed, 'What's this? Maupassant had the audacity to ask you to dance, Marie? He's just a pup – and a very forward one at that – asking a married lady to dance.'

Marie replied, 'Edouard, you forget your own wicked reputation as a womaniser and yet I would still dance with you.'

Manet's expression softened. 'Well, I insist then that I dance with you immediately after Maupassant so he can't detain you any longer than necessary.'

Marie laughed. 'Very well Sir Galahad, you may rescue me from Guy's arms on the dance floor, but only if you are nice to him.'

At that moment Paul Gauguin approached and bowed to Marie. 'Madame, may I claim the next dance?'

'Certainly, Monsieur Gauguin; I would be delighted to make your acquaintance. I have heard so much about you.' She stood up and took his proffered hand and headed to the dance floor.

Manet exclaimed, 'She's not safe in his company either, Charles!'

Charles replied, 'She is more than capable of coping with young Gauguin. You can't blame him for claiming a dance with her when she is the only woman at the table.' He said in a louder voice, 'The Empress asked why so few artists were married and I told her the truth – that at least half of you have mistresses but would not legally marry them.'

Zacharie Astruc said, 'Duran if we all had mistresses as beautiful as your wife then we would all be married.'

Paul Cézanne growled, 'A wife is the last thing I need in my life.'

Courbet replied, 'Thank God for that, the poor woman would need rescuing from your black moods as you would likely murder her.'

Marie danced with all her partners, who all behaved themselves. Guy de Maupassant was rather overawed by her but they had a slow waltz and she chattered away to him whilst he gazed at her with his puppy dog eyes. True to his word, Manet accosted her on the dance floor to take over the next dance and Guy could only kiss her hand and leave.

At 12:30 p.m. the final dances were being played and as was tradition, Charles and Marie danced the last dance with Napoleon and Eugenie.

As they left the dance floor, Napoleon turned to Charles. 'I understand you walked here from the Hôtel de Ville with Manet and Monet and there was a lot of press interest. My guard informs me that reporters and members of the public are waiting outside. I insist you have two armed guards escort you to the Hôtel de Ville to ensure your safety.'

Charles bowed. 'If you insist Sire, to ensure my wife's safety I will accept.'

Napoleon said, 'Well with 5000 francs worth of emeralds round her neck you can't be too careful.'

They said their formal goodbyes and thanked them for a wonderful evening. Manet and Monet caught up with them and Marie went to fetch her cloak. He told them that they were to have an armed escort and they could hear the crowds outside shouting as guests left the palace.

They waited until everyone else had filtered out and then went through the door together. Barriers had been erected to keep the public back and they were blinded by the press cameras as they flashed. Charles took a firm hold of Marie's hand and Manet did the same on her other side. People were shouting at Marie and trying to climb the barriers. The press was calling for them to pose and it was beginning to turn into a scrum. However, within seconds, an armed guard of twelve soldiers marched out and went to the barriers to keep the crowd back. Another four soldiers joined them at the top of the steps and once the press had taken their photos, two of them led the way down the steps and two took up position behind them. Although some of the crowd followed, they did not dare come too close.

28

It was a five-minute walk to the Hôtel de Ville, which had already put barriers up and they had their own security guards on the steps. They all remained quiet, just taking in what they were encountering as they found it very hard to believe. As they walked inside, Charles remained outside, thanking the soldiers.

As Charles rejoined the group, the hotel manager said, 'Monsieur Duran, the hotel is full of guests and if you would like some privacy for a late drink I can make a salon available for you down here? Your wife looks rather overwhelmed by all the attention.'

Charles put his arm round Marie and spoke to Manet and Monet. They decided they would just have one last drink and then they would leave for home so they went into the bar, where the waiters cleared them a private table in the window and brought over a bottle of brandy and three glasses.

Marie had a small glass of brandy as she had gone rather pale, and they chatted about their experience.

Marie said, 'Well, if that's what being famous is all about then I will settle for anonymity any time.'

Charles said, 'My dear, I don't know whether that

will be quite possible now Pandora's Box has been opened. Those pictures are going to go worldwide, not just be headlines in *Le Figaro* for one day. The interview we did will also be published in the press and in art magazines too. I suspect we could all be fending off the press for a while but on the plus side, we could all receive commissions and sell paintings because of it.'

Manet said, 'Well that would be a welcome boost but I won't tolerate press attention every time I step out of my studio, with my whereabouts being made public.'

Monet laughed. 'Could that be because you might get caught visiting your many female admirers? Perhaps you could be receiving many more after the ball hits the press.'

Manet replied, 'Exactly, so what do I tell Suzanne if this happens? She will go mad; she can't stand crowds at the best of times and what if they start hanging around my house?'

Manet and Monet were soon ready to leave and they all felt slightly uncomfortable about being observed closely by so many people in the bar. Charles and Marie accompanied them into the foyer and then took the lift to their top floor suite. Charles wrapped her in his arms and kissed her lips tenderly. 'You were a star, my darling, tonight. I am so proud of you; that was a huge task for a young woman to cope with but you carried it off superbly.'

As they entered the lounge, steaming hot coffee

and tea had been laid out for them so they paused to have a drink. Marie was going to go and take her dress off but then realised she would need help with the crinoline skirt and hoops so Charles helped her out of it in the lounge and she was relieved to be free of the weight.

Charles said, 'When we have had our coffee I will undress you like I did on our wedding night. But first of all, tell me what Napoleon said that upset you. Did he proposition you?'

Marie blushed and said, 'No, not exactly. He noticed I wasn't drinking and rather than offend I told him I was *enceinte* and although he suggested he would want me as his mistress if he was forty years younger, he didn't really mean it. However, he suggested that as I had now done my duty as a wife I should be taking a lover and bed-hopping around Paris.'

Charles roared with laughter. 'Oh, my precious one, what did you say to him? I am thankful you didn't slap his face.'

'I told him through gritted teeth that such behaviour was totally unacceptable to me. The fact that I vowed before God to remain faithful to you, the man whom I love truly and deeply and would never offend, had not even occurred to him. To be fair he did apologise, but tell me is this really what Parisian women do? Would they really take lovers once they are pregnant?'

'Perhaps if they were in loveless marriages or if their

husbands were also having affairs then they might, but I am very grateful you find it so unacceptable. It highlights the dangers of leaving the marital bed once the wife is pregnant, something we both find abhorrent. Now I am just going to get out of my uniform and then I will be your personal maid when I return.' He kissed her cheek as he got up and went into the dressing room.

He soon reappeared in his wrap and as she was in her chemise he suggested they move into the bedroom and he led her to the dressing table and she sat down. Expertly, he unpinned the tiara from her hair and released the sides and combed it through, kissing the nape of her neck as he finished. He opened the jewellery boxes and took her bracelet, earrings and ring off and placed the tiara inside. He then turned her to face him and removed her stockings and drawers, gently running his finger down her thighs and she gasped with pleasure. He stood up and pulled her to her feet.

She said, 'But the necklace needs removing, Charles.'

He led her over to a large mirror and replied, 'The necklace stays exactly where it is. Do you think I would miss the opportunity to make love to you while you're wearing that expensive emerald and diamond necklace?'

'Knowing you Charles, I can understand why you would like that, but we will have to be careful not to damage it.'

Carefully, he undid her chemise and they both watched in the mirror as it fell to the floor and revealed her naked body with the emeralds and diamonds shimmering in the light. He ran his hands down her stomach and said, 'How is my little baby? Has he fallen asleep with all the music and dancing?'

Marie responded quickly. 'You said "he". Does that mean you will be disappointed if it's a "she"?'

'No, it just means I will have to keep trying until a boy arrives and so if you don't want to spend the next ten years pregnant, you had better quickly produce one.' He then scooped her up into his arms, walked to their bedroom and laid her in the centre of the bed. He removed his wrap, knelt beside her on the bed and bent down and kissed her tenderly on the lips, running his hands through her hair and watching the sparkle of the light in the emeralds. He put his right knee over her and was astride her waist.

He whispered to her, 'Tell me if I am too heavy for you sweetheart, and we'll change position.'

He was caressing her left breast with one hand and had her right nipple in his mouth. She groaned with pleasure and buried her hands in his hair. He kept moving south down her body, caressing her with his tongue as he went. When he reached her pubic hair and touched her intimately with his tongue she screamed and came instantly and then he entered her and took his pleasure. He came powerfully and every fibre of his skin that touched her screamed with pleasure. He was now in danger of his face being ripped by the emeralds so he pulled away from her, rolled over and lay panting next to her, his head on her right breast.

When they had both got their breath back she said, 'Who were you looking at in the mirror, me or you?'

Charles hesitated but then said, 'Why you of course, darling.'

Marie leant over him, wagging her finger in his face. 'Don't lie to me husband, you were watching yourself not me; I could see you!'

Charles laughed. 'Well I don't often get the chance to appraise my performance in a mirror.'

'Well now you have been caught lying you will have to surrender to my wishes. I will give you an even better view of the emeralds now.' She pushed him over onto his back and then sat astride him.

Charles whimpered, 'Please give me a little longer to recover, ma cherie.'

'Are you saying you cannot recover within five minutes, husband? I am sure that Renoir, Fauré, Zola, Degas and even young Maupassant would have no trouble in performing again.'

'You little witch, Marie. How dare you insult me so?' He tried to move his arms but she had pinned one under his hip and had her hand on his other shoulder.

'Lie still now, Charles. I am going to be doing all the work and I will have you ready for action in no time.'

He laughed and said, 'Very well Madame, I submit to your superior authority; my body is yours for the taking.' He lay back and marvelled at her skill and he could have burst with pride and happiness as she coaxed him to an earth-shattering climax in less than five minutes.

Afterwards, they lay side by side with her in front and he ran his finger down her profile from breast to bottom.

He whispered in her ear, 'You are so perfect, my darling. Promise me you will never leave me.'

'Leave you – why ever would I do that? I could not exist without you by my side; you're my soulmate, friend and lover.'

'Then tell me, of all the men you danced with tonight, who did you like best?'

'Charles, I didn't desire any of them but to me the most interesting was Auguste Renoir. He was not like most artists are – self-centred and arrogant – but he was anxious to be accepted and desperate to learn.'

'How surprising, Manet also spoke highly of him and he doesn't praise other artists often. Perhaps I should invite him to my studio and take a look at what he can produce. But you Madame, I shall lock in the cellar, for fear you will ravish him like you just did me.'

She put back her hand and slapped him hard on his backside. 'Don't ever think I would do such a thing with another man. Take the necklace off now so I can go to sleep.'

He undid the necklace, pulled back the covers and deposited her on the soft pillows and covered her up. He put the necklace in the box and went into the dressing room, put on breeches and a white shirt, slipped out of the room and gave the box in at reception, watched it being placed in the hotel safe, then signed the receipt.

By the time he got back, Marie was fast asleep.

29

He woke the next morning as the sun streamed through the window. Marie was still fast asleep, as they hadn't retired till after 2:00 a.m. He slipped out of bed, trying not to disturb her, put on his wrap and went out into the lounge to admire the magnificent view over Paris. He heard footsteps in the corridor and asked a maid to send coffee as he thought it would be a while before Marie was ready to go down to breakfast. A few minutes later he heard a loud rap on the door and he went quickly to answer it, fearing he would disturb Marie. As he opened the door he was astonished to see Manet with several copies of *Le Figaro,* accompanied by Zola with a tray of coffee and cups.

'Manet, what in God's name are you doing here at this time on a Saturday morning?'

Manet flew in and headed towards the open lounge door. 'We met the waiter in the lift and offered to deliver your tray. I have come to warn you that I have just been past your studio and there is already a crowd of press and people outside demanding to see 'L'etoile de Paris.' With a flourish he unfolded *Le*

Figaro and held up the front page with a large photo of them on the steps of the Hôtel de Ville with the headline in large type above it.

'There are even people outside my studio so I thought I had better wake Zola up and get his advice on how to deal with this situation.'

Charles groaned but took the copy to the large round table in the window and saw that a full report on the ball occupied three inside pages of the paper. There were pictures of their interviews the previous week and he quickly read through them to check their wording. There was a column by the woman who had interviewed Marie and although some of it was totally inaccurate, it was generally very complimentary. It basically raved about Marie's beauty, intelligence, bluntness, independence and defence of female artists.

Manet had been busy pouring coffees and passing them round.

Charles turned to Zola, 'What can we expect from this then, Zola?'

Zola smiled. 'Well as far as press reports go it is very complimentary about all of you, but of course your wife has created a huge stir. I suspect this will lead to a barrage of requests for interviews, not just here but from all over Europe. You can also expect her to receive letters and flowers from men who, although they have never met her, have fallen in love with her... not to mention women who want to invite her to their salons for tea.'

Charles interrupted, 'But she's a married woman; surely she won't receive that sort of attention. She's not an actress, singer or dancer, for heaven's sake, she is my wife.'

Just at that moment, Marie appeared barefoot in her white silk nightgown with her hair flowing down to her shoulders. She looked slightly shocked and said, 'I heard voices and recognised Manet's but what are you doing here so early? Oh, and Monsieur Zola too!'

Charles said, 'They have come to warn us that you appear to have become an overnight sensation.' He lifted *Le Figaro* up to show her.

Marie said, 'Oh, don't be ridiculous. I am just a plain ordinary woman; who would think I was a raving beauty?' She moved over to the table and leant over the newspaper and at that exact moment a shaft of sunlight filtered through the window to the side of her and lit the outline of her profile through the silk nightgown and gave them a perfect view of her lithe athletic body in all its glory.

Manet gasped and Zola nearly dropped his coffee cup. Charles was further back in the room and could not initially see what was happening.

Marie turned to look at Manet. Startled by his look of incredulity, she said, 'What on earth's the matter with you, Manet? You look as though you have seen a ghost.'

'Not a ghost Marie, just the most beautiful woman I have ever laid eyes on.'

Suddenly, Marie realised what had happened and pulled the curtain over the window and said, 'For heaven's sake Manet, you must have seen prettier women than me in the flesh.'

Manet replied, 'I've told you before you are the vision of the goddess Diana'.

Marie interrupted, 'Don't be ridiculous Manet, you are just creating a myth; tell me what makes me so damned special?'

'Your beautiful blue eyes, tiny pert nose, near symmetrical face, long elegant neck, lustrous auburn hair, lithe body, long legs, elegant walk and most important of all, your look of calmness and freedom and your strong bond with nature.'

Marie laughed. 'And you, Monsieur Zola, surely you can't agree with Manet that I am a goddess?'

Zola replied, 'Oh, Madame, your beauty has rendered me speechless. Thank God I make my living as a writer, but I agree with every word Edouard uttered.'

Marie said, 'I give up. I cannot understand what all the fuss is about.'

Charles moved over to her and kissed her nose and said, 'Well I am delighted that Manet has confirmed my opinion of how very special you are, my darling. I suggest we get breakfast sent up here but I think we both need to dress first.'

Marie said, 'Oh, if you are going to breakfast in here then I am going for a bath before I start to feel sick. Perhaps you would bring me a coffee in when it arrives, Charles? She picked up a copy of *Le Figaro* to take with her.

Manet said, 'I will bring the coffee to you!'

Marie walked over to him and said, 'No you won't, Sir Galahad. I don't want your armour tarnishing in the water.' As she moved off she let her right hand trail across his cheek and shoulder to soften his dismissal.

Breakfast arrived and they all tucked in and it was Charles who took Marie her coffee.

They discussed what the repercussions from all the publicity might be and Charles stressed that Marie would find any restrictions on her freedom a burden. She would hate people recognising her as she really did not think she was anything special. Zola said they would have to be very careful how they handled it as the public could just as easily turn on her as revere her, if she did not behave as they expected.

Manet laughed and said he could hardly see Marie attending ladies' coffee mornings. Zola said that as the article referred to her being an artist and working in the studio they could try and portray her as a working woman rather than a model wife. He would be able to follow up the article in *Le Figaro* with his reminiscences of the night and portray her as a shy, introverted woman who shuns publicity, but he didn't have much hope of it working.

'The trouble is, the public put their own stamp on how they expect their idols to behave. The women will hate her because of her beauty and see her as a threat, but men will idolise her and want to see more of her.'

Charles replied, 'But by January she is going to be visibly *enceinte* and French etiquette would expect her to withdraw from the social scene anyway.'

Zola replied, 'Well that could help our cause but she cannot refuse every invitation she receives. You will both be invited to every important dinner, opera, concert and gallery exhibition in Paris, possibly even abroad.'

Charles said, 'But I have my work to do and students to teach and I need her organising my pupils and studio. You have no idea how much administration she has already taken off my shoulders but neither of us have the time to be socialites.'

Zola said, 'But if you offend them by turning down their invitations then you could find your reputation as an artist and teacher suffers too. Certainly once these pictures go round the world, you could have art students camping out to be part of your studio if your wife is there.'

Manet said, 'Yes, that's a good point; you don't want the wheel to turn full circle. You know how vicious the tongues of Parisian society can be. Look how I have been vilified since I produced "Le Déjeuner" and "Olympia".'

Zola said, 'What we need is some advice from someone who knows how the system works. How about Judith Gautier, daughter of the writer and poet Theo Gautier? She is only 23, married and a very good looking girl herself with a talent for writing, playing the piano and sculpting. She would be able to coach Marie on dealing with the public – fervent male admirers in particular. She has been fending off the advances of Flaubert, Baudelaire, Poe and Dore, who all visit her father regularly, since she was a child.'

Charles said, 'She has not been involved in any scandal, has she? I would not want Marie being associated with someone who has loose morals. Is she a Catholic girl?'

Zola replied, 'Well she was educated at a convent school but you know as well as I do, that doesn't necessarily mean she will be a nun in later life.'

Manet interjected, 'Certainly not; one of the best lovers I had was a girl of 17, fresh out of a boarding convent school and her best subject was definitely biology, rather than theology.'

Charles muttered, 'Trust you, Manet. Remind me to lock up my daughters, if I have any, when you are around.'

Manet parried with, 'You know I am an honourable man at heart. I just can't resist beautiful women who tempt me, but I would never go that far with any of your family, especially not your wife. I worship her as a goddess and would die protecting her, but you know I would never lay a finger on her. She has a right punch as strong as any man and she kicks and bites like a horse and I am a total coward at heart.'

Zola and Charles roared with laughter just as

Marie came in wearing the blue and gold Worth day dress.

Manet said, 'And here is L'étoile herself, looking divine in another Worth creation. Do you realise Charles, you could get free dresses for Marie for life after all the publicity you have given him over the ball gown?'

Charles replied, 'Yes, perhaps I should ask him for a refund.'

oOo

They all took a hansom cab from the back exit of the Hôtel de Ville, to attempt to slip into Charles's studio unnoticed. However, having left the cab in the next street and walked through an alleyway to Rue du Montparnasse, they were amazed to find the studio now had about 100 people outside, including the press. Propped against the stone frontage were six bouquets of flowers.

Marie had a black cloak on and a hood pulled over her and Charles and Manet held onto her on either side and Zola walked directly in front. They had got within ten feet of the door when someone shouted, 'Here is Manet and Duran with his wife!'

All hell broke loose and they had to fight their way to the door, which to Charles's horror, was locked. However, Antonio was behind it and as he saw them he opened it and they all tumbled into the narrow entrance hall.

Charles shouted at Antonio, 'Why did you lock

the bloody door and what are those flowers doing outside?'

Antonio screamed, 'I have been under siege for two hours and had to lock the door; we were being invaded. The world has gone nuts. Come and look in your studio.'

Charles ran to the top of the stairs with his suitcase still in his hand. Zola and Manet ran up after him and Marie made a more dignified ascent. They all stood in the double doorway of the main studio staring open mouthed as the entire floor was covered in bunches of flowers of every description. There were huge bunches of roses, chrysanthemums, lilies of every variety and the main colour seemed to be white, although there were a lot of red roses. There were also exotic orchids and the smell was intoxicating.

Charles gasped, 'Oh my God, where have all these come from?'

Antonio said sharply, 'Charles these are for Marie, not you!'

Charles barked, 'I realise that you idiot!'

Manet picked up a beautiful white orchid and opened the card attached and read, 'Thank you for a wonderful dance; you looked stunning. Looking forward to singing with you at Notre Dame. Regards Gabriel.'

Charles picked up some smaller bouquets that had no cards attached or just said "from an admirer". Marie sat down in a chair, staring at the rows of flowers, speechless.

Manet picked up a huge bunch of two-dozen pristine white roses and read the card: ' "To a beautiful angel who turned a pauper into a prince last night – Auguste Renoir." Well at least he sent white roses for purity, not red.'

Charles exploded, 'If he had sent red roses he would be looking down the barrel of my gun tomorrow morning!'

Manet laughed. 'Oh Charles don't be so cruel, he is only besotted with her just like the rest of us.'

Zola waved a boxed single red rose and shouted, 'I thought I recognised the writing. When I left Maupassant last night he was drunk and proclaiming he would never wash his left hand again as it had been touched by the beautiful Madame Duran. However, he must have slept outside the florist because he has sent this rose and said, "To the belle of the ball – a new star is born. From your devoted servant, Guy de Maupassant." He is going to be an excellent writer when he matures.'

Charles had opened a bouquet of white calla lilies tied in a green velvet bow. '"To Diana the hunting goddess, from a mere mortal who is transfixed by her beauty. Paul Gauguin." Not bad for a 20-year-old artist I suppose.'

Marie said, 'Manet, is it really considered appropriate for men to send flowers to a married woman?'

Manet said, 'Well probably not under old French

society rules but for a young single man to send flowers to a lady who has honoured him with a dance would not be considered inappropriate now and none of them have made indecent proposals.'

Charles said, 'Thank God for that, you mean some of them might? You and Zola didn't send any flowers and you danced with her.'

Manet said, 'Well, precisely. I am 43 and have my wife Suzanne and Émile is the same age and has Gabrielle. As you know, I am Marie's Sir Galahad and your best man so I take her welfare very seriously and was just keeping a watchful eye on your wife while all these young pups fawned over her.'

Marie said, 'But what are we going to do with all the flowers? They cannot be wasted on me and left to die. Am I expected to pen thank you notes to those who have sent them and left a card?'

Manet said, 'Yes, it would be expected for the recipient to respond.'

Zola said, 'Well how about we check all the bouquets and if there is a card, we write on what was sent and then remove the cards for Marie to send thank you notes and then find a home for the flowers.'

Charles said, 'But where?'

Manet said, 'I've got it; Fauré has given me the answer. It's Sunday tomorrow; let's send them all round in a hansom cab with a handwritten note from Marie donating them personally to Notre Dame. Word is bound to get out and that shows that

"L'étoile" cares about nature and religion.'

Zola clapped his hands. 'Inspirational, Edouard – the perfect answer to the problem. However, you may find that by Monday you have received more flowers than today. There will also be numerous letters of requests pouring through the door for both of you to attend the opening of an envelope and who knows what else. Perhaps you could send the next batch of flowers to the hospital.'

Marie said, 'What a good idea but I am keeping those from my dance partners as a memento of a wonderful evening. You won't be offended Charles, if I do?'

Charles said, 'No darling, you may keep them. You deserve them; you were sensational after all.'

Zola replied, 'I would expect you to receive some form of acknowledgement from the Emperor for being principal guests.'

Charles said, 'Like the odd spare palace or yacht?'

Zola laughed. 'Perhaps you should lower your sights a little, unless of course he wants Marie for himself.'

Marie yelled, 'Enough! I won't be spoken of as if I am a painting for sale to the highest bidder!'

Charles looked at her and said, 'Everything has a price, Marie.'

She wagged her finger at him. 'You sir, had better watch your manners or I may retire into confinement and do as Napoleon recommended.'

Manet quipped, 'What exactly was that then

Marie?'

Marie replied, 'He suggested that now that I have done my duty as a wife I should enjoy myself with whomever I may fancy.'

Manet said, 'How dare he insult you so. I've a good mind to challenge him for that remark.'

Zola said, 'For God's sake Edouard, you are in enough trouble for duelling as it is without challenging the Emperor. Do you honestly think you would win? He will have someone shoot you with a rifle before you can even turn round.'

Marie said, 'And I would be left bereft without my Sir Galahad. To be fair I would feel safer in a room alone with Napoleon than I would with Edgar Degas.'

Charles immediately retorted, 'Why, what did he do?'

All three men looked at her questioningly.

Marie replied, 'Nothing inappropriate, I just felt instinctively aware that he was very dominant, used to getting his own way and he made me feel uneasy. To me he just did not seem to relate well to women; he dismissed me as he would a servant.'

Manet said, 'Well he came from a rich family so you would expect him to have better manners, but maybe he just doesn't like women.'

Zola said, 'How could anyone not like women? I couldn't sleep at night without being curled up next to one.'

Marie retaliated, 'So your sole use for women is

merely to warm your bed, Monsieur Zola?'

Zola laughed and said, 'Trust you Madame, to twist a poor man's words. The world would be a miserable place without women, especially one as beautiful as you.'

30

Charles went to check from the front window to see if the crowds had lessened, and sent Antonio to fetch a hansom cab for the flowers while Marie hastily wrote a note for Notre Dame Cathedral. Antonio, Zola and Manet loaded the flowers into the cab and Charles and Marie remained safely inside as a large crowd was milling around and shouting for Marie.

Charles wrapped his arms round her. 'Don't worry, ma cherie. I promise no harm will befall you or my precious child; this may just be a storm in a teacup and will soon die down. I will not ask you to do anything you do not wish to do. I will slip out and get another cab after the flowers have gone and take you safely home. You look like you need a rest. I don't think there will be press at home as it is not general knowledge where we live.'

Zola promised to contact Judith Gautier and see if she would meet Marie and advise her of how to deal with her new-found fame. He said he would call at the studio on Monday afternoon to see what other letters, invitations and presents had arrived.

Marie and Charles were smuggled out and loaded into the cab with her selected flowers and off home they went. Thankfully, when they arrived at the chateau there was no press around. Marie managed to eat an omelette for dinner and then he took her upstairs, undressed her and put on her silk nightgown and tucked her up into bed and sat next to her stroking her hand until she fell asleep.

He then went back downstairs, poured himself a large brandy and sat in the semi-darkness going over the amazing scenes of the last two days. He already knew that Marie could not be allowed to wander the streets of Paris alone anymore. She just would not be safe; some unhinged lunatic might try to kidnap her and at the thought of what may befall her, a shiver ran down his spine. His precious wife and unborn child could be in danger and he felt totally responsible for not anticipating this.

oOo

The next morning, he woke early and gazed down at her sleeping body in her usual dishevelled state, in danger of falling out and taking up three quarters of the bed. He gathered her up and turned her onto her side, lying next to him, with his arm resting on her right breast. She started to come round and she took his hands, kissed his palm and nuzzled his fingers.

She said, 'Oh, I have had some weird dream of being pursued by an army of soldiers on horseback but they weren't wearing French uniform. I was all

434

alone and they captured me and took me back to their headquarters and locked me in a cell.'

'It was just a dream, darling. You are home safely in bed with me at your side.' He stroked her luxurious hair and kissed the nape of her neck.

She turned over towards him and said, 'Make love to me, darling. I need to feel closer still to your body for comfort and security.'

'Oh my darling angel, your wish is my command.' He then made love to her as gently and reverently as he could, ensuring he worshipped every part of her body until she was sated.

After they had recovered, he got up and went down to prepare breakfast as there were no house servants on a Sunday. Marie came down in her riding breeches and white shirt. Charles stared at her in disbelief.

'Where are you thinking of going?'

'Well, it's a cold, sunny, frosty Sunday morning and I thought I would have a good gallop on Favorit to clear my head.'

'Sweetheart, we agreed you could continue riding, but I think now is the time you switch from Favorit to Merlin and you must not ride unaccompanied at all. I will happily escort you as we don't know whether the press have found out where we live and we don't want a recurrence of yesterday.'

They ate breakfast and then Charles went back upstairs to change into his breeches and boots to go riding. He also took the precaution of fetching a pistol from the gun cabinet and attaching it to his belt for added security. After what had happened yesterday he wasn't taking any chances with Marie's safety.

They walked down to the stables and Favorit heard Marie's voice long before they got there and whinnied a welcome. Their groom had fed, hayed up and mucked them out earlier but would only return to feed them in the evening.

Favorit was clamouring for Marie's attention, especially when Marie appeared with tack in her hand and went into Merlin's stable. She kicked the door in her jealous protest. Charles arrived with Shadow's tack and after observing Favorit, he put his head over Merlin's stable door.

'Do you think she will behave with me if I ride her? I am concerned she may try to jump out if we leave her on her own.'

'Well, you may find her challenging as she has not been ridden by men but it will certainly make the ride more interesting for me, watching you cope with her.'

Charles laughed, 'Well I tamed her mistress so she will have to learn to accept my authority as you do.'

He opened the stable door and took the tack in. He undid her rugs and was thankful the groom had given her a hunter clip so she would not get too hot. She allowed him to put the bridle on but when he was girthing up the saddle she whipped round and bit him on the hand.

'Bastard!' and he gave her a resounding slap on the neck for her cheek.

Marie had already pulled Merlin out into the yard and Charles opened the door and led Favorit out, who was rolling her eyes at him. He knew this was not going to be an easy ride and tightened the curb chain on her bit one notch before he mounted.

Marie was observing them with a big grin but resisted the temptation to speak, as she knew Charles was rattled enough already. Merlin walked gently out of the yard whilst Favorit bounced out, ready to explode at any minute. Charles realised that it would take all his skills learnt as a boy riding bareback to control this hot-tempered mare. He kept his leg on and forced her up into the bridle and she became shorter in stride and very collected.

As they went through the gate out into the quiet lane, the first signs of sweat appeared on Favorit's neck. Even Merlin turned to look at her as he could not understand why she was getting so excited. They came to the first path that ran for a good mile over grassy turf.

Marie said, 'Do you think you can manage her in a canter? She may settle after she has stretched her legs.'

Charles replied through gritted teeth, 'Well, you go first but not too fast and I hope I can hold her.'

Marie set off at a trot and Favorit instantly tried to leap into canter and dropped her head to snatch the bit. Charles was ready for her and pushed her forward with his legs but raised his hands to keep her head from dropping to give her the freedom to buck. As he let her move up into canter she gave one massive buck, which he ignored and just kept pushing her forward and blocking her speed with his hands. By changing his weight in the saddle she changed from one leading leg to the other and he had her under control. His balance in the saddle was so light and his long legs soon had her admitting defeat. She realised he was not going to be an easy rider to disobey and so she settled down and relaxed into a canter, allowing him to dictate the speed.

Marie pulled up at the end of the track and said, 'Well, you coped really well with Favorit as she had to admit defeat in the end.'

'She is no different from you, Madame; she needs a firm hand on the reins to curb her exuberance without stifling her freedom.'

'You really are quite a philosopher Charles but it demonstrates just how much you know about the female psyche.' She pushed Merlin close into Favorit, stood in the stirrups, turned his chin towards her and kissed him passionately on the lips.

They moved on into open country and cantered side-by-side in perfect harmony. Favorit had learnt her lesson and behaved herself. Any lesser rider she would have deposited on the ground before they had even left the chateau, but she had met her match this time.

Apart from one or two families returning from

church they had encountered nobody on their ride so far. However, as they were nearing home he could see in the distance a lone rider standing by their gate. As he spotted them he cantered towards them and Charles checked his gun. As he got nearer, Marie suddenly recognised him and shouted, 'Oh Charles, it's Henri!' and set off at canter to meet him.

Favorit expected to follow but out of sheer devilry, he made her walk. She tried to take off, half rear and do her utmost to follow but every time he held her tightly in halt and then let her walk on and if she attempted to speed up, he stopped again. Eventually she learned that she would make quicker progress if she walked rather than bounced, plunged or trotted and she had to obey the master on her back.

When he reached the pair of them Marie was overjoyed to see her brother. He told them he had a week's leave from the barracks and he was going to stay at home with his parents. On Saturday morning he had been astonished to see their photo all over *Le Figaro* and read the report on the Arts' Ball.

'Marie, do you realise how famous you are now? All my troop are captivated by just seeing your picture and are madly in love with you. When they realised I was your brother I suddenly became the most popular man in the barracks, all demanding to meet you.'

Charles said, 'Unfortunately, this is exactly the problem we face as we were surrounded by press and people outside the studio and inundated by flowers sent by admirers. Would you do me a big favour and consider spending your week's holiday here where you can chaperone your sister around Paris and stay here with her when I am at the studio? She really is not safe left alone.'

Marie said, 'Oh, what a wonderful idea. Please say yes Henri, I am *enceinte* now and all the pushing and shoving we experienced yesterday made me concerned for the baby.'

Henri laughed. 'Of course I will, I spent my youth protecting you and extracting you from dangerous situations; this can't be any harder. Congratulations to both of you. I hope motherhood will calm you down, dear sister. I suppose we can visit Mother for a day, as any longer will have you both fighting in lumps, especially when she sees all the press coverage.'

Charles laughed. 'I doubt for one minute that motherhood will calm her down.'

Henri said, 'I see you are riding Favorit so Marie can be on the quieter Merlin. It looks like you had an interesting experience.'

Charles grinned. 'Shall we just say I was reminding her of her manners and showing her who the boss is, in just the same way I have to remind your sister occasionally.'

They returned the horses to the stable and Henri automatically went to see to Marie's horse.

Marie said, 'Henri, I am perfectly capable of unsaddling my own horse. I am not an invalid.'

Henri replied, 'Sorry sister, I didn't mean it to

look like that; it is an automatic response as I spend most of my day dealing with horses. However, you should start to consider whether you should ride at all now.'

Marie said, 'Henri, don't you start cosseting me. I have enough trouble with Charles fussing about my safety.'

'You should heed Charles; he is only concerned about you and he is your husband whom you vowed to obey.'

Charles put his head over the door. 'Henri, you are wasting your breath; she will only listen to me when it suits her. She is still the same headstrong independent woman she has always been.'

'Ah, but I know how to bring her to heel. Send her home to our mother for a couple of weeks and she will beg you to let her come back. But make her promise to obey your every word before you release her from Mother's clutches.'

'Thank you Henri, I will bear that in mind. It could prove useful information.'

The horses settled, they went back into the kitchen and Charles sorted out coffee for them all and croissants for Henri.

Henri said, 'So how did you find my illustrious leader then? Did he steal any illicit kisses or touch you inappropriately?'

Marie said, 'Henri, how could you think that? He was a gentleman as befits his position and don't forget he was in full view of everyone, including my dear Charles. The only impropriety was when he suggested that as I had done my duty to Charles I would now be free to bed-hop around Paris with anyone who takes my eye.'

Henri roared with laughter. 'I hope you gave him one of your tongue lashings for that remark.'

Marie replied, 'I most certainly did as I was so shocked as it never occurred to me that any married woman would even consider doing that.'

Henri responded, 'Well, you my dear, you do not know how very lucky you are to have such a wonderful husband as Charles. Not many men are as trusting with their wives and if you ever misbehave Marie, you will have me to answer to as well as him.'

Marie retorted, 'You know very well I would never contemplate such behaviour; did we not see enough relationships ruined in Russia by extra marital affairs to put both of us off for life? Besides, I love Charles with all my heart and could never contemplate destroying our perfect relationship.'

Charles said, 'Good, sweetheart, I am glad to hear it.'

Henri said, 'What plans have you for this week, Charles? We will have to visit Mother on one day.'

Charles answered, 'Well, actually with all the fuss over the ball everything is a bit up in the air. I would be grateful if you would give your sister some self-defence lessons and teach her to shoot a pistol at short range and handle a dagger.'

Henri laughed. 'She already knows, as in Russia

she had a dagger concealed in her boot from the age of 12 and she will only need a short retraining lesson to get her up to scratch.'

Marie said, 'Charles, do you really think this is necessary? This is Paris not Moscow.'

'Yes I do, darling. Although I don't wish to frighten you, you have to be aware that there are unhinged people out there who may contemplate kidnapping you, or worse wanting you for their own perverted pleasure, and the fact is that I am a mere artist with little money – how would I raise capital to pay a ransom?'

Henri said, 'I do think you are right to consider having weapons on her person at all times. Marie is no timid woman and has one huge advantage in surprise, as her attacker would not expect her to fight back. However, if there is more than one person intent on kidnap she will be quickly overpowered. I have recently done a course in self-defence and can teach her what I know, but it all hinges on whether she would be able to carry out these moves under duress and possibly with a knife at her throat.'

Marie said, 'Big brother, have no fear; you know I have an animal instinct for survival.'

Henri replied, 'Yes I know Marie, but in having access to weapons you could risk being killed. There is a fine line between courage and death and no man would expect to be attacked by a mere woman… but in fighting back you could end up dead.'

Marie interrupted, 'Well death is a better option

than being raped or kept as a sex slave for some lunatic.'

Henri said, 'But think of your baby, Marie; you have to consider its wellbeing.'

Charles was busying himself in the kitchen putting a piece of pork in a roasting tin and peeling potatoes, carrots and cauliflower.

'I just wanted to put this meat in the oven as we have no servants today – I am in charge of cooking on a Sunday.'

Henri laughed but joined Charles and chopped up the cauliflower. 'And what about you Marie, don't you do the cooking?'

Marie laughed. 'No, I seem to burn everything I do. I put it on and then wander off and forget about it. Charles is so much better than I am at cooking. However, I will just go upstairs and check the guest room bed is made up and put a warming pan in the bed to air it.'

Henri roared with laughter. 'Such domesticity Marie, I never thought I would see the day.'

As Marie went upstairs they discussed the safety situation as Charles had already realised he would have to improve security at his house as it would not be long before the press sniffed out where he lived. Henri suggested Marie brought her two Borzois from home as house pets as they would at least raise a warning if somebody broke into the house and would be gentle enough with the baby when it arrived.

They discussed their plans for the week over their evening meal. On Monday, Charles would walk to the studio and survey the scene and Henri would bring Marie in the carriage at around 3 p.m. after dropping off the cloak at Worth's. Zola and possibly Manet, had promised to call late afternoon to see what the post had brought. Henri would write a note to his father explaining why he would be staying with Charles and advising that he and Marie would call to see their mother on Wednesday, and Charles would send Antonio to the Conservatoire with it in the morning.

Charles thanked Henri for the two horses, Merlin and Shadow and said he could not have given them a better wedding present as they were both fully sound and had taken well to being carriage horses in the busy streets of Paris.

Henri spoke about life in the barracks. He was delighted to have been recognised for his shooting and sword skills. He had been top of his troop in both skills recently and had been put into a small group of soldiers training on the newest rifle model. His long-range accuracy was to some extent down to his excellent eyesight but mainly due to his practice in Russia when he had gone out hunting in his teens.

Marie told him about their honeymoon in Lille and how she had loved being immersed in the countryside surrounded by horses and dogs at the farm. She told about Gustav and Freya and Charles admitted that his nephew, young Louis

Odin, had made him seriously want to be a father. They told him of the scholarship at Lille Academy and that Jacques would be joining them at home in January. Henri was highly amused by Francois's depiction of Marie in the nude and gave him credit for his courage and daring. After dinner Marie chose to retire early as the fresh air encountered in the morning ride had made her tired.

Charles and Henri remained in the small kitchen by the glowing fire and drank brandy. He was a huge admirer of Henri and was delighted he was doing so well in the cavalry. He feared that he would be in the firing line at some point but hoped he could stay alive with his talents in sword fighting and shooting. He had similar features to Marie in both eyes and mouth, although he had Pierre's thick curly black hair but was blessed with Marie's beautiful pale complexion and skin tone. Henri said married life was obviously suiting them both as he had never seen Charles so happy and relaxed and Marie was positively blooming. He took him to task about being too lenient with her as Henri remembered his father could never chastise his beautiful daughter as she only had to look at him with a fake tear running down her cheek and threats of a good smacking disappeared.

Charles laughed and told him his father had admitted that on their wedding day, but he pleaded that she had not given him too much cause for concern so far. Henri asked him how he would cope with all the male attention she was now bound to receive and he said that he trusted her not to misbehave and to go no further than harmless flirting. He told him about young Guy de Maupassant claiming he wouldn't wash his hand again because Marie had danced with him… and about the red rose he sent. He explained that part of Marie's beauty was in the way she perceived herself as being nothing special and could not understand why men swooned over her. Henri shook his head and said she had been like that from the age of 12.

At 10 p.m. they both retired and he found Marie fast asleep, in danger of falling out of bed, but she didn't wake when he rearranged her so he could get into the bed.

oOo

He woke early, slipped out of the bed and quietly got dressed in the bathroom. He intended to go straight to the studio and he smiled when he realised he might actually catch Antonio and his girlfriend in the flat as Antonio didn't expect him in before 9 a.m. at the earliest. However, he was more concerned that there might be people milling around outside still, expecting Marie to be there.

To his surprise, Henri was already in the kitchen with a steaming pot of coffee.

'You're supposed to be on holiday, Henri. What are you doing up so early?'

'You forget Charles, that as cavalry we are

responsible for our own horses and have to be in the yard by 6 a.m. to feed. I also have my commanding officer's mount to attend and because I am used to caring for horses I am the first port of call should anything be amiss with a horse as the vets don't start until 9 a.m. There are grooms around during the day but every man has to be capable of caring for his own horse out in the field, so we are not permitted to hand the day-to-day chores over to grooms in the barracks.'

'I suppose that is a very good rule as some of the soldiers will have never cared for a horse when they are recruited.'

'Precisely, and we who do have stable management experience are responsible for teaching those who don't. I once saw a trooper come back from a hard training session with a horse lathered in sweat and he shoved him in the stable, untacked him and then was drawing cold water from the well and was about to leave him sweating and without a rug in the middle of winter. Suffice to say he never did it again and really, I should not have stepped in as he wasn't in my regiment.'

Charles told him of the luxury that the Duc de Beauchamp's stallions were kept in and his beautiful set-up for breeding both racehorses and hunters. Cook arrived and so Charles donned his cloak and boots to set off walking and Henri went down to the stables to check on his horse.

Henri was happy to help the groom with the four

horses and warned him that Merlin and Shadow would be required for the trip into Paris after lunch. A young stable lad did the heavier jobs and the groom set to ensuring the harness was clean and in good repair while Henri gave Favorit a good grooming session. Favorit knew Henri of old and remembered that no liberties could be taken with this young man and so she stood to attention and behaved herself. The groom said she could be a real bitch and often attempted to nip him. He laughed and said he would have a word with her about it.

He went back in ready for breakfast at 9 a.m. and Marie, who had only just woken, joined him in her night attire.

Henri joked, 'What's this, Madame, oversleeping and breakfasting in your nightgown? Would you dare do this if your husband was home? Is this not the sister who said only yesterday "I am not an invalid," are you turning into a slovenly woman when your husband's back is turned?'

Marie fired back, 'Oh brother, give me a break; you have no idea how distressing morning sickness can be and you know I loathe being sick. I daren't dress until I know whether I am going to keep my breakfast down.'

Henri laughed. 'Well you don't look pregnant yet although there is a charming increase in size up top since your wedding day.'

'Trust you to notice brother; along with all men you are only interested in my breasts. How is your love life or lack of it?'

'When do I get the opportunity to pursue women in a barracks full of men? I get the odd night out in Paris with my troop but it's generally a drinking night rather than a womanising night.'

'Oh, Henri you will forget how to behave in front of a young lady and ruin your marriage prospects.'

'Not all of us get the chance to dine with royalty, my dear!'

'Oh, stop teasing me Henri. You know it wasn't my choice; I was doing it for Charles and the other French artists and I had to make a good impression for their sake.'

'Oh, I think you managed that alright; you certainly went above and beyond the call of duty. Now half of Paris is in love with you and even my regiment have put the *Le Figaro* picture up in the canteen and I will have to live with their leering comments for the foreseeable future.'

'Henri, explain to me why men find me so attractive. You must remember me when I was as thin as a waif, had sticky out ears, my legs were too long and I couldn't balance on my toes in ballet class.'

'Oh Marie that was when you were about 12, but now you have grown from a leggy colt into a beautiful filly that is now going to transform into a beautiful brood mare.'

'That's it exactly. I told Charles I feel like one of his father's brood mares and yet I am now being pursued as if I was Venus personified.'

'Your only hope then little sister, is that you are carrying twins and will become so gross that the public won't love you anymore.'

'Twins, Henri? Oh please don't tell me there are twins in our family history that I don't know about. I shall die if I am having twins and God forbid how I'll get them out, if there are.'

Henri roared with laughter. 'It is wonderful to tease you now like you teased me when we were in Russia, little sister. I find it astonishing that you are even pregnant; I did not think you would have wanted to start a family so young.'

'I didn't intend for this to happen so soon; I expected it to take ages. I didn't even think I was fertile as my courses were so intermittent. Charles never mentioned children when we got engaged he was so fixed on forging his career, I assumed the last distraction he would want is a family.'

'But Marie as soon as you were married you must have known that a baby was a strong possibility.'

'No, I was just too busy learning what sex was all about and enjoying it to consider the consequences. We could hardly leave each other alone for a moment on our honeymoon but it looks as though I may have conceived within 48 hours of the wedding.'

'He has taught you from the start how wonderful an experience sex can be between two people who love each other. He worships you. Don't ever risk losing him by being unfaithful; you would be so disappointed. No man would ever treat you as well as he does, you are a very lucky woman.

'I do know that Henri, I love him to bits as well. We got caught "in flagrante" by his mother over the kitchen table one morning and that is the only time he could not perform his duty.'

Henri roared with laughter. 'You really are incorrigible, Marie. What would Mother think if she knew?'

'I don't give a damn what Mother would think; she's not the angel you think she is Henri. Perhaps I get my wanton sexuality from her and since I have become *enceinte* I am getting worse.'

'Oh, Marie surely not, Mother has always been a dignified lady.'

Marie rolled her eyes at him but refused to say more.

31

At 2 p.m. they left the house by carriage and drove into Paris to deliver the cloak back to Worth's. As they arrived, several other carriages were outside and Marie thought she would just pop in and leave it with one of his girls. Henri insisted on coming in with her and just as Marie was handing over the green cloak, Charles Worth came running into the reception.

'Madame Duran, what an absolute triumph you were at the ball. The dress looked perfect in the picture and I have already been inundated to produce hundreds more, but I won't do it, only you shall have the original. I know I could sell them but I am prepared to sacrifice them to the copyists rather than sully my reputation. Nobody else will be able to reproduce it anyway and certainly nobody else as pretty as you would ever look as good in a fake. How can I be of service to you, Madame?'

'Monsieur Worth, I only came to drop off the beautiful cloak you loaned me. It also had a fair share of the limelight.'

'But Madame, you must keep the cloak; you have

done me such a service. Anytime you wish for a gown for a special occasion you must come to me straight away. You are going to be the toast of Paris now and invited everywhere.'

'Monsieur Worth I don't have time to indulge myself in a social life. I am a working woman just like my husband.'

She turned to leave but Worth grabbed the cloak and ran after her. 'But Madame you must accept the cloak; you may want to wear the dress again.'

'Very well Monsieur Worth if it pleases you so, I will keep it. Thank you very much.'

Henri had gone over to the door as he had seen several people milling about and word had obviously spread that Marie was in the salon. He told Marie to wait and went outside to observe the scene. Thankfully, the crowd was held at bay by the line of carriages but he spotted a photographer positioned to the left of the door with his camera ready. He dashed back in, put Marie's hood over her face, put his arm round her and ushered her out of the door. Shouts went up and he managed to shield her from the camera on the left and they ran to the carriage door and he flung it open and they jumped in. The groom wasted no time in pulling the horses out of line and trotting them smartly up the road.

Henri said, 'That was within five minutes of you stopping. I think I will get the groom to drop me behind the studio and I will check out whether it is safe to get out from the carriage. We may be better walking in from the street.'

As they reached the Rue du Montparnasse he leapt out of the carriage and doubled back down an alleyway and sure enough, there was a melee of press and photographers. He went back for Marie and they walked towards the door with Marie on his inside, hoping to pass as pedestrians. They got within two feet of the door before somebody spotted them but he was able to get her inside without too much effort.

They went upstairs and yet again the studio had a layer of flowers strewn across the floor. Charles came to greet them and his students put down their brushes and gaped at the newly crowned "Star of Paris".

Charles exploded, 'For heaven's sake get on with your work, you have seen my wife before.'

He ushered them into the salon and gave Marie the cards from the flowers. 'Most of these are unsigned but there is one large bunch from Worth and plenty of invitations; we will go through those when Zola gets here. Would you mind taking the flowers to the hospital and depositing them there? I have the cards from all those that were signed.'

Henri went off to bring the carriage to the door and Charles went back into the studio and instructed his front row of students to gather as many bouquets of flowers as they could carry down to the door. Marie followed them down and prepared to run to the carriage. Henri came and held her tight and whisked her into the carriage.

They set off on the short ride to the main hospital and as they pulled up outside Henri offered to go and check whether they would accept them and where they wanted them delivering to. He returned with two orderlies in tow and helped Marie out of the carriage while they offloaded the bouquets. Just as they were nearly finished, a very tall man in his thirties approached them from the main door and offered his hand to Marie.

'Madame Duran, Dr Pozzi at your service. I just had to come and feast my eyes on the new star of Paris and your natural beauty far exceeds the photos in *Le Figaro.*' He took her hand and raised it to his lips and deposited three kisses on it.

Marie responded, 'I apologise Dr Pozzi but I have a tight schedule today and must depart immediately.'

As they approached the carriage Henri got in first as it was obvious Dr Pozzi intended to help her up the step. She took his proffered hand and put her left foot on the carriage step and as she turned her back to enter she felt his hand on her, pinching her bottom. Anxious to be off, the groom already had the horses trotting off as she sat down next to Henri.

He said, 'Marie, whatever is the matter?'

'He just pinched my bottom but he had his hand under my cloak, dress and chemise – he was actually touching my drawers.'

Henri gasped in horror. 'Should we go back and confront him?

'No, because he would deny it outright and say I was a fantasist… but the cheek of the man. If I ever see him out in public I will humiliate him in exactly the same way, except I shall make sure everyone sees me doing it.'

As they got back to the studio the carriage dropped them outside the door and remained to wait for them to go home. As she came up the stairs she was met by Antonio, who said Manet and Zola were in the salon with Charles.

Zola had Judith Gautier with him and he jumped up to introduce her to Marie and Henri. She was smaller than Marie in height but had a fair complexion with bright blue eyes, a small nose and mouth, a mane of brunette curls and was full of confidence.

She said, 'Madame Duran I am so pleased to meet you and I am happy to help you with your newly acquired star status. You really do have a natural beauty and elegance.'

Marie replied, 'Why thank you, Madame. I really do not see what all the fuss is about and why there are crowds outside the studio shouting my name. I can see the whole scenario becoming very tiresome.'

Charles said, 'Marie, you have received several cards and letters from people who I don't even know as well as some who state "from an admirer". We also have invitations to attend the opera, concerts, plays and private dinners. Émile and Judith have volunteered to take them away and discuss their merits and she has offered to come to our house tomorrow to help you compose some suitable replies. She knows how little time we have to pursue a social life but we have to be careful not to offend.'

Marie replied, 'Oh thank you Madame, that would be so helpful. Henri and I have just delivered a carriage full of flowers to the hospital and I met Dr Pozzi who left his patients to come and see me.'

Charles said, 'Oh yes? Dr Pozzi is the new rising star in Gynaecology at St. Nazarre Hospital.'

Marie turned to Henri and raised her eyebrows but neither of them spoke.

Marie said, 'I tried to drop the cloak off at Worth's but he would not let me return it, he has given it me. He has also been inundated with requests for the dress but he has decided not to make another even though the copyists will sell hundreds – he wants to keep his reputation for high-class individual gowns intact.'

Zola and Madame Gautier left and Manet remained for a few minutes. He turned to Marie and said, 'Has Diana taken another guardian and thrown Sir Galahad out in the cold? I cannot bear the thought of being banished from your side.'

They all laughed and Marie replied, 'Don't worry Galahad, you will have plenty of opportunities to protect me when Henri returns to his post. Charles is insisting he gives me self-defence lessons whilst he is at home.'

Manet responded quickly, 'Are you mad, Charles?

She is lethal enough with her hands and feet, what damage will she inflict with a knife or pistol?'

Most of the students had left the studio and they returned home by carriage.

oOo

The next morning before breakfast, Henri turned one of the newly decorated downstairs rooms into an improvised gym as it had no furniture in it yet. He covered a square in the centre with some spare carpet and commandeered some cushions and pillows from Jeanette. At breakfast he told Marie to wear an old dress as she may get it ripped in their play fighting, and to put her hair up. Charles had been out yesterday and purchased a 4" dagger and a tiny pistol and had left Henri with the key to his gun and sword cupboard.

He started with a round of fencing using épées to test how much she had remembered from her lessons in Russia. Although Henri was far superior he complimented her on her speed and agility and challenged her to a round of twelve. She managed to beat Henri to a hit five times as she immediately became extremely competitive.

After the bout they collapsed onto the floor and propped the pillows up against the wall.

Henri said, 'Not bad for a pregnant 18-year-old girl; some of my opponents at the barracks would struggle to get five points against me. The problem is, dear sister, you are unlikely to be challenged by a

459

swordsman in broad daylight on a Paris street. If you are attacked in the home then you may have time to get a sword but you would need to use a sabre to make enough impact on an opponent and if kidnap is the motive then they will have guns and there will be more than one of them.

'So how do I survive a kidnap attempt at home?'

'Well the first thing you need to do is bring your two Borzois here from our house and keep them indoors at night. They won't be strong enough to prevent an attack but they should hopefully warn you if someone breaks in. If it is at night Charles should be here to protect you and you would be better trying to hide rather than take them on.'

'You are joking Henri, do you really expect me to leave Charles alone to fight them off?'

'Well, most women would, but not you Marie. I can understand that. But your greatest asset is your speed and courage and the fact they won't expect you to fight back. You can pretend to be the terrified woman and faint with fear, if it allows you to get the pistol or dagger into action, but you need to be very close to your target to cause enough damage.'

He showed her the dagger and sheath and told her it would need to be tied on a ribbon to her silk stockings or sewn onto her chemise at waist level, or tied round her wrist or tucked into her sleeve.

'This dagger will be your weapon if a single man grabs you to kiss you and has his hands round your neck. You will have to decide what his intention is. If he is just being over-amorous you can just knee him in the groin but if you think he is intent on raping you then you need to get the dagger into your hand and pretend to faint backwards, bring your knee up into his groin and then use the dagger in his eyes or throat.'

They had a few practices with Henri grabbing her from both in front and behind, and she managed to avoid kicking him directly but they had a few near misses. He showed her how to pretend to faint if he had his hands round her throat, and then to clasp her hands together and bring them upwards very quickly and break his hold around her neck. He warned her that if she had the pistol on her, she would need to be close to her opponent to have any chance of killing him as it may disable him for a few seconds and in that time she must run for her life.

Marie said, 'Oh God, Henri, do you really think I am in danger?'

'No, not if you behave sensibly and are on alert at all times; but gone are the days when you could wander around Paris alone, certainly for the time being until this fervour has died down. The problem is you are now on the press hit list and they will be watching for any credible news.'

Henri replaced the weapons and they both went to shower and change before Madame Gautier's arrival for lunch.

Marie asked Henri what his initial thoughts about her were. He said he thought she was very like

Marie in that she spoke her mind and did not bow to convention and they would be likely to become friends.

She arrived at 1 p.m. and they had lunch, which gave them a chance to get to know one another better.

Marie said, 'Well Madame, what advice have you for me to deal with all these men who seem to have gone mad and fallen in love with me without even meeting me?'

She replied, 'Well, you are going to have to be careful not to inflame their passion so they neglect their manners. I have found that older men tend to covet you and assume that you will be open to them touching you inappropriately and that you should be grateful for their attention. The best way to deal with this type of man is to either ridicule him verbally… or if he goes too far, a quick stamp on his toes usually suffices. You can also claim to be best friends with his wife, or better still his mother-in-law, which may put a few younger men off overstepping the line.'

Henri and Marie roared with laughter and Marie said, 'But why do they assume you want to be touched when you are a married woman and your husband is in earshot?

She replied, 'Marie, you are dealing with French men who think any woman that breathes is a possible target for their bed.'

Marie responded, 'But surely not all French men are like that?'

'Age has a lot to do with it. I discovered from the age of 8 that sitting on a man's knee was not a good idea. Older men can be openly sexual even whilst your family is in the room. They just seem to think it is their right to dominate women. It is total fabrication that French men are chivalrous and honourable towards women. In fact, English men score best in that department. They have a strict class code and they respect women and would certainly not approach a married woman with the intention of bedding them.'

Henri asked, 'But surely the higher class the man, the better his manners?'

'No, Henri, it is generally the opposite. The old French aristocrats are where this sort of behaviour emanates from… think of Louis XIV. The more sheltered, privileged and spoilt they are, the more their attitude to women deteriorates.

Marie asked, 'Is it acceptable that married women who are *enceinte* are fair game to men?'

'Historically, yes as many marriages were made out of convenience not love and most kings and princes had mistresses as well. But don't think that this practice has died with Louis XVI's death. It is very much still alive and kicking in France. You only have to look at Napoleon and his mistresses to know that.'

Marie replied, 'But I would never consider doing such a thing. I love my husband and would never be unfaithful.'

'Good for you, but you are in the minority and married for love. I should also warn you that your husband will also be a target for women who are in loveless marriages. You were not the only one to be revered when your picture went Europe-wide. Manet, Monet and your husband are all good looking men and artists have a reputation as excellent lovers and are easily available to women to paint their portraits at a price.'

Henri laughed. 'Perhaps it is Charles I should teach self-defence moves to.'

Marie, having reflected, said, 'But Manet will not paint portraits; he will only paint what he wants. But then, he is not dependent upon making a living. Monet has a lover and child now and he prefers painting "en plein air" and does not take portrait commissions as he paints his friends for pleasure. That only leaves my husband at the mercy of these rich harlots.'

Henri interrupted, 'Marie, do not concern yourself. Charles is devoted to you and his religious ethics would not allow him to forsake you.'

'Madame, when do pregnant women withdraw from public attention?'

'Marie if you were an aristocrat, after six months or when the baby becomes too obvious. You would not be expected to reappear until you have been churched at around six to eight weeks after the birth and you would not be breastfeeding either.'

'And when should men leave the marital bed?'

'Around three months into the pregnancy and for up to two months after the birth.'

'Charles and I have no intention of following any of this ridiculous rubbish and he will be at my side when I give birth as well.'

'Well, I am delighted to hear that; he sounds utterly devoted to you. I am sure your husband has already experienced amorous advances from some of his sitters so he will be more than capable of coping with a few more.'

With lunch finished, the table was cleared and Judith laid out the cards and letters Marie had received.

'I have divided them into three piles; the first pile is from people who sent flowers and gave their name. I have written a draft template of a short note that would be deemed an acceptable response. If you know them personally then you can add more lines. The second pile is invitations you have received and those Zola and I think you should consider before rejecting; these include any Arts related events. The third pile is for events like coffee mornings or daytime things that would distract from your work and I have drafted a reply for those.'

'Madame, you have been very efficient in your appraisal. I can't thank you enough.'

'Émile was anxious that by turning down events you don't lose public sympathy, as we don't want them to turn against you. There is such a fine line between success and failure. We have been very careful to portray the image of you as a working woman who assists her husband in his career. Of course this does not sit well with the aristocracy, who consider a working wife to be abhorrent, but you are not a model or actress so we have a difficult tightrope to walk. He is certain you will be receiving scores of requests for interviews from art magazines but recommends caution in whom you allow access.'

Marie replied, 'I am sure Charles will discuss it with Manet and Zola before we consider these approaches and we can have a firm idea of what we are seeking to cover.'

'I have also brought you some printed stationery with your address embossed in gold, which will make it much easier to pen short thank you letters; if you like, we can make a start on them? Perhaps Henri would help us too so as to ease the burden?'

Henri laughed. 'How could I refuse such a polite request, Madame? I suppose it beats galloping around muddy fields, practising battle charges in the freezing rain, which is what I would be doing if I was working.'

They all got to work penning thank you notes and turning down invitations to coffee mornings. At 4:30 p.m. Madame Gautier's coach returned for her and Henri escorted her to the door. She promised to return later in the week.

When Henri returned to the dining room Marie gave him a searching look and said, 'Do you find Judith attractive, Henri?'

Henri laughed. 'Marie, coming from you that's priceless. Yes, of course I find her attractive; what man would not? But I have no time to pursue a relationship whilst in the cavalry.'

'I daren't ask her as I don't know her well enough yet but Zola told me she has a lot of admirers. So what that means, I shall have to find out… but she seems impressed by you.'

'She is three years older than me, intent on a career as a writer and a married woman. She is hardly likely to consider me as an ideal suitor now, is she?'

'Oh, Henri I just want you to be happy and to have a wife and a family.'

'I need to get further up the career ladder first before I look for a wife and I fear that I may be facing war before too long.'

'Oh, don't say that. I cannot bear the thought of you dead on a battlefield in some foreign country.'

'You know being in the hussars has been my life's dream and if death happens then so be it. I can't expect a woman to raise a family when I might not be around to provide and protect them, so I am best leaving the ladies alone. You can produce my share of children, Marie – nobody could be better parents than you two.'

Marie hugged him to her. 'My brave big brother… I can understand but it does not make it any easier.'

Charles returned from the studio and they had dinner together and Marie explained what Madame Gautier had done with all the invitations. She insisted Charles reimburse her for the stationery and her time, which had been invaluable.

32

The next morning, Marie and Henri prepared to go to their family home. They were staying the night so she could see her father, so Charles had taken the opportunity to arrange to go to Café Gerbois and meet up with the other artists and stay at the studio as Marie would not be at home.

They drove over in the carriage but Marie's sickness recurred due to the swinging motion and they had to stop several times on the way. Henri found it amusing but she was mortified.

After her third stop she clambered back into the carriage and proclaimed, 'I am never getting pregnant again. Charles will have to take a mistress to produce his heirs; I can't cope with this and the prospect of giving birth and breastfeeding fills me with even more horror!'

Henri laughed. 'You were the one who wanted to know what sex was all about, now you have to take the consequences of your actions, lady!'

'Henri did I ever once state that I wanted to be a mother when we were growing up? I was only every interested in reproducing horses and dogs; babies never entered my head.'

They stopped ten minutes from home and she insisted on taking a short walk to clear her head as she knew her mother would be waiting to greet her and cast her critical eye over her wayward daughter.

As they pulled up the drive, the grooms were already on standby to see to the horses. Her mother appeared at the top of the steps as Henri helped her down from the carriage.

Louise surveyed her daughter as she approached. 'Well Marie, haven't you been making a name for yourself in Paris.' She stiffly hugged her and kissed her cheek but her attitude changed completely as she embraced her darling son.

Marie watched them both with years of bitterness boiling up inside her. She knew exactly where she stood in her mother's affections and vowed that she would never treat one child differently from another.

On the way, she had begged Henri not to leave her alone with her mother but Louise cleverly engineered a reason to show her daughter something upstairs.

Feeling like a fox caught in a trap, she resigned herself for the showdown with her mother that had been boiling for a long time.

Louise opened with, 'So you are now "la belle étoile de Paris," Marie. It pleases me to know that my predictions have become true but you couldn't wait, could you? You had to throw yourself at the first man that paid you attention – and an artist at that. You could have had a king but you chose an artist who will tire of you within a few years and move onto his next model whilst you are in the nursery rearing his brood.'

Marie gasped and could feel tears pricking her eyelids but she would not stand and take this outburst from her mother.

Her mother continued, 'The press tells me you are already carrying his child. Congratulations, you are obviously fertile. I would have preferred to hear it from you personally, but then you never were a model of convention, were you?

Marie raised her voice. 'Don't you dare lecture me on the subject of morals and convention; you are the last person that I will tolerate lecturing me.'

'I should have taken a horse whip to you when you were younger but you had your father wrapped round your little finger and he spoiled you rotten.

'Well one of us had to love him because you clearly didn't! You proved that by having an affair with Capitan Nikolai Kavischof and before you try to deny it, I actually saw you in bed with him when I was 13.'

Her mother stared at her in disbelief and struggled to speak.

'Did you tell your father and Henri?'

'No, of course not! Not out of any loyalty to you but because I could not break their hearts. But reflect on this... If I knew it was going on, then other people must have known too. The fact you openly entertained him in your marital bed was hardly conducive to secrecy. Henri adored him and he taught both of us to ride, shoot, hunt and fight and he is one of the reasons Henri is in the cavalry; Nikolai was his hero. But if any harm befalls Henri, I shall hold you responsible for that too.'

'Marie, you don't understand the circumstances under which this affair started.'

'I don't want to know. There can be no excuse; you did it because he flattered you and you were bored. You skilfully ensured that Henri and I were being educated at the Lycée and Father was busy teaching and you had plenty of time to indulge him. You weren't stupid enough to think you were the only one, Mother? He visited two other women at the same time as romancing you.'

Her mother gasped and had to sit down on the bed and Marie actually felt sorry for her.

'Then when I was 14, he turned his attentions on me!'

The shock on her mother's face was horrendous. 'God forbid, Marie. Did he take your virginity?'

'No, because I knew the minute he touched me inappropriately that I was not going to be his next victim. I held a dagger to his throat and threatened that if he touched me I would tell everybody about his sordid affairs – including his Commanding Officer.'

'Marie, he could have raped and murdered you.'

'No, he had some feelings for me and he knew I would carry out my threat. Don't forget he taught me the survival skills that I turned on him. Like Henri, I worshipped him too until I discovered what you were both up to. So don't ever lecture me about morals. I love Charles and he loves me; neither of us would ever break our marriage vows and he is worth far more to me than any king would ever be.'

'Oh, Marie you are so naïve and inexperienced. Every girl likes to think her husband will love her forever, but life intervenes and time moves on. Men take sexual opportunities that are presented to them without thinking of the consequences. You threw yourself in his bed two months before your wedding.'

Marie rounded on her. 'I know it was a foolish thing to do now but he sent me packing unfulfilled because he wanted me as a virgin on our wedding day. He didn't take that opportunity, did he? Don't forget, he is a wanton artist skilled in sexual conquests in your eyes.'

'Marie, most men want virgins for wives and harlots for mistresses!'

'Well Charles is very lucky then because he has got both in one package!'

She then marched out of the room, ran down the stairs out of the front door and down to the stables. Henri heard the noise and came out and saw her running down the drive, obviously in distress. Louise came downstairs and Henri looked at her.

'Mother, what have you said to upset her now? She really is in a fragile state of mind at the moment with everything that's happened since the ball, and

473

being pregnant as well. The last thing she needs right now is you giving her any more grief.'

'Henri why must it be something I have said or done? In fact it is her that has mortally wounded me.'

Henri fetched his coat and Marie's cloak and ran out of the door and down to the stables.

Marie had arrived in the yard and the head groom had been startled by her wild appearance with no coat on a cold November day and came running to her side.

'Madame what is the matter, can I be of service?'

'I just wanted some time and space to collect myself, Jean. Where are my two horses?

The groom could tell she had been crying. 'Over here, Madame.' He ushered her to the stables. 'I shall see you are not disturbed.'

Marie went into Merlin's stable and he was munching away at a rack of top grade hay.

'Oh, Merlin, what a tangled mess life can be. I think being a horse would have been an easier option.' She stroked his black velvet nose and sleek, taut neck. Tears poured down her face as the horror of the confrontation with her mother played over in her mind.

Henri arrived in the yard and he approached Jean.

'Madame Duran is over in the stable with her horse, Master Henri. She seems a little distraught. I said I wouldn't let anyone disturb her but if ever there was anyone who could put a smile on her face it was always you. She shouldn't be out in the cold for much longer, either.'

'Jean, could you have Marie's Borzois ready to go in the morning with a supply of feed? She's taking them home now as I think she needs them in the house for protection.'

Henri went quietly over to the stable and peeked over the door. Merlin sensed his presence but did not move, instinctively knowing that Marie needed comforting.

Henri opened the door, walked up to Marie and placed the cloak around her shoulders.

'Marie, I know you have deep animosity towards Mother and I think I know why. Did she insult Charles? Is that why you are angry?'

'Yes, she did, she said he would be unfaithful to me and leave me rearing his brood of children and I should have waited instead of throwing myself at the first man who flattered me with attention. I won't tolerate her lecturing me about morals. I know she was aiming for a good marriage for me but I chose who I wanted to marry and it was always going to be for love, not money.'

'Marie, has this got something to do with Nikolai?'

She turned round to face him in complete shock and he pulled her into his arms.

'I probably knew around the same time as you. I overheard the servants gossiping and to confirm it I followed him one day and he went to our apartment and stayed for three hours.'

'Oh, Henri and I discovered them in bed when I was off sick from lessons one day. She must have forgotten I was at home in bed. I knew how you worship mother and hero worshipped Nicolai and I just couldn't destroy your feelings for either of them.'

'Father knows too Marie, but he never raised it with her or anyone else.'

Marie gasped in shock. 'But how could he carry on, knowing what she had done?'

'He loved her of course. I know in your idealistic mind it should never happen but Marie, we are all human and make dreadful mistakes and he had our future to consider. Would you not forgive Charles too, if he made a mistake and was unfaithful?'

'No I wouldn't. I'd kill him and her if he ever deceived me.'

'Marie, life is not that black and white – other people are bound to be affected – what about your child? Would you want to rear a family on your own? I know your beliefs have been swayed by what you have seen and I understand that completely, but don't be too quick to judge. We are all open to temptation and one day it could be you that's tempted. Come on, we need to get you warmed up and you need something to eat.'

'Oh, Henri how did you become so wise at 22?'

'I grew up with you Marie, who always reacted to everything in the extreme. I am more like Father and think of the consequences before I act. I hope that will make me survive in battle rather than get my head blown off in the first charge.'

They went back to the house and sneaked into the kitchen and persuaded Cook to supply them with tea and cake, which they ate downstairs. Marie did not want a repeat performance with her mother. They avoided each other until Pierre arrived home for dinner.

As he came in he had some newspapers rolled up under his arm. He held his arms open and Marie ran to him and nearly squeezed the life out of him.

'My dear child, you haven't done that for years.'

He gave Henri a hug and said, 'Well it seems I have not one, but now two children making headline news.'

He unrolled a copy of *Le Figaro* and on the front page there was a picture of Henri with his arm round a hooded Marie, taken outside Worth's salon. The headline read "Has L'étoile taken a lover already?"

Marie and Henri stared at the newspaper in complete amazement.

Henri said, 'How dare they publish something like that without checking the facts?'

Pierre replied, 'Oh, don't worry. Charles and Zola were round at the newspaper offices by 9 a.m., threatening to sue them. It seems the editor turned down one of Zola's articles in the past so he was raring to rip them to shreds. God, Marie are you alright? You have gone as white as a sheet.'

He ushered them into the salon while a servant took his coat. Louise came over having heard the commotion and he passed her a copy.

Marie sat down and stuttered, 'But all of Paris will think I am an adulteress.'

Pierre said, 'No sweetheart, they will have to print an apology and Zola will ensure it is on the front page. I am sure he will procure some payment for damages as well.'

Marie said, 'But some people will still believe it and be denouncing me.'

Pierre responded, 'Marie as long as we all know the truth, what does it matter? I called round at the studio before I left and saw Charles, and Manet was there. He was incandescent with rage and threatening to challenge the editor to a duel.'

Marie said, 'But so he would be, he is my Sir Galahad and protector. He would not want anybody thinking ill of me.'

Henri groaned. 'Oh, am I going to be facing some ribbing when I go back to the barracks?'

Marie said, 'Henri, I am so sorry but this is what I meant about it impacting on innocent people.'

Louise said, 'You will have to be careful now, Marie – wherever you go, the press will be out for a story.'

Marie replied, 'The next thing is they will say I am Napoleon's mistress because I danced with him at the ball.'

Pierre said, 'I think that's stretching the bounds of fantasy a bit too much my dear.'

They went into dinner and at least the subject

detracted from the atmosphere between the two women. Afterwards, the women left and Henri and Pierre were left to their port.

Pierre said, 'What's wrong with Marie, she looked pale and distraught?'

'I think the press attention since the ball has taken the wind out of her sails and combined with the pregnancy, it has just been too much. She was badly sick on the way over in the carriage this morning and her hormones are all over the place. It didn't help when she had a row with Mother over her insulting Charles and saying he will be unfaithful to her and confine her to the nursery.'

'Charles would not do that to her I hope, but he is expecting a lot of her to become a wife and mother so soon at only 18 and then to cope with the fallout from the press.'

'I don't think any of them realised what effect Marie would have at the Arts' Ball so you can't blame Charles for that and he is well aware of the can of worms that has been opened and he is desperate to protect her. I'm just glad I was here when needed. He's worried for the baby's sake and I know he thinks they should have waited before starting a family but Marie didn't think it would happen this quickly. She also doubts whether she will be a good mother, which is perfectly normal but it all adds to the stress.'

'Do you think she would be better staying here for a rest?'

'No, she and Mother are like warring cats and she

needs to be with Charles to comfort her. He really is wonderful with her; I just wish she would appreciate him more.'

'Now, how are you faring at the barracks?'

'I am fine and have come top in shooting and sword fighting in my regiment again. I have been drafted in to test the new rifle design and have been given extra instruction in scouting. I am also the first port of call when any of the horses are sick or sorry; although I have no veterinary training, I am constantly alert and spotting lame horses on exercise and rescuing them before they are permanently damaged.'

'Is it what you expected, son?'

'More or less, but I would prefer to see some action soon; until I have faced death I don't know how well I will cope with it.'

'You, my boy, will be as steady as a rock and a credit to your regiment.'

'My shooting skills have elevated me to the post of personal bodyguard to Napoleon and Eugenie over the Christmas social scene. I won't be in uniform but will have to dress according to the event so I should get to the ballet, opera and concerts with my clothes provided by the State. However, I won't see much of what's going on as I shall be watching for anyone acting suspiciously.'

'Charles tells me Eugenie is a delight and Napoleon thought Marie was a breath of fresh air. He did of course mention that if he had been 40 years younger he would have liked her for his mistress, but then what can you expect.'

'It was the fact he suggested that now that she was pregnant she should take a lover that offended her most. She had no idea that married women would even contemplate doing such a thing.'

'I do hope Marie will be able to cope with the pressure. Would you mind asking her to join me in here? I could do with speaking to her alone and I am sure your mother would relish some time alone with you.'

A few minutes later Marie came into the library and Pierre was sat on one of the settees.

'Come here my darling and let me give you a good cuddle, and I want you to tell me what worries you?'

'Oh Papa, what would I do without you?' She snuggled up to him with her head on his shoulder.

'I thought you had replaced me with Charles. Now, don't tell me married life is becoming a burden already? I hope he is not making too many demands on you, especially now you are *enceinte*.'

'No Papa, if anything it is me making sexual demands on him since I became pregnant.'

Pierre roared with laughter. 'Oh, have you no shame? You are far too honest and outspoken. Women are not meant to reveal they enjoy sex.'

'Papa, I didn't think the baby would happen so quickly and Charles is more than aware he is going to turn me into a mother at only 18.'

'I would have thought since your honeymoon

your ardour would be slowing down now Charles is back working. Does he intend to move out of your bed when you reach six months?'

'No Papa, neither of us wants that as he wants to be by my side throughout the pregnancy and birth and I could not contemplate him leaving my side either.'

'I hope you haven't imparted that information to your mother just yet, dear. Charles is a braver man than I thought if he is intending to cope with you during childbirth.'

'He wants me to breastfeed as well and I know mother will be outraged. But if it delays a future pregnancy then it will be worth it.'

'Let's not impart that news to your mother just yet either, Marie. I was hoping for a quiet Christmas! Daughters are usually expected to take advice on marital relationships from their mother, not their father. Charles would be appalled if he knew you were discussing your sex life with me.'

'Well, I have already discussed it with Henri as we are so close.'

'Good god, child; your brother is not even married yet! What does he know about the marital bed?'

'Probably more than you think; Henri is very wise for his age. He thinks about the consequences of his actions before he does it whereas I just jump in without any thought whatsoever. Don't worry, he is not planning to get married for a while yet.'

'Your mother was right, Marie. I should have

confined you to a convent in Paris when you were 12.'

'Oh, you know I wouldn't have stayed. I would have run away or the nuns would have expelled me for bad behaviour.'

'I think that would have been highly likely dear, but you obviously gained too much freedom in Russia and it sounds like you were learning about subjects I never intended you to study.'

'Well I did learn about Greek and Roman sex lives when I should have been studying politics and philosophy and I did research human biology from a Russian medical book but that was very hard going as I had to translate it into French to understand it.'

'Good grief child, please refrain from informing Charles about this – he will wonder what a brazen hussy he has married!'

'I think he has already found out Papa, and I don't hear him complaining.'

Pierre nearly fell off the sofa, laughing at her.

'Child, I thought I was supposed to be cheering you up but you have certainly cheered me up! Have you and Charles discussed how many children you would like?'

'When we looked at the house and there was a nursery with four bedrooms Charles suggested we fill them. However, he only said the other day that if I keep producing the same sex we will have to carry on. Don't worry Papa, Charles may be a Catholic but as he says, "The Church doesn't pay for the upkeep of children," and there are ways of preventing conception as neither of us have any intention of abstaining.'

'Marie, don't you say another word; your husband would take a horsewhip to you if he knew what you had been discussing with his father-in-law. Don't worry, I won't inform your mother of this conversation either; she would have a major heart attack!'

'Papa, you know I love Charles very much. Do you think he will remain faithful to me?'

'What can I say, Marie? He loves the bones of you and has a deep-set moral code but who can know what temptation life throws at us? But he refused to succumb to temptation when you went to him before your wedding day and that must have taken an iron will.'

'I didn't know you knew… Do you think the less of me for it?'

'You were just being young, presumptuous, inquisitive and in love, Marie. I just hope it will sustain you for life.'

oOo

After breakfast the next morning, Marie and Henri got ready to take their leave. Monty and Lily, her two Borzois, were loaded into the carriage along with a food supply and their baskets and rugs.

Her mother gave her a hug and told her she would have to grow up fast now and prepare for motherhood.

As they drove home, Henri told her about being Napoleon's bodyguard over the Christmas period and how he was looking forward to enjoying the social scene at court. Marie said he should look for a potential wife but he just laughed.

Marie couldn't wait for Charles to get home for dinner as the two days without him had felt like a long time. The two hounds jumped all over him and gave him an enthusiastic greeting before he even got to Marie.

He said, 'You have some work to put in Madame, reminding these two of their manners if they are to become hounds at my fireside. However, I can't quite see them making reliable guard dogs.'

She ran over to him and hugged him. 'I have missed you, Charles. I didn't like sleeping alone in my old bed; I missed the security of having you by my side.'

Spotting the parcel under his arm she said, 'What's that – a token of your undying love for me?'

'Not *my* love, dear – a gift from Napoleon and Eugenie for both of us.' He opened the package, which contained two jewellery boxes and opened the smaller one, which contained a diamond cravat pin, two diamond collar studs and two diamond cufflinks.

Marie gasped and said, 'Oh, Charles, they are exquisite!'

He replied, 'Not quite in the same league as your

present.' He opened the jewellery box and both Marie and Henri gasped in amazement. Inside lay an emerald and diamond necklace shaped in a five-point star with two identical earrings.

'I can't accept that even though he is a king; its value is too high.'

'Ah but wait till you hear what he has written on the card. "To ma belle étoile de Paris in recognition of your services in raising the profile of France in Europe. Don't ever change, ma cherie; remain true to yourself." What did Eugenie say in her card? "To a true gentleman who reminded me of my homeland and danced like a prince."'

Marie said, 'Can we really accept these gifts?'

'Well Zola says as they have been given in recognition for service then it would be considered an insult to turn them down. He will have realised the emeralds you were wearing were not your own. We will have to send suitable thank you notes, which Zola said he would help compose.'

After dinner they retired to bed and Charles asked her how she had got on at home with her mother as he had picked up on some negative vibes when the subject had been mentioned.

Marie said, 'Is it true that men want virgins for wives and harlots for mistresses?'

Charles reacted with shock. 'Good God, who said that, surely not Henri?'

'No, my mother… She said you would be unfaithful and leave me raising your brood in the nursery.'

'And what was your response to that?'

'I told her that you were very lucky then because you had got both in one package!'

'Oh, God forbid, Marie. That whiplash tongue of yours will get you into real trouble one day. No wonder Napoleon said, "don't change" when he sent you the emeralds. We both knew, right from the start that I was not the ideal candidate for your hand in marriage, which is why I thought I would never get you. I do have sympathy for your mother's opinions especially in view of my occupation, but I am determined to prove her wrong and why would I look elsewhere with you in my bed? Now you stop worrying and get down to proving to me that you are the harlot you described.'

He pulled her into his arms and kissed her passionately. Marie took up the challenge with relish.

33

It was three weeks before Christmas and Marie received a letter from Fauré in Brittany asking if he could see her over the coming weekend to discuss the Christmas concert at Notre Dame. She showed it to Charles and he suggested they invite Fauré, Manet, Renoir, Zola, Madame Gautier and Guy de Maupassant to dinner on the Saturday night, to stay over until Sunday. If Fauré came in the morning, they could discuss the concert and rehearse the songs. Marie agreed, provided she could draft in some of her parents' staff to cook and serve the meal. She despatched personal invitations to each guest and a note to her mother. She and Jeanette prepared the guest bedrooms and gave the house a massive clean.

She was delighted that she would be surrounded by her admirers from the ball but hoped that she and Madame Gautier would be able to cope with the male testosterone. Thankfully, her sickness had receded unless she drove in the carriage first thing in the morning. She planned the menu with Cook and ordered the ingredients and wine. She had asked her mother for the loan of a dinner service and glasses, which would arrive with the serving staff on Saturday morning.

She searched her wardrobe and selected one of the evening dresses she had picked at Worth, which was intended for dinners, operas or concerts. She picked the red dress – the one she had first seen when she had been shopping for her ball gown. It was burgundy velvet with puffed sleeves to her elbow and had overlaid lace on the bodice and back. It was well fitted at the waist and just had a puddle train. The great advantage was that no voluminous hoops or tulle petticoats were required. She had been given a ruby necklace by her father when she was 16 and this would work well with the neck of the dress, which wasn't too low as even she had noticed the increase in size of her top line since her pregnancy had started.

oOo

On Saturday morning, the extra cooking staff arrived and she had a meeting with them in the dining room to go over the menu and drinks. The serving staff would be arriving at 5 p.m. along with two maids and a butler to cover the dinner. The flowers she had selected had arrived and she and Jeanette filled all the rooms with white roses, chrysanthemums, calla lilies and orchids. One of the kitchen maids made her some table decorations from the remaining flower heads and pinecones.

At 11 a.m. prompt, Gabriel Fauré arrived by hansom cab straight from the station. Both Charles and Marie greeted him on arrival and as Charles prepared to leave them in the music room, Fauré asked him to stay.

'Charles, I have been discussing the concert with Pierre as he will be conducting the Conservatoire Choir and Orchestra in my absence as I will not be released from my school until the 18th December. He suggested that as you have such a fine tenor voice you might join the choir at rehearsals with Marie and then you will be there to chaperone her to and from the venue.'

Charles replied, 'Well I can see the sense in that because I don't let Marie walk alone in Paris since all the excitement after the ball.'

Fauré said, 'Well it makes sense because you two can rehearse our duet pieces at home. We also have special guests coming this year – Napoleon and Eugenie – so everything has to be perfect. The other favour I have to ask both of you is that Notre Dame produces a nativity tableau at the end of the concert and the key players are from the musicians, singers and conductors. We would like Marie to be Mary and you to be Joseph.'

Marie gasped. 'Oh Gabriel, I couldn't possibly do that. I am not worthy of taking on such a part.'

Fauré interrupted, 'But Marie, you would not even need to speak because that is covered by the narrator, interspersed with the carols. You just have to look beautiful and tend the baby in the crib and carry him during the procession out of church to a press shoot at the top of the cathedral steps.'

Marie intervened. 'Look after the baby? But what if it screams the place down?'

Fauré responded, 'Oh, don't worry; we have two babies and their mothers are angels in the stable with you. We usually use one in the crib and then the other for the procession. Charles will have the donkey to lead down the aisle as we use real sheep and a donkey.'

Marie laughed. 'A donkey? But they can be stubborn as well... and what if it gets away and tramples the rest of the cast? What part do you have in all this, then?'

'Gounod, Pierre and I are the three kings.'

Charles laughed. 'How very convenient for you all to be portraying kings while I am groom to the donkey.'

Fauré fired back, 'No, you are the husband of Mary.'

Marie intervened, 'But I cannot portray the sainted Virgin; my baby was conceived naturally and is no way a virgin birth.'

Fauré replied, 'But, conceived within the sanctity of marriage as prescribed by the Church. Marie you are perfect for the role and so is Charles.'

'I just need time to think about it Gabriel; it's a terrific responsibility and I don't want anything to go wrong. I have no experience of dealing with babies.'

Charles replied, 'The decision is yours, my dear. If you don't want the added pressure of being in the nativity that is entirely up to you.'

Fauré produced the programme for the concert and Marie was down to sing the soprano part as a solo in the Bruckner 'Ave Maria', two opera duets with him and finally he had rearranged 'O Holy Night' and written a soprano solo for her to sing along to with him and the choir. Marie was delighted and he played it for her while she read the music.

Charles left them to become acquainted with the new music and to sort out the wine, which had just been delivered.

After Marie had sung her soprano part through a couple of times he sang with her and their voices blended perfectly. They moved on to the opera duets, which Marie would need time to learn as she had never sung them in public before.

He asked her, 'What is the reason you doubt you are suitable to be Mary?'

'I just don't feel that I am a suitable representative of the Virgin Mary. The press will be bound to make comparisons between my life and hers and I am just not in her league.'

'I thought it might be because you were not a virgin on your wedding day that it worried you.'

'Gabriel, I was most certainly a virgin at the altar, believe me. Charles would have it no other way.'

'I'm sorry Marie, forgive my impudence. I should not have asked you that; it is none of my business.'

Marie smiled at him. 'I must be maturing as two months ago I would have slapped your face for being so forward, Gabriel. I think the furore over the ball and the subsequent press interest has just made me hesitant about revealing myself to the public.'

Charles returned and Fauré played him 'O Holy Night' and said he would have to accompany Marie both on the piano and take his tenor part so they could rehearse together.

After they had finished, Marie asked him what she should wear for the concert. The choir would be dressed in simple black dresses as was customary but Fauré said as a soloist she was free to choose whatever she wanted bearing in mind it was Christmas and the special guests were Napoleon and Eugenie and it was based in a cathedral setting. She thought she would consult Worth but she had some ideas of her own she wanted to discuss with him.

oOo

Their first guests arrived around 7:30 p.m. and it was Zola, Judith and Guy.

Marie smiled as Guy's face turned slightly red when she shook his hand and she bent forward and whispered to him, 'Don't worry, Guy. I won't let Zola tease you mercilessly; I will protect you.'

'Oh thank you, Madame. May I say how beautiful you look tonight?'

'Well thank you Guy, you are so kind.'

Charles watched her with a smile on his face as she had taken the trouble to make him feel at ease among his peers and he had nothing but praise for her.

Manet and Renoir arrived together and Marie saw the devotion in his eyes as he kissed her hand. Manet didn't miss it either but he kissed her cheek and whispered, 'You look divine as always, my dear.'

After drinks in the salon they went through to the dining room and took their places at the table. Charles sat at the head with Marie on his left-hand side and Manet on his right. Judith sat next to Manet, with Zola on her right. Marie had Renoir on her left and Guy next to him. Fauré sat at the bottom of the table.

During the soup course they all talked about the ball and its repercussions and Manet admitted that he had sold paintings as a result. Charles said he had been inundated by requests from students from all over Europe that he could not possibly accommodate, not to mention the requests for portraits. Monet had also sold paintings since the ball and had gone to Auvergne for a rest.

Charles confirmed that he, Manet, Monet and Marie had been asked to judge a prestigious art competition in London in February, courtesy of the Tate Gallery, and the *Illustrated London News* wanted to interview them at the same time.

Zola told them about the debacle with *Le Figaro* printing a picture of Henri and Marie trying to intimate that they were lovers. This had ended in a compensation claim and a printed apology in the newspaper but had caused a sensation in the magazine world. Many requests for interviews with Marie had ensued but she had declined to be interviewed.

Fauré mentioned the Christmas concert and about Marie singing solos and duets with him as well as Charles joining them.

Zola said, 'So you are an accomplished singer and pianist too, Marie. Is there no end to your talents?'

She replied, 'I really never thought I was a good singer but it appears Fauré thinks so.'

Fauré said, 'You sing like a songbird, Marie, and have done since you were a child. Your father told me that you sang your first solo in Russia at the age of 5.'

Marie replied, 'Well, I can't quite recall it but fathers always exaggerate their offspring's talent.'

Manet said, 'I can concur that at your own wedding you pulled off 'Ave Maria' to critical acclaim.'

Marie blushed and said, 'Ok I give in but I really don't count myself as anything other than a good choral soprano singer and would never make my living from singing.'

Madame Gautier told them a story of when she was asked to sing a solo at a school concert when she was 14 and completely froze and could not utter a word.

Marie directed her attentions to Renoir. 'And you, Auguste. Do you have any hidden talents?'

Renoir replied, 'Not that I have discovered yet. However, having started painting on porcelain I have produced some miniatures, which I believe is also one of your interests.'

Marie said, 'In that case I shall show you some of my work tomorrow and ask for your advice on technique.'

Manet could not resist flashing Renoir a scowl as he did not want him spending any time alone with Marie. Charles had seen Manet's reaction and he smiled. He had no fear that Renoir was pursuing his wife and it amused him that it rattled Manet.

As the meal ended the ladies retired to the music room and left the men to their port. Marie asked Judith what she thought about her invitation to be the Virgin Mary at the Christmas concert. Judith was amused that Marie did not think of herself as worthy to portray the Madonna.

'But why, you haven't done anything wrong, Marie?'

'I just feel slightly ill at ease with the fact that I don't fit the profile of a virgin mother. I enjoyed every moment of becoming pregnant with Charles and I feel like a sinner rather than a Madonna.'

Judith laughed. 'I do see your point but it was an inevitable result of becoming married. You were young, fertile and in love; it was bound to happen.'

'Trouble was I expected it to take more time than it did as I would have preferred more time alone with Charles before I became a mother as I don't feel I will be a natural mother.'

'Of course you will; once the baby arrives you will make a perfect mother and Charles seems intent on being a hands on father, which is quite rare. He has already dispensed with ideas of leaving your marital bed so it's not like you're going to be on your own rearing a child as most women are.'

'I know, I suppose I should count my blessings but do you think I will get any increased press coverage because of it?'

'Probably, but it will hardly be negative publicity, just the usual headlines like "L'étoile stars as Madonna in the Notre Dame Nativity Play". Your own pregnancy is hardly showing yet, but even if they mention it, there is nothing unusual about it.'

'What if they suggest it is Henri's child?'

'Good grief Marie, after what happened last time they would never dare make any reference to that. *Le Figaro* had a lawsuit on the table within hours of them publishing their faux pas and believe me all the other newspapers and magazines will know that.'

'I suppose you are right and I don't want to disappoint Fauré but to be honest I would rather I had control over the donkey and Charles looked after the baby, as I am sure it will scream the place down in my arms.'

They both howled with laughter and then the men joined them. After a little more chit-chat, Zola suggested Fauré, Marie and Judith serenade them at the piano and sing their repertoire. Blushing profusely, Marie sang 'O Holy Night,' along with Fauré, and it was well received.

They were then inundated with requests to sing

and thankfully, Fauré could reproduce most of the songs requested by ear, without the need for sheet music.

Manet took the opportunity to speak to Charles in the window bay and said, 'Marie looks different now, have you noticed?'

'Well the pregnancy is hardly visible except up top, which is certainly pleasing me.'

'No I meant when you look at her now she exudes sensuality rather than the innocent look she had before. You can tell that she is an uninhibited woman who loves sex. You have certainly stamped your authority on her by reproducing so quickly but in releasing her sexuality, more men than ever will desire her.'

'As long as it's from a distance I don't mind men worshipping or desiring her as long as it is in my bed she lays. Woe betide any man who thinks he can steal her from me.'

'You know I worship her as a goddess although that vision of her naked body courtesy of the sunlight shining through her silk nightgown at the Hôtel De Ville, prevents my sleep on some nights.'

'Come off it Edouard; you have your wife Suzanne as well as numerous other women. Surely you can find a suitable alternative?'

'Charles, as you well know being an artist, perfection is very difficult to find and once seen, never forgotten.'

After a leisurely breakfast the next morning Zola, Judith, Fauré and Guy left as they had other commitments. Renoir and Manet were not leaving until later.

Renoir asked Charles, 'Do you have your own studio at home? Have you any of your work here? I would love to see some.'

He replied, 'I only have some of my personal canvasses that I have been working on here, but I can show you.'

He led Manet and Renoir up to his studio and Marie said she would join them after she had thanked the staff.

The only pictures he had in his studio were the self-portrait of their wedding day and his recreation of Freya's portrait. Renoir was captivated by the dappled shadows from the tree caused by the sunlight on Freya's hair. They talked at length about how he had managed to recreate it without the branches visible on the canvas. Charles showed him his preliminary sketches where he had drawn the tree and shown the direction of the sunlight as it shone on Freya's head. He pointed out that it had to be accurate and how he used three different colours in the strands of her hair and then painted the shadow over the top.

Manet and Renoir discussed his technique with him until Marie shouted asking him to come downstairs and Manet went with him to bring them up some coffee. Renoir was left alone and he took the opportunity to look through Charles's honeymoon sketchbook. He saw the preliminary sketches of Marie naked at the waterfall and those of Freya feeding Louis… and the ones Marie had done of Caesar and Louis and the new foal. He knew he should not be looking but he could not resist.

He moved away from the easel as he heard Manet coming back upstairs with the tray.

Manet said, 'What do you think of Freya's portrait?'

'I love it and can't believe the detail in her face and hair; it must have taken him hours to do the hair and then overlay it with shadow from the leaves and it is just exceptional. Will he exhibit this at the Salon?'

'I don't know, but I hope so; it would create quite a stir as it is such an unusual portrait. However, the judges will pan it for being "en plein air" and they will probably say that showing her bare thigh, legs and feet is indecent. I think it's wonderful as he is a master at portraying the spirit of the sitter. You just look at her and can feel her Viking heritage and the snow and ice of Scandinavia. Don't forget that the canvas was covered in black charcoal to start with so to get such a refraction of light on her face is astonishing. I believe it comes to life when the moon shines on it. He does have this knack of making it feel almost alive. His horse portraits were the same – you wanted to touch them because you felt they were really there.'

Charles returned and they drank the coffee.

Renoir asked him how he had managed to paint the wedding day self- portrait and Charles described his mirror technique. However, he explained that it required the ability to be able to flip the image in his mind by 180-degrees and that took some practice.

Marie came in and produced some of the miniatures she had made to show Renoir. They spent a contented half hour discussing miniatures while Charles and Manet chatted.

Manet asked, 'What are you doing for Christmas?'

Charles answered, 'We are going to Marie's parents for four days and then coming home for New Year because Gustav, Louis and Freya are coming and bringing Jacques with them from Lille.'

Manet exclaimed, 'Oh, you must introduce me to Freya so I can see how close your portrait is to her in the flesh.'

Charles replied, 'As accurate as I could make it. She is pregnant again to Gustav so I hope he has learned his lesson. You are welcome to come over any time. What about your plans over Christmas?'

'I am going home to my mother's and taking Suzanne and her brother Leon for a couple of days. My brother Eugene is joining us but it really is just to make Mother feel less alone at Christmas since father died six years ago.'

34

The day of the concert at Notre Dame arrived on the Sunday, two days before Christmas Day. Marie felt slightly nervous, but not about the singing. The prospect of dealing with the baby caused her far more concern. She looked at her dress hanging on the wardrobe, and smiled.

She had gone to Worth with a sketch of the type of style she wanted and they had worked together on the design. She had wanted the dress to be a combination of black and white with the white extending from her shoulder, over to her right hip. Worth had used white silk embroidered with sequins and pearls. The remaining skirt was black silk and framed her body with only one hooped petticoat underneath. Although she was now a full three months into her pregnancy and her waist and chest had increased by two inches there was no visible bump. Her hair had been swept up and pinned into a French pleat to ensure it did not impede her singing. Her costume for the nativity was a light blue shift dress, dark blue cloak and white headdress.

Charles had attended most of the rehearsals and

was actually quite enjoying the singing. He had rehearsed the duets she was to do with Fauré and then on Saturday they had the dress rehearsal and Fauré took over. He explained to Charles that the two opera pieces required some acting and asked if he would mind if he kissed Marie on the cheek and held her hand. He could hardly object as Fauré cleverly asked in front of the entire choir conducted by her father, so he did not really have a choice. At the first attempt Marie had blushed when he kissed her but as it fitted the context of the song it looked charming.

Charles and the donkey were on good terms and he had been given some treats to keep him quiet if he started making any noise during the service. He had been left without hay until he was put in the pen so thankfully, he should be quiet munching that through the play. The lambs also had their mothers to keep them occupied in their pen.

The baby boys were both around four weeks old and had behaved impeccably at the rehearsal. While one fell asleep in the crib another was substituted for the procession down the aisle and it had gone well so far. Their mothers were in the stable scene as angels, with Gabriel, who was male. Charles slightly annoyed about the sumptuousness of the kings' costumes compared to his Joseph costume, especially as Fauré was one of them.

As Napoleon and Eugenie were attending they had asked to meet Marie, Charles, Fauré and Philippe before the concert started as at the end they would all be outside, in the nativity scene. The concert tickets had sold out within a day of being released and Charles hoped it wasn't because everyone was desperate to see Marie. Over 1200 people had bought tickets and this did not include the performers, choirs, musicians and clergy.

At 5 p.m. they changed into their clothes. Charles was delighted with her dress. The white jewel-encrusted top looked stunning, sparkling in the lights. He was pleased that the neckline was higher than on a ball gown and he noticed the increase in her breast size. Marie had chosen to wear the green velvet cloak to keep her warm on the carriage drive. He was in a dress suit along with the other male choir members. They left the carriage before Notre Dame as it would have taken far too long for them to queue to unload at the main cathedral entrance. They slipped in unnoticed, from a side entrance to the vestry.

oOo

At 7 p.m. the Emperor's coach pulled up at the door and Napoleon and Eugenie were ushered into a small room to meet the organisers. To Marie's delight Henri was with them in his role as bodyguard and he managed a quick word with them while Napoleon and Eugenie were meeting the clergy. He looked very handsome in his tail suit and white silk shirt and cravat. Two of the royal guards were in attendance but Henri was in charge of them overall, should any incident occur.

Finally, it was their turn to be introduced and Marie curtseyed deeply at Napoleon's feet. He took her hand and kissed it.

'Madame Duran we meet again; last time you were my dance partner and now you are to be my songbird. What a beautiful talented lady you are and looking blooming with health on this cold winter's night.'

Marie replied, 'And now you have my brother at your side.'

Napoleon said, 'Yes, he is a delight to have around and the time spent in Russia learning to shoot has not been wasted. I believe your father is also directing the choir and orchestra. What a talented family you have, Madame.'

Eugenie spoke to Charles. 'Monsieur Duran, how well you look, and I see you are serenading us too.'

Charles replied, 'Actually, I am really enjoying it although I am only here to chaperone my wife from the press.'

Eugenie said, 'Yes, I understand the press rather got out of hand after the Arts' Ball. I hope it did not frighten Marie with its intensity?'

The royal party moved back out into the cathedral and they took their places. Marie was pleased when the 'Ave Maria' was completed as this was the most difficult piece and any mistake would be highlighted. She was also performing at the top of the nave, which was quite a distance from the church choir that was accompanying her.

For the two opera pieces she had Fauré with her and she enjoyed his flirting and acting skills. She prayed the press would not suggest there was anything going on between them. She joined the soprano section of the choir to sing some of the other pieces, which included Vivaldi's 'Gloria' and Fauré's 'Jean Racine', both of which had been performed on her wedding day. She looked over towards Charles in the tenor section and as the Gloria ended he blew her a kiss.

Their final piece was 'O Holy Night' and she loved singing above Fauré in the duet piece he had written especially for her. The audience went wild with clapping after they had sung it. Fauré took her hand and led her down the steps to the top of the nave and she curtsied and was met with the audience on its feet. She noticed Napoleon had also stood up in tribute. The interval was next and they rushed back to change for the nativity. She was pleased to see that both babies had just been fed and changed so they should hopefully settle down during the play.

She put her costume on and used the mirror to pin her headdress and she prayed she would not do anything to offend God. The responsibility of her role weighed her down and she was glad she was not singing any solos. The usual Christmas carols would be sung during the tableaux. They just had a scene at the inn door where they were ushered into the stable and Charles had to put the donkey in its pen. She smiled when she thought of the baby appearing in the next scene. If only her impending birth could be as quick and quiet as this.

The nativity started with the Angel Gabriel telling her she was going to conceive a child but as the music portrayed the scene, she only had to stand serenely. She had a reprise whilst the shepherds and the kings were informed of the impending birth. They took up their positions and Charles led the donkey and held her hand as they approached the inn door. The donkey hesitated about going into his pen but Charles slipped him a titbit and when he spotted the hay, he was soon in. When the shepherds brought the sheep there was an amusing bit when one of them jumped back out of the pen and was tackled very quickly by Charles before it escaped down the aisle. Her baby had been handed to her fast asleep so she carefully laid him in the crib and he slumbered on. Fauré winked at her as he presented his gift of myrrh and her father gave her a chest of gold.

As the end drew close and they started to prepare for the procession, she left the first baby in the crib and collected the second baby who was in his mother's arms and also asleep. Charles collected the donkey that had to be parted from his hay with a titbit. As they set off down the aisle the baby woke up and started to wriggle in her arms. Soon a loud wail ensued and she panicked. Before it could get louder Charles thrust the donkey's lead at her and grabbed the baby out of her arms. He gave him a hug and kiss and then settled him in his arms and the child just looked up at him and gurgled. The huge entrance door was wide open and as they reached it, cameras exploded with light. Charles then handed her the baby and took control of the donkey, who was slightly phased by all the lights. They only paused for five minutes outside for the photos, as it was freezing cold. She was able to hand the baby over to its mother and the donkey's owner relieved Charles of its care.

As they went back through a side entrance they passed the Lady Chapel and Charles pulled her in and led her to the altar rail where they knelt and prayed for a few moments. They both prayed for a safe delivery of their own baby. The peace and tranquillity of the small chapel was a delight from the busy nave of Notre Dame.

As they turned away from the altar and walked down the steps Charles said, 'You really were sensational tonight, sweetheart. I was very proud of you.'

She kissed him and said, 'And you didn't do a bad job as Joseph yourself.'